Dating Games

USA TODAY BESTSELLING AUTHOR

T.K. LEIGH

DATING GAMES

Published by Carpe Per Diem, Inc. / Tracy Kellam, 25852 McBean Parkway # 806, Santa Clarita, CA 91355

Edited by: Kim Young, Kim's Editing Services

Cover Image Elements:

kiuikson © 2019

Mexrix © 2019

Anntuan © 2019

Used under license from Adobe

To all the survivors...

Chapter One

I'VE ALWAYS HAD an affinity for the number three.

Third time's a charm.

Past, present, future.

Beginning, middle, end.

Three is considered the perfect number, and not just by me. Many religions view it as a sacred number, a holy number. Even Plato recognized the idealism in it, dividing his Utopian city into three populations — Laborers, Guardians, and Philosophers.

Three is also the "magic" number in fairy tales. A hero or heroine is often given three choices, or they overcome the obstacle on the third try. Think back to the beloved tale of *Cinderella*. When the prince searches for his perfect match, with the aid of a glass slipper, Cinderella's is the third foot he tries after unsuccessfully attempting to shove it onto her darling step-sisters' feet. There's a tension inherently built into this number that has always spoken to me on an ethereal level. Throughout my life, everything always happened in threes, perhaps due to my own insistence.

I graduated third in my high school class. Granted, there were only a whopping ten people in my graduating class, but that made it even more significant, considering I was in the top 33.33%. I kept my circle of best friends small, only three of us. And up until now, I've only had sex with three people.

The first was my neighbor, Brent. There was no romantic attraction. I was almost eighteen and thought it best to have a practice round so I'd be fully prepared when it counted. Plus, we both felt like we were the last two virgins our age in all of Nebraska. Years later, I found out Brent was gay. I hope it wasn't his experience with me that made him realize this.

My second sexual encounter was with Christian Murphy. He was the one I wanted to practice for. (Thank you, Brent.) Handsome. Popular. Smart, without having to try. I thought he was the man I would spend the rest of my life with, which concerned me, because he was only my second.

But when Trevor Channing walked into my History 101 class freshman year of college, it was suddenly goodbye, Christian, and hello, Trevor!

You know those scenes in movies where the heroine locks eyes with the leading man the first time and an explosion of orchestral music fills the background? That's what happened with Trevor. Without saying a word, I knew he'd forever be my number three. My perfect match.

Which is why it feels like all the wind has been sucked from my lungs as I stare at him incredulously. I must not have heard him correctly. There's no way those words came out of his mouth, not when we're celebrating my thirtieth birthday at the sushi place where we shared our third meal after moving to New York.

All day, I'd been confident this was the night he would pop the question. After all, we've been together over ten years. Not to mention the fact I often said I wanted to wait until I was thirty before I got married. Surely, Trevor would have taken the hint that this meant he should propose on a birthday of such significance. Every sign pointed to me screeching "yes" after he got down on one knee in front of a restaurant full of strangers and poured his heart out. Hell, in my fantasy, he even shed a few tears because of how overwhelmed he was.

As is typically the case, my fantasy was so far from reality.

Perhaps Chloe brought the wrong batch of brownies to the office and this is the result of having mistakenly consumed one of her "special treats", as she refers to them. Perhaps it's the lack of sleep from pulling an all-nighter to rewrite my article for the magazine. Perhaps it's due to the shot of Jameson I threw back to settle my nerves before heading here. But as I stare into Trevor's deep-set hazel eyes, his expression filled with pity and something else I can't quite put my finger on, I know none of those circumstances are true.

The truth is my boyfriend just broke up with me.

The man I moved my world for so I'd be near him during law school.

The man I supported by working two jobs while he studied for the bar exam.

The man I imagined for myself when all other girls were dreaming of marrying that year's boy band lead singer.

"Evie?" He cuts into my thoughts, snapping me back to the present. I used to enjoy listening to him talk. Now it oozes with betrayal. "Please, say something."

I place my hands on the small wooden table, bracing myself as I draw in a deep breath. "Are you seriously breaking up with me?" My voice rises in pitch, unable to reel in my disbelief at this turn of events. My jaw tenses as I peer at him with an unfocused gaze. I'm convinced

I'm in some alternate universe, like when Alice daydreamed about a world of pure nonsense, then ended up in Wonderland where everything wasn't as it seemed. That's got to be what's going on here, too. Any minute, the White Rabbit will come scurrying in front of me. Right? *Right?*

Trevor leans closer, hushing me, not wanting to make a scene. He's always been this way. He's not boring, per se, but he can be quite…serious, perpetually worried about even the most subtle hint of impropriety. After all, he is a lawyer. His maturity was one of the many things I found attractive about him.

Until Trevor, I was convinced the entire male species was the same. That they only cared about when the next *Call of Duty* would be released, despite my naïve hope they'd eventually outgrow that kind of thing when they sprouted hair on their balls. It was a rude awakening when I went away to college and walked through the hallways of my dorm to see my male counterparts huddled in front of a screen, their fingers glued to game controllers in a way that solidified my suspicion they'd probably never touched a clitoris with such excitement. Hell, they probably couldn't even *find* a clitoris. At least I'd never let them near mine.

Then I met Trevor.

Handsome.

Intelligent.

Mature.

I thought this was it. *He* was it. The person I was meant to be with. My Bogart, my Grant, my Gable.

"Please, Evie," he implores. My stare only becomes more harsh as I recall everything I've done for him, everything I've sacrificed for him…just so he can walk away after twelve years. "You have to understand how difficult this is for me."

"For you?" I blink repeatedly. "You think this is only difficult for...*you*?"

He glances over his shoulder, anxious about anyone overhearing. If he wanted to avoid a scene, he should have considered that before breaking up with me in public. The restaurant isn't too busy yet, considering it's only a little after five. I'd originally thought it odd he asked me to meet him for dinner so early, but I figured he wanted to devote as much time as he could to celebrate my birthday.

Apparently, he forgot about that, too.

"I gave you over a decade of my life, Trevor. I did everything to support you, to make you happy, to make this relationship work. I sacrificed my own dreams so you could pursue yours. I worked two jobs while you went to law school so you wouldn't have to worry about working and could focus on your studies. I've done *everything* for you. Every decision I've made over the past twelve years has been for *you*, for *us*."

"But that's the thing..." He blows out a breath, running a hand through his dark hair. "We started dating when we were eighteen, too young to experience life."

"We've experienced life. Together." I reach across the table and cover his hand with mine. The familiar warmth of his smooth skin comforts me. But it's fleeting. Too soon, he pulls his hand away. The corner of his mouth twitches, a nervous tick I've grown accustomed to over the years.

"We're not the same people anymore."

"People change all the time. It's part of being in a relationship. We all grow, regardless of how long we're together. The important thing is that you love the person you're with. I loved you back then. I still love you now. And I know you love me. That's why this is so hard for you. Because you know you're making a mistake."

He shakes his head, slowly, deliberately. "I'm not, Evie. We've grown apart. We no longer want the same things."

"All I want is you," I say, grasping at straws.

Standing, he re-secures the button on his suit jacket. Then he retrieves his wallet, throwing several bills onto the table to cover the tab. At least he didn't break up with me and expect me to pick up the check.

"But I no longer want you. I need to think about my future. I work for one of the top firms in the state, if not the country. If I want to be taken seriously for partner, I need to consider the type of woman they'd want me to be with."

His words are like a knife to the heart, yet he manages to hold his head high, acting as if he hadn't inferred he was choosing his job over me.

"And you don't think they'll take you seriously dating me." The truth leaves a sour taste in my mouth, one even the aroma of ginger in the air can't alleviate.

"Can you blame me, Evie? This is a very conservative firm with a client list that includes direct descendants of the Vanderbilt's, Rockefeller's, and Kennedy's...to name a few." He lowers his head, avoiding my gaze. "Didn't you ever wonder why I never asked you to come to any of the firm's events?" He glances up, chewing on his lower lip. "I can't exactly tell them what you do for a living, not when it entails doling out ridiculous dating advice or recommending vibrators."

I blanch, my mouth growing slack, my eyes wide. "You

always knew I wanted to be a writer. I was an English major when we met. The fact I'm doing what I set out to do shouldn't come as a huge shock to you, Trevor."

"It's not. It's *what* you're writing. You were one of the few girls I'd met who seemed to know precisely what she wanted and had a plan to achieve it. I knew you wanted to work in the magazine industry. I thought you'd want to do more than pen fluff pieces about how a woman could tell if a guy's really into her. Maybe your parents are right. Maybe you'd be better off if you got your teaching certificate. Then you'd have a more respectable profession."

He holds my gaze for a moment longer, then steps back. "You can stay in the apartment until you find a place of your own. I'll be working long hours over the next month anyway. I'll sleep on the couch for the time being. You'll barely notice I'm even there."

"You're kicking me out?" I practically screech.

"Don't say it like that. Technically, it *is* my place. I pay the mortgage. My name's on the title. But there's no rush. We can be roommates until you're able to find your own place."

"Roommates?" I ask, still unable to wrap my head around this.

"I don't want this to ruin our friendship. We started out as friends. I hope that doesn't change."

I shake my head, at a complete loss for words. How can we be friends after this? I'm pretty sure we crossed that line, oh, about eleven years ago when he told me he couldn't imagine his life without me. I still can't imagine my life without him. Why did he suddenly change his mind?

"I've got to get back to the office," he says after stealing a glimpse at his watch. "I'll see you..." He stops short of saying anything more than that. Then he turns from me, everything about his stride confident, as if he didn't just end a twelve-year relationship.

Chapter Two

HEART POUNDING AND fists clenching, I burst through the doors of a bar a few blocks from Columbus Circle, finding Chloe, Nora, and Izzy sitting at the bar, a drink in front of each of them. Chloe's about to take a sip of her martini when I plop into the empty chair to her left.

"I need tequila." I wave down the bartender, Aiden, ignoring the inquisitive stares coming from the women who've become my best friends since I uprooted my life and moved to New York for Trevor. And for what? For him to break up with me because I may not be as stuffy as the other wives and girlfriends of the people he works with?

"The usual?" Aiden's brows furrow as he assesses my appearance. There's a benefit to being a regular at your weekly happy hour watering hole. However, right now, that benefit allows Aiden to realize something's off. I'm not sure how to explain the events of the past hour. It still seems surreal, like I'll wake up and all of this will be a nightmare.

"Yes. And a shot of tequila."

He eyes me skeptically at first, then fills my order, placing my manhattan in front of me, followed by the shot glass filled with a clear liquid. Thankfully, he remembers I like the silver stuff best.

Without offering a single word of explanation, I grab the shot and raise it, meeting my friends' confused expressions. They *should* be confused. I'm supposed to be out celebrating my engagement to my fiancé, possibly drinking ridiculously expensive Champagne in a suite at the Ritz he booked for the occasion. Instead, I'm sitting at the bar I go to every Thursday night, trying to reconcile the drastic turn my life's taken.

"Here's to wasting nearly twelve years on a man who no longer wants to be with me because I'm not *serious* enough." Rolling my eyes, I down the liquid, grimacing as it burns my throat. I bang the glass back onto the bar, asking Aiden for another shot. The only thing that will make tonight better in comparison is waking up tomorrow with a hangover that will leave me cursing the gods who invented alcohol.

"He *broke* up with you?" Chloe asks, aghast, her nose scrunched up in repulsion. Her medium-length, gray and lilac ombre-colored locks still hold the perfect beach wave, her makeup freshly applied. There isn't a single wrinkle on her black pencil skirt or silk blouse, despite having worn it all day at work.

I met Chloe when I started working at the magazine several years ago. Her cubicle is next to mine, and we became fast friends. She's the go-to on all things involving every celebrity out there. Hell, I haven't even heard of some of the people I hear her discussing. Thanks to our friendship, I also grew close to Nora, Chloe's college roommate, who now runs a yoga and meditation studio in the Village, and Izzy, Chloe's childhood best friend.

"Happy fucking birthday to me!" I lift my next shot, throwing it back, this one burning a little less.

"Why?" Nora inquires, her doe-eyes wide, strawberry

blonde hair perfectly coifed.

"I thought you were happy," Izzy adds. I'm thankful she's here, so I'm not the only one who looks like the didn't just step off the runway, like Nora and Chloe do. She's still dressed in her scrubs, evidence that she must have come here straight from the hospital, where she works as a pediatric oncology nurse. Her long, dark hair is pulled back into a tight ponytail. She doesn't wear much makeup, but she doesn't need it, her Latina heritage giving her a naturally tanned complexion.

I face my friends, offering them a tight smile as I smooth my frazzled red hair. "I guess I'm not serious enough for him." I roll my eyes.

"What do you mean?" Chloe presses, her lips formed into a tight line.

"Start at the beginning," Nora instructs. "I want to know everything."

The last thing I want is to rehash what just happened. I'm surprised I made it out of that sushi restaurant without having a complete breakdown. There's no telling how much longer I'll be able to keep it together. At least I'm in a place with an endless supply of alcohol.

"When I got there, he was sitting at a table in the corner. His legs were bouncing as he chewed on his nails. I thought he was nervous about popping the question. I guess the first clue should have been when I leaned in to kiss him and he turned so I kissed his cheek instead."

"He did not!" With wide eyes, Nora slams her hands on the bar, drawing the attention of several people.

"He's working on a huge case and the trial starts next week. I figured he might be worried about getting sick. I didn't even think twice about it. He always turns into a germaphobe right before trial. When I sat down, he was still visibly anxious, which was absolutely adorable. I mean, he was about to propose. At least that's what I thought." I take another long sip of my manhattan, the effects of the alcohol loosening my lips.

"Then he grabbed my hand and toyed with my ring finger. Or maybe I imagined he did because, in retrospect, there's no way he'd do that. It doesn't make sense. Anyway, he went on and on about how he'd been thinking about doing this for a while but didn't know how I'd react, blah blah blah. I mean, the entire lead-up...the way he held my hand, the way he was so excitable, the way he made it sound like this was a monumental time in our relationship...made me think this was it. He was finally going to pop the question."

The more I speak, the louder my voice becomes. Gone is the heartbreak that consumed me when I watched Trevor walk out of my life without a single glance back. Now I'm annoyed. Annoyed that I gave twelve years to a man who tossed it aside because he didn't think I was serious enough to be the wife of a partner at some stuffy law firm. Annoyed that I put so much effort into being the perfect girlfriend I believed he deserved. Annoyed I didn't see the signs he wasn't happy.

"What did he say next?" Nora pulls her left hand away, hiding the engagement ring on her finger. When she first told us she was getting married, we were all shocked. She'd only been dating her fiancé for three months, not to mention he started as a Tinder hookup that turned into more than a one-time thing. Although I doubt I'd personally be able to overlook the idea that my partner had been a player before me, he makes Nora happy. That's all I care about.

"What do you think? I was so wrapped up in the moment, it didn't register he broke up with me at first. I was about to squeal 'yes' at the top of my lungs, but as I opened my mouth, I replayed his words in my mind. That's when I realized he wasn't reaching into his jacket for some ridiculously expensive ring. Instead, he said it was time we both went our separate ways. That if he wants to be partner, he needs to be more 'serious'," I explain, using air quotes.

"More serious?" Chloe's voice is laden with disgust. As far as friends go, she's the cynical one. Nora's the romantic one. Izzy's the career-driven one. And me... Well, I'm not sure what I am. They'd probably say I'm a mixture of all three.

"Apparently, he doesn't consider a woman who writes about sex and dating for a living as serious, at least not to his standards. But that's complete bullshit! I'm serious! Look at me." I gesture at my business attire. Then I raise my martini glass. "I'm drinking alcohol out of a glass with a stem. If that doesn't say maturity, I don't know what does. If I were immature, you two would be holding my legs in the air while I did a keg stand or something like that."

"I don't think he means you're immature," Izzy assures me with all the sympathy and compassion I've come to expect from her. "You're sophisticated, motivated, not to mention talented. Don't mistake immaturity as having a sense of humor. You have the latter in spades. Regardless, you're also driven. How many other people can claim to be doing exactly what they set their mind to when they were just a teenager?"

I shrug, brushing it off.

"You made your own way in this industry," Chloe adds. "The only reason I got the job I did was because my dad works for the *Times* and made phone calls. Not you. You didn't know a soul. You got in on talent and drive alone. So don't let Trevor make you think you lack motivation."

"Oh, but I do." My voice oozes sarcasm. "Obviously, since I have a degree in English, I should be doing something more than writing articles about sex. But I *like* having a sex and dating column."

"He's a prick for not supporting you, especially if you enjoy what you do. I don't see you giving him a hard time for not making partner yet."

I scoff. "Well, according to him, at least he has a *real* job." I dig my fingers through my hair, yanking at it, groaning in frustration. "Couldn't he have chosen a different day? *Any* other day? Now I'll forever equate my thirtieth birthday with the day he broke up with me."

I reach for my drink, about to take another sip, when I spy a handsome man in a suit walking past the bar, his hand on the lower back of a beautiful woman wearing a cocktail dress. The alcohol loosening my inhibitions, I call out to him. "Hey! You!"

Surprisingly, he pauses, both he and who I assume to be his date looking at me. They probably stopped here to grab a drink before heading off to the theater or some romantic dinner. Hell, he may even be proposing tonight.

"You look like a person with good judgment, someone who's not a complete moron."

"Thank…you?" he replies with a wavering smile, unsure what to make of my statement.

"Would you ever break up with your girlfriend on an important date, say… I don't know. I'll just pull something out of thin air. Her birthday?"

"God no." He laughs, peering down at the woman beside him. There's a warmth and affection between them. I had that. At least I thought I did. Now what am I supposed to do?

I don't know life without Trevor in it. I've never imagined the possibility. Am I supposed to pretend I'll be okay, that I can fall out of love as quickly as he did? We were together longer than most married couples. At least longer than Brittany Spears' marriages.

He looks back to me. "I'd never live to see another day if I did that."

"Thank you, sir!" I lift my glass, toasting him. "You are a gentleman. My boyfriend, well...ex-boyfriend is not. It's my thirtieth birthday today."

The bar erupts in applause and congratulatory shouts of happy birthday. I'm not sure why, but something about the combination of their applause and the alcohol flowing through me has me standing and curtseying to my new friends.

"Thank you. Thank you. And do you know what my boyfriend of twelve years gave me as a birthday present?"

I scan the bar area. Now that it's close to seven on a Thursday night, the booths and tables in the remodeled industrial space are filled with a mixture of locals and tourists. Despite that, the background chatter has become almost non-existent, everyone interested in what I have to say. I suppose learning about a stranger's pathetic heartbreak is infinitely more interesting than discussing the unstable markets.

A woman calls out from the opposite end of the bar. "It better have been a ring!"

I point at her. "After this long, I thought it would be. I earned that much. We met during my freshman year of college. The instant I saw him walk into my history class, I no longer cared about the Battle of Bunker Hill. I just

15

wanted him to bunk my hill."

A roar of laughter tears through the space, causing me to smile for the first time all evening. I look at my friends, who wear amused expressions on their faces. Maybe this is what Trevor referred to when he said he needed to be with someone more serious. I thought he liked the fact I'm on the eccentric side, that I don't mind being the center of attention. After all, I minored in theater. Hell, my bold personality is what caught his attention all those years ago.

"When he smiled at me that day…" I trail off, placing my hand over my heart, sighing. "I swore I heard music. I know what you're thinking," I add quickly, hoisting myself up onto the bartop so I can address the crowd.

Aiden doesn't stop me. A smirk forms on his lips as he crosses his arms over his chest. Too bad he's gay. He would be a great rebound, if I were into that kind of thing.

"That I had probably just come from a meeting of what we called the 420 Club." I lock eyes with a table full of twenty-something men, who nod in understanding. "You guys know what I'm talking about, don't you?" They lift their beers, laughing, as I address the rest of the bar once more. "But honestly, I heard music. If hearing music in your head doesn't mean you've just found your fucking soul mate, I probably belong in a straitjacket. Which may be the case anyway, but I digress." Grabbing my glass, I take another sip of my drink, before continuing.

"I've always been a planner. My mother claims I was the one who put her on a schedule for my feedings as a baby, not the other way around. So even when I was a little girl, I knew the type of man I wanted to spend the rest of my life with. Just my luck that man went to the

University of Nebraska, too."

"Go Huskers!" a voice shouts, and I look in its direction.

"You're from Nebraska?" I ask a man I estimate to be in his mid-fifties. His skin is pale, gray hair thinning.

He nods. "Kearney."

"Ah, so you had electricity."

Chuckling, he nods once more. "Most days."

"Well, I grew up in a little town called Hickman." I pause for emphasis, which I learned in some of my acting classes. "Let me repeat that for you. Hick...man, Nebraska. I mean, if that doesn't scream we marry our cousins, I don't know what does."

Laughter fills the space once more. I glance behind me, meeting Aiden's eyes as he leans against the back counter and winks. He probably didn't expect there to be an opening act for the band scheduled to play later. I hand him my glass, an unspoken request for him to fill it. Two manhattans and two tequila shots in the span of less than an hour isn't a smart idea, but being smart isn't in the cards for me tonight.

"Now, something I should mention is that I have a slight affinity for the number three." I hold up a hand. "Don't ask. And no, I'm not OCD and have to lock and unlock the door three times. Except on the third day of the third week of the third month of the year."

There's another burst of laughter and applause. Once it dies down, I continue. "I like to think it was a sign when Trevor walked into my history class at exactly 3 PM on September third and proceeded to sit in the third row of the lecture hall... Which also so happened to be the row I sat in because, well, it was the third row. I *always* sat in the third row."

I feel a tap on my back and glance behind me to see Aiden handing me a fresh drink. I thank him with a smile, then take a sip before placing the glass beside me on the bar.

"Our relationship began like all good relationships do… By me pretending to be inept at U.S. history so he'd tutor me." I bat my eyelashes, passing everyone a demure look. "But after our first test and he saw I got the top grade in the class, he realized it was all a ploy. So he asked me out, and the rest is history.

"Fast forward four years. Trevor graduated with a degree in finance. I graduated with a degree in English and a minor in theater, which is probably why I have absolutely no problem telling a bar of complete strangers about my breakup. And my mother said theater would be useless." I roll my eyes, my expression oozing sarcasm. "I'm proving her wrong this very second. Anyway, after graduation, Trevor was accepted into Columbia Law here in New York. There wasn't even a question in my mind. I would move to New York with him."

A nostalgic smile lights up my face as I recall those early days of living in the city. For the longest time, I thought I made a mistake, especially when I was forced to take a cold shower in the middle of winter because the building superintendent hadn't fixed the hot water heater. Or when the smoke alarm went off anytime I tried to cook because it was placed right above the stove. Or when we lost power on Christmas and had to order Chinese takeout because the meal I'd planned was a lost cause without electricity. At the time, all the disasters made me long for the comfort and space of Nebraska. I now look back on everything and laugh.

"I worked as a bridal assistant for a wedding planner during the day. Honestly, it was the perfect job for someone as obsessed with planning and organization as I am. Essentially, I was the bride's bitch. 'You need Voss water instead of Evian? At your service.' 'You don't want your maid of honor to look better than you, even though she's prettier on the inside and out? That can be arranged. We'll be sure to pick a dress style that doesn't complement her body type.' 'Don't want the groom to find out you had one last fling with his best man the night before the wedding? There's the morning-after pill for that.'

"However, being a wedding planner's assistant didn't pay enough to cover all our bills, not to mention my student loans, so I got a second job as a bartender. All to support Trevor so the only thing he had to worry about was studying. I figured he'd return the favor down the road. I suppose he did, in his own way. After he passed the bar and got a job at an incredible firm, we eventually moved into a great apartment in Brooklyn. One he paid for, which he reminds me regularly." I pinch my lips, shaking my head at how blind I've been. "My support of his dreams has been nothing short of unwavering. I don't think he's ever truly supported me in mine."

I jump off the bartop and grab my glass, pacing as I attempt to come to terms with how Trevor could be so callous as to break up with me without even a hint of remorse or regret.

"I was the perfect girlfriend. I kept our place clean, despite working long hours. On those nights he worked late, I often dropped by the firm to bring him dinner. I was so convinced if I did everything right, we'd fly off into the sunset like Danny and Sandy and live happily ever after. Hell, I even *waxed* for him." I gesture to my crotch area. "Do you have any idea how much that hurts? That shit feels like someone just doused gasoline all over your nether regions, then lit a match and tossed it, forcing you to wallow in agony for hours with no relief in sight." I pause, allowing the laughter to swell, then die down. "But I did it for him. Because that's what people do when they're in love, isn't it? They do everything to keep the other person happy."

Everyone seems to nod in agreement.

"What they *don't* do is break up with them on their thirtieth...*fucking*...birthday because they no longer think their partner of twelve years is serious enough."

"Fuck him," a man shouts above the silence, his New York accent thick. I look in his direction as he raises his beer toward me. "He doesn't deserve you anyway."

I nod, smiling in appreciation. "You're probably right. Because everything he's done tells me I deserve someone so much better than what I allowed myself to settle for, all because he checked off every box the teenage version of myself said she wanted in a potential husband."

I blow out a long breath, blinking back the tears forming. "But how do you tell your heart to stop loving someone?"

My expression turns pleading, inwardly wishing someone has the secret to this. The atmosphere shifts, becoming more solemn. I hate ending my story on such a sour note, so I force a smile, although it doesn't reach my eyes.

"I'll tell you what you do, Evie." My voice wavers. "You take a page from Scarlett 'Fuck All Men' O'Hara. A lovely Irish lass, much like myself. You worry about it tomorrow." I lift my glass and practically the entire bar follows suit. "Because tomorrow is another day," I finish in my best Scarlett O'Hara impression.

In an instant, the deafening sound of cheers and

applause surrounds me. By morning, I may regret consuming the amount of alcohol that provided me the loose lips to share my heartache with a room of strangers. Based on the phones that have been pointed at me the past several minutes, I'm sure I'll be a viral sensation by tomorrow. Right now, none of that matters. All that does is trying to salvage what I can of my thirtieth birthday.

With a smile, I curtsey once more, slowly turning to each corner of the bar to offer my thanks for their rapt attention.

And that's when I notice *him*.

Outwardly, there's nothing unique about him.

Except for the disheveled light brown hair that curls over the collar of his perfectly tailored suit.

Except for the penetrating blue eyes that remain locked on me, the heat in his gaze making me think he can read my innermost secrets.

Except for the way he's the only one not clapping, simply assessing everything about me.

He's sitting by himself at a table in the corner, away from the regular Thursday evening revelry. While this isn't a complete dive bar, he still seems out of place with his Armani suit and Tag Heuer watch. Needless to say, I'm intrigued. Who is he? Why is he peering at me in a way that makes me feel like he can see straight through the mask?

"What are you going to do about your living situation?" Izzy asks once the laughter and applause die down.

I snap out of my daze and lower myself back to my chair. My limbs are jittery as I take a deep breath, unable to shake the heat of a pair of blue eyes staring at me.

"I'm not sure." My voice is distant. "He said I didn't

have to move out right away. And maybe I shouldn't. Maybe Trevor needs some time to realize what a mistake this is."

"You honestly think it's a mistake?" Chloe presses, obviously annoyed.

"He *is* under a lot of pressure with that big trial coming up. If this one goes well, he could be on a fast track for junior partner. I think…" I toy with the stem of my glass. "I'm *sure* he'll eventually come to his senses. I mean, if he didn't want to be with me, why wouldn't he insist I immediately find somewhere else to live? He knows I could crash on the pullout in your den. Instead, he told me to stay as long as I need." I'm probably grasping at straws, but I'm not ready to give up on Trevor yet. Maybe he needs to know that. "Perhaps if I'm still living there, he'll be reminded of exactly what he's throwing away."

"Oh, I know what you should do!" Nora exclaims, her eyes brightening as if having an epiphany.

"What's that?" I ask. "And no. I am *not* putting up a profile on Tinder."

She laughs. "No. I wasn't going to suggest that, although there is nothing wrong with meeting someone on Tinder. I was going to suggest you hire August Laurent."

I pinch my brows together, shaking my head. "August Laurent? Who's that?"

"He's this guy…" She looks at Chloe. "I'm not sure how to explain. He provides a…boyfriend experience, so to speak."

"Boyfriend experience?"

"Yeah," Chloe answers. "Women pay him to pretend to be their boyfriend for however short or long a time as necessary."

"So…an escort," I scoff.

"Not just any escort." Nora smirks, her eyes dancing with excitement. "He's, like, the most sought-after escort on the East Coast, if not the country. And he lives right here in Manhattan. Women line up to hire him."

"Sorry, but I don't need an escort. Or to pay someone for a 'boyfriend experience'. I have an *actual* boyfriend."

Chloe lifts a finger. "Had."

"Yes. Had. But like I said, my situation with Trevor is just temporary."

"This guy specializes in that kind of thing."

"What do you mean?"

"What's one of the biggest motivators out there?" Chloe narrows her gaze.

I stare blankly at her.

"Jealousy, Evie." Nora looks at me like I'm a complete idiot. I've just been out of the dating world for so long. True, my job entails doling out relationship and dating advice on a regular basis, but I've never had to play any of these games myself. The mere thought exhausts me. "I'm sure hiring a ridiculously hot guy to pretend to be your boyfriend would have Trevor banging down your door in no time."

"So he takes advantage of women who've had their hearts broken?" I bring my glass back to my lips, inhaling the oaky aroma of the whiskey before taking a sip. "Real stand-up guy."

"People swear by him." Chloe arches her brow. "For what it's worth. They say he helped them realize their true value. Helped them feel worthy of being loved again, whether it be by their ex or someone new."

"He must have a magical penis." I laugh, wavering a little in my chair. "Super penis." I snort, amused at the image I've concocted in my head of a penis wearing a cape. "Faster than a premature ejaculation," I joke, coming up with his superhero tagline. Ideas for a feature in my column swirl in my head.

Martini spews out of Izzy's mouth as she chokes on the sip she had just taken. I swipe at my face, removing a few droplets.

"Didn't that super model hire him?" she asks Chloe once her coughing settles down.

She nods. "Holly Turner."

"Holly Turner?" I repeat. "Why would she have to hire an escort? The woman's stunning! You'd think she'd have a line of men vying to take her ex's place."

"She refused to confirm she did, in fact, use this guy's services," Chloe explains, "but she did admit that had it not been for the help of a 'dear friend' during her separation and eventual divorce, she never would have realized how unhappy she'd been. This 'dear friend' made her feel beautiful again."

I straighten my spine, finishing my drink. "I don't need someone to help me feel beautiful again. And I certainly don't need to hire some escort to pretend to be my boyfriend. I'll handle Trevor on my own. I just need..."

"Yeah?"

"I just need to celebrate my thirtieth birthday and forget that Trevor ruined the day for me."

The girls pass a devious grin amongst each other. I have a feeling I'll regret this tomorrow, but for now, I need a night with my two best friends.

"You got it, Evie." Chloe signals Aiden. A line of shots appears in front of us within a few seconds.

"Here's to thirty." Izzy raises her shot, Chloe, Nora, and me mirroring her, gulping down the liquor.

Just as I take a sip of the water Aiden's thankfully placed in front of me, a body brushes against mine. A shiver rolls down my spine, making me breathless. I glance behind me to see Mr. Armani Suit walk toward the door. Everything tells me to look away, to return my attention to my friends, but the tipsy version of Evie doesn't listen, keeping her eyes glued to his tall physique instead. This is the best suit porn I've seen in a while and I can't get enough.

As he's about to walk out the door, he stops. My heart skyrockets to my throat when his gaze locks with mine. A blush builds on my cheeks as I snap my eyes forward, doing everything to pretend he didn't catch me ogling him. But he did. And the smirk on his full lips confirms this fact.

Bastard.

Chapter Three

SUN STREAMS THROUGH the windows, bathing the room in light, rousing me from unconsciousness. I squint, having difficulty adjusting to the brightness. I don't remember my bedroom being this bright, considering it faces west. Then again, the last thing I probably thought about last night when I stumbled back to the apartment was closing the drapes.

Rubbing my eyes, I try to shake off the cobwebs, my tongue feeling like sandpaper. Thankfully, drunk Evie must have predicted I'd wake up with a hangover to rival all hangovers and left a water bottle and a couple aspirin on the nightstand. Drunk Evie really is thoughtful.

I reach for the pills, pop them into my mouth, and chase them with a huge gulp of water, practically downing the entire bottle to dull the fire. After returning the bottle to the table, I collapse back onto the bed, the cool, silky sheets comforting against my skin.

As I stare at the ceiling, I exhale a long breath, the reality of yesterday slowly trickling back. Trevor really did break up with me. On my thirtieth birthday. Because I'm not serious enough. I'll show him how wrong he is. I just need to nurse this hangover, then I'll begin Operation Prove Trevor Wrong. If he wants a serious girlfriend, I can be that. I can tone down the jokes. I can stop making snarky comments. I can even write some different articles for the magazine. Less raunchy, more smart humor. What I can't do is throw away over a decade of our relationship because he doesn't think I'm the type of girl he can be with if he wants to make partner. I've always been a problem solver. Right now, this issue with Trevor is simply a problem I vow to fix.

Closing my eyes, I wrap the comforter around my body. I expect the remnants of Trevor's scent to infiltrate my senses. But it doesn't. One night and his aroma has already faded from the bed we once shared.

As I try not to think about that, my foot brushes against another body. I still, inhaling sharply. Did Trevor forget he broke up with me? Was he so exhausted after working all night he was on autopilot and climbed into bed? Better yet, did he already realize what a mistake he made and changed his mind, but I was in too much of an alcohol-induced coma to remember him telling me as much?

Hope building, I glance beside me, expecting to see Trevor's impeccable dark hair. Everything about him is always perfect, right down to the lack of bedhead when he gets up in the morning. He makes me feel like Cousin It next to him.

When I see a full head of disheveled, sandy brown hair instead of Trevor's pristine locks, I bolt up. The duvet falls around my waist, revealing my underwear-clad body. Then I look up, realizing I'm not in my bedroom.

"Shit, shit, shit," I whisper shout, wracking my brain for a clue as to how I went from having a girls' night to sharing a bed with a stranger. Maybe it's not that bad. Maybe I told him my sob story about what happened earlier in the night and he offered me a place to sleep so I didn't have to go back to a home full of memories.

But practically naked?

Nice try, Evie. There's a better chance of it snowing in Florida than that being true. There's only one explanation why I'm scantily dressed and in another man's bed after a night of drinking.

I had a one-night stand.

With a stranger.

Hours after the man I thought I'd marry dumped me.

No wonder it seems like the world's out of balance this morning, aside from the dizziness consuming me due to the alcohol I'm sure still flows through my bloodstream. I've now slept with four men.

Surely this can be excused as a result of some relationship-related PTSD. I'm not trying to make light of the severity of actual PTSD, but I need something, *anything* to make me feel better about the situation. I don't have one-night stands. I just...don't. Especially with someone I met at a bar. What kind of man takes home a drunk girl and sleeps with her anyway? No one worth sticking around to find out about.

Mumbling a silent prayer that I can escape unnoticed, I carefully lift the duvet off me and step onto the chilly hardwood floor. As I tiptoe around the large room, every muscle in my body aches, probably due to the previous night's calisthenics. I search for my dress, expecting to find it crumpled on the floor, along with a trail of his clothes leading to the bed. Instead, it's neatly slung over a chair in the corner. Maybe he's a neat freak.

When I tug the dress over my head, a whiff of a powder-fresh scent filters into my nostrils. I'd anticipated it to smell like alcohol and sweat, not as if it had been recently laundered.

Curiosity piqued, I glance at the bed to get a better look at the man I found irresistible in my alcohol-induced fog. When I see his chiseled face, I release what I hope is a noiseless gasp, my hand flying to cover my mouth.

It's him. The man I noticed sitting across the bar after telling the entire place about my breakup. The man who caused a jolt of electricity to course through my veins when he brushed against me. The man whose blue eyes I couldn't get out of my mind all night, even after he left. How the hell did I end up here?

Cautious, I step closer to the bed, hoping something will trigger a memory. If nothing else, at least I went home with an attractive guy. Well, attractive isn't an accurate descriptor of this man's beauty. The way he looks so peaceful, yet still incredibly masculine as he sleeps causes a tingle to spread through me at the thought of what we did last night. I can almost hear his deep voice whispering his most carnal desires into my ear. I imagine he was a sensual lover, one who put my needs first, making sure I was taken care of. Maybe it's a good thing I can't remember. Then I can pretend it never happened. Pretend I've still only slept with three people.

My eyes rake down his naked torso, confirming what I'd imagined last night as I ogled his physique. Broad shoulders. Sculpted pecs. Chiseled abs. And the cherry on top… An intricate tribal tattoo of a phoenix covering his back. This is a man who obviously takes care of himself. He's not one of those guys who's too muscular that it's unattractive. His muscles are firm and defined, but not overly so. He's pure perfection, making it nearly impossible to look away.

That's when I notice the triangle of scars on his abdomen near his hipbone, an imperfection on an otherwise flawless physique. They're pink and faded from the obvious passing of years, but I'm intrigued by the story behind them.

Instantly, my mystery man shifts, letting out a raspy groan. It hits me deep in my core, a heightened desire filling me. It almost makes me want to crawl back into bed to see if we can recreate what happened last night in the hopes of jumpstarting my memory. But I can't do that to Trevor. Not now that I'm coherent and thinking clearly again.

Hastily collecting my shoes and purse, I hurry from the bedroom, praying I'm able to escape before he wakes up. I have no desire to face him, not when whatever happened last night was a giant mistake. I need to get out of…wherever I am before whoever he is notices I'm no longer in his bed and comes looking for me. Then I can pretend this never happened. New York is an enormous city. The likelihood of our paths crossing again is nonexistent.

Quietly shutting the bedroom door behind me, I pause, holding my breath, listening for any movement from within. Thankfully, all I hear is silence. I blow out a slow exhale and continue down a long corridor, wondering where I am. Whoever this man is, he must do pretty well for himself. His place is bright and modern, sleek wood flooring coupled with immaculate walls containing well-appointed black-and-white framed prints of famous landmarks in New York. The Brooklyn Bridge. The Empire State Building. Ellis Island.

As I emerge into the luxurious living room, I'm caught breathless at the view from the expansive windows filling the far wall. The sun shines through them, the breathtaking sight of Central Park several dozen stories below us.

"Wow." I can only imagine what a place like this cost. The mortgage on the apartment I shared with Trevor in Brooklyn was over $3,000 a month. A place overlooking

Central Park in Columbus Circle? It must cost several million.

Even more intrigued as to who this mystery man is, I consider snooping to see what else I can find out. Hell, I can't even remember his name. I wonder if I asked for it, or if I agreed to sleep with him regardless of whether I knew it. I'd like to say I'd never do such a thing, but all bets are off.

I shift my attention to the enormous kitchen island and spy a stack of mail on the corner. When I start toward it for no other reason than to learn his name, I discern the faint echo of footsteps from down the hallway.

My pulse soaring, I spin around, hurrying out of the apartment, leaving my one-night stand where it belongs... Behind me.

Chapter Four

WHEN I EMERGE onto the street, I'm enveloped by the fevered pace of midtown Manhattan, the sidewalks moving with the energy of this place I've grown to love. Sirens blare, horns honk, truck brakes squeak and moan. But as I revel in the mass of people walking in every direction possible, coupled with the strength of the sun on this summer day, the panic of waking up in a strange man's bed is overshadowed with a new reason to panic... It's Friday. And I'm most likely late for work.

Reaching into my purse, I retrieve my cell, thankful it still has a little battery life left, and spy the time. 9:35.

"Crap," I mutter, dashing through the crowd of men and women in suits, as well as the occasional tourist snapping photos, not paying attention to the people trying to skirt around them. At least I had the wherewithal to have a one-night stand with someone who lives only a few blocks from the office. As much as I hate showing up in the dress I wore yesterday, I don't have enough time to go back to Brooklyn and change if I want to be on time for the weekly check-in with the magazine's editor. Thankfully, I have extra clothes at work.

I reach the building in record time and run through the lobby, my heels clicking on the marble tile. After scanning my ID badge, permitting me entry through the turnstiles, I join the mob of people waiting for an elevator. When one arrives, we all pile in, everyone glued to their phones as we ride up to our respective floors.

Having no idea how I must look this morning, I pull out the compact I keep in my purse, checking my reflection. I cringe, the bloodshot eyes staring back evidencing a night of overindulgence and lack of sleep.

I do my best to adjust my appearance with the few tools I have. I secure my wavy red hair into a fashionable messy bun on the top of my head, then pull out a few ringlets to frame my face, making it appear the haphazard style is intentional. After I put a little powder on my fair skin and line my lips with gloss, I pop a mint into my mouth to rid myself of rank morning breath, hoping it will be sufficient until I can get to the toothbrush I keep in my desk.

The instant I'm done readjusting my appearance, the elevator comes to a stop on my floor. I straighten my spine, holding my head high as I emerge into the magazine's busy newsroom, smiling as I pass the chipper receptionist who, just like the rest of the entry-level staff, is waiting for her big break in the modeling industry. The place is bright and buzzing with energy, phones ringing off the hook, nails tapping against keyboards, music playing from a few desks.

As I continue through the rows of cubicles, I exude all the confidence I can muster in the hopes no one realizes I dragged myself out of a stranger's bed and am wearing the same dress I had on yesterday. What am I thinking? Of course they'll notice. This is a women's fashion magazine. For many of these people, fashion is their life. They could probably tell me what I wore on a certain date better than I can.

Bypassing my cubicle, I head straight for the break room, needing caffeine before I face what I imagine will be a day from hell. I enter the space, the aroma of coffee making my mouth water. As I pour myself a cup, I hear a familiar whistle, followed by the sound of drawn-out clapping. I groan silently. There's only one person it could be.

"Did you just slow clap my walk of shame?" I slowly turn around, stirring sweetener and creamer into my coffee.

"You bet your ass I did, sweet cheeks," Chloe retorts, annoyingly chipper for what seems like an early hour.

Her hair is sleek and lustrous, her outfit stylish, her gray eyes bold and refreshed. I hate her for not suffering from the same hangover as me. Then again, she exhibited something called self-control last night, whereas I fired for effect. I didn't drink to take the edge off. I drank to forget. It worked...a little too well.

"Based on your appearance..." She gestures to my dress, more than aware it's the same one I wore yesterday, "it looks like you never made it home last night."

I take a sip of coffee, briefly closing my eyes as I savor the nutty flavor.

"So if you didn't go home, where did you have your Uber take you?"

I arch a brow, looking over my mug at her. "Uber?"

"Yeah. Uber." She peers at me as if I'm a complete idiot. "You tried to take the subway, but we convinced you that you were too drunk, so you called for an Uber."

"Of course! I took an Uber!" I place my coffee on the counter and withdraw my phone from my purse. Ignoring the multiple texts from my mother, I bring up the app and search my latest trip.

Chloe grabs my arm, tugging me from the break room.

Thankfully, my reflexes are quick enough that I grab my coffee before she drags me through the offices.

"Do you not remember what happened between leaving the bar and waking up this morning?" she asks softly so no one can overhear.

"I vaguely recall wanting to go home and sleep off the alcohol…" I suck in a breath, my eyes flinging to my phone. "But when the Uber driver pulled up in front of our place, I couldn't go inside." I shove my cell at her. She takes it, looking at the map of my trip, which appears to be one large circle. "I must have had him take me back to the bar."

"Why?"

"All I know is I couldn't go into that apartment and be surrounded by memories of Trevor. Maybe I went back to find you and crash at your place for the night."

"Instead of having the Uber driver *take* you to my place?"

I shake my head. "I can't attempt to rationalize what went through my brain last night, other than way too much alcohol."

"I guess I can understand that. And I said you could crash with me as long as you need to, not just one night. I'm barely there anyway."

"That's unnecessary." Once we reach my cubicle, I place my mug on the desk, then open the storage cabinet in the corner, pulling out a fresh bra, panties, and wrap dress, as well as my toothbrush and toothpaste. "Like I said yesterday…" My steps are quick as I walk toward the ladies' room, Chloe following. "I'm sure once this trial is over and Trevor is less stressed, he'll realize what a mistake he made."

I lock myself in one of the stalls and rip my dress over

my head. I almost want to keep it on since it smells like my mystery man.

"Evie, wh—"

"I don't remember making it back to the bar," I interrupt, knowing all too well she's about to ask what my plan is if Trevor doesn't believe he made a mistake. I'm not going to think about that right now. It's not an option. Everything about my relationship with Trevor had gone according to plan…until now. We've gotten derailed. I need to get us back on track. That's all.

"Then where did you go, because the Uber dropped you back off at the bar." She pauses. "Or at least close to the bar." I imagine her scrutinizing the trip map on the app. "Actually, he dropped you off in Columbus Circle."

I gasp, straightening my spine.

"What is it?"

I hastily pull the wrap dress over my body, tying it around the waist. "That's where I woke up this morning." I collect my things and step out of the stall.

"Where?"

"Columbus Circle. More specifically, on the seventy-something floor in an apartment overlooking Central Park that had to cost millions." Finding my toothbrush, I squeeze some toothpaste on it.

Her eyes widen as she gapes at me. "Who the hell did you sleep with last night? A goddamn Rockefeller?"

"I have no idea, but he was at the bar," I say as I brush my teeth.

"He was?"

I nod, then spit into the sink, wiping the residue from around my mouth. "Sitting alone at a table in the corner. I noticed him after I did my little…act."

"You did, did you?" She waggles her brows, crossing her arms as she leans against the counter.

"Not like that." I turn my attention to the mirror, fixing my appearance the best I can. "But he wore this gorgeous designer suit and had even more gorgeous eyes. Any female with an interest in the male population would notice this guy."

"*I* never noticed him."

"Well, you're missing out, because this guy…" I peer at my reflection, recalling the electricity that filled me when his body breezed by mine. The touch was so subtle, but hit me deeper than anything had in recent memory, even when Trevor and I were intimate. I blame it on the combination of the alcohol and my heartbreak, refusing to consider the possibility there's a different reason for my reaction.

"Yes?" Chloe presses.

"Beautiful. Absolutely beautiful, Chloe."

She places her hand on her hip, analyzing me. "Okay. So he's gorgeous. That doesn't explain how you ended up in his apartment in Columbus Circle."

"I don't know how I ended up there." I snatch my phone out of Chloe's hand and stare at the map of my Uber trip, seeing it wasn't a complete round trip. The car dropped me a few blocks shy of the bar. I lean against the tile wall, wishing something would trigger a memory. As I rest my head on the cool tile, I inhale a breath, blinking repeatedly.

"What? What is it?"

"All the stop and go of the car. He was a typical New York driver, gunning the gas before coming to a screeching stop at a light." I snap my eyes to Chloe. "It made me sick, so before I threw up in his car, I had him let me out by the Time Warner Center."

"And did you throw up in his car?"

"I don't think so." I pinch my lips together, thinking. "No. I definitely didn't." I squint, pieces of the previous night trickling back like raindrops. "I remember feeling dizzy after getting out of the car, so I grasped a bus bench to steady myself, but it didn't help. The world kept spinning. I think I mumbled something about never drinking again." My eyes widen as his voice fills my mind. "That's when I heard someone say, 'That's probably a good idea', or something like that."

"Who?"

"Him. Mr. Armani Suit." I smile dreamily at the memory of looking up to see my knight in shining armor standing before me, his blue eyes emblazoned in my mind. Noticing Chloe smirking, I quickly wipe the smile off my face, pretending not to be affected. "After that, I don't remember much."

"You like him," she comments after a brief silence.

"What?" I step back, aghast. "No. Absolutely not. I don't even know his name."

"That's never stopped me before," she answers dismissively.

"I was under duress. I drank far too much, made the mistake of going home with some random guy, then woke up practically naked in his bed. Just goes to show you what kind of slimeball this guy truly is, sleeping with someone who's obviously drunk. So not only did my boyfriend dump me, I get to end my week with a visit to the clinic to get tested because who knows if this guy put on a condom."

"How do you know you slept with him? You said yourself you don't remember much."

"I woke up in my bra and panties."

"All the more evidence you *didn't* sleep together. Who in their right mind puts their bra and panties back on after sex? Especially drunken sex. Who sleeps with a bra on anyway?"

"Again, I can't attempt to rationalize what I was thinking last night. And trust me. I know how I get when I've had too much to drink. I'm sure once I saw this guy without his shirt on, all thoughts of Trevor went out the window and I only cared about one thing...getting laid. Or maybe I did it to spite Trevor...a revenge screw, so to speak...which I must have thought was a *brilliant* idea with all the alcohol I drank last night."

She smirks, amused by my misfortune. I guess I deserve it. I've repeatedly claimed I would never have a one-night stand. That I would only sleep with someone I felt a strong connection to. I'm not a prude. While I enjoy sex as much as any other woman, I don't feel the need to sleep around.

Then again, when most people are at the age where they're exploring their sexuality, I was already dating Trevor. We explored our sexuality together. Is this what my life will be like without Trevor? Having to sleep around and hope to find someone I connect with? God, I don't even want to think about having to date, especially in New York City.

"So..." She grins deviously. "What *did* he look like without his shirt on?"

"An Adonis," I answer before my brain can tell my mouth to shut it. "Fuck, Chloe. Male perfection. Broad shoulders. Sculpted chest. Abs you want to lick. With a body like that, I'm sure I was all over him. Which makes me feel even more guilty."

"Why? Trevor broke up with you."

"Yes, but—"

"Oh, there you two are," a voice interrupts. We whip our heads toward the door. Maggie, the editor-in-chief's assistant, stands there, a self-important expression on her face. Sometimes she forgets she's the editor's assistant, not assistant editor. Big difference. "The meeting's about to start. Viv's waiting on you guys."

"Sorry, Mags. We're coming." Grateful for the reprieve, I smile at Chloe as I follow Maggie, dropping off my clothes from yesterday at my cubicle on the way.

As I'm about to walk into Viv's office, a hand covers my arm. I look at Chloe, her slate-gray eyes narrowed on me. "Listen, Evie. I get that you're hurting over what happened with Trevor, and you have every right to be. Maybe this is the opportunity you need to have a little fun and figure out who you are."

"I already know—"

"Who you are?" Her voice is low, her expression filled with skepticism. "If you do, why are you willing to change that just so Trevor will want to be with you? I get you have a history. I can't even imagine how difficult the next few weeks…hell, months will be trying to adjust to a new normal. I'm the last person you should take relationship advice from, considering I avoid them like the plague. But instead of wasting time concocting a plan to win Trevor back by becoming the type of person he wants to date, you should focus on finding someone who wants to date you as you are right now."

She places her hands on my biceps, her eyebrows pulled down. "Because the Evie I know is a complete badass. And any guy who doesn't see that doesn't deserve you."

Chapter Five

CHLOE'S WORDS LEAVE me questioning whether salvaging my relationship with Trevor is the right move. How could it not be? Like she said, she's the last person I should take relationship advice from. In the five years I've known her, she hasn't been in a single committed relationship. She doesn't understand the dynamic of a real relationship. It's all about give and take, being in a partnership. Sometimes one person has to shoulder more of the weight. Right now, I need to do the heavy lifting. I refuse to give up so easily.

Resolved, I step into the conference room, coming to an immediate stop when my eyes fall on the spread of flowers covering the table, cards and chocolate interspersed among the extravagant display.

"What's going on?""

I want to believe this is merely a birthday celebration for me. It probably started that way, but as I spy the sympathy covering my coworkers' faces, coupled with the balloons that say "I'm sorry" and "Get Well Soon", I'm positive that's not the case.

"It appears condolences are in order."

Vivian Wood, Editor-in-Chief of *Blush* magazine, is the picture of sophistication. Then again, I'm fairly certain she could make a paper sack look like this year's latest fashion trend. Not a single strand of her platinum

41

hair is out of place. She's in her sixties, but her youthful complexion, devoid of wrinkles, makes it appear as if she's not a day over forty. She's slender, dressed in skinny jeans, gorgeous heels, and a suit jacket. I consider myself on the tall side at five feet, nine inches, but that's no match for Viv. That's probably one of the reasons she's remained single most of her life. Her six-foot height must intimidate most potential partners. Let's face it. The majority of men would feel emasculated standing next to a woman who's taller than them...especially a woman as confident and successful as Viv.

"Sorry about the breakup, Evie." There's an air of authority about her as she strides toward me, a devilish smirk crawling across her thin, pink lips. "Or I should be sorry, but the opportunist in me looks forward to how this will affect your perspective in some of your articles."

"It won't."

Her smile widens. "We'll see about that. For the past five years, you've been writing about sex and dating from the safety of what you thought to be a secure relationship. That's not the case anymore. Trust me. I've been single in this city for thirty years. It's a jungle out there. I'm looking forward to what new and exciting things you'll bring to the table now."

"I'm sure it's not that bad."

Chloe snorts a laugh and I shift my gaze to her. "The men in this city are a different breed altogether."

"She's right," Lenora, the editor for health and beauty, offers. I head toward Chloe, sitting beside her on the couch. "Most of them are glued to their phones."

"And forget about being chivalrous," Dawn, one of our graphic designers, adds. "I can't tell you how many dates I've been on with a guy who didn't even open the door or pick up the check."

Chloe turns to me. "So if you come across a man who takes care of you, go after that." She winks, an unspoken reminder in her gaze about last night's mystery man.

"I'll keep that in mind," I say. "And thank you all for your kind thoughts. But honestly, I'm okay. I have a plan."

"Of course you do," Viv quips as several other people snicker or groan, accustomed to my quirks. "Evie Fitzgerald, the girl with a plan."

I suppose after working here this long, she's gotten accustomed to my idiosyncrasies, particularly my love for plans and itineraries. I've always preferred structure. Whereas Chloe loves waiting until the last minute to get her work done, often sending her final piece to Viv mere seconds before it's due, I work ahead, not rushing anything. Hell, I have pieces I intend to write for the magazine and blog planned out for the next six months. My planner is a work of art, and my lifeline. Structure keeps me grounded, focused.

"Speaking of which, let's hear what you have planned for the August issue."

I blow out a relieved breath, happy to concentrate on work instead of my breakup for a moment. With a smile, I discuss my idea of exploring the world of dating in five major cities across the country. An idea that just came to me, thanks to Chloe. Viv thinks it's brilliant, since she's under the impression I'll be rejoining the ranks of single people.

Once she gives me the go-ahead, she continues going around the room, everyone pitching different story ideas for the next issue. She nixes a few, approves others, or reworks some to make them more compelling. Her ability to know a brilliant idea when she hears one has kept her at the helm of this magazine for over a decade.

When I was a teenager, I scrambled to the shelves for my monthly copy of *Blush* magazine. I always knew I wanted to work in this industry, so I did what anyone with a dream would do. I studied. Working for *Blush* was the end goal. One I didn't think I'd ever achieve. It's continually been the top women's magazine in the country, always on the cutting edge. While I didn't see myself offering dating tips, it's a stepping stone to being able to write things I really want to, things of interest to all women. Reproductive rights, equality, economic justice... Just to name a few.

Once the meeting ends and we have our assignments for next month's issue, about half of which will never make it to print, we disperse. I hang back to collect the gifts my irreverent coworkers bestowed on me. As I read one of the cards that went along with a bouquet of roses, Chloe sidles up next to me.

"'Sorry for your loss. Wishing you moments of peace and comfort as you remember all the good times you had together.'"

She snort-laughs at the ridiculousness of it all.

"Did I just get a sympathy card for a breakup?" I muse as I toss it back onto the pile.

"It appears so."

This shouldn't surprise me. Since accepting Viv's offer to work here, I've come to learn many of the employees have a rather dark and cynical sense of humor. When the mouse that roamed the office, evading all the traps the exterminators set out for it, had finally been outsmarted, one of the fashion columnists declared a day of mourning. He even went so far as to plan a memorial for our fallen friend. There's no such thing as a normal day at *Blush* magazine.

"How did everyone find out?"

She shrugs as she helps me gather everything. "News travels fast around here. You should know that by now. It's a miracle you didn't find out Trevor was breaking up with you *before* he told you. That happened to Maureen over in beauty."

Arms full, we head out of the conference room with what we manage to carry.

"At least I get chocolate out of it. Like a parting gift after picking the wrong door on *Let's Make a Deal*." I imitate my best announcer's voice. "Instead of a beautiful diamond or a lifetime of security, we'll be sending you home with a box of drugstore chocolates. Better luck next time!" We turn into my cubicle and I deposit the first batch of flowers, cards, and chocolates onto my desk.

"Oh, come on. You got a lot more than just a crappy box of chocolates."

"You're right. I got sympathy cards meant for the death of a loved one, flowers, and a few balloons."

"Don't forget the sausage."

I frown. "Sausage?"

"Yeah." She waggles her brows, making an obscene gesture with her hand. "Mr. Armani's sausage, on the off-chance I'm wrong and you *did* sleep with him. Regardless, I'd take that consolation prize any day over some schmuck who didn't realize what he had."

"Trevor's under a great deal of stress." I repeat the same argument, although my words lack the conviction they had earlier. "He knows what he had." I avoid what I can only assume to be Chloe's annoyed stare. "I just

45

need to remind him of that."

I step out of my cubicle to get the rest of my breakup gifts when I almost run straight into Viv. I inhale a sharp breath, stopping in my tracks.

"Sorry, Viv. I wasn't looking."

"That much is clear, Evie. I'd like a word."

"Of course." I force a smile, pass Chloe a nervous look, then follow Viv, curious as to her sudden need to speak to me. Normally, all magazine-related problems are addressed at our weekly meetings. Then again, Viv's known to use her employees' real-life issues in concocting new, edgy story ideas. I worry she's about to ask me to do something crazy, like sign up for online dating apps and journal my experience. Or apply to *The Bachelor*. Or something that would rival the premise of *How to Lose a Guy in Ten Days*.

Once we're in her office, she closes the door, putting me even more on edge. "Have a seat, Evie." Her voice is even as she gestures across the desk.

"Is everything okay?" Tentative, I sit down in the bright orange chair. Her workspace is decorated in a stunning mid-century modern design. Vibrant colors. Sleek lines. Uncluttered shelves. Every time I step into this room, I feel like I've just walked onto the set of *Mad Men*. In fact, Viv bought many of the items here in a prop auction.

"Everything's great. I wanted to speak with you in private about an...opportunity."

She opens one of the desk drawers and withdraws a file. Placing a pair of dark-rimmed glasses over her eyes, she scans the papers in the folder.

"Since we hired you, our readership has seen a steady increase. These days, every other magazine similar to ours struggles to capture the market's attention. But your wit, coupled with your love of social media, has helped us stay modern. Prior to bringing you onboard, our sex and dating column was the least popular. Most people overlooked it as being the same stale advice women have received for decades. But you gave it a fresh coat of paint, so to speak. You write stories real women can relate to, although I've yet to be the lucky recipient of a penis picture over the Internet."

I laugh, recalling my most recent blog post that garnered hundreds of thousands of shares on social media. "That's all I wanted when I took over the column. To make dating and relationships more relatable. To help people realize relationships don't have to be as hard as we make them."

"And you've done an incredible job. We all know this industry can be tough, having wide swings from quarter to quarter. But it hasn't been that way lately, and I think a lot of it has to do with your ingenuity. You bring a fresh perspective to a platform we all feared would soon die."

She removes her glasses and places them on the desk, pinching her lips together. "As you know, Grace is pregnant and will be leaving at the end of the year. She's decided not to return to work, which means I'm now looking for a new assistant editor. You interested?"

My eyes fling wide open as I sit in shock. I thought I'd have to work here much longer and gradually move up the ladder. I'd be more than happy if she offered me a transfer to the current events desk, with Margo being promoted to assistant editor. But to consider me for the position? This would be a huge promotion for me, not to mention the exact thing that could show Trevor I can be the serious, professional type. What's more professional than working as assistant editor at the top women's magazine in the country? For someone with a degree in English, there's not much higher I can go.

"Vivian," I breathe, shaking my head, covering my mouth with my hand. "I don't know what to say."

"Say you're interested."

"Of course I am. This is… This is amazing. I promise I won't let you down." I make a move to get up, but her voice stops me.

"Well, the job isn't yours yet."

I cock my head.

"Grace will be staying through December, but we'd like to start exploring our options now. So we're prepared. I'm sure you can appreciate that."

"I can." My shoulders fall. The likelihood of me getting chosen over people with more experience and seniority is slim to none. "And who are your other options?"

"Judy from celebrity news."

I nod. That doesn't come as a shock. She's been in the magazine industry for nearly twenty years. I'm surprised she wasn't promoted the last time an assistant editor left.

"Margo from current events."

Another obvious choice. Another woman who's made a career out of working in magazines. A woman whose job I've coveted for years.

"And you."

"Okay. So what do you need me to do?"

"Show me you can fulfill the duties of this role — conceptualizing and pitching stories for all sections of the magazine, as well as researching, interviewing, writing and editing the copy. You'll also oversee all the social media accounts and develop a content calendar for those."

I place my hands in my lap, wishing I hadn't gotten as drunk as I did last night. I would have much preferred having this conversation with a clear mind and a full night's sleep.

"I'm more than ready to take on all those responsibilities. I may not have the experience Judy and Margo do, but I'm a damn hard worker and won't be satisfied until I've perfected my craft. Not to mention the idea of planning content for our social media accounts gets me all sorts of excited."

"I knew it would. That's why I'm considering you. Now I need you to prove you're up for the job." She grins, sitting back in her chair, tenting her fingers in front of her. "Pitch me a story. Something no other magazine has written about. Something we can blast all over the cover and people will be lining up to grab their copies."

"Right now?" I fidget with the silky material of my dress, toying with the hem.

"Yes, right now. As my assistant editor, you'll need to be on your toes. Show me you can pitch something without advance warning. There are times a story doesn't pan out at the eleventh hour and you'll have to scramble to put something together, perhaps even a featured story, in little time."

"Okay." I look around her office, doing everything to get my creative juices flowing. I'm a writer. This is what I do. I find inspiration in the most obscure places and turn it into a story. Maybe if I weren't still nursing the mother of all hangovers, I'd be able to come up with an idea, but my brain is still cloudy. Then again, maybe something from last night could be my source of inspiration.

I flash my eyes back to Viv. "August Laurent."

Intrigued, Viv narrows her gaze on me. "Excuse me?"

"August Laurent," I repeat. "From what I understand, he's the most sought-after escort on the East Coast, possibly even the country."

Her lips turn into a conniving smile. "I'm more than aware of who August Laurent is. I'm also very aware he values his anonymity and privacy. He's never agreed to an interview. And despite repeated attempts by other reporters to unmask this mystery man, no one's been successful. What makes you think he'll allow you to interview him?"

"I don't know." My voice wavers, a sinking feeling forming in the pit of my stomach that I've just pitched Viv an impossible story. I don't want her to pick up on that, though. "Isn't part of being assistant editor seeking out those difficult stories? Imagine having a man dressed in a beautiful suit on the front page, not showing his face, with the headline 'August Laurent: Unrobed', or something like that. This guy is like Keyser Söze."

"Who?"

"Keyser Söze. The mystery man behind all the shit that goes down in *The Usual Suspects*."

Viv looks at me with quizzical eyes. Apparently, she's never seen one of my all-time favorite movies.

I shake my head. "It doesn't matter. All that does is this guy is a legend, but also a ghost. Imagine being the first magazine to get the inside scoop or, better yet…reveal his true identity."

Viv studies me for another long moment, then says, "Okay, Evie. Run with it. Let's see what you can do. Treat it as if it *will* be a feature, because whoever turns in the best article gets the feature story *and* the job. I'm giving you plenty of time, so I expect nothing less than absolute perfection. Don't let me down."

"I won't, Viv." I raise myself to my feet. "Thank you again for even considering me." I head toward the door.

"Oh, and Evie?"

I glance over my shoulder, meeting her eyes.

"Just a reminder. We deal with real facts, not sensationalized falsehoods." She gives me a knowing look. "Make sure you only write the true story. I won't accept anything less."

Chapter Six

MY FEET CAN'T carry me as quickly as I need them to as I hurry from Viv's office. All I do is pray I didn't just set myself up for failure by pitching Viv an impossible story. How is it everyone seems to know the name August Laurent, yet I've been blissfully unaware my entire life? Now I'm even more intrigued.

Out of breath, I round the corner into Chloe's cubicle, her peachy perfume wafting in the air. Her space is much more cluttered than mine. A celebrity news columnist, she always has various tips she's received scattered across her desk, hoping to be the first to report on whatever this month's big story will be, usually a pregnancy or new birth. Our audience loves reading about the children of the rich and famous. I can't blame them. I like reading about it, too. It normalizes them, apart from them having enough money to hire a nanny to help with midnight feedings, dirty diapers, and meltdowns.

"Evie, are you okay?" Her brow wrinkles in concern when she sees me.

I sit in her spare chair, my eyes zeroed in on her. I grab a notepad sitting on her desk and flip to a blank page, pulling out the pen I perpetually keep in the bun in my hair, readying myself to scratch down every word Chloe says. So many of my colleagues have forgone notepads for the ease of digital recorders. There's something about putting pen to paper that energizes me, makes me feel like I'm a participant in the story instead of a casual observer.

"I need you to tell me everything you know about August Laurent. Don't leave out a single thing." My firm voice relays the seriousness of the situation.

"Reconsidering Nora's idea from last night?" She winks.

"What? No," I answer quickly. "I don't need to pay someone to date me."

"Then why are you interested in August Laurent?"

I roll my chair closer to hers so no one can overhear, needing her to understand the depth of the hole I just dug for myself. "Because Viv is considering me for the assistant editor position when Grace leaves."

She releases a shriek of excitement, and I hush her, unsure if I'm supposed to discuss it.

"I'm as surprised as you. I honestly never gave it much thought."

"But Viv's giving it to you?"

"Not exactly. She wants to make sure I can handle a wider range of assignments first."

Chloe arches a brow. "Meaning?"

"Meaning she kind of put me on the spot and asked me to pitch her a story that would sell hundreds of thousands of copies." I fight a yawn. I don't know how I'll make it to five o'clock. All I want is to crawl into bed and sleep all weekend. Then the reminder I don't really have a bed anymore hits me, depressing me even more. If this is a sign for what awaits me in my thirties, I'd like to return them for a refund. Or maybe just skip straight to forty. "She's also considering Judy and Margo. Whoever produces the best story gets the job."

"So you pitched August Laurent?" Chloe's voice is a

mixture of surprise and superiority, almost like she knew I'd eventually want to know more about this guy. The concept is appealing, particularly from a sex and dating standpoint. What pushes a woman to such extremes that she doesn't think she has any other option but to hire someone to date her, or give her a "boyfriend experience", as they referred to it last night? I don't care how bad things get. I'd never stoop to that level.

"It was the first thing that popped into my head. To be honest, my brain isn't exactly firing on all cylinders today. I'm lucky I was able to come up with anything at all."

"You honestly think you'll get him to agree to this story?"

"Why not?" I shrug, trying not to feel dejected by the constant uncertainty facing me. "Why wouldn't he want to set the record straight on why he does what he does? I know I would. Unless he really is just a sleaze."

"He's remained anonymous for years," Chloe repeats the same warning Viv offered. "He's like the Keyser Söze of the escort world. A name you say that forces a certain reaction."

"See!" I exclaim, slamming my hands on the notepad, causing Chloe to startle. "I told Viv the same thing! But she never saw *The Usual Suspects,* so the analogy was lost on her."

"Instead of being some scary spook story you tell your kids so they eat their vegetables, it's more a threat to your spouse. 'Take me on vacation or I'll hire August Laurent to do it.'"

"'If you don't go down on me, August Laurent will!'" I offer, getting in on the game.

"'Let me use a strap-on with you, or I'm calling August

Laurent!'"

I laugh, then stop, her words registering with me. "Wait. A strap-on?" My forehead creases.

"Too far?"

"Yeah, a little. Weirdo," I joke before fixing my expression. "So, tell me what you know."

She sighs, leaning back in her chair. "I don't know much more than what you'll find online, which is next to nothing."

"But you know everything about everyone! And didn't you say Holly Turner hired him when she went through her divorce?"

"She never came right out and said she did, but she insinuated she spent a month in Fiji with him to escape reporters when news of her separation hit the papers."

"That's all? Nothing else? She must have said more than that. Anything to help me track down this guy."

"She was pretty tight-lipped about the entire thing." She pulls her bottom lip between her teeth, sucking on it.

"What is it?" I ask urgently.

"Nothing. It's probably nothing."

"Or it could be something."

Turmoil covers her expression.

"Come on, Chloe. You're the gossip queen! You must know something!"

She sighs in resignation. "Fine, but there's no guarantee there's truth to any of this. All I get are bits and pieces from people."

"Yes, but you get *lots* of bits and pieces, all of which could eventually fit into one puzzle."

Rolling her chair closer to mine, her voice becomes practically inaudible. "He's careful not to give out too much personal information to any of his clients. He makes it all about them, which I suppose is what they're paying him for. The guy's interested me for a few years, but with my column the way it is, I can't stop to hunt down a ghost. Still, you hear rumors."

"And did you hear a rumor about this mystery man sharing a piece of personal information with one of his clients that could potentially help me?" I grin wide, to which she nods.

"When Holly was here for a shoot a few months ago, we got to talking. Of course, she never mentioned *who* helped her through her divorce, but I read between the lines. It had to be August Laurent. She said he told her the importance of establishing a routine, some sort of normalcy in her life when it feels like it'll never be normal again."

I pinch my lips together, his advice resonating with me. I like having a routine when my life hasn't been uprooted. Now, after Trevor, I crave it even more. In fact, the thought of spending a few hours updating my planner has me more excited than I've been in a while.

"I'd mentioned how I prefer to be spontaneous, that I doubt I could ever do the same thing every single day. She said he claimed you could find normalcy in something small. Then she shared the example he gave her."

"And what was that?" I scribble down a few notes on my pad before looking back up at her.

"He apparently lost someone very close to him and had trouble coping with the loss. What helped was starting his day by going to the same coffee shop and ordering the same pastry. It gave him something to look forward to. To this very day, when he's in town, he still goes to the same coffee shop and orders the same chocolate hazelnut pastry."

She shifts her attention to her laptop, scrolling through a folder that must contain thousands upon thousands of images. Finding one, she turns the screen toward me. It's a blurry photo of a woman in a sleek pink dress, dark sunglasses covering her eyes, her face downturned.

"Who's that?"

"Carly Jensen. She's rumored to have hired August Laurent." She points to a man walking a few feet behind her, his eyes also obscured by dark sunglasses. "That man."

I squint, trying to make out his features, but it's impossible. Nothing about him stands out, not to mention he's walking several feet behind Carly.

"Chloe, I—"

"Wait. There's more." Keeping the photo on the screen, she searches for another one. When she finds it, she clicks on it, the image similar to the previous one. Another celebrity walking on the street wearing sunglasses. Another man in a dark suit trailing behind.

"This proves nothing."

"It may not, but it's a start."

I shake my head. "I don't see how. "There's nothing—"

"Because you aren't looking close enough," she interrupts. "Part of getting the scoop before anyone is being attuned to the details everyone else overlooks. Like this."

She zooms in on the man's hand. I squint again, faintly able to make out the familiar logo of Manhattan's famous Steam Room etched on the coffee cup. Then she does the same to the other photo.

"Isn't the Steam Room famous for their chocolate

hazelnut pastries?" she asks, a smirk on her face.

"They are."

"Bit of a coincidence, don't you think?" She sits back and folds her arms in front of her chest.

I stare at the two photos. It could be nothing, but it could be everything.

"I guess I know where I'll be spending my time now."

Chapter Seven

OVER THE NEXT few weeks, I make myself a cozy little home at a corner table in the Steam Room on Fifth Avenue. Based on the sheer number of people who frequent this place, it seems to be a popular spot among locals and tourists. I'm not surprised, considering it's located across from Central Park.

When I first concocted this plan, I didn't think it would be too difficult to figure out who August Laurent was — note whoever ordered a chocolate hazelnut pastry every morning, then see who was a repeat offender. I underestimated how popular that particular danish is. August Laurent probably knows this, too, which was why he didn't mind sharing this piece of personal information with his client. The entire population of Manhattan orders these damn pastries, which has made my job even more difficult. I've resorted to focusing on men without wedding bands whom I consider attractive enough to be a male escort. Shallow? Perhaps. But I have to narrow down the pool somehow.

On the last Thursday in June, as I sit in what's become my satellite office, I hear a deep voice order an Americano and the chocolate hazelnut pastry. I tear my eyes away from my laptop, hope building inside me that this may be the man I've been looking for.

The instant I do, I inhale a sharp breath, understanding why the timbre of the man's voice made

59

my thighs involuntarily squeeze together. There he is…
Mr. Armani Suit.

Dumbfounded at my horrible luck, all I can do is stare,
although all reason tells me to look away, to hide, to
pretend I have no idea who he is. What are the freaking
chances? Of all the coffee shops in this city, the one
person I hoped to never see again walks into this one.
Then, in confirmation of my belief that the universe is
out to get me, a pair of vibrant blue eyes shifts to mine, a
sly smile curling his lips.

"Shit." I lower my head and stare at my laptop screen,
wishing I could disappear into the background. I've
always loved the unique shade of my red hair…until this
moment when I'd give anything to blend into a sea of
blondes and brunettes.

As I pretend to read the words I've written over the
past hour, the aroma of citrus mixed with spice invades
my senses, reminiscent of the morning I woke up in a
strange man's bed. I pinch my lips together,
concentrating even harder, as if it will make him
disappear. Then I hear his voice — low, deep,
hypnotizing.

"I thought it was you. But maybe you should get up
and run away so I can be certain." There's dry
amusement in his tone.

I reluctantly look up, about to reply with a snarky
comment when I'm rendered speechless. I'd forgotten
how captivating this man is. At least drunk Evie doesn't
skimp on good looks, even when she's had a few too
many. Sandy, disheveled hair. Vibrant azure eyes
framed with lashes any woman would kill for. Olive skin
that appears to have been kissed by the sun. Strong face
with angular cheekbones. Broad nose. Two-day scruff
along his jaw. And full, lush lips surrounding gleaming

white teeth.

I lick my lips as I scan the rest of his frame, the navy blue suit he's wearing just as impeccable as the one he wore the night we first saw each other. But that's not what has my mouth salivating. It's the memory of what lies beneath — firm muscles, intricate tattoo, and mysterious scars on his otherwise flawless physique.

"Evie?"

I snap my eyes back to his, pretending I hadn't been ogling his body. The smirk pulling on his mouth is all the evidence I need to know he caught me in my mental undressing of him. Again.

"Hello," I say, exuding all the confidence I can, not wanting him to realize I can't remember his name...if he even told me. The cocky, self-assured way he carries himself gives off the impression it's not a stretch to think he *didn't* tell me his name. That he saw some drunk girl nearly passed out by his apartment and brought her up to take advantage of her.

But something about the way he gazes at me with heat and a hint of relief gives me pause. Perhaps Chloe was right when she suggested we may not have slept together. Now would be the perfect time to ask him, but I'm too embarrassed to admit I can't remember much of that night.

"It's good to see you again."

He narrows his eyes, unnerving me. "Is that so? From where I'm standing, you seem...flustered."

"Honestly, when I walked in here earlier this morning, the last thing I expected was to run into someone I made the mistake of going home with after drinking far too much. So, as much as I've enjoyed this awkward little reunion, you'll have to excuse me. I have work to do."

I return my eyes to my laptop, pretending to look incredibly busy and important. My muscles tense as I wait for him to walk away. Instead, he takes the seat across from me.

I stare at him, annoyed by his rashness. "What part of 'get lost' did you not understand?"

"I didn't exactly hear you say 'get lost'."

"No." I glower at him, then check over his shoulder to make sure I haven't missed anyone who looks like he might be an escort ordering a chocolate hazelnut pastry. "I was trying to be polite. It seems manners aren't your thing."

"Hmm... Manners. Like saying goodbye?" He arches a brow.

"Yes."

"It seems we both have a lesson to learn in manners then. Where I'm from, we say goodbye when we leave. Is that not customary where you grew up?"

He leans back, brushing his thumb against his lower lip. My eyes float to his mouth and I salivate at the idea of how they might taste. I squirm in my seat, hoping he doesn't pick up on what a tangled bundle of hormones I am.

"What did you say the name of your hometown is? Hickman? Do you not say goodbye in Hickman?"

"We do," I answer sheepishly.

He rests his elbows on the table, inching toward me. "Then why did you leave without saying goodbye?"

I open my mouth to respond, but he cuts me off.

"And don't say because you didn't want to wake me."

I snap my jaw shut. His formerly arrogant expression now carries a hint of vulnerability, at complete odds with the image I'd painted of him in my mind. "Maybe because I was embarrassed."

"Embarrassed?" He cocks his head at me. "Embarrassed about what?"

"Oh, I don't know," I shoot back sarcastically. "Because I got raging drunk and woke up in a stranger's bed."

He parts his lips to say something, but I hold up my hand. Now it's my turn to interrupt him.

"I'm sure you have no qualms about picking up drunk girls at a club or a bar and taking them home with you. What happened a few weeks ago... That's an isolated incident. I was drunk and dealing with some personal stuff, which caused me to make the horrible decision of going home with someone I don't even know."

"You know who I am. I told you. My name's Julian."

I blink repeatedly, something about that name sparking a memory. I snap my fingers. "That's right! Julian! Now I remember. I kept calling you Julius Caesar." I laugh, recalling the numerous times I'd slurred "*Et tu, Brute*", to which he responded that his name was "Juli*an* not Juli*us*".

"You didn't remember my name?" He appears genuinely hurt.

I shrink into myself, a momentary feeling of guilt washing over me before I brush it off.

"Listen, Julian, I appreciate you taking the time to come over to say hi and not ignore me. If I were in your shoes, I would have done just that. Hell, I *tried* to do that. But I'm here to work on a story that could land me a promotion." Agitated by his presence, I fidget with my hands. "As you overheard at the bar, my boyfriend broke up with me because I'm not serious enough. So this promotion can certainly prove otherwise."

"A story?" He gives me a wry smile, causing his dimples to pop. If he weren't irresistible enough to begin with, he has to have dimples, too? It's like the big guy upstairs put together everything I find attractive about a man, then gave him the opposite personality I need. And as much as looks are important, personality trumps all.

"Yes. I'm the sex and dating editor for *Blush* magazine."

"But you're up for a promotion?"

"Assistant editor of the entire magazine. As long as I nail this story."

He peeks over my laptop at my notepad, squinting to decipher my chicken scratch. "August Laurent?"

Indignant, I cover my notepad with my hand, pulling it toward me and flipping it over so he can't see. "He's the subject of my story."

He doesn't react. I take his silence for confusion.

"He's the most sought-after escort in the country. Apparently, he lives right here in Manhattan," I explain. "No one's been able to nail down this guy for an interview, so that's what I'm trying to do. My sources say he frequents this place, so if you'll excuse me…" I lock eyes with him, hoping he gets the hint that I have no desire to continue this conversation.

Finally, after a stare down that feels like it lasts hours, he reluctantly gets up. "Well, I'll leave you to your work."

"Thank you." I reach for my coffee, taking a long sip, trying to calm my overwrought nerves. The last thing I need is to be distracted and miss spotting the man who could be the mysterious August Laurent.

"For the record…" When I hear Julian speak, I lift my head, meeting his sincere eyes. "It was nice to see you again, Evie." His lips curve up at the corners. "Really nice." Then he disappears into another section of the coffee shop.

Chapter Eight

I CAN'T GET Julian out of my mind the rest of the morning, despite a valiant effort on my part to do so. Every time I think of his sapphire eyes and the earnestness in his voice when he confessed he was happy to see me, my body heats as my stomach erupts in flutters I haven't experienced in too long now.

Whenever I consider the possibility that maybe there's something more there, I remind myself it's all part of his game. Men like Julian crave the chase. Once they've captured their prey, they'll either destroy it in a way that makes it unrecognizable, or release it back into the wild with the hope of finding something tastier, perkier, younger. I'm too smart to allow Julian to capture me again.

Since my focus is essentially nonexistent, thanks to one Julian…whatever his last name is, I decide to call today a loss and return tomorrow, refreshed and rejuvenated. After collecting my things and shoving them into my laptop bag, I do like all New Yorkers do and check my social media on my phone to avoid eye contact as I head out of the coffee shop, paying no attention to the couple walking in.

"Evie." It's not a question. More like a statement of surprise.

I lift my head, admiring the long, sleek lines of the suit-clad body, sucking in a breath when I peer into a pair of familiar hazel eyes. Eyes that once looked at me with such devotion as the owner declared his love. I swallow hard through the lump in my throat at the comfort I once felt whenever I peered into them. Now I only feel inadequate.

"Trevor…," I breathe, unsure what else to say.

"Hey." He looks as uneasy about our unexpected meeting as I do.

I've been living in our apartment the past few weeks, but we haven't seen each other. Every night, I prepared a dinner plate for him, thinking he'd be hungry whenever he got home from the office, yet I was always asleep when that happened. By the time I woke up in the morning, Trevor would already be gone, his plate in the dishwasher. It probably sounds like nothing, but the gesture fills me with hope that this separation won't last. That he'll see how much he needs me in his life.

Until I see the woman clinging to his arm, their hands intertwined. If seeing him for the first time since he broke up with me isn't hard enough, now I have to look at him while another woman holds his hand, feels his skin, enjoys his warmth. That's supposed to be *my* hand, *my* skin, *my* warmth.

When a throat clearing sounds, Trevor tears his eyes from mine, looking at the petite woman at his side. She can't be more than five-foot-two, and probably a perfect size two. She's pretty, I suppose, but nothing stands out that makes her remarkable.

Her dark hair is pin straight, not a single strand out of place, as opposed to my wild red locks I have trouble taming. It fits my personality — bold and a bit reckless. Her clothing choice is a complete juxtaposition to my love of color, her conservative charcoal suit something I wouldn't even wear to a funeral. Her makeup is simple.

Not over the top, but enough to add color in all the right places. I like making a statement with my makeup. My mother once told me a great red lipstick could make everything better, advice I've carried into adulthood. She doesn't seem to have a single curve on her body, compared to my shapely hips and ample chest. The combination of my physique and red hair causes many people to comment that I resemble the character Joan from *Mad Men*.

Is this *really* what Trevor wants? Someone boring and...ordinary? It's almost like he purposely found someone who's the polar opposite of me. I'm not sure if I should find satisfaction or sadness in that fact.

"Sorry." He licks his lips as he tugs at his tie, a nervous tick of his. I wonder if his new friend even knows that yet. "Evie, this is Theresa. Theresa..." His Adam's apple bobs up and down, "this is Evie."

She stares me down, her mouth forming a tight line. Her lukewarm reception gives the impression that Trevor must have mentioned me. I can almost hear her disapproving thoughts, wondering what he could have seen in someone like me.

Likewise, girlfriend. Likewise.

In an attempt to be the bigger person, I reach my hand toward her. "Theresa. So wonderful to meet you."

She plasters a fake smile on her face, although she can't fake it like I can. She better practice because she'll need to fake some orgasms if she plans on staying with him. Sex is...okay, but she'll need some extra assistance if she wants to get off on a regular basis.

"I've heard so much about you."

I look from Theresa to Trevor. Even their names are similar. It's creepy. "I wish I could say the same." I keep my tone upbeat, not wanting anyone to catch on to how hard it is for me to see him with another woman, especially mere weeks after he broke up with me. "I didn't realize you liked this place. It's out of the way from your office. What is it? Fifteen blocks from Thirty-Fourth and Fifth?"

"Actually, it's closer to twenty. But Theresa's never had one of their chocolate hazelnut pastries. I stop by every morning for one before heading into the office."

"You do?" I try to hide the hurt in my voice over the fact that I didn't know this about him. And that I haven't noticed him during the weeks I've been camped out here. Who else haven't I noticed? What if my propensity to be easily distracted by cute puppy videos on the Internet caused me to miss August Laurent?

"Yeah. But I haven't been able to get here recently because of the trial."

"Right," I breathe in a drawn-out voice, relieved. "The trial."

I don't even bother to ask how it went as we stare at each other in uncomfortable silence. I do my best to pretend the idea of him sharing a chocolate hazelnut pastry with Theresa doesn't break me even more. He's supposed to want to share these things with me. Hell, my office is only a few blocks away, yet not once did he ask me to meet him here.

"Well…," I say, my tone upbeat. We had the spark once. I have to figure out how to get it back. Then he'll come to his senses, and I'll be there waiting. "I need to get back to work."

I'd normally make a joke about having to take a few vibrators for a test drive for an article I'm working on, but I don't, choosing the mature route. Although it's hard... *Really* hard.

"It was nice seeing you." I skirt past them and push my way through the glass doors. The instant I'm outside, I lean against the brick wall of the building, exhaling a breath. People move along this busy section of New York as if I don't matter, don't exist. Like Trevor just made me feel, despite our lengthy history.

"That's him then, is it? Your ex?"

I whip my eyes to my left, watching with a furtive stare as Julian strolls toward me.

Great. Just what I need. Sometimes I wish my life had background music so I can understand what the hell is going on. Right now, I'm at a complete loss. All I know is it seems like the universe is conspiring against me.

"So what if it is?" I cross my arms in front of my chest, acting as if seeing Trevor had no effect on me.

"Hope you don't think it rude of me to say——"

"The fact you lead off with that statement means whatever's about to follow is rude."

He closes the distance between us, his gaze searing my flesh, causing it to prickle. Trevor never stared at me with this much heat, this much want, this much raw need. When I first met Julian, I figured I imagined the connection. But it's here. And I'm sober, despite my burning need for a drink after running into Trevor, then Julian again. Both within minutes of each other.

"He doesn't seem your type."

"Great." I roll my eyes. "Yet another person who thinks Trevor's too good for me." I push past him, but stop in my tracks, the Irish temper I'm normally able to keep under wraps exploding from me. Whirling around, I narrow my fiery stare on him, my jaw tense, my fists clenched. "Who do you think you are anyway? You know nothing about me, other than how I am in bed, which you shouldn't have found out in the first place. I can't do anything to change that now, though. So while I appreciate your little pep talk, I am *so* not in the mood today."

I turn from him, my hair nearly smacking me in the face with the force as I walk in the opposite direction of the magazine's office.

"I can help you!" he calls after me.

"With another romp in the sack?" I shout over my shoulder as I cross the street, swept up in the sea of people heading toward Central Park. "Thanks for the offer, but I'd rather keep our one-night stand to just that. One night. Goodbye, *Julius*."

Chapter Nine

THERE ARE TIMES I've often longed for the simple and sparsely populated life I lived back in Nebraska. The sheer amount of people who live, work, or play in New York City can be suffocating. Right now, I use that to my advantage, allowing everyone heading into the park to shield me from Julian.

Once I'm certain I've evaded him, I break off from the crowd and walk down one of the meandering paths, mature trees shading me from the hot June sun. The sound of runners' feet hitting the pavement is coupled with birds and the background noise of Manhattan, but there's still a tranquility here you can't find anywhere else.

Dogs pull their walkers along the trails, tourists stop for a picnic on a grassy area. A few locals on their lunch break sit on a bench and read. I even spy a couple having their engagement photos taken. It causes me to slow my steps, unable to look away. I had planned this very thing for Trevor and me.

I even had a list of shots I wanted our photographer to capture. Thanks to my time working for a wedding planner, I knew exactly what I wanted. Now, I stare at this couple with longing, faced with the possibility that I've truly lost Trevor, that this breakup may not be due to stress, as I tried to claim it was.

My legs seeming to give out as I confront this new reality, I fall onto a bench, recalling the distance that seemed to stretch between us, even when we had first moved here. I always excused his behavior, considering he was in law school. Maybe we fell out of love all those years ago, but neither of us would admit it, not wanting to prove our parents right when they warned us moving to New York together was crazy. But I remember all the happy moments we shared, too.

Like when we'd order a pizza and sit out on the fire escape to eat it, the view of the city more mesmerizing and exhilarating than any movie could be.

Like the time we got lost when trying to figure out the subway system and ended up somewhere in the Bronx. Instead of asking someone for help finding our way back, Trevor insisted we figure it out on our own. Together. And we did.

Like the way all the tension slowly rolled off his body when he'd climb into bed beside me after a long day of studying. He'd wrap his arms around me and fall asleep. In those moments, everything was worth it.

I have to believe it still is.

"You're giving me a complex, ya know," a voice startles me from my quiet reflection.

I snap my head to my right to see Julian helping himself to the vacant space beside me. He drapes his long arms along the back of the park bench, resting the calf of one leg on the other thigh.

"How many times are you going to run away from me, Evie?"

"Not used to a woman telling you no?"

He narrows his steely gaze on me. "I'm not used to *anyone* telling me no."

Rolling my eyes, I stand. "Well, get used to it because the only answer you'll ever get out of me is no. Have a nice day, Julian." When I spin from him, I almost run into a group of cyclists flying by. Thankfully, their reflexes are quick and swerve out of my way, allowing me to avoid any additional embarrassment today.

"Even if I said I may have a way to help you with your predicament with your ex?" he calls out.

I halt, gradually turning to face him, tilting my head to the side. A voice in my head reminds me that I barely know this guy, so there's only one reason he'd want to help me. But there's something about the way he looks at me that keeps me here. A genuine affection that's been missing from Trevor in recent days.

I place a hand on my hip, pinching my lips into a tight line. "Well, are you going to share how? Or do you hope I pick it up telepathically?"

With a smile that can only be described as panty-dropping, he gestures back to the park bench, an unspoken request for me to sit. I hesitate, but eventually acquiesce, ignoring the buzz of energy that sparks in my body as I pass him, inhaling a hint of his aroma.

Once we're both situated, he glances at me. "You're serious about getting back with your ex?"

"Of course!" I exclaim, indignant. "We were together twelve years. You don't throw away twelve years overnight. He probably didn't think he had any other option if he wanted to be taken seriously as a possible candidate for partner. All the other partners' spouses have more serious jobs. I get that giving sex advice isn't something to be proud of."

He rests his forearms on his thighs, considering my words. "I believe it shows you have no problem talking about uncomfortable topics, a trait Trevor should find valuable."

I struggle not to react to his compliment, failing miserably as heat covers my cheeks.

"So let me help you prove that to him."

"How?"

"Date me."

I straighten my spine, leaning farther away from him. "What?"

The expression on my face is probably akin to that of a child who prematurely learns Mommy or Daddy is actually Santa Claus. Nothing could have prepared me to hear Julian suggest we date to help me win back Trevor.

"Sorry if I sound blunt, but are you fucking crazy? I just told you I want to get back together with my ex and you ask me to date you?"

"It won't be real." He laughs, causing his eyes to sparkle. It's the first time I've heard him laugh, and it's just as hypnotic and seductive as I imagined it would be. "Just for show. To make him jealous. He's moved on. You should make him think you've done the same."

I shake my head, thinking the entire idea absurd. It reminds me of my conversation with Chloe and Nora that night at the bar when I first heard the name August Laurent. They suggested I hunt him down to do the very same thing. I was against it then. I'm still against it now.

"It would never work. The chance of running into Trevor in a city this size is slim to none. Hell, I haven't even moved out of our apartment yet and today was the first time I've seen him since we broke up two weeks ago."

He whips his head toward me, his brows pulled in. "Wait a minute. You're *still* living with him?"

"Yeah." Chewing on my lower lip, I shrug. "I figure if

I don't move out, he'll realize how much he needs me in his life, how big of a mistake it was to walk away from me."

Julian shakes his head, pinching the bridge of his nose before returning his impassioned gaze to me. "That's exactly *why* you should have moved out by now. Don't give him the satisfaction of knowing you'll always be waiting for him." He shoots to his feet and grabs my hand, tugging me off the park bench. I'm too off balance from the sudden movement to fight him. "Come with me. This appears to be a bigger task than I originally thought."

I fight to keep up with his long strides as he leads me through the park. "Oh, really? And what makes you an expert in how to win back a boyfriend? Forgive me if I don't see you as the romantic type."

"You don't think I'm romantic?"

"This shouldn't come as a shock to you," I argue, but am quickly cut off when he stops walking and yanks me against his hard body. Initially, I struggle in his arms, but when he leans toward me, his breath warming my neck, I melt, becoming a ball of clay in his rather capable hands. That spark is back, that unyielding rush of need filling me, urging me forward.

"You may not think I'm romantic," he begins, his tone low and seductive. I exhale a shaky breath as my eyes roll into the back of my head, my nerve endings firing. "But if that's the case, do you think I would have cared that you were no longer in my bed when I woke up the morning after our chance meeting?"

I stiffen, shooting my gaze to him.

"Because I did," he continues, barely pausing for a beat. "For days, all I could think was I should have gotten your number. So I did what anyone would do in this digital age. I scoured Facebook to find you. I searched for anyone with every variation of the name Evie. Evelyn. Yvonne. Yvette. Everything remotely close to Evie, hoping I could track you down and see if…"

"If what?" Floating my eyes to his, I lose myself in deep pools of blue.

"If you feel this, too."

His mouth inches closer to mine, the anticipation of feeling his lips on my tender flesh unhinging me in a way that erases all sense of what's right. I've reverted to pure animalistic desire. No emotions. No reason. Just the urge to be satisfied.

"Feel what?" My heart pounds violently against the walls of my chest as I brace for his kiss, praying it will be as incredible as I imagine.

"How much you want to say yes to my little proposal." Before I have a chance to react, he pulls away, straightening his jacket, acting as if he weren't just about to kiss me.

I'm wound tight, a bundle of sensation in desperate need of release. It doesn't help I've been celibate for two weeks. It's the longest I've gone without sex since I met Trevor. That's got to be why I'm ready to agree to anything. It's desperation. That's it. Nothing more.

Recovering quickly, I run my hands along my dress, fixing my expression. "Your proposal is ridiculous. In order for it to work, Trevor needs to see us together."

He passes me a sly grin. "You really have no idea who I am, do you?"

"I know who you are." I square my shoulders. "Your name's Julian. *Not* Julius."

Bemused, he smirks. "Do you know anything else?"

"Just the fact you must have a shit-ton of money, or at least a really wealthy sugar mommy...or daddy. I'm not one to judge."

He chuckles, the corners of his eyes creasing. "Definitely no sugar mommy...or daddy. I can assure you of that." When his laughter wanes, he narrows his gaze on me. "Suffice it to say, Trevor *will* hear about us. A lot of people will. They'll all wonder about the mystery woman on my arm. It's summer. Party season is under way in the Hamptons."

"The Hamptons?" I swallow hard. I'd heard stories about those parties, mostly from Chloe, but you have to know someone to get an invitation. Hell, I've never even been north of Jones Beach on Long Island. The Hamptons is like a different world than what I know.

"Precisely. Men are protective and territorial by nature. In his mind, he can still stake a claim over you because you haven't moved on. Attend enough of these parties on my arm, he'll come to believe you have moved on. If his so-called 'ownership' over you is threatened, he'll realize his mistake. He'll never do that as long as you remain in his apartment, cook and clean for him, do his laundry like the status quo hasn't changed. It *has* changed. And he needs to feel that change or he'll never admit he fucked up. Trust me on this."

I ponder his words for a moment, something not adding up. Maybe living in New York has made me more cynical. "I find it hard to believe any guy like you would proactively want to help a woman he's slept with get back with her ex unless he wants a repeat. So, as enlightening as this entire conversation has been, it's over. I'm not interested in a replay." I turn from him, my legs not moving as fast as I wish they could.

"Evie, wait!" he calls, but I ignore him, continuing

down the path. Then I hear him bellow, "We never slept together!"

I come to an abrupt stop, my pulse quickening. Passersby look in our direction, a few snickers and gasps ripping through the air, but I don't pay them much attention, too shocked by his admission.

"What did you say?" I ask over my shoulder.

He advances toward me. "We never slept together."

"But—" I square my shoulders, fully facing him.

"But then why would you wake up in a strange man's bed in just your bra and panties?"

I nod, still shell-shocked by this revelation.

"Because you threw up all over your damn dress... And my shoes."

Embarrassment fills me as I close my eyes, cringing. "I did?"

"Sure did."

"But how—"

"When I headed up to my place, I saw someone who looked alarmingly like this beautiful, charismatic woman I'd witnessed tell an entire bar about her breakup that evening. So, out of curiosity, I walked up to her. That's when I overheard you say you were never going to drink again."

"To which you said, 'That's probably a good idea.'"

He smiles. "I did. To which you responded by emptying the contents of your stomach."

I bury my head in my hands. "Oh god. I really am never drinking again. I'm so sorry."

His arms wrap around me...unexpected, yet comforting. I inhale a breath, my muscles relaxing at his familiar aroma. "It's okay. We all have those nights

79

where the only cure is bourbon or tequila. Nothing to be embarrassed about. Not the first time I've had someone throw up on me. And it probably won't be the last."

"Unless you have some sick fetish, it should be." I tilt my head up at him. "You don't have some weird fetish where you pay people to puke on you, do you? That's not why you want to do this, is it?"

He chuckles as he drops his hold on me. "Certainly not. No sick fetishes here." He raises his hand. "Scout's honor."

I pinch my lips. "Why do I get the feeling you were never a Boy Scout?"

"Very observant of you. I wasn't."

There's a brief silence before I speak again. "So you saw me drunk on the street, then what? You decided to take care of me when the rest of the city just walked right by?"

"What can I say? I know how it feels to be overlooked, to think no one notices you. Plus, you'd just had a horrible night. The last thing you should do on your thirtieth birthday is spend it in the drunk tank at the local police precinct. I brought you back to my place to make sure you were okay, that you weren't about to pass out and choke on your own vomit."

"You washed my dress," I breathe. It's not a question.

"You probably thought the worst of me when you woke up in my bed. I considered sleeping in one of the guest rooms, but the reason I brought you to my place was to keep an eye on you. I couldn't do that if I slept in a different room. When I woke up and you weren't there, I panicked. I could only imagine what you must have thought, and I hated the idea of you walking around thinking we slept together. I needed to track you down and explain. That's why I searched for every name close to Evie on Facebook. I even went to the bar I first saw you at in the hopes I could find you."

"I haven't been in the drinking mood after that night. Plus, once my boss told me about the possible promotion, that's been my focus."

"I don't take advantage of women," he states with determination, his jaw firm. "Particularly drunk women. I just..." He blows out a breath. "I just wanted you to know the truth."

I stare into the distance, reflecting on this new information. No one in the city cares about each other. It's always every man for himself. The idea that Julian took it upon himself to make sure I was okay has me rethinking my original assumption.

"You really are a good guy," I murmur, more to myself than anyone else.

"I'm no saint, but I try to be a decent human being. Okay?"

"Okay." It's all I can manage to say as relief fills me. Trevor's still my number three. There's no number four. But now the idea of there being a number four doesn't seem to be the apocalyptic event I once believed it to be. For two weeks, I'd carried on like there was a number four. There were no flooding rains requiring me to build an arc. No swarm of locusts. No great famine, apart from that between my legs. Life went on. And I get the feeling it will continue to go on even if there were to be a number four.

"So, what do you say?" He runs a hand through his hair, drawing my attention back to him. "Want to be my fake girlfriend?"

To anyone else, I'm sure it sounds like a great offer.

Pretend to date some ridiculously good-looking, presumably wealthy man who looks incredible in a suit. But it's not that easy for me. Even though Trevor's moved on, there's still a level of guilt.

"I apologize if I appear skeptical, but I just don't see what *you* get out of this."

"Simple. I get a seat at the table."

I scrunch my brows together. "Excuse me?"

"Listen…" He licks his lips. "I didn't always have money. Because of that, there are a few prominent people in my circle who are bitter about my windfall. I'm typically relegated to the 'kid's table', so to speak. Old money versus found money kind of thing. A dear friend who's been around this life for more years than she cares to admit suggested a girlfriend might help. Showing up at many of these events as a bachelor could be working against me. I'm in the middle of a few huge projects for my company, but there's a lot of bureaucratic red tape I need to cut through to get them off the ground. Some of the nation's most powerful people summer in the Hamptons."

"And if they see you're in a committed relationship and aren't just some bachelor playboy pissing away his fortune, they'll take you more seriously."

He nods. "Like I said, it'll be a win-win. I can conduct some much-needed business. You can make Trevor so jealous that he'll come crawling back to you."

I chew on my bottom lip, considering his offer. Julian certainly makes it sound appealing. But he doesn't know Trevor like I do. He's always had an uncanny ability to weed through the bullshit, which is why he's one hell of an attorney, even for only being thirty. He'll see through this bullshit, too. When he does, it will only reaffirm his reasons for breaking up with me in the first place — that I don't take anything in life seriously enough.

"I really do appreciate the offer, but Trevor will see right through our game in a flash. It will never work. I'm sorry. But I'm sure you can find someone else to help you." I lock eyes with him, feeling a twinge of guilt at the disappointment crossing his brow. "Goodbye, Julian."

When I turn from him, a part of me hopes he'll call my name once more. He never does.

Chapter Ten

"I CAN'T BELIEVE you're actually trying to figure out who August Laurent is," Nora says Friday afternoon as we unpack all the boxes containing possessions from my former life.

After my run-in with Julian in Central Park yesterday, I went back to the apartment I shared with Trevor instead of heading to the office. All I heard was Julian's warning that if I kept living with him, I'd only give him the satisfaction of knowing I'll always be around and waiting. I refuse to do that any longer. He needs to know I'm ready to walk away, too. A part of me hoped Trevor would reach out to talk when he walked into the apartment last night and saw the stacks of boxes containing my things. He never did. So, after our weekly meeting at the magazine earlier today, I convinced Chloe to play hooky. When I told Nora of my plans, she volunteered to help, as well. The only one missing from our circle is Izzy, but treating kids with cancer is more important than helping me move.

"Yeah," I groan. "And it's proving to be impossible. The man's a ghost."

"Like Keyser Söze."

"Exactly!" This is why we get along so well. We all think the same thing. It can be a little scary at times, but being able to anticipate what each other is thinking and feeling makes things easier.

"I wonder what he looks like." She grabs a magazine off the stack of back issues of *Blush* and flips through it.

I've kept a copy of every single issue since I started there. I remember holding the very first one in my hands and seeing my name in print. The feeling was indescribable. I even slept with it on my nightstand that night. Trevor never even asked to read the article.

"Maybe he appears differently for everyone who hires him. You know, like the Mirror of Erised in *Harry Potter*." She stops flipping through the pages, turning the magazine around to show us an image of Brad Pitt and Angelina Jolie when they were still "Brangelina". "Brad Pitt would be *my* August Laurent."

Chloe laughs. "I don't think it works that way, Nora. I don't think he changes his appearance based on what the person who hires him wants to see."

With a frown, Nora returns the magazine to the pile, then places them on a small bookshelf. "Pity. Wouldn't that be nice?"

"Sure," I say with an eye roll.

"How did you figure out he frequents the Steam Room anyway?" she presses.

I avoid her speculative gaze as I remove a few of my favorite coffee mugs from bubble wrap. Trevor always hated my affinity for mugs with snarky sayings on them. He drank out of the same boring black mug, said most adults don't drink out of mugs with profanity. I guess I'm not like most adults.

"Just a hunch based on a few tips."

"Hmm..." Her lips form a tight line. "Those tips wouldn't have come from our very own gossip queen, would they?" She waggles her brows, nodding toward Chloe.

I open my mouth to respond just as my phone rings. I glance at the screen, my breath hitching when I see Trevor's face smiling back.

"Who is it?" Chloe asks, noticing my reaction.

"Trevor," I answer hesitantly.

"What do you think *he* wants?" Nora sneers.

It took my friends no time at all to go from Team Trevor to Team No One, especially after I told them about seeing him yesterday. Of course, I left out any mention of bumping into Julian and his little proposition.

"Maybe to tell me he realized he made a mistake."

"You're not going back to him after this, are you?" Chloe presses.

Unsure how to respond to her, I shrug. I should just write him off. If we'd only been together a few months, I'd do just that. But it's been twelve years. There's a certain level of patience, understanding, and forgiveness that increases over time.

"Trevor," I say when I answer. It's strange to greet him this way. Normally, I'd say "Hey, baby" or "Hiya, sweetie". I hate I can't do that anymore.

"Oh, Evie. Hey," he responds, like he's surprised to hear my voice, even though he was the one who called.

"Is there something you need, or was this a butt dial?" I quip in a sarcastic tone when he doesn't say anything more.

"Right…" There's a pause and I hold my breath. Something's different in the timbre of his voice. Regret? Remorse? Sorrow? "I stopped by the apartment to change suits for tonight." Hope builds inside me that my plan has already had the intended effect. "There was a delivery for you."

"A delivery?" I can't remember the last order I placed.

I normally have everything sent to the office, unless it's a big item.

"Yeah. It's... Well, someone sent you flowers."

I roll my eyes, thinking it's someone else from the magazine who decided to send me flowers in condolence for my breakup. Most likely one of the contributors who doesn't regularly come into the office.

I'm about to explain what my coworkers do during a breakup, when he cuts me off. "Who's Julian?"

My jaw falls open, a rush of adrenaline causing my skin to tingle from the name alone. "Julian?" I swallow hard.

In an instant, Chloe and Nora kneel directly in front of my position on the floor, their curious eyes trained on me. *Who's Julian?* Nora mouths. I hold up a finger, hushing them. This is as much a mystery to me as it is to them. Why would he send me flowers after I turned him down yesterday?

"I didn't mean to read the card, but it wasn't in an envelope. It was kind of hard to miss. Are you already seeing someone else?" His voice is low with a hint of jealousy. I shouldn't smile at the pain I hear, but it gives me a taste of vindication. Now he knows how it feels. Even if I'm *not* seeing Julian, he doesn't need to know that.

"You've already moved on. You can't expect me to sit around and wait for you, can you?"

"Well... No. I guess not." He blows out a long breath. "I just thought—"

"Actually, you didn't, Trevor. That's the problem. You didn't think. You didn't think I'd ever get over you. Well, maybe I have."

"Is that the only reason you're dating him?" His voice becomes strained, turning into almost a growl. I picture him pacing in front of the entryway table, tugging at his hair, sneering at the flowers Julian sent. "To piss me off? To make me jealous?"

"Do you really think so little of me that I'd stoop to such levels?" I keep my tone calm, refusing to show any hint of emotion. "Maybe I'm with Julian because he makes me laugh, makes me smile, makes me feel like I matter." I stand, pacing in the little free space between all my boxes. "And you know what? He likes that I'm a bit eccentric. He likes that I don't fit into the cookie-cutter mold it appears you want. He likes I don't have a size two body. Not to mention he *really* likes that I have more than a handful up top."

Nora snort-laughs, her wide eyes sparkling with amusement. I may have dug the knife a little deeper than necessary, but it feels good. Who knew? Apparently, Julian did.

"So am I doing this to make you jealous? No. I'm doing this to give me the happiness I deserve." I draw in a deep breath, my own words surprising me. I think they surprise my friends, too. They gape at me for a moment, then they both jump to their feet as they give me a silent standing ovation.

I glare and wave my hands at them, warning them not to make me laugh as I return my attention to my phone. "As you probably already noticed, I've packed up my things and brought them over to Chloe's. You shouldn't receive any additional deliveries for me over there, but text me if you do and I'll swing by to pick them up. There are a few more things I need to get out of the apartment this weekend. After that, you'll finally have me out of your life. I'm sorry it's taken so long."

A lump builds in my throat at the double meaning. I want him to beg me not to go, to tell me he doesn't want to come home to an apartment without tripping over my shoes, or seeing my collection of coffee mugs that haven't yet made their way into the dishwasher. But he doesn't. He doesn't say anything.

"Goodbye, Trevor."

I stay on the line a moment longer, praying he'll admit he made a mistake. But he doesn't. I go to end the call to see he already has. I remain motionless for a moment, simply staring at the phone as I try to process what just happened. Is this officially the end of Trevor and Evie? Trevi? I'd even planned for us to honeymoon in Rome just to go to the fountain bearing the same name as our couple name. Will I ever find someone I'll have an awesome couple name with again?

"Want to tell us what the hell is going on?" Chloe's voice pulls me out of my thoughts.

I glance to see her standing beside me, her arms crossed.

"Who's Julian?" Nora adds. "Why didn't you say anything about a new suitor?"

I shake my head, unsure where to even begin with this. I still can't wrap my head around it myself. "Julian isn't a suitor," I begin, then my phone rings once more.

"Is it Trevor telling you there's another delivery of flowers from yet another gentleman caller?" Nora giggles.

Rolling my eyes, I look at the phone to see my office line number, indicating it's a call forwarded from there, something I do whenever I'm away from my desk during normal business hours.

"It's a work call." I grit a smile. "Just a second." I bring the phone back up to my ear, squaring my shoulders and plastering on as professional an expression as I can, even though whoever's calling can't see me. "Evie Fitzgerald."

"Hello, Evie," a deep baritone responds.

The instant that voice comes over the line, my core clenches, my breath quickening as desire builds inside me, low and deep. My cheeks heat, so I look away from Chloe and Nora, hoping they don't notice the sudden change in my demeanor.

"Good afternoon, Julian."

Nora squeals and I glare at her. She quickly silences herself, but that doesn't stop her and Chloe from making obscene gestures, the occasional moan of "Oh, Julian" thrown in for added emphasis.

"Is it?" There's a hint of amusement in his voice, leading me to believe this was all part of his plan to begin with.

"It is now." I walk away from my two best friends, who seem to be acting like they're in middle school instead of professional adults, and head to the bay windows in Chloe's living room, looking out at the streets of Greenwich Village.

"And why's that?"

"Oh, I don't know." I lower myself to the window seat. "Maybe because my ex-boyfriend just called me in a jealous rage because someone happened to send me flowers."

He chuckles, the sound still having the same effect as it did yesterday. "Is that right?"

"That's right."

"I told you I can help, did I not?"

"All you did was send flowers," I retort. The last thing I want is to sound overly eager to agree to his proposition. I'm still not convinced it's the right way to go about this. "You were lucky Trevor was even home when they were delivered. He's been practically sleeping at the office these days."

"You call it luck. I call it due diligence."

"Due diligence?"

"Precisely. I promised that if you agreed to help me, I'd do everything to help *you*. Randomly sending you flowers doesn't cut it. If I simply wanted to send you flowers, I would have sent them to your office. I wanted *him* to know I sent you flowers. Which is why I paid the delivery person to sit outside your building and wait until he saw Trevor walk in."

I'm momentarily speechless by the length it appears Julian went in order to make Trevor jealous. I have to hand it to him. It certainly worked.

"Do I want to know how long the delivery man was sitting outside?" I'm unsure if I should consider this a creepy form of stalking or if it is simply a demonstration that he's a talented manipulator.

"Probably not. So, what do you say, Evie? Did I prove you wrong?"

I brush my hair behind my ear, ignoring the questioning stare of my two friends, who are now squeezed on the opposite side of the window seat, their gazes seemingly glued to my every move.

"What do you mean?"

"You said Trevor was too smart to buy into the idea of us being a real couple."

"And he is."

"You still believe that?"

"I do. He asked if I was only dating you to make him jealous, so he's certainly skeptical."

"But he *did* think you were dating me." His voice is

light and playful. "I think my column deserves points for that alone."

"This isn't a game, Julian."

"Of course it is. Life is merely a game. So are relationships. It's all about strategy."

"Is that what this is? Your strategy to get me to agree to your proposition?"

"And if it is?"

I pinch my lips together, carefully considering my words. "Then it seems you're going to awful lengths when I'm sure you have your choice of women who'd gladly agree to be your arm candy at a few parties in the Hamptons."

Nora shrieks again, but Chloe jabs her in the side, silencing her. Still, they both stare at me like I'm the three-headed dog from *Harry Potter*.

"But I don't want any of them. I want a stunning, irresistible woman who can hold her own in a room full of stuffy businessmen and their stuck-up wives."

"You're barking up the wrong tree because I—"

"Don't think you fit that description?" he interrupts, finishing the thought on the tip of my tongue. "Well, you're wrong. Maybe in your ex-boyfriend's opinion you don't, but from what I've seen, you're the perfect person for the job. I'm not looking for someone who can't form an intelligent thought if her life depended on it, or someone who will only speak when spoken to. I'm looking for someone with edge. Someone who has confidence in spades. That's you. So let's do this. I help you. You help me. Tit for tat."

I chew on my bottom lip, torn. On one hand, I don't have anything to lose by agreeing. It could work, considering how jealous Trevor sounded just from the idea of me receiving flowers from another man. But on the other hand, there are too many variables, too many ways for this to turn from a strictly business relationship into something…more.

"It's unwise to agree to this without ironing out all the details. Despite what you may think you know about me, I prefer when there's a concrete plan."

"I couldn't agree more. I'll make dinner reservations for seven o'clock tonight. Shall I pick you up from your place or the office?"

"Tonight?" I look to Chloe and Nora for guidance. Their eyes are bright with excitement over the prospect of me having dinner with a guy tonight.

Chloe mouths, *My place*, then winks.

"How about you tell me where and I'll meet you there."

"I had a feeling you'd be a challenge." I can hear the smile in his voice. "If this is to work, we need to give off the appearance of being a real couple."

"Real couples meet at restaurants all the time, especially in this city. I met Trevor constantly. In fact, I can't remember the last time we went out when I *didn't* meet him there." The second the words leave my mouth, a pang squeezes my heart.

"And that's precisely why I'll always pick you up for every single one of our outings," he responds, not allowing me to dwell too long on my realization. I wonder if he knows this. "No exceptions. So, again, your place or the office?"

"How about my friend Chloe's?"

"Is there a reason you don't want me to pick you up at your place?"

"I moved out."

"Good girl." The way he caresses those two words forces me to squeeze my legs together, an ache building as my overactive imagination goes to places it shouldn't, not when I'm still supposed to be pining for Trevor. "Program this number into your phone. Let me know when you're ready."

"Hold on." Jumping off the bench, I head into the bathroom, wanting some privacy. I put him on speaker, then switch to my contacts. "Ready."

He rattles off his number and I input his information into my phone. "That's my cell. Text me her address."

"I will." I save his number and take him off speaker, bringing my phone back up to my ear.

"No. Right now."

I groan. "Seriously? Been stood up too many times?" I open the door, stepping back into the living room, only to be met by my friends' scowls.

"Never, but you're different from the usual women I find in my company."

"Fine." Continuing past Chloe and Nora, I pull the phone away and switch to the message app. After typing out a quick text with Chloe's address, I hit send, then return my cell to my ear. "Is that a good or bad thing?"

"Only time with tell." I hear the ping of an incoming message in the background. When he speaks again, his tone is low, almost seductive. "I'll see you at seven, Evie."

"I look forward to it." I stare blankly ahead, about to hang up when I think of something. "Julian, wait!"

"Yes?"

"What's your last name?"

"My last name?"

"Yeah. In case you turn out to be a serial killer, I'd like

Chloe and Nora to know the full name of the man I was last seen with. That way, the police have a head start on tracking down my body to some old, abandoned warehouse in Jersey City you've re-purposed as a kill room."

"Dammit. You've figured me out."

I laugh, a lightness in my chest at how effortless it is to joke with him. I almost don't want to hang up.

"Gage," he says finally. "My last name is Gage."

"Okay."

"Okay," he says.

It's silent for a moment. Then I blurt out, "Guinevere."

"Excuse me?"

"My real name's Guinevere. That's why you couldn't find me online. Evie's a nickname. I had trouble pronouncing my name when I was a little girl and called myself Evie. It just kind of stuck."

"Guinevere… I like that." He pauses, then says, "See you in a few hours, Guinevere."

Chapter Eleven

"WHAT THE HELL is going on?" Chloe asks once the line goes silent. I clutch the phone for a moment longer while I attempt to recover my composure enough to face my friends.

"And who is Julian?" Nora teases.

I turn around, meeting their curious eyes, at a loss for words.

"Based on your conversation, he sent you flowers, which made Trevor jealous, and now you're going to dinner with him. Who is he and where did you meet?" Chloe presses.

I worry my bottom lip, rubbing my hands along my jeans. What do I tell them? What *can* I tell them? If I'm supposed to pretend to date Julian, won't we have to keep up appearances? But this is Chloe and Nora, my two best friends. We're the three amigas. Three musketeers. Sisters from another mister. Am I expected to keep up the charade in front of *everyone*?

"Okay." I blow out a long breath. "But you can *not* tell a soul. No one else can know about this." I narrow my gaze on Chloe, my stare harsh, trying to relay the severity of the situation. "This is so far off the record, it would be akin to career suicide if you were to print it."

"You have my word." Her light eyes are bright and filled with all the sincerity I've come to expect from her, especially when discussing private matters. There are few people I believe when they make me a promise. Chloe's one of them. "This will stay between us. No one else."

Secure in her assurance, I walk to the couch and sit down. Chloe and Nora follow, sitting next to each other on the opposite end. Once they're situated, I face them.

"I spent yesterday morning in the Steam Room, like I have been all week."

"Yeah, I know," Chloe says.

"What you don't know is that as I was trying to figure out who August Laurent is, Mr. Armani Suit came in."

"Shut up!" Nora playfully jabs me. "He did not! What are the chances?" She bounces with excitement.

Ever since I'd shared the story of waking up in a strange man's bed and struggling to remember what happened, she made it her mission to get to the bottom of who he was. She'd even asked Aiden, the bartender, if he knew, to no avail.

"Apparently pretty good." I roll my eyes, feigning annoyance with the idea of seeing the man I swore I had no desire to cross paths with again.

"What did you do?" Chloe inquires, not as excitable as Nora.

"I did what any self-respecting thirty-year-old woman in my shoes would do when facing a man whose bed she woke up in after a night of drinking."

"You tried to hide, didn't you?"

"Do you blame me? I hoped to never see the guy again. So I did my best to act disinterested, although... Holy hell, girls." Warmth radiates through me as I melt into the couch, unable to contain my smile. "On a scale of ten, this guy is, like, a solid eleven. He was even hotter than I remember. Usually, it's the other way around.

And bonus, I learned his name is Julian, so there's that."

"What did he say?"

I stare into space, recalling our conversation in the coffee house. One thing stands out above all others. "He wanted to know why I left without saying goodbye. He appeared genuinely upset by it."

"Aww...," Nora and Chloe say in unison, passing each other an endearing look.

"No. Not *aww*. This is not an *aww* moment."

"It is," Chloe insists.

"No."

"It's destiny, Evie!" Nora beams as she clutches my hand, squeezing. "You get wasted and sleep with who I can only imagine to be God's gift to the male form, can't remember a thing, then cross paths with him two weeks later. I'm not sure the odds of something like that happening, especially in a city the size of New York, but it's got to be unheard of!"

"It's not destiny." I brush off the idea, even though I'd briefly considered it. "And..." I trail off.

"And...what?" Chloe leans in, clinging to my every word.

I expect them to break out the popcorn as they take in the story I've kept from them for twenty-four hours. I'm not sure why I thought I could keep it from them forever. Maybe because I assumed yesterday was the last time I'd see Julian. Boy, was I wrong. Maybe it *is* destiny.

Returning my attention to them, I admit, "You were right."

"Right?" Confused, Chloe's brows pull in.

"We *didn't* sleep together."

"I knew it!" She pumps her fist in the air. "I mean, who

in their right mind would have the wherewithal to put her bra back on after having sexy times? Hell, what woman would fall asleep with her bra on in the first place, unless they were completely incapable of taking it off? And there's no way he wouldn't take it off to get a look at those girls." With a laugh, she gestures to my chest. "You have fantastic boobs."

"Thank...you?"

"Start at the beginning," Nora orders. "And don't leave out a single detail."

With a grin, I run them through yesterday's unexpected events. Seeing Julian and learning his name. Dismissing him so I could work on finding August Laurent. Being unable to focus after our encounter. Running into Trevor with another woman as I left the coffee shop. Bumping into Julian again. Him telling me what happened the night of my birthday, then proposing a little arrangement.

"An arrangement?" Chloe waggles her brows deviously.

"Like a friends with benefits thing?" Nora smirks. "No strings, but you still get treated to a rocking orgasm when needed? Trust me. Those are a lot of fun." She looks to Chloe, who nods in agreement.

"No... Well, I don't think so. We still have to iron out the details, but if I agree to be his date to a bunch of stuffy dinner parties and events he has coming up, he'll help me win back Trevor. I turned him down, claiming Trevor was too smart to believe I'd be dating someone like Julian, especially so soon after our own breakup, but then..."

"Julian sent flowers to you at Trevor's while he was conveniently present," Chloe sings, filling in the blanks.

"Exactly."

"And it made him jealous."

"Sure did."

"So Julian wanted to prove you were wrong about Trevor being too smart. Now you're considering his proposal."

"You hit the nail on the head. But I haven't agreed yet. I still have my doubts—"

"Despite the fact that Trevor was jealous after only a bouquet of flowers?" Chloe tilts her head at me. "Imagine if he caught you guys doing it? He'd come crawling back to you in a flash."

"I don't know about that. Even if he *is* jealous, there's no guarantee it'll make him want to be with me."

Chloe and Nora share a look, shrugging.

"The reason Trevor broke up with me is because he doesn't think I'm serious. Lying to him and pretending to date someone else?" I grab one of Chloe's colorful throw pillows and hug it to my body. "That will most likely only solidify his original opinion."

Squinting, Nora considers my words for a moment. "Then why didn't you tell Trevor you *weren't* dating Julian? And why didn't you refuse to meet Julian for dinner tonight?"

I stare forward, shaking my head as I give the only answer that seems fitting. "I couldn't say no to him."

Chloe jumps to her feet, tugging me off the couch and into the den, which has become my bedroom, Nora following close on our heels. "Well, what are you going to wear?" She proceeds toward a hanging rack, shifting through all my clothes.

"I have no idea. I don't even know where he's taking me tonight." I plop down onto the bed.

"Ask him." She nods at my hand, which still clutches my cell.

"What? I can't do that."

"Sure you can," Nora encourages.

"Then he'll think I'm excited about tonight, and I can't be excited about tonight. It's strictly a business dinner. A glorified negotiation, so to speak."

With a groan, Chloe steps toward me, taking the phone from my hand. "Then I'll text him. While I'm at it, I'll ask him what kind of panties he prefers. Briefs, thongs, or commando. Ya know... So you can dress appropriately...in all respects."

My reflexes have never been so quick as I rip my cell out of Chloe's hands. "Fine. I'll text him." I open my messages to see he responded to the one I'd sent with her address.

The Village? My mother always warned me about dating a village girl.

A smile builds on my face as I respond.

Well then, it's a good thing I'm a Nebraska girl. Is there a dress code for dinner?

She warned me about Midwest girls, too. And wear something nice. A dress. Nothing too formal, but nothing too casual, either.

What will you be wearing?

Are you sexting with me?

I blush at his comment, drawing a blank as I try to come up with a witty response. Normally, I'd have an entire arsenal of possibilities. But something about Julian unnerves me, like I'm not myself.

If I were sexting, you'd be squirming in your seat, itching to drive over here and see me. I'm simply asking as a point of reference. And so I don't pick out the same Brooks Brothers' suit. It's happened before, and it was the embarrassment of the century. So I made Trevor go home and change.

Chloe bursts out laughing. I glance over my shoulder to see her and Nora peering at the screen.

"You're horrible," Nora comments.

"Everyone uses comedy in awkward situations."

"But you use it in *all* situations."

"What can I say? I live an awkward life."

When my phone buzzes, we all fling our eyes back to the screen.

Oh, Guinevere. I do enjoy your wit. No need to worry about us wearing the same Brooks Brothers suit. I don't own any. Most of mine are Tom Ford, which I'll be wearing tonight. I think slate gray. I'll see you at seven.

I'm about to type a response when Nora snatches the phone from me. "Don't."

"What? Why?"

She blows out a breath, pinching the bridge of her nose. "You've been out of the dating world for too long."

"No, I haven't," I protest. "I've been working in it for years."

"Working in it and living it are two different things." Chloe gives me a knowing look.

"I—"

"You need to make him want you."

I stand up from the bed, heading to my rack of clothes to find something suitable for tonight. "This isn't a real relationship. It's not even a relationship. Plus, I haven't agreed to his proposal yet. I'm not sure I *want* to. Using someone to make Trevor jealous? It's definitely a bit juvenile, if you ask me."

"Fuck Trevor," Chloe interjects harshly. "Don't do this for Trevor. Do this for you. Have some fun this summer instead of moping around with a broken heart. And maybe this Julian is just the person to help you do that and get over Trevor."

"I doubt that." I stare ahead, avoiding her eyes. "We have absolutely no interest in each other."

Nora stands, walking toward me. "I find that hard to believe. For both of you. You blushed the entire time you spoke to him. And Julian? He digs you. Mentioning sexting? He's flirting with you. I told you not to respond to his text because he *wants* you to. By leaving him hanging, you'll have him thinking about you all afternoon until he sees you tonight. He'll be so on edge, he won't be able to contain himself."

I pull a yellow polka-dot dress from the rack, holding it up to my body. It's a fun, flirty, summer dress, reminiscent of a pinup girl style. Both my friends simultaneously shake their heads, grimacing. I groan. I want to go for something that screams just friends. I have a feeling they want me to wear something that makes me look like a temptress.

"Like I told you…," I begin with a sigh.

"Yeah, yeah. It isn't real." Nora does her best imitation of my voice.

"It's not.

"Trust me." She narrows her gaze on me. "He's into you. If he weren't, he would never have proposed this arrangement. I have a knack for picking up on these things. It's, like, my superpower or something."

I scoff, averting my gaze so my friends can't see the twinge of hope building over the idea of someone like Julian Gage being interested in me. He's so mature, so mysterious, so…sophisticated.

"In fact, I can prove it to you." She jumps up, shifting through my dresses.

"How?" I place a hand on my hip, arching my brows.

"I guarantee, before we've all agreed on a dress for you to wear tonight, he'll text again. He's probably staring at his phone, waiting for you to respond. Eventually, it'll be too much, so he'll message you something he hopes you won't be able to ignore. But you'll do just that. When you see him tonight, *you'll* have the upper hand. *You'll* be the one in control."

She returns her attention to my clothes, stopping to look at a few dresses before moving on. I'm about to argue, yet again, that her experience on Tinder doesn't make her a dating expert when a loud chiming rips through the quiet space.

We stop moving, all eyes zeroing in on the phone on the bed. Nora faces me, wearing a self-satisfied smirk. She crosses her arms over her chest.

"Did someone text you, *Guinevere?*"

My mouth growing dry, I slowly walk toward the bed and grab the phone. "Sorcery," I murmur as I unlock the screen.

"Who's it from?" she asks in faux curiosity.

"Julian."

"And what does it say?"

I'll never hear the end of it after I read this to her. "'And as far as your earlier comment that I'd be itching to see you if you were sexting... I already am.'"

Her expression is smug as she turns from me, looking through my dresses once more. "Dating is one strategic game. Even fake dating."

On a hard swallow, I remain silent, her words mirroring what Julian said. How all of life is simply a game.

"Play your cards right, you might just end up with a royal flush."

Chapter Twelve

"HOLY CRAP, EVIE!" Nora squeals when I walk out of Chloe's bedroom and into the open living area.

The two girls took it upon themselves to give me a makeover as we opened a bottle of chardonnay. It was reminiscent of adolescent slumber parties, apart from the wine. We gushed over the prospect of a date with a ridiculously attractive man while they perfected my hair and makeup. And, of course, being the list-maker I am, I jotted down a list of pros and cons for Julian and Trevor, hoping it would help sway my decision. It didn't.

"You're smoking hot. I barely recognize you." She gets up from the couch, bringing her half-filled wine glass with her.

"Thanks... I think."

"It reminds me of my first date with Jeremy," she gushes as she leads me over to the full-length mirror hanging on the far wall, checking her handiwork.

"How?" I turn to her. "You met him on Tinder. Your first 'date' was a no-strings hookup. This is nothing like that."

"Whatever you say, Evie." She squares my shoulders, forcing me to face the mirror once more as she smooths a few of my flyaways. "Unlike what you think, you can't plan for everything. I wasn't looking for anything serious.

Neither was Jeremy. You can't deny chemistry. Now look at us." With bright eyes and a brilliant smile, she holds out her left hand where a stunning diamond sits on her ring finger. "I'd say that's a pretty damn big string. All because I stepped out of my comfort zone, veered away from my *plan*, and allowed life to take the wheel."

"I'm happy for you, Nora." Despite their unconventional beginning, they are perfect for each other, not to mention Jeremy treats her like a queen. That's all any woman wants. Too bad there appears to be a lack of kings around these days.

I return my eyes to the mirror to do one last check. Nora was right. I don't look like myself. I wear makeup on a regular basis, but don't spend this amount of time on all the shading and contouring. The pallet Nora used makes the green of my eyes pop even more. Couple that with my red hair, the pouty, red lips, and the slim-fit black dress that hugs all my curves in the right places, which Chloe insisted I wear, and I've never felt so glamorous, so...beautiful.

"You don't think it looks like I'm trying too hard?" I spin around to face my friends. "I mean, this isn't a date."

"We know," Chloe groans. "You've only reminded us every minute since you hung up with this guy. And it's not about trying too hard. It's about using your natural...assets to come out on top in your negotiation. With a dress like that and your fantastic curves..." She gestures down my frame, "this guy will be eating out of the palm of your hand. Trust me."

"I don't—"

The buzzer rips through the apartment, interrupting me, and we all jump. My pulse skyrockets as I fling my wide eyes to the door, my breath quickening. I've never wanted to run away and hide as much as I do right now.

I don't remember being this on edge when Trevor picked me up for our first date. Then again, we were friends first. Not to mention, all he had to do was take the elevator down a few floors in our dorm.

"Evie…" Nora places her hands on my arms, soothing me. "Relax. You remember all the conditions we discussed earlier?"

I nod quickly. "I made a list in my phone."

"Good. Remain firm. Keep the ball in your court."

"How do I even do that? I haven't been on a date, real or fake, in over a decade. Not like you guys."

"Well, then…" Chloe approaches and slings an arm along my shoulders. "If you ever find yourself in an uncomfortable situation and aren't sure what to do, ask yourself, 'What would Chloe do?'"

My two best friends burst out laughing. It's no secret what Chloe would do. It's what she always does.

With a groan, I push away from them. "That would end with me beneath him. And we are *not* going there. It's on my list." I hold up my phone before dropping it into my clutch. "No sex."

"It wouldn't end with me beneath him," she argues, then winks. "I much prefer being on top." With that, she spins, heading toward the door.

When her hand touches the doorknob, about to turn it, she glances over her shoulder, her brow arched, giving me one last chance to call it off. This is why I love her. No matter what, she'll always have my back. As much as she's exhibited her excitement over the idea of me going to dinner with Julian, she'll support me if I decide to cancel. Friends like Chloe and Nora are nearly impossible to find. I'm grateful I did. Navigating the stormy waters of my break up with Trevor would have been infinitely more difficult had it not been for them.

On a deep inhale, I nod. Time seems to stand still as she opens the door, revealing Julian on her front stoop. The instant my eyes lock with his, all the breath leaves me. He parts his lips slightly, his gaze darkening as he takes in my appearance, scanning me from head to toe. He doesn't even pay attention to Chloe, which is different. Whenever the three of us go out, Chloe seems to get the majority of the attention, what with her slender physique and unique shade of hair. It's difficult *not* to notice Chloe. But Julian doesn't even give her a second glance. I *like* that he notices me.

"Hi," his voice cuts through the silence.

I'm not sure how long we've been staring at each other. All I know is I can stare at this man all night and not be tired of the way he looks. A pair of dark jeans hang from his waist. Not too tight, but not too baggy, either. A beige jacket is slung over a white button-down shirt, the top two buttons undone, revealing a few tufts of chest hair. The previous times I've seen him, he's been in business attire — perfectly tailored suit, tie, shoes that cost more than I make in a year...including the ones I threw up on. While I like him in a suit, I love this dressy, yet casual look.

Nora nudges me and I snap out of my stupor. "Hi."

He bites his lower lip, reluctant to rip his eyes away from me, but he eventually does, addressing Chloe. "You must be Chloe." He holds out his hand.

"And you're Julian Gage." Her tone is borderline accusatory. I furrow my brow. I don't remember telling her his last name. Then again, the entire afternoon is a whirlwind. It probably slipped out while they helped me get ready.

"Guilty as charged." He laughs politely as Chloe steps back, allowing him to enter the apartment, but keeping her furtive stare trained on his every move.

As he walks toward me, his eyes rake over me in a way that makes me think he's seeing me for the first time. Or maybe, thanks to my impromptu makeover, he's seeing me in a different light. During our previous encounters, I was dressed well, but not like this. Not in a dress that clung to my curves. Not with my hair styled. Not with my makeup impeccable. I don't even feel like that same woman anymore. Maybe that's a good thing.

"Guinevere," he murmurs as he leans in, kissing my cheek, his lips lingering on my skin, turning the exchange from a friendly one into something more sensual. My heart seems to do backflips in my chest, his proximity overwhelming me. "You're stunning." He inhales deeply, a subtle moan escaping his throat on the exhale. "And you smell even better, if that's possible." He pulls back, his delectable smile disarming me. "I get the feeling with you, *anything* is possible."

The innuendo in his tone sends a shiver down my spine. I remind myself of the list I'd made of conditions that must be in place for me to agree to this. No sex is right at the top. Perhaps I should add no sexual innuendos to that list.

Remembering my friends' advice that I keep the ball in my court, I smile coyly, increasing the distance between us. "I thought you said you'd be wearing a suit. That's more of a blazer and jeans."

When he flashes a devious grin, I have to fight the urge not to jump on him and ride him until he erases every last trace of Trevor from my life. The old Evie would never think such a thing, but the energy buzzing between Julian and me is electrifying. Add in my sudden ability to only get off with the assistance of inanimate objects, and I'm on edge.

"Would you hold it against me if I admitted I lied just so you'd wear a dress?"

I pass him a demure look, batting my lashes. "You *wanted* me to wear a dress? Any reason for that?"

My breathy voice surprises me. Is this how people act in relationships? Like whoever they think the other person wants them to be? How will that work? Won't they get tired of pretending to be someone else, causing the relationship to go up in flames?

Isn't that what I'm doing with Trevor? Aren't I trying to convince him I can be serious instead of wanting him just to love me for me?

"I'm staring at the reason for that." Julian leans even closer, his breath dancing on my skin, intense, warm, thrilling. "You're exquisite, Guinevere. And any man who couldn't see what he had doesn't deserve you."

I meet his heated gaze, losing myself in the darkening blue. For a second, I almost believe his endearing words. Then I remember it's all an act. He's putting on a show, making my friends think this is a real date. He has no idea they know the truth. Stepping back before I do something I'll regret, I glance to my right, Nora grinning at me.

"Julian… This is my other friend, Nora."

"Pleasure to meet you," he says, reaching for her hand and taking it in his. "Do you live here, too?"

"No. I live in Queens with my fiancé, but when Evie said she was moving out of her old place and needed our help, we were more than happy to take time off and lend a hand. It's a worthy cause."

"I couldn't agree more." He shifts his gaze from Nora,

looking between the three of us.

"Well, we should get going then, shouldn't we?" I look to Julian.

"Where are you going?" Chloe demands, her tone surprising me.

"Chloe," I hiss, furrowing my brow, an unspoken question as to the origins of the stick that now seems to be firmly shoved up her ass.

"It's a fair question," Julian responds with authority, not even batting an eye. "I'm sure you're both skeptical about her going out with a guy she barely knows, but I promise, you have nothing to be worried about." He adjusts his posture, the smile gone from his face. Now his expression appears all business. "I'm taking Evie to dinner at Maison Noir in Hell's Kitchen. After that, I'll bring her straight back here."

"Or maybe you should take her back to your place," Nora interjects, waggling her brows.

"Okay then!" I interrupt, nudging Julian toward the door. This is officially becoming more awkward than when I brought Trevor home to meet my parents. "Time to go! See you girls later."

I hurry onto the stoop, wanting to get out of here before it gets even worse. However, I'm not used to the three-inch heels Chloe dressed me in and my ankle catches. Everything happens in slow motion as I try to right myself, but my weight is already crashing forward. Suddenly, I'm stopped mid-collapse, a pair of strong arms wrapping around me and pulling me upright. My heart is caught in my throat as I stand chest-to-chest with Julian, peering up into his eyes.

"Got ya." His smooth voice sends a shiver through me.

"Thanks." The safety of his embrace and passion in his

gaze turns me into a blubbering fool, unable to form a coherent thought.

"I have a feeling you're going to keep me on my toes."

"Me, too," I whimper.

He holds me a moment longer until he's confident I have my footing, then releases me. I don't say anything as he helps me inside an idling town car, a driver standing next to it. Once the door closes, giving me a moment to myself as he runs around to get in beside me, I blow out a breath.

I'm in deep trouble.

Chapter Thirteen

"AM I OVERDRESSED?" I ask as the car pulls up in front of a building in Hell's Kitchen, Maison Noir etched on a gold plate next to a nondescript wooden door. The nearly thirty-minute drive through the typical Manhattan traffic was unnerving as I attempted to ignore the sizzling electricity between us.

"Are you kidding me?" Julian leans toward me when the driver steps out. "I haven't been able to keep my eyes off you yet. You look incredible."

"We're alone," I remind him with a trite smile. "You can drop the act."

My door opens, allowing me a brief reprieve from Julian's intensity before he rushes out of the car himself, hurrying to catch up.

"What makes you think it's all an act?" His hand rests on the small of my back as he leads me toward the building.

Now that we're on display, I pass him an enamored look, doing my best to give off the impression I'm head over heels in love with him. I can play his game just as well as he. A minor in theater not a wise choice, Mom? Well, I'm about to put all those acting classes to use.

"Let's not pretend this is anything other than what it is, Julian." My voice is sickly sweet, a complete contradiction to the words I speak. Facing him, I stand on my toes, my lips hovering near his. I sense his composure crack when I exhale, my breath ghosting over his mouth. His grip on me tightens, his jaw clenching. His reaction gives me an added boost of confidence.

"And what *is* this, Guinevere?"

"Two people who agreed to have dinner to discuss the potential of entering into a business arrangement." I move my lips along his jawline, every inch of him seeming to harden as I lean into the crook of his neck. "Nothing more."

I linger for a moment longer, then abruptly pull back, swaying my hips as I head into the restaurant without waiting for him. I can sense the heat of his gaze on me and silently thank Chloe and Nora for their dating advice. I still have the upper hand. That's exactly what I need if I'm to get through tonight without this guy becoming number four. Officially.

When Julian finally joins me, he acts as if he weren't about to slam me against the wall and kiss me in a way Trevor never did. I hoped he'd be on edge and out of sorts, just like I felt when I first saw him stroll into Chloe's apartment. Instead, he's as collected as I remember him from our first meeting, an air of authority in his voice when he gives the *maître d'* his name.

"Of course, Monsieur Gage," he says in a thick French accent, winking. There's a hint of familiarity between the two. I wonder if Julian brings all his dates here. Worse, I wonder if he's proposed this sort of arrangement to other women in the past. I have no reason to believe he hasn't. Why does my chest tighten at the idea of me being another one in what I can only assume to be a long list of women?

"Guinevere?" Julian's voice cuts through. I dart my gaze to his, his brow wrinkled in concern. "Are you okay?"

"Certainly, darling." I grit a smile and step toward him.

As we follow the *maître d'* into the dining area, I focus my attention on the décor in an effort to ignore the warmth emanating from Julian's hand resting just above my waist. The place is all dim lighting, intimate tables, and mirrored walls, making the room appear bigger than it actually is. With it being New York, space is at a premium, but we're tucked away in a corner, giving us privacy, which will prove useful for our discussions.

Once we each have a glass of wine in front of us and have placed our orders, I pull my phone from my clutch and open the "notes" application, scanning the points I'd typed out earlier.

I look at him, my expression serious. "First, if I'm to agree to this, I'd like to establish boundaries. Obviously, there will have to be a certain level of physical contact, but there needs to be a line. Sex is absolutely out of the question." I look down, my face heating, the confidence I'd felt earlier dissipating now that we're getting into the nitty-gritty of what will and won't be permitted in our fake relationship. "I'd prefer we not—"

"Guinevere," Julian's soft voice interrupts as his hand grabs mine. I snap my eyes to his, an innate response my brain has somehow learned in only a few days' time. "Put the phone away."

"But—"

He brings my hand up to his lips, his gaze unwavering. The seconds stretch as he nuzzles against my knuckles, but doesn't kiss them. Regardless, the roughness of his unshaven jaw against my flesh causes a tingle to trickle down my spine. Then he looks out of the corner of his eye, as if trying to tell me something.

As cautiously as possible, I shift my gaze toward the entrance of the restaurant, my breath hitching when I see Trevor walk in with Theresa, his hand on the small of her back as they're led toward a table. He holds out the chair for her, something he's never done for me, at least not that I can remember.

"How—"

"Don't you want him to think we're together? Considering he appears to have moved on, as well."

"I suppose, but—"

"Then you need to put the phone away. People who are into each other don't spend dinner on their cells. We'll have this discussion, which appears to be extremely important to you, but we'll do so without the talking points you've already made notes of. Like I said, dating is simply a game. The ref just blew the first whistle."

Doing my best not to look at Trevor to see if he's noticed me sitting here with Julian, I pull my hand away, discreetly pushing my phone back into my purse before reaching for my wine glass, swirling it.

"I still haven't agreed to anything," I remind him.

"I think you just did, baby doll." He winks.

"I—"

"You could have easily ignored my request. But you didn't. So that tells me there's a part of you, however small, that *wants* Trevor to think we're together."

I raise my glass, taking a sip of the full-bodied red, allowing it to warm my stomach. It's robust with a hint of spice, the perfect pairing for the filet mignon I ordered. If Julian's treating me to dinner, I may as well take advantage and go for the gold.

"What I *want* Trevor to think and what he actually *does*

117

are two different things. Yes, he was jealous when he intercepted the flowers you sent. However, as I pointed out during our conversation, he did accuse me of only dating you to make him jealous. So, regardless of what I agree to, that will always be in the back of his mind. That we're only together for a juvenile purpose."

"Juvenile?"

"Yes. Juvenile." I lean closer, lowering my voice. My expression remains amorous, as if I'm murmuring my deepest desires to this intriguing man. "Even you must admit it's something you'd do in high school. Your smart, studious, perfect boyfriend breaks up with you, so you get back at him by dating the school flirt. The one who seems to go through women like toilet paper. The one who could get any girl he wants, but he somehow decides to clean up his act with the theater geek. I've already seen that movie. Hell, I *lived* that movie in high school. I'm not sure I'm interested in a sequel."

Julian's gaze remains resolute, unaffected by my outburst. When he brings his hands in front of his face, he tents them, his fingers brushing against his lips in quiet contemplation.

"Then perhaps we should forget about my original proposal altogether."

My mouth grows slack as I cock my head at him. "Forget about it?"

I'm not sure what my end game was, but I didn't expect him to call it quits before our meals even arrived. And I was really looking forward to that steak. Did I overplay my hand? I wish Chloe and Nora were here to tell me what to do.

I've spent the past five years dishing out relationship advice, but I never took any of it seriously. It was more a comedic outlet for my writing, a way for me to poke fun at how crazy and stressful dating could be. No one would think I'd actually advocate starting a collection of your date's toenail trimmings and present it to them on your first anniversary. At least I hope they wouldn't.

"Yes, Guinevere. No matter what I say or do, I fear I'll never be able to convince you this idea is anything but juvenile. And maybe it is. I simply saw it as a way to solve *both* our problems. I was already on the lookout for someone who might be interested in posing as my girlfriend. When I heard you share your troubles that night at the bar, I thought you'd be perfect. And I still think you'd be perfect for what I need."

I worry my bottom lip, absorbing his words. "Why me?"

"Why *not* you?"

"I can list a thousand reasons. I'm sure there are plenty of women who would gladly agree to pretend to be your girlfriend. Hell, you might even get laid, which one would argue would be a nice bonus. You won't get that with me."

He leans closer, gazing thoughtfully at me with his penetrating blue eyes. It almost feels like he's able to peer into my soul.

"Did you ever stop to think that's exactly why I asked you?"

"Because I *won't* sleep with you?" I push out a laugh, then sip my wine. "Most men would probably expect sex from this kind of arrangement. Unless, of course, they were gay…" My breath hitches, wide eyes darting to Julian. "Oh, my god!" I whisper-shout, glancing around the restaurant, ensuring no one's paying attention. Apart from Trevor's occasional wandering gaze, no one seems to care about our conversation. "You're gay, aren't you? You need me to pretend to date you to keep your sexual orientation a secret so some conservative politician will back whatever project you're working on. That's why you didn't take advantage of me when I was drunk and in your bed."

He chuckles, his expression brightening with amusement. "I've been called a lot of things in my life, but I've yet to be accused of being gay."

"It's okay if you are. There's nothing wrong with it. No one cares these days, especially in New York. Are you from a religious family? Is that why—"

"I am *not* gay. That's *not* why I'm looking for someone to pose as my girlfriend. And that's *not* why I didn't take advantage of you. I didn't take advantage of you because I'm not an asshole. I don't take advantage of women. Period." His voice is determined, his eyes steadfast.

At that moment, the waiter approaches with our meals, cutting through the tension. The aroma of garlic and meat invades my senses as my mouth waters from the beautifully prepared steak in front of me. I pick up my knife and slice into it, meeting Julian's eyes as he cuts into his lamb, the meat falling off the bone.

"*Bon appetite*," he says in a perfect French accent, which piques my curiosity, but not enough to press him about it. Not with my steak inches from my mouth.

I take a bite, moaning at the buttery flavor of the impeccably prepared filet.

"You really know how to tease a man, don't you?"

"Why? Am I teasing you?" I bat my lashes, thankful for the flirtatious atmosphere between us once more.

"You have no fucking idea."

The tone of his voice hits me deep in my core. As much

as I want to tear my eyes from his, I'm unable to, the tension cracking and sizzling. Why don't I remember it being like this with Trevor?

"So..." I clear my throat, my brain finally communicating with the rest of my body to look away from Julian before I throw myself at him without a single regard for the fact we're in public. "Getting back to why we're here."

"Yes?"

"Why me? Especially considering you know I'm not exactly over my ex."

"That's one of the reasons," Julian answers nonchalantly. "Less drama. Less headache. I get the pleasure of the company of a woman who's familiar with what it takes to be in a committed relationship and will be able to sell the idea that we're in one. And I won't have to worry about you wanting more than I'm willing to give."

"This begs the question of why you need to pretend to be in a committed relationship. Why aren't you in one? You're not one of those guys who thinks it's his civic duty to screw as many women as possible, yet refuses to commit to anyone, are you?"

"Certainly not," he answers with a chuckle. "I'm just not interested in a relationship."

"At all?" I arch a brow. It reminds me of Chloe's take on relationships. Maybe I should suggest they get together since it seems he has more in common with her. "Life is full of relationships," I continue, pushing down the jealousy bubbling at the idea of Chloe and Julian hooking up, "even if they're not the intimate type. You appear to be rather successful in whatever it is you do. You don't get there unless you build business relationships."

"That's different. We leave all emotions out of things to get the job done. It's not personal."

"So you're just not interested in a relationship that requires you to get too personal."

His expression pensive, he considers my statement for a moment before nodding. "Yes. I suppose that's correct." He brings his fork to his mouth, taking another bite of his lamb.

"May I ask why?"

"I'd rather you didn't."

I sigh, lifting my glass. "Then I suppose you'll have to find someone else to be your fake girlfriend."

His gaze turns steely, his jaw tightening. I've hit a nerve. "Suffice it to say, I don't buy into the requirement that in order to be happy, you have to be in a relationship with someone. Some people aren't cut out for that."

"And you think you're one of them?" My voice is timid as I press on. The more I do, the greater the chance he'll walk away.

"I know I am. And that's all I'll say on the matter."

Silence falls between us, awkward and stiff. It's the most distant I've felt around him since we met. In an attempt to ignore it, I push my food around my plate, my appetite disappearing.

"As far as the other reason…"

When I hear him speak again, I lift my eyes to meet his. "Pardon?"

"I said one of the reasons you're perfect for this is that I don't have to worry about you falling for me. But there's more."

"And what's that?" My heart drums in my chest, his

tone a stark contrast to the anger with which he spoke mere seconds earlier. I marvel at his ability to flip the switch so quickly.

With extreme grace, he swirls his wine before bringing it to his mouth. My eyes instantly focus on his lips. I'm mesmerized by everything this man does. I should find comfort in the fact nothing will ever happen between us. Hell, these were my conditions, after all. Regardless, a twinge of disappointment settles in my heart at never knowing him on a more intimate level.

"There was something in your voice as you informed the entire bar of your breakup. I can't quite explain it. After twelve years, you'd think there would be anger, sadness, disappointment. But there was something else instead."

"Sarcasm?" I offer, recalling the bitterness that prompted me to share my heartache with complete strangers. I'm sure the alcohol didn't hurt in that regard, either. No need to give me a truth serum. Give me a shot of tequila and I'd tell you the location of Jimmy Hoffa…if I knew it.

"That's not it." He shakes his head. "I heard hope."

"Hope?"

"Yes. And determination. Your ability to find humor about what could only be described as one of the most heartbreaking events of your life shows your strength of character. You didn't go home, watch *When Harry Met Sally*, and gorge on Ben & Jerry's."

I scoff, "Not by choice."

He studies me for a moment before speaking again. "I think it was. I may not know you as well as Chloe or Nora, but I've picked up on a few things. One of those is you only do what you want. If you didn't want to spend time with me, you wouldn't be here."

I lower my eyes, not wanting to acknowledge his statement bears a hint of truth. Two days ago, I never would have expected to be sitting here with him in this restaurant while Trevor looms a few tables away. Now I've barely thought of Trevor, all my focus on Julian. Maybe that's how it's supposed to be.

"Have I answered all your questions?" Julian asks when I remain silent. "Is there anything else you need to know before you agree to my proposal?"

Lifting my head, I do my best to appear collected, as if he hadn't weaseled his way under my skin throughout the evening by simply being honest and upfront with me. It's more than I can say for Trevor as of late.

"If I agree, I don't want you to think it's an open invitation to make out with me whenever it suits you.

"I'll be escorting you to fundraisers, charity dinners, galas, things like that. Not to a sex club."

"Well, that's a shame. I'll need to return my flogger and ball gag."

After momentarily scrutinizing me, Julian breaks into a hearty laugh, attracting the attention of a few of our fellow diners, Trevor included. There's a hint of jealousy mixed with longing in his gaze. It makes me feel somewhat vindicated. A frazzled aura surrounds him, like he's having trouble focusing on whatever Theresa's saying because I'm sitting a few tables away with a very handsome, successful man. Then, not paying attention, he knocks his wine glass over, the red liquid spilling all over Theresa's white blouse. Waiters rush to help clean up the mess, but the damage is already done.

I turn my eyes back to Julian, struggling to reel in my smile. Maybe we *can* kill two birds with one stone.

"In all seriousness, I promise not to do anything you're uncomfortable with."

"Even if I say no kissing?"

He blinks repeatedly, taken aback. "No kissing?"

"Yes. At least on the mouth. I'm agreeable to a kiss on the cheek or forehead, but I'd rather we draw the line there."

He recovers his composure. "Any reason for that?"

"It's too…personal." I fidget with my napkin in my lap, the soft texture comforting. "It seems I'm not built like you. I do get attached to people. As long as we have the line drawn at no kissing, I won't forget what this is…a business arrangement."

"Okay." He nods curtly after a moment of contemplation. "You have my word. No kissing on the lips."

"Really?" I cock my head.

"You sound surprised. Why wouldn't I agree?"

"Oh, I don't know. Won't people think there's something amiss if they don't see us kiss?"

"Trust me, Guinevere." His voice is smooth and confident. "There are other ways to demonstrate your desire. Kissing is the easy way out. There's nothing suggestive about one mouth pressing against the other. No. Desire is in the way your bodies find each other, the way your eyes darken with unmatched hunger, the way a shiver runs through you at the promise of what's to come."

I swallow hard, doing my best to make it appear as if I'm not slowly losing my composure at his sensual words, to pretend I don't already react that way whenever I'm in his presence. "Says the man who avoids committed relationships."

"I never said I was perfect." He dabs his napkin against his mouth, making me incredibly jealous of a piece of fabric. "So no sex, no kissing. What are your other conditions?"

"Right." I square my shoulders. "An itinerary."

"An itinerary?"

"Yes. I don't like the unexpected. I've been a bit of a planner my entire life. Hell, I'd already planned my wedding to Trevor before we even met." I laugh under my breath. "I tweaked a few things once we *did* meet, but that's beside the point." I return my gaze to Julian. "I like having a plan, knowing what's expected of me so I can anticipate...things."

"Things?"

"Yes. I'd like to know precisely the type of event and when I'll be required to be...at your service."

"You'll never be 'at my service', Guinevere," he responds quickly. "But if a list of events makes you less on edge, I'm happy to provide one. I understand your job is important to you, so I'll limit the events to weekends and holidays. I just ask you set aside Fridays through Sundays."

"We have our weekly staff meeting Friday mornings."

"Then you'll leave right after. Is that agreeable?"

"Yes. That's fine. Viv is flexible with us working out of the office."

"Any other conditions?"

I chew on my lower lip, recalling the list I'd come up with earlier in the evening. "A firm end date."

He nods. "No sense dragging this out longer than necessary. Come Labor Day, you're free to return to your normal life. Anything else?"

"No." Those were my non-negotiable conditions. I thought he'd put up more of a fight over no sex or kissing. I guess I was wrong.

"Okay then. Agreed on all points. Now I have a few conditions of my own."

"Such as?"

"First, you'll be staying in my beach house with me." He leans closer, lowering his voice. "Don't worry. You'll have your own room and space. Anytime we're not scheduled to be somewhere, you can do whatever you'd like. You won't need to spend extra time with me. You can sit by the pool, go to the beach, whatever you like. Your free time is just that...yours."

"And your other conditions?"

"It's more of a...request."

I arch a brow. "And that is?"

"I'd appreciate your word that you'll commit to me for the duration of the summer and not end this arrangement early. I need a woman by my side for all the social events that fill the summer season in the Hamptons. So in the event Trevor has a change of heart and wants you back, I'd request you hold him off until the end of summer. After that, we walk away and never have to see each other again. By then, I'm hoping this project will be underway. I'll make up a story about how you're still in love with your ex, which isn't a stretch, and we'll go our separate ways.

"So... What'll it be, Guinevere? Will you be my fake girlfriend?"

I stare into space, considering his proposition. Out of the corner of my eye, I catch a glimpse of Trevor. Instead of the frantic energy that surrounded him before, he's calm, he and Theresa seeming to laugh off the mishap.

He brings her hand up to his mouth, peppering soft kisses against it. I don't remember the last time he looked at me that way.

Resolute, I return my attention to Julian. What do I have to lose? Trevor's already moved on. Why should I torture myself by waiting for him to come to his senses? After twelve years, maybe I deserve to have some fun myself. A summer in the Hamptons at what I can only imagine to be a luxurious beach house may be exactly what the doctor ordered to mend my broken heart. What could possibly go wrong?

"Yes, Julian. I'll be your fake girlfriend."

Chapter Fourteen

"**D**O I WANT to know whether tonight was just a coincidence?" I ask once we're in the back seat of the town car and on the way to Chloe's apartment.

"Whatever do you mean, Guinevere?" Julian flashes a conniving smile.

I blow out a breath, crossing my arms. "You know *exactly* what I mean, Julian. Trevor showing up at the same restaurant we happened to be dining at is a bit suspicious, wouldn't you agree?"

"New York's not as big as people think."

Not saying a word, I narrow my gaze at him like my mother always did when she knew I was being purposely evasive.

"And what would you say if I *did* plan it?"

"First, I'd say you have impeccable stalker abilities. Perhaps that's your true calling."

He curves his body toward me, grinning deviously. "Who said it's not? You did figure out I have a secret kill room in Jersey City. You don't lure people to a kill room without properly doing your research...or, as you referred to it, stalking." He winks before leaning back against the seat.

"That's right. How could I forget about the kill room? Okay then, Dexter..."

He laughs at my nickname for him, a twinkle visible in

his eyes, even in the darkened car.

"Care to share how you knew Trevor would be dining there tonight?"

"Simple." He rests his elbow on the center console, drumming his fingertips against the leather. "Theresa is actually a close friend of my neighbor in Southampton. They went to prep school together or something. I just so happened to see her post on Instagram yesterday that she'd bought a new dress for a dinner date with her beau. Friends asked where she was going, and she spilled. No information is too difficult to find out these days. Not with social media."

"So you *did* stalk her."

"Again, I prefer to call it research."

"Okay. So you knew where they'd be. How did you get a reservation? From what I know of that place, they have a waiting list a mile long. You need to book months in advance."

"That's true, unless you know someone."

"And you know someone."

"I know a lot of people."

"But does Trevor know people?" My voice is low and wavers slightly. "Or did Theresa just go in my place?" I suck in a breath, another possibility crossing my mind. A more heartbreaking possibility. "Or was it Theresa's date all along?"

I never even considered that Trevor had cheated on me. He didn't seem the type. Plus, we lived together. I would have noticed if he came home smelling of another woman's perfume. Then again, there were plenty of nights he never came home at all. Was he lying to me the whole time?

"Does it matter?"

"What?" I shift my gaze to Julian.

"Does it matter?" he repeats, this time more forcefully. "At this moment, right here, right now…" He brings his hands to cup my face, an intensity in his eyes causing a surge of desire to pool in my stomach. "Does…it…matter?"

I swallow hard, trying to calm my racing heart, on the brink of insisting it does. Whether Trevor made that reservation for me or Theresa is the difference between me opening my heart to him again or constructing a wall and never allowing him in. But Julian has a point. All evening, I barely thought of Trevor and Theresa, despite them sitting mere feet away. Every ounce of my attention was devoted to Julian. I was in the moment with him. He was all that mattered.

"No," I say softly. "It doesn't." My words come out sounding surprised, and I am a little. Regardless, they're true. Right now, there is no Trevor or Theresa. It's just Julian and me.

"Good." He keeps my face in his hands for another moment before pulling away. The sudden lack of contact leaves me longing for more.

Not wanting to let on, I clear my throat, pulling my cell out of my clutch. "Are there any pressing dates I should be made aware of now? Like within the next week? I don't have any vacation planned, and am able to work from out of the office, but I have a few big projects going on."

I shift my eyes to him when he doesn't say anything right away. His brows are pulled in, an analytical gaze on his face as he seems to assess me. I'm not sure what to make of it. Then he sighs, relaxing into the seat.

"This coming Thursday is July Fourth. The

celebrations go all week, starting tomorrow."

"Tomorrow?" My mouth becomes slack. "I have things I need to get done this weekend. I need to have a life outside of our arrangement."

"And I understand that. I'm not asking you to attend every single party with me. Just the important ones."

"And July Fourth is important."

He nods. "The annual Red, White, and Blue Gala."

"Gala?" I arch a brow. "Am I going to need a dress?"

He laughs, his eyes dancing in amusement. "You're going to need a lot of dresses, swimsuits, stuff like that. Some of these events will be formal, like Fourth of July. Others will be less so. There will be charity auctions, boat christenings, perhaps even some Ladies' Tea luncheons you'll most likely be invited to once word gets around you're my girlfriend."

My stomach suddenly feels weighted down. Lowering my head, I fiddle with the hem of the dress I bought at a discount clothing store, inadequacy washing over me.

"Do you honestly think this will work, Julian? This lifestyle you lead is vastly different from mine. Hell, for all intents and purposes, I'm homeless right now. The only reason I'm not on a street corner holding up a cardboard sign is because Chloe's letting me sleep on the pullout couch in her den. The idea of anyone in your social circle accepting me is ridiculous. Don't you think you'd be better off finding someone who knows the difference between the salad and fish fork?"

With a smirk, he grabs my hand, stopping me from fidgeting. "The fact that you know some settings have both a salad and fish fork shows you're not as inexperienced as you'd like me to believe. We may not know each other well, but the instant I saw you, I knew you were the only person who could do this with me. The only woman I'd *want* to do this with." He brings my hand to his lips, treating my skin to a delicious kiss. "So bury your doubt. Your unabashed confidence is what caught my attention. Don't let the idea that you're not good enough, like Trevor made you think, take it away. You *are* good enough. Hell, you're better than most people can ever dream to be. Don't forget that. Okay?"

I slowly turn my eyes from his, breathless from the passion and genuine affection in his words. "Okay." It's all I can manage.

After a few silent moments, the car comes to a stop. I glance out the window to see we're already at Chloe's building. Julian and his driver step out at the same time. When my door opens, I smile in thanks at his driver before turning to Julian. He places his hand on my lower back, leading me toward the brownstone.

The closer we get to the front door, the more my heart rate increases. What's the proper protocol for saying goodnight to the man you're pretending to date? I doubt I'd find the answer in any rule book. Perhaps this entire experience will give me more material for the column. Instead of just giving advice on normal relationships, I can give tips for fake relationships, too. I'm already writing it in my head...*Fifty Rules for Pretending to Date an Undateable Man.*

Not wanting to endure any more awkwardness than I already have, I take control of the situation, facing Julian and extending my hand toward him. "Thanks for dinner. I thoroughly enjoyed it."

Squinting, he eyes my hand, a bemused smirk forming on his lips. "A handshake?"

"Yes. Your driver obviously knows about our arrangement, as does Chloe, since she and Nora were sitting next to me when you called. There's no need to put on an act right now. So, thank you for dinner." I extend my hand even farther, making it clear that I'm serious about the handshake. When he lifts his hand, I exhale a small breath of relief, only to let out a surprised squeak when he grabs my hip instead, pulling me against him.

In an instant, the desire I'd struggled to suppress all evening flickers back to life as my body fuses into his. He brings a hand to my face, tilting my head back, forcing my eyes to his. They're so intense. So consuming. So vivid. The hair on my nape stands on end, every inch of me aching with raw need.

"Do you honestly believe the only reason I touch you is to put on a show? To keep up an act?" His voice is deep and lustful as he lowers his mouth toward my neck. A slave to his unspoken command, I crane my head, this dance between us feeling like one we've done dozens of times over. Instead, we're two strangers.

"The thought's crossed my mind."

"Well, get the thought *out* of your mind. Yes, I had certain criteria I was looking for in approaching someone about the prospect of this little arrangement. Smart, funny, confident. Most importantly, *attractive*." He nuzzles against my skin, the roughness of his scruff jarring, exciting, and everything I need but didn't realize it.

"Even though you want to keep emotions out of it?" I murmur, my eyes rolling into the back of my head as his breath tortures my skin. It's pure agony, but in the most addicting way.

"That doesn't mean I don't want to be attracted to the person." He lightly runs a finger down the curve of my neck, his breath following the same path, so close yet still not crossing any line. "And I am *profoundly* attracted to you." His hands cup my cheeks and my eyes flutter open, staring into his enamored gaze once more. "You're one of the most alluring women I've seen in a very long time. You have a classic beauty to you. One women would pay thousands of dollars to have, but it's natural for you."

I part my lips, my breath coming in pants the longer his body remains pressed against mine.

"And you're confident in your own skin. Skin thousands of men would love to taste." He smooths my hair behind my shoulder, his hand brushing the exposed flesh. "But what had me absolutely mesmerized was this mouth." He shifts his eyes from mine, focusing on my mouth.

When he brings his lips within a breath of mine, my knees weaken. Desperate for some sort of release, I squeeze my thighs together. Mr. Winky, as I've named my battery-operated boyfriend, will definitely be getting a workout tonight.

"The things that came out of it were witty, charming, and full of hope. With each word you spoke, I was hungry for more. More of your words. More of your mouth. More of you."

He leans even closer, his lips hovering so near to mine I can practically taste them. Wine. Spice. And a hint of chocolate from the soufflé we shared.

"No kissing," I murmur, my teeth chattering. "You agreed."

I sense his mouth curve into a smile. Then he drops his hold on me. I open my eyes to see him retreating down the stairs.

I'm unable to move, to breathe, to think, a statue frozen in time as I watch him walk toward the car. Before he ducks inside, he glances back at me, a mischievous grin on those lips I was a whisper away from kissing, despite insisting we not.

"Kissing is for amateurs, Guinevere. You're in the big leagues now." He holds my gaze a moment longer, then winks before disappearing into the car.

As his car drives off into the night, I lean against the door, placing my hand over my racing heart, trying to calm it down.

One thing is abundantly clear… I am royally fucked.

Chapter Fifteen

"HOW DID THE date go?" Chloe asks the following morning when I emerge from my makeshift bedroom. I head toward the one-cup brewer in the tiny kitchen and pop a pod into it. Instantly, the aroma of coffee fills the air. Just the smell of this magic potion helps erase the cobwebs from my restless and frustrated night, thanks to one Julian Gage.

"It wasn't a date, Chloe." I avoid her eyes as I answer. "Just dinner to discuss a mutually beneficial arrangement."

"So you said yesterday." She looks up from her laptop where she's probably working on a story about some celebrity gossip that hit the wires within the past few hours. Chloe typically pulls all-nighters on Fridays and Saturdays, since that tends to be when all the juicy stories happen. "Have you come to a decision about this 'arrangement'?"

After adding a bit of milk and sweetener to my coffee, I join her on the couch, keeping my head held high. "I have. And I've agreed to help."

"Hmm." Her lips press together.

"What?"

"Nothing." She waves a hand dismissively, returning her attention to her laptop.

"No. It's not nothing. You don't *hmm* unless you want

to say something but are holding back. What is it? Why did you go from wanting me to jump Julian's bones to giving him the stink eye the instant he showed up at the door last night? Is it because he's ridiculously good-looking and you don't think it makes sense for someone like me to be with him?" With each word, my voice gets louder. "Because I'm more than aware I don't fit the mold of the cookie-cutter, waif-like model a guy like him would normally be with. But I—"

"Evie, no. It's not that. It's just…" She blows out a breath as she pulls her gray and lilac locks into a messy bun on top her head. "Why didn't you tell me it was Julian Gage?"

I furrow my brow. "Why does it matter? And how do you know his last name? I don't think I told you."

"You didn't."

"Then how—"

"You don't know who he is, do you?"

I shrug, feeling like an idiot for not Googling him before going out with him. Last time I was single, Myspace was still a thing. That's how long it's been.

Pushing out an exasperated sigh, Chloe types on her laptop before turning it toward me. Heat rushes through me when Julian's vibrant blue eyes stare back from a Wikipedia article. The ache I'd momentarily relieved with the use of my battery-operated boyfriend is back and more intense than it was last night.

"Evie?"

I refocus on Chloe, discreetly wiping at my lip in the hopes that I'm not drooling. Thankfully, I'm not.

"Should I leave you and the laptop alone for a minute?" She giggles.

Rolling my eyes, I zero in on the screen and read a

rather lengthy biography of the man who left me a quivering pile of hormones last night.

Julian Gage was completely unknown until Theodore Price, a distant relative of the Vanderbilt family, passed away, leaving the majority of his vast fortune to him. This prompted a fierce contest over the will by Mr. Price's children, who assumed they'd inherit everything. While Mr. Price didn't disinherit them altogether, providing each of his three children a rather generous testamentary gift...in most people's standards...it was nothing compared to the billions of dollars he'd gifted Julian.

Mr. Price's children tried to allege the will was invalid and that Julian exerted undue influence over an old man who wasn't of sound mind. However, the court found that his children wouldn't know whether he were of sound mind, considering they'd rarely spoken to him over the past few decades. Mr. Price's housekeeper testified to that fact. She also stated that Mr. Price and Julian become acquainted when Mr. Price saw him in a local park and offered to teach him how to play chess, since he seemed interested in the game. I can't help but smile at the image in my mind of a sixteen-year-old Julian befriending an older man over a game of chess. When I was sixteen, most boys only cared about video games. I can't see Julian as someone who was ever interested in video games.

Upon Mr. Price's death, Julian took the helm of the Price-Young empire. Hotels. Restaurants. Commercial buildings. There are hundreds of properties in New York City alone. It's all incredibly impressive, but what catches my eye is the mention of a non-profit he's tied to. An organization aimed at helping victims of domestic violence. It certainly piques my interest, another puzzle piece of who Julian truly is sliding into place.

I should have stopped reading there, but the section labeled "Personal Life" grabs my attention and I scroll down. Labeled one of the most eligible bachelors in the country, there are various photos of him posing with beautiful woman after beautiful woman. Models. Actresses. Heiresses. Every single one of them is all legs with barely an ounce of fat, a complete one-eighty from my ample chest and curvy hips. It again begs the question I posed last night... *Why me?*

"Are you thinking what I'm thinking?" Chloe asks when I push away from the laptop, a sickness forming in my stomach.

"Why would he pursue me if he has his pick of any number of gorgeous women?"

She shrugs, silently agreeing. "I just don't want to see you get hurt, Evie. That's all."

"What do you know about him?" I meet her eyes, unsure if I want to hear her answer.

"No more than what you read about in that Wiki article. There's no information at all about his younger years. He's an extremely private guy. People try to get details about him from those he's closest to, but they all stay tightlipped. There's a great deal of speculation about why he's never had a serious relationship, although he's been photographed with plenty of gorgeous women, as you see. My vote is he's gay."

I choke on my coffee. "I accused him of the same thing," I say through a fit of coughing.

"You *did?*"

The tense atmosphere slowly wanes. Now we're just two friends dishing about my date last night. Who cares if Julian has a Wikipedia page? Hell, even I have one because of my position at the magazine, although there's not much information on it. That doesn't make me someone worth knowing. Granted, Julian probably has a few billion reasons why he's worth knowing, but that doesn't make a difference to me. I'd still find him endearing, regardless of the size of his bank account.

"Trust me. There is absolutely no way that man is gay."

This catches Chloe's attention and she smirks. "Is that so?" She crosses her arms over her chest. "I thought you weren't going to sleep with him. Hell, you said even kissing was off the table."

"I didn't sleep with him. We didn't even kiss." I waggle my brows.

"You didn't? Then—"

"I told him my conditions, and he agreed to all of them. I thought for sure he'd insist on kissing me if we're pretending to date."

"It *is* a bit of a challenge, isn't it?"

"Not to him, apparently. He said kissing's for amateurs. And after the goodnight kiss that wasn't last night, I'd say he's right. Kissing *is* for amateurs." I bite my lower lip, reeling in my smile. "And Julian Gage is certainly no amateur." I fan myself, causing both of us to break out into a fit of giggles.

When our laughter fades, her expression turns serious once more. "So you're going to do it? You're going to be his fake girlfriend?"

"I am," I respond thoughtfully before my eyes harden. "But you can *not* tell a soul the truth, that it's just for show. You can't use this in any of your articles. This is incredibly off the record."

She reaches across the couch and clutches my hand. "You have my word. If you say it's off the record, it's off the record. I like my job."

I laugh slightly, knowing how seriously Viv takes this kind of thing.

"But I value our friendship even more. I just don't want you to get hurt."

"I won't—"

She quickly holds up her hand. "I know you, Evie. You get attached to people. Hell, you were with Trevor for twelve years."

"That's different."

"Still, you're not the type of girl who does random hookups. You're either all in or all out. There's no in-between with you. I just…" She blows out a breath. "I don't want you to fall for this guy and end up getting hurt because this is only a business deal for him."

"It's nothing more than a business deal for me, too. Weren't you saying I deserved to have some fun this summer?"

"That is true. And Trevor certainly does deserve to have the fact that you're dating one of the most eligible men in New York shoved in his face." Her eyes focus on me. "And it will be shoved in his face. Not by me, but Hamptons' parties are a hotbed for gossip columnists. Gossip websites *will* publish photos of you together. You won't be able to keep it quiet for long."

"Julian doesn't want it to be kept quiet. He wants us to act as if it's real."

"And there's no part of you that wishes it were?"

"Of course not," I respond quickly. "I'm not interested in him." I straighten my spine, exuding all the confidence I can muster just as the sound of my phone ringing rips through the space. I dart my eyes to the screen, a warmth filling me when Julian's name pops up.

"Not interested, you say?" Chloe teases, getting up from the couch. "Your wide smile and increased breathing indicate otherwise, Evie." She narrows her eyes on me. "Just be careful."

With that, she disappears into her bedroom, allowing me to speak with Julian in private.

Not wanting to sound overly eager, I blow out a long breath, then bring the phone to my ear, answering in a sultry tone.

"Good morning."

"Good morning, Guinevere. As requested, I've emailed you an itinerary for the next two months."

His tone is clipped, formal, almost as if I'm merely another call he has to make in conducting business. It's like he's a different person than the man who left me a panting mess on Chloe's front stoop last night. Did I imagine it all?

"Please check your calendar and let me know what conflicts you may have. I prefer to know in advance. Like you, I'm not fond of surprises."

"All I have planned this summer is work," I answer in a tone matching his own.

"There are some events that may occur during the week, so I'll need you to take the time off, if it can be arranged."

"I don't foresee a problem. Like I said last night, my boss doesn't mind if I work out of the office, as long as all my work is turned in by my deadline."

"Also, my personal stylist needs your measurements to pull things for you. She'll be reaching out to you sometime today. She's located in Midtown. You can either go to her or she can come to you."

"Personal stylist?"

"If you're to act the part of my girlfriend, you need to dress the part. Don't worry. You can keep the clothes when the summer is over. My stylist has a list of things you'll need. I'll see you Wednesday."

"Wednesday?" I ask, feeling overwhelmed as I not only attempt to absorb the difference in demeanor, but the reality of what pretending to be this man's girlfriend will entail. "But—"

"Take a look at the itinerary. I'm sure it will answer all your questions. If not, the number for my assistant is included. Goodbye, Guinevere."

"Goodbye, Julian."

But the line's already dead.

Chapter Sixteen

THE STEAM ROOM is particularly busy Monday morning as I sit at my usual table with the perfect view of the counter and dining area. The murmur of low conversation competes to be heard over coffee beans being ground and employees shouting orders to each other. I've yet to indulge in any of their pastries, but I feel my hips getting bigger simply from sitting here these past few weeks... Calories by osmosis or something like that.

I do everything I can to focus on how to determine which of the men on my list of possibilities is the real August Laurent, like I'm playing my own version of *To Tell the Truth*. Instead, all I can think of is Julian. How sweet and charming he was Friday night, then how cold and distant he seemed during our brief phone call. All weekend, I reminded myself it shouldn't matter, that it's only a business relationship, that it's not real. But I *felt* something. Was he really that good of an actor?

The itinerary he sent is quite extensive. There's something requiring my presence every weekend. It boggles my mind to think people live this way. Galas. Fundraisers. Art auctions. Pool parties. Bonfires. And this is a normal summer. I already feel like I don't belong, and I haven't even stepped foot in the Hamptons yet.

I try not to think too much about it, concentrating instead on the copious notes I'd made the previous week. As I flip through them, I'm unable to shake the feeling I missed something. None of the men on my list scream escort. Maybe August Laurent isn't in town. Maybe something came up and he had to take some bored housewife off to a remote island in exchange for a ridiculously obscene amount of money.

As I'm about to pull up the web browser on my laptop to sort through another one of the dozens of articles I found online theorizing about who he could be, my cell rings, the number to my work line popping up, indicating it's a forwarded call.

"Evie Fitzgerald," I answer. There's no immediate response. When I'm about to speak again, a voice interrupts.

"A little birdie said you've been looking for me." The deep baritone hits me in my core. Gravelly. Mysterious. Bemused. There's a hint of an accent. French maybe? It's not obvious. Just enough to make me believe he's not American-born.

"And does this little birdie have a name?" I ask coyly as I scan the coffee shop. It could have been someone else, maybe a wrong number, but it's too much of a coincidence. My gut says this is *him*, that he somehow heard I've been sitting in this café every morning on a quest to figure out who he is.

There's a chuckle on the other end, a low rumble. I picture him in a perfectly tailored suit, leaning back in the chair of his office, the beautiful cityscape of New York in the background, the brilliant summer sun beaming through the windows. Or maybe he's like the rest of wealthy Manhattan society and spends his summer in the Hamptons, which would account for why I haven't seen him. Perhaps he's just now waking up at ten in the morning with a view of the Atlantic Ocean and is calling me from the balcony of a luxurious beach house he purchased with the proceeds of taking advantage of women.

"I never reveal my sources. But I'm intrigued to know how you found out about my little secret."

I smile, lifting my coffee to my lips. "Like you, I never reveal my sources. Your story caught my attention, and I'd like to learn more. As would my readers."

"I'm sure they would. Do you realize how many people have been where you are? Sitting in that very café at a table close to the counter, yet still with a great view of the dining area, notebook out, scribbling down notes about every man who's come in to order a chocolate hazelnut pastry?"

I swallow hard. I don't know why I assumed I could outsmart this man who appears to take his privacy to a level I've never seen. It hadn't even crossed my mind that other people had done this very thing. And where are they now? Did they give up because the man truly is a ghost? Did he call them and tell them it's a lost cause?

"You're not the first, Miss Fitzgerald, although I will say you're the first who doesn't scream 'reporter'."

"No?"

"Trust me. That's a good thing, considering the editor at your fine magazine doesn't want her staff to be like normal reporters, which is why her publication's kept circulation high, despite the changed environment."

"You've done your research."

"I always do."

"Well, since I don't scream reporter, what do you say to sitting down for a one-on-one interview?" I waggle my brows, even though he can't see.

"So you can write an article cheapening what I do, claiming something ridiculous, such as I take advantage of women?" There's a teasing quality to his tone.

"*Do* you take advantage of women?"

"Absolutely not."

Excitement bubbles in my veins as I flip to a blank page in my notepad, jotting down the date. "You answered a question. Does this mean you agree to be interviewed?" There's no masking the hope in my voice.

"Not yet. I'm sure you've realized by now the importance of anonymity in my line of work."

"I do… To an extent. But I'd like to understand better. That could be more effectively accomplished face-to-face. Perhaps an interview and a photo shoot."

He laughs once more, the sound light and natural. Not forced, like you hear so often during initial meetings. "I have to give you credit, Miss Fitzgerald. You certainly are persistent."

"No. Just stubborn. I am Irish, after all."

"I had a feeling you were."

"What gave it away? The last name?"

"No. Your fiery personality."

"You don't even know me," I quip back.

"Ah, but I do. You familiar with the old saying, 'You write what you know'?"

I chew on the inside of my cheek, not answering.

"Well, I've read your column. In fact, I've read everything you've ever published at that magazine…print *and* online."

My jaw drops. "I've been there over five years now," I say, dumbstruck. "I've written hundreds of articles."

"Just like I'm sure you've been scouring the Internet for information on me, the instant I learned a woman named Evie Fitzgerald from *Blush* magazine was looking for me, I did some research of my own."

"Is that right? And what did you find out?"

"That you, Miss Fitzgerald, are extremely talented. Actually, I was able to skip a few days of ab exercises from the workout I got laughing at your work. You have a gift."

I blow out a laugh. "Sure. Tell my ex that."

"Your ex?" His voice rises in pitch, curious about my statement. I hadn't meant to say anything like that. It just kind of slipped out.

"It's nothing. I shouldn't have said that. I didn't—"

"It's obviously not nothing. Tell me."

"Thanks for the offer, but it's okay."

"You want to understand what it is I do, why I do what I do, this is part of it. What I do isn't as black and white as accompanying a beautiful woman to one event or another. It's giving them the confidence they need, for whatever reason, to help them see what any man with half a brain should. So if you want greater insight into August Laurent, tell me about your ex."

"Are you *bribing* me?"

"Not a bribe. But if I'm to agree to an interview, I'd like to know we're on an even playing field. If you expect me to share personal information about myself with you, and the rest of the world, I'd ask you do the same in return…minus the rest of the world. So, if you tell me why your ex doesn't think you're talented, I'll answer one of your questions."

I hesitate, considering his offer for a moment. I could tell him I'm not comfortable with this, but I really want this promotion. I want to finally write something with meaning, something people will talk about for weeks.

"Because he doesn't think what I do is something to be

proud of. I suppose that's why this interview is so important. This story can get me promoted to assistant editor…of the entire magazine. That will show him I *am* good at what I do, that I *am* a talented writer."

"Why does it matter?" August asks after a brief silence. "If he's your ex, why do you care what he thinks?"

"It's not just proving it to my ex," I respond, not wanting to admit I'm holding out hope that Trevor and I still have a chance. "It's proving it to everyone who ever told me I should use my English degree to become a teacher instead of writing."

"Let me guess. Your parents perhaps?"

I exhale a long breath. "You have to understand. Mom was an English teacher and shared her love for the written word with me. When most parents read their children *Green Eggs and Ham*, she read *Pride and Prejudice*. My father's a former English teacher, but is now the principal of the high school. Even my older brother's an English teacher. They thought I was crazy for wanting to use my degree in English to be a writer. They *still* don't think I'm a real writer, since all I write is sex and dating advice. So the opportunity to write an article like this, then getting promoted where I can write more interesting and compelling articles… I finally *will* prove them wrong."

"Okay then," he says after a protracted pause. "What would you like to know about me?"

"Where to start?" I laugh, lightening the tension.

"I find the beginning is usually best."

"I agree. So, Mr. Laurent—"

"Please, call me August."

"Okay. August… How did you start doing…" I wave a hand around, "whatever it is you do?"

"The local Escorts R Us was hiring, and I seemed to be what they were looking for."

My eyes widen. "Really?"

"Certainly not." He chuckles, something about it causing a shiver to roll down my spine.

It's an unexpected response and I adjust my posture, squeezing my legs together. He does have a smooth, pacifying voice. I could picture him as a sex phone operator, if that were even still a thing. *Is* that still a thing?

"I hope you're not always this gullible."

"Not usually, but there isn't much reliable information on the Internet on how to become a high-priced and extremely sought-after escort."

"Why? Looking for a career change? In case the promotion doesn't work out?"

"I'd rather not sell my body for money."

"Ah, but that's where you have it wrong, Miss Fitzgerald. Yes, men are typically only interested in one thing when they hire an escort."

"Sex."

"Precisely, although that's technically illegal in most states. Escort services get around it by claiming the client is simply paying for the company of the employee."

"And why do women hire an escort, if not for sex?"

"Companionship. That's it. Women just want to feel something. They want to be romanced, feel adored. That's what I do. On the record, I never set out to be in this profession."

"Is that right?" I jot down notes as he continues telling his story.

"I doubt anyone says they want to be an escort when

they grow up," he jokes. "It just…happened. It was never about taking advantage of women when they're feeling unguarded. I understand how it looks, especially when I'm selective to whom I offer my services."

"So you agree you specifically only choose women who are vulnerable?"

"Their vulnerability means they need my services more than someone else. I come in not simply as a piece of 'arm candy', but to empower women who are at a time in their lives when they need to feel like they have value. At the end of the day, my goal is to make every single woman who hires me feel beautiful, like they're worthy of being loved. That's it."

"And it works?"

"I like to believe it does. I help these women realize their worth. Realize they're meant to be more than just something nice to look at while accompanying their powerful husbands to whatever society event is going on that week. Many of my clients grew up in wealth. From their earliest days, they were raised to believe their only role in life was to marry someone of equivalent social standing. It sounds antiquated, especially in these modern days, but trust me when I say the caste system is still alive and well, even here in the land of the free and home of the brave. The haves of this country want to keep the have-nots out of their circle. They're the equivalent of American royalty. They marry their daughters off to people in their circle, and the cycle is repeated through the generations.

"These women are strong, resilient, and highly educated, but they've been mentally — and sometimes physically — abused for so long, they truly believe their only worth in life is offering a nice smile and making sure their bodies are in top physical condition so their husbands don't stray to something younger...which I know for a fact they do anyway. Hell, I've even had some of my clients tell me their husbands offered them up to their associates in order to make a deal on a valuable piece of real estate or something else, viewing them as a piece of property. Nothing more."

"And you think what you do helps break the cycle?"

"I hope so. Before many of these women sought my services, they believed their only option was to stay in a loveless, often abusive relationship. Their husbands made them feel like they were disposable. Some of them have never worked a day in their lives. Their husbands made them believe if they left the marriage, they'd have nothing. So they stayed, resigning themselves to a life of unhappiness. I give them the strength and confidence they've never felt, which helps them with the next step, whether it be filing for divorce or trying to make things work with their spouse."

"How do you claim to not take advantage of these women then? It sounds like they've been taken advantage of their entire lives. Now you come in and use their vulnerability to sleep with them."

"Who says I've slept with them?"

"Have you?"

"I believe that may be a question for another day, Miss Fitzgerald."

"Okay, but you didn't answer my question about how you started doing this. Obviously, something must have happened in your life that made you become the Keyser Söze of the escort industry."

The line's silent for a moment. Then he breaks into a throaty laugh. It's deep, intense, and all-consuming. Everything I get the feeling this man is in real life.

"The Keyser Söze of the escort industry?"

"You *do* know who that is, don't you?"

His laughing gradually dies down. "Yes. I have seen *The Usual Suspects.*"

"Then you know why I call you that. You're like an enigma, a ghost story wives can threaten their husbands with if they act like assholes. 'Better treat me well, or August Laurent will come to my rescue.' So how does one become August Laurent? Or is it a combination of Keyser Söze and the Dread Pirate Roberts?"

"The what?"

"The Dread Pirate Roberts," I repeat. "Please tell me you know what that's from; otherwise, I'll have to question my faith in the human race."

He laughs again, and I find myself melting into my chair from the sound. "*The Princess Bride.* One of my absolute favorite movies. But the book is better."

"It always is. So, did you get taught the ropes from the August Laurent who came before you? Like in *The Princess Bride?*"

"No. It's just me. But you do give me an idea for when I'm ready to hang up my hat."

"Hang up your hat?"

"I can't do this forever. Unfortunately, what I do has a time limit. Or an age limit."

"And that's the only reason you'd walk away? When you age out, so to speak?"

He considers my question for a moment, then answers, "Yes."

"But what about finding a wife? Settling down to have a family of your own?"

"You assume I don't already have one," he jests,

bemused. I picture him leaning back in a chair, brushing his masculine fingers against his lips, much like Julian does when I say something amusing.

"I think it's a valid assumption. Not sure how practical it is to do what you do *and* be married. I doubt any woman would put up with that. I wouldn't."

"And you're right. Which is why I'm not involved. Nor do I plan to become involved with anyone in the near future."

"Don't you want that?"

"Want what?"

"A real relationship."

"I'm happy with my current situation. It satisfies me in a way you'd only be able to scratch the surface of."

"I understand that," I say quickly. "Obviously, you enjoy…whatever it is you do. Otherwise, I doubt you'd be doing it. But aren't you lonely?"

"How can I be lonely when I have the pleasure of keeping beautiful women company?"

"You keep them company. But who keeps you company?" I press. When he doesn't immediately respond, I continue. "Everyone wants to find love. Real love. True love. It's what wars are fought over. That and religion, but I suppose one could argue love would enter into that equation, too. Throughout our adult life, every decision we make is generally for the purpose of love. What is so important about remaining on this path that you're willing to sacrifice finding love?"

There's a pause on the line. When he finally speaks again, his voice is a bit softer than it was mere seconds ago. "I'll tell you what, Miss Fitzgerald, since you seem to believe so strongly in the concept of love… If I ever find someone worth giving this all up for, I'll gladly grant your magazine an exclusive photo shoot and you can plaster my face from here to kingdom come."

"Really?"

"Yes. Really." I remain silent as I absorb his words. Then he clears his throat. "I believe we've gotten off track again."

"Right." I snap out of my daze. "We were talking about how you became August Laurent." I bring my pen back to my notepad.

When he speaks again, he sounds different, less emotional, more business-like. "As I mentioned earlier, it just kind of happened."

"There must have been some propelling event that made you stop and say, 'I'm going to be a male escort for a living. I'd be damn good at it.' What was yours?"

"I promised a friend I'd take her to her brother's wedding."

"A wedding date turned you into an escort?"

"She'd recently broken up with her boyfriend, who also happened to be the best man. She was the maid of honor. To say it was awkward is an understatement. Since she was still upset, she was anxious about seeing him. I offered to go as her date and do everything to make her ex regret leaving her. I did just that."

"You pretended to date her? And no one caught on?" This has my curiosity piqued, considering the agreement I'd made with Julian.

"I suppose you could say I'm a good actor. But I was a good actor because I knew how important this was to her. And it worked. During the entire ceremony and reception, he couldn't keep his eyes off her. He even suggested they give the relationship another shot. But after one weekend with me, after I spent the time to treat her the way I believed she deserved to be treated, she realized what she felt for her ex wasn't love. That she deserved so much more from a relationship than a guy who refused to support her dreams."

There's something in his tone, almost like he's silently asking if his story sounds familiar. And it does. Then again, he could be making it up to get me to sympathize with what he does for a living.

"So how did one wedding date turn into a career of empowering women, as you like to put it?" I ask, not wanting to dwell on my recent breakup with Trevor.

"Not long after that weekend, I started getting other requests to accompany more women to important events, mostly weddings. Now, over fifteen years later, it's evolved into more than accompanying them for a weekend wedding. Some women hire me for a month at a time to help them through a difficult time in their lives. As you've found out, you can't run an Internet search and book me. It's all by referral. My clients require a certain level of privacy, as do I. What keeps me in business is the fact that the only people who know who I am are my clients. To everyone else, I'm simply an old friend of the family or wealthy donor to whatever cause the family is championing at the moment."

"And no one's put the pieces together?"

"I do believe that's another question, Miss Fitzgerald."

"No. Simply a necessary follow-up."

There's a lightness in his tone when he answers. "I like you. I have a feeling I'm going to enjoy talking to you."

"So you agree to do the story?"

"I swore I'd never do this, but there's something about you that intrigues me, so yes, I'll agree."

"And I can publish what you tell me?"

"Unless I tell you it's off the record. And I'll require strict approval before it's printed. This is non-negotiable. Under no circumstances are you to reveal any information that may allow people to figure out my true identity. My anonymity is all I have, the only thing that keeps me doing this."

"Absolutely. Not a problem." I can't help but beam, my eyes lighting up. I want to dance, shout, tell the world I was somehow able to get August Laurent to agree to have a story written about him. I have no idea what angle this will take, but from this brief conversation, I get the feeling he's interesting enough that any angle will have women flocking to read the article.

"On that, I'll let you get on with your day. I always say to leave on a high note. And I'm not sure I've ever seen anything as beautiful as the smile on your face right now."

A warmth spreads through me at his words. It takes me a minute to grasp the hidden meaning. When I do, I shoot up, my heart racing as I feverishly scan the crowded coffee shop for any man on his phone.

"Have a good day, Buttercup."

"Wait!" I beg, but my plea is met with silence. I look at my screen to see the call's been disconnected. I hastily gather my things, shoving them into my bag, when a woman wearing the café's uniform approaches.

"For you, miss." With a smile, she places a white plate containing a chocolate hazelnut pastry on my table. "Enjoy. It's our most popular item."

I frown. "I didn't order this."

"A gentleman did. Requested it be sent to you."

"Who?" I ask frantically, my voice bordering on desperation.

She stands on her toes, trying to peer over the heads filling the busy coffee shop. Then she inhales a breath, pointing toward the doors.

"That's him. Right there. Brown hair. Sunglasses. Gorgeous suit."

"Thank you!" Adrenaline pumping through me, I sling my bag over my shoulder, dashing through the coffee shop, trying to keep him in my line of vision. When I step onto the sidewalk, a body slams into me, causing me to lose my balance, propelling me forward onto my hands and knees.

"Watch where you're going next time, lady. Fucking tourists."

"I'm not a tourist, asshole!" I shout, getting back on my feet, no thanks to anyone walking by. Dusting myself off, grateful the only injury is to my ego, I scan the bodies passing, not one of them matching that of the man I observed leaving the café.

Frustration fills me. I was so close to unmasking *the* August Laurent. Still, I know more about him than I did an hour ago. But now I'm desperate for even more information, to find out what makes him tick, why he feels the need to hire himself out as a companion. He says he empowers women. That's a reason *they* hire *him*. I want to know his reasons, too.

As I'm about to head toward Central Park to see if he went in that direction, even though I know it's probably futile, my phone pings with an alert. It's not unusual. I get dozens of emails every hour. But something makes me pull my phone out of my bag and open my email.

To: Evie Fitzgerald
From: August Laurent
Subject: Special Place in Hell

159

Dear Miss Fitzgerald,

You do realize there's a special place in hell for people who walk away from the Steam Room's famous chocolate hazelnut pastries. They are quite...sinful.

Kindest regards,

A

Smiling, I type a reply as I walk, no longer frantic about finding him now that I have his email address.

To: August Laurent
From: Evie Fitzgerald
Subject: Already Going

Dear August,

I'm already going to hell. I figure either go big or go home. So I'm going big, starting with leaving that pastry on the table. In my experience, delayed gratification only heightens that first taste.

E

I hit send, unsure what came over me to act so bold. I suppose we all feel a level of power behind the safety of a computer or, in my case, a phone, which pings again.

To: Evie Fitzgerald
From: August Laurent
Subject: Deal with the Devil

Dear Miss Fitzgerald,

Now I'm intrigued as to what you've done to have earned a ticket on the proverbial Highway to Hell. And even more intrigued by your interest in delayed gratification.

I hope you have a productive Monday. I'll be in touch soon and we can continue our conversation...speaking of delayed gratification.

A

Damn. He's smooth.

Chapter Seventeen

MY EYES ARE transfixed out the window of the town car on Wednesday as Julian's driver, Reed, maneuvers along narrow streets where the wealthiest members of society play for the summer. High hedges and security gates prevent the outside world from peeking in, but it doesn't stop me from gawking at the sprawling estates that pop up every quarter-mile. The closer to the shore we get, the larger and more impressive the properties. This is some serious money.

When I don't think the houses can get any more extravagant, Reed pulls off the main road, stopping outside a secure gate. After punching in a code, the impressive steel gates open, allowing us entry. My heart thumps in my chest as he continues up a long, stone driveway.

I haven't seen Julian since Friday. Hell, I haven't even spoken to him since our conversation Saturday, apart from an email from his assistant telling me that his driver would pick me up today at ten in the morning. At first, his curt tone left a sour taste in my mouth. Maybe it's a good thing. I've already felt myself wanting to blur some of the lines I insisted we draw. How much longer will they remain if he continues to flirt with me?

As the house comes into view, my jaw grows slack. It's a sprawling three-story, shingle-style historic home that's obviously been updated and taken care of rather well over the years. The pristine exterior has a sweeping lawn out front, the grass greener than any I've seen recently. Then again, I've been living in New York for the past several years. The only grass I see is when I visit Central Park, which isn't often. It's amazing how much you take the little things, like grass, for granted until they're no longer part of your daily life.

Reed brings the car to a stop, then hurries to open the door for me. Immediately, a woman in her fifties or sixties rushes out of the front door, hustling along the stone walkway. She wears a dark suit dress, her hair pulled into a tight bun at her nape. Her kind blue eyes are filled with joy as she approaches me.

"You must be Guinevere." She holds her hand out toward mine, shaking it excitedly. "I'm Camille, the head of staff."

"Head of staff?" I repeat. "You mean there's more than one person?"

She laughs merrily at my question. "Of course, dear. At least during the summers. Someone must ensure the household runs smoothly, particularly during parties. But the rest of the year, it's just me keeping his Manhattan apartment in order. Reed will bring your things up to your suite while I give you the tour."

With wide eyes, I follow her up to the front door, unable to mask my complete awe and amazement when she pushes it open and we enter a grand foyer, the ceiling over thirty feet high with a stunning crystal chandelier. It's a circular room with a single round table holding a floral centerpiece of red roses, white lilacs, and blue orchids, tying in with the Fourth of July theme of the weekend. I step closer, the familiar aroma of powder-fresh flowers floating through my senses.

Camille leads me past a curving staircase and into an

open living area. The cream-colored walls have wood and stone accents, the high-end furniture made of heavy wood. It's a stark contrast to the tiny room and pull-out couch I've been sleeping on, which seems ready to collapse if I breathe too hard.

"This is the living and informal dining area." She brings me to an expanse of floor-to-ceiling windows lining the eastern wall and I take in the panoramic views of the pool deck overlooking the ocean. I find it a bit of overkill to have both an ocean view and a pool, but what do I know?

"Wow." It's all I can manage.

I've seen places like this in the movies or online, but never in my wildest dreams would I have imagined being here myself. It's crazy to even consider that this will be my life for the next two months. I wonder if this is how Cinderella felt when Prince Charming whisked her away to his castle after he finally found her. Did she realize her life would be forever changed when she called her Fairy Godmother and went to the ball? Is my life about to be forever changed, too?

"It's pretty amazing, isn't it?" Camille comments.

"I don't think I've ever seen anything so...majestic."

She places a hand on my bicep, her smile warm as she meets my eyes. Her soft-spoken and caring demeanor reminds me of my grandmother. "Wait until tomorrow morning."

"What's tomorrow morning?"

"Sunrise. I checked the weather report. It's supposed to be a clear day, which means the sun coming up over that horizon..." She points out the window, "is sure to be fantastic. If you want to get up early to watch, I'll make sure to have coffee prepared. If you like coffee, that is. I'll need a list of any allergies and food preferences, as well as any other items you'll need on hand during your time here."

"And you'll get them for me?"

"Of course," she answers, as if it's no big deal.

"So if I say I like to snack on apples dipped in peanut butter, you'd get them?"

"What kind of apples? And do you have a preference for brand of peanut butter?" She withdraws a notepad from her suit jacket and proceeds to jot down notes.

I blink repeatedly at her proficiency. The closest I've ever been to this level of pampering was the one time I'd ordered room service. I thought having someone bring food to my hotel room was magical. That's nothing compared to this.

"I… It was just an example."

With a warm smile, she returns the small notepad to her pocket. "It's Mr. Gage's desire that you have everything to make your stay comfortable. So anything you need, please let myself or any of the other staff members know. Okay?"

"Okay." With every second that passes, I feel more and more like Julia Roberts in *Pretty Woman*. Well, if she weren't a prostitute. Still, there are similarities, like the way she gawks at his lavish lifestyle, not used to anyone waiting on her. The way she's confused about which fork to use. I can completely sympathize with her struggle there.

I continue to follow Camille as she shows me the formal dining room, library, theater room, game room, and even a gym. I want to ask for a floor plan of the house so I can find my way around. Or at least a bag of breadcrumbs.

Finally, we head up the staircase and down a long hallway lined with what I assume to be expensive artwork, coming to a stop outside a wooden door. When she opens it, revealing a large bedroom, I step onto the lush carpet. The aroma of fresh air mixed with the sea breeze flows in from an open window, and I walk to the far wall, the views of the ocean just as breathtaking up here.

"There's a balcony," Camille offers as she strides toward a pair of French doors, pushing them open. "Right out here."

I follow her out onto a large wrap-around balcony. A pair of chairs sits in front of the windows to my room, a small side table placed between them. Another pair is placed several hundred feet down, as well, in front of windows to what I assume to be another bedroom.

"That's Mr. Gage's suite," she explains, gesturing toward the end of the balcony to the north. Then she nods in the opposite direction. "And those are additional guest bedrooms, but will not be occupied during, well…during your little arrangement."

"Our…arrangement?" I repeat, making sure I heard her correctly.

"Yes, dear. Don't worry. I'm the only one aware of the truth, other than Reed, of course. It was my idea, after all, although my motivation may not have been completely innocent."

I square my shoulders as I face her. "What do you mean?"

"I've been on the household staff longer than you've been alive, dear." She smiles. "Even longer than Julian's been alive."

There's a familial affection in her tone as she caresses

his name, like a mother would her child. It's the first time she's referred to him as Julian instead of Mr. Gage. I can't help wondering if their relationship is more than employer and employee.

"I see things. I hear things. Mr. Price's children are still around, and they like to make things difficult for him, unduly influencing people who can help him. It's been several years since Mr. Price's passing, but no thanks to his children, who like to perpetuate the rumor that Mr. Gage took advantage of an old man, people still view him as a billionaire playboy, a passing fad who will end up blowing his fortune. Regardless, being around so long, you hear things. Many people's biggest criticism is that he's thirty-eight and isn't married. So I suggested he finally date someone."

"Well, I guess he must really look up to you since he took your suggestion."

She bursts out laughing as she leads me back into the room. "He certainly did not. Much to my dismay, he shot me down right away at the mere mention of him dating anyone. So I suggested he *purport* to date someone instead. He was hesitant at first, but he eventually figured it was worth a shot. At the very least, it would get the social clingers off his back for a summer."

"Camille?" I ask as I follow her past the four-poster bed, the sheer material draped over the sides billowing with our movement. Everything about this room is peaceful and serene. I'm not going to want to leave at the end of the weekend.

"Yes?"

"What *is* this project he's working on that appears to be so important to him?" I lower my eyes. "Or at least important enough to ask a complete stranger to pretend to be his girlfriend?"

She avoids my eyes as she continues toward a door just past the sitting area. "Oh, he never discusses his business plans with me." Her response comes fast and shaky. "They'd go right over my head anyway. Dana, Mr. Gage's stylist, has already been by to organize all the clothing she's selected for you. It's all here in the closet." She doesn't even pause to take a breath as she changes the topic, opening another door along the far wall.

I want to push and find out what the big secret is, but I'm rendered speechless at what she referred to as a closet. I have to stop myself from laughing. If Chloe and Nora could see me now, they'd piss their pants. This "closet" is bigger than my old apartment. Instead of only a handful of items for me to choose from over the course of the next few months, the walls are lined with a wardrobe suitable for any occasion imaginable, along with several dozen cubbies filled with shoes.

"Mr. Gage provided Dana with a copy of your itinerary for the summer," Camille explains. "She's taken the guesswork out of everything." She heads toward a table in the center of the room and opens a binder. "Each article of clothing is labeled with a number that corresponds to an event in here." She points to the first page in the binder. I see today's date, the event, followed by a list of numbers, indicating what I'm to wear. "Sometimes things come up, so in the back are a handful of outfits in case of an emergency." She closes the binder as she faces me, her stare harsh and direct. "Under no circumstances are you to wear the same outfit twice. Do you understand?"

I'm overwhelmed as I take in everything. The house. The staff. The clothes. When I'd agreed to be Julian Gage's fake girlfriend, never in a million years did I expect it to be like this. Rules about what to wear and when. But the planner in me appreciates it. There are no surprises. I find comfort in that fact.

"Perfectly."

"Wonderful." She clasps her hands together. "Well, I'll leave you to get situated. Can I bring you anything? I'm sure you're hungry after the long drive."

I place my hand over my stomach, which is in knots. "Actually, I had a big breakfast," I lie.

"Okay, dear. Just dial 2111 on the house phone if you change your mind. I'll be back to check on you a bit later." She begins to retreat.

"Camille?"

"Yes?"

I pinch my lips together, unsure what I even want to ask. Perhaps I'm feeling a little out of my element and want someone to tell me I didn't make a colossal mistake in agreeing to this.

"Never mind," I say quickly.

"Certainly." She continues toward the door. When she's about to close it behind her, she catches my eyes and speaks again.

"Don't worry. You'll do fine. Mr. Gage wouldn't have asked you to do this if he didn't think you could handle it. It may seem overwhelming right now, but once you get settled in, you'll forget what life was like before you came to the Hamptons." She gives me an encouraging smile, then closes the door, leaving me alone to absorb this strange life I've been thrust into.

"That's what I'm afraid of," I sigh.

This would be most women's dream come true. A gorgeous bedroom overlooking the Atlantic Ocean, complete with palatial walk-in closet, which is stocked with designer clothes and shoes. So why am I having such a hard time with this?

Restless and unnerved by the unusual silence, particularly compared to Manhattan, I head back into the elaborate closet, flipping the binder open. I scan the first page to find the pre-selected outfit for today's event — a pool party beginning at three o'clock. Turning my attention to the clothes, I locate the items Dana indicated and place them on a railing by a 180-degree mirror, scowling at the navy-and-white polka-dot two-piece bathing suit. At least she chose more of a vintage, pinup style with a high waist and full coverage for my girls.

"Well, I guess I should shave my legs," I say to myself, spinning around and going in search of the bathroom. Thankfully, it's right next to the closet.

Like the rest of the house, it's impressive and extravagant. Marble tile. Spacious shower with several showerheads. Tempered glass behind an enormous claw-foot tub overlooking the ocean. I can't remember the last time I've lived somewhere with a tub, so I opt for a bath.

I turn on the faucet, spying a canister of bath salts sitting on a shelf above the tub. After sprinkling some into the steaming water, the fragrant aroma of lavender fills the air. I twist my hair into a knot on top of my head, then rid myself of my clothes.

Once I step into the bath and lean against the porcelain, tension rolls off me as all my worries about what this afternoon may bring evaporate. So what if these people don't think I fit in? That's never bothered me before. It's just a few months. After that, I'll never have to see any of them again.

Basking in the serenity of my luxurious bath and surroundings, I all but lose track of time until I notice the water's gone tepid and my skin's begun to prune. I shave quickly and grudgingly step out of the tub. After toweling myself off, I set about readying myself for my first event of the summer. I'm surprised how well the bathing suit Dana selected fits. Then again, she was rather meticulous in measuring me. I expected nothing less.

After applying copious amounts of sunscreen to my fair skin, I accentuate my natural peachy hue with a hint of blush. Then, as per Dana's instructions, I smooth my signature red lipstick on my lips. It brings together the vintage look. I tie a band around my head, knotting it at my nape, allowing the excess material to fall in front of my chest. I complete the look by draping a sheer white, floor-length coverup dress over my body.

When I step in front of the mirror in the closet, I gawk at my reflection. I still look like myself, but I don't feel like myself. Normally, I loathe wearing bathing suits. That's the benefit of living in the city — there's no real reason to wear one. But Dana chose one that accents what I consider my best assets — my hips and chest — without revealing too much skin. If she was able to work her magic on selecting the perfect two-piece, I can only imagine the gown she chose for tomorrow night's gala.

Curious, I spin from the mirror and head to the binder, about to turn the page to see exactly what I'll be wearing, when there's a knock on the door. Assuming it's Camille to check on me, I simply call out, "Come on in."

As I round the corner into the bedroom to meet her, I stop in my tracks when Julian stands in front of me. All six-foot-four of pure Julian Gage. Sinewy muscles. Consuming stare. Perfect lips turned into a subtle hint of a smile. He wears a white, short-sleeved, button-down shirt paired with blue checkered swim trunks. Yet again, it's another new look for him. Is there anything this man can't wear and make absolutely delicious? I doubt it. His skin appears darker than a few days ago, the ends of his hair lighter, kissed by the sun.

"Remind me to give Dana a raise," he murmurs as he circles me.

If anyone else regarded me in such a way, I'd probably feel like a prize pig on display during the annual county fair. That's not the case with Julian. He makes me feel coveted, admired…beautiful, something I never thought I would by wearing a two-piece bathing suit.

"A very *large* raise." Instantly, his hand clutches my hip and he drags my body against his. I gasp, taken aback by the gesture, particularly after our phone call Saturday.

"We're back to playing nice, are we?"

"Playing nice? What do you mean?"

I lower my head, feeling more exposed than I already am. "Nothing."

His thumb and forefinger grip my chin, forcing my eyes back to his, his deep pools of blue piercing me. "I don't keep secrets and don't expect you to, either. It's important we're both honest with each other about this arrangement. It's the only way it will work."

"It's nothing," I say once more, pushing away from him. I fold my arms over my chest.

"Guinevere…" His voice is a warning.

"You were…different when you called on Saturday. I guess I wasn't sure which version of Julian Gage I'd see today." I shrug half-heartedly, not wanting him to think his demeanor was a big deal, and turn from him.

"Which Julian Gage? You don't mean…" He trails off. I glance over my shoulder as he closes his eyes, dragging his fingers through his hair. When he looks up, he catches my gaze, his expression apologetic. "You thought I was short with you because I'd gotten you to agree to my proposition and no longer had to pretend to like you?"

172

"The thought crossed my mind." I face him, placing my hands on my hips.

He approaches me and tilts my head back. There's a power and earnestness as he stares deeply into my eyes. Unwavering. Determined. Honest.

"Listen to me, Guinevere. Everything I told you Friday is true. I *am* profoundly attracted to you. I was the instant I laid eyes on you. And I've only become more so with each second I spend in your presence. I'm sorry if I made you feel like you're anything but the beautiful, charming, witty woman I'm thrilled to spend the next few months with." He holds my gaze for a moment longer before stepping back, releasing his hold on me. "I was working Saturday. We all have our faults, and one of mine is being unable to switch from business mode to…pleasure mode."

I laugh slightly as the stress about the situation rolls off me. "And what exactly is 'pleasure mode'?" I smirk, chewing on my bottom lip.

He leans toward me, his voice a low growl. "Keep sucking on that lip and you'll find out."

Bringing my hand to his chest, I gently push him away. "I thought you said kissing's for amateurs."

"Who said anything about kissing you?"

I open my mouth to argue, but snap it shut. He's certainly got me there.

"That's what I thought." He flashes a devious smile before straightening his posture, extending his hand. "So, are you ready to convince the world you're my girlfriend?"

I pass him a flirtatious look as I link my fingers with his, his skin rough against mine. "Let the games begin."

Chapter Eighteen

"SO WHAT'S OUR story?" I turn to Julian as he drives along the streets of Southampton. It's the first time I've seen him behind the wheel. There's something incredibly sexy about it. The natural confidence he exudes as he shifts from third to fourth, his free hand resting leisurely on the wheel. For most people, driving is a necessity, a way to get from point A to point B in the shortest amount of time. Julian makes it appear like an art form.

And let's face it, his car is ridiculously hot, too. I practically had an orgasm when we entered his garage and I feasted my eyes on a fleet of luxury cars — Land Rover, Porsche, Mercedes, Tesla, Bentley, Jaguar. But when Julian clicked a key fob and the lights to a red Ferrari Portofino convertible blinked, I all but had to wipe the drool off my lower lip. When he asked if I wanted to take it for a spin sometime, I offered to give him a blow job in return. Jokingly, of course. But that's how amazing this car is in the hierarchy of hot cars. It truly is blow-job worthy. The hum of the engine as he revved it to life only solidified my original assessment.

"What do you mean?" His smile is bright against his tan skin.

"People are bound to ask how we met. I can't come out and tell them the truth."

"Why not?" He's so cavalier about it, composed and

in control, acting as if we're not about to walk into a party where we'll try to convince the Hamptons' elite we're an item.

"For one, we met in a bar. I'm sure you'd rather we make up something, like we met at a Sotheby's auction or doing something else people with a ridiculous amount of money do." I squint at him, pinching my lips together. "What is it you people do for fun?"

He laughs, shaking his head as he shifts into fifth. "*We* people…" He playfully lifts a brow, "do the same kinds of things you do for fun."

"Except you probably smoke better weed and do keg stands on twenty-four karat gold kegs with diamond-encrusted taps."

"Actually, the taps are hard to come by this year, but twenty-four karat kegs are a dime a dozen up here." He winks, his response taking me by surprise. Whenever I'd make a joke like that to Trevor, he'd scold me for being absurd, that I should be more serious. It's refreshing to be with someone who can appreciate my sense of humor.

"Thank God, because there is no way I'm drinking Natty Ice out of anything other than a keg that's plated in gold. A broad's got her standards."

"Of course."

It's silent before I speak again. "But seriously… Shouldn't we make sure our stories line up?"

"What's there to line up? We met in a bar." He glances at me. "*Not* at a Sotheby's auction."

"Horseback riding?"

"Definitely not."

"Golfing?"

"Hate the sport."

"At the racquetball club?"

"It's for men only."

"Chauvinistic bastards."

"They certainly are. Only men would make a competition out of smacking balls against a wall."

I shift my eyes to his, fighting against my smile. "Did *the* Julian Gage just make yet another joke? I thought the first one was a fluke, but a second one in so many minutes?"

"Why do you sound surprised?"

I face forward, allowing the strong rays of the sun to warm my face. I wonder if Dana knew which car Julian would take to the party and that's why she instructed that I tie a wrap around my hair. It does go with the vintage style of the rest of my wardrobe, but it has also proved to be rather practical.

"I had this image in my mind of you being so serious, like you were born shitting caviar and pissing Champagne."

"That's not true."

"I know." I fidget with the line of my coverup, hesitating before blurting out, "I Googled you."

"I figured you would." His voice shifts, no longer playful. Now it's more serious, cautious. He clears his throat. "Find anything interesting?" He steals a glimpse at me before staring straight ahead, his Adam's apple bobbing up and down in a hard swallow.

"No," I respond thoughtfully. "It simply solidified my opinion of you."

"Do I want to hear what that is?"

"That you're a good person, despite what some tabloids would lead people to believe."

Out of the corner of my eye, I notice his grip on the steering wheel tighten. According to my research, Julian came into his fortune nearly ten years ago now. I can't believe he's still dealing with the quiet whispers and upturned noses, even after all this time.

"I like to believe that karma rewarded your generous spirit."

Upon hearing my words, he flicks his gaze toward me as he lifts his hand from the gear shift and grabs onto mine, squeezing.

"Thank you." The corners of his mouth turn up in a gentle, heartfelt smile. It's not the sensual, flirtatious one I'm accustomed to. It's real, genuine, pure, a peek into who Julian Gage truly is.

"Of course."

He keeps his fingers intertwined with mine for a while as he drives. As we approach an intersection, he withdraws his hand to downshift, causing my shoulders to fall. But once he turns down another street and is back up to speed, he returns it to my thigh.

I snap my eyes toward his as a fluttering erupts in my stomach. My breathing increases, the skin beneath his fingers tingling.

"Is this okay?" he inquires in a low, smooth tone.

"Yes," I whimper.

"Good." His pupils dilate as he steals a glimpse at my exposed leg. Then he looks forward, squaring his shoulders. "Because we'll need to touch each other quite a bit over the next few weeks. If we're to make people believe what we have is real, we need our interactions to appear natural."

"Right." I form my mouth into a tight line, suppressing the flicker of hope his gesture gave me. "So is there anything I should know about the people who will be there today?"

"This is more of a casual get-together at David Gittney's house."

"Old money or found money?"

He passes me a sly smile as he shifts into fifth, then returns his hand to my thigh. "Very good. You remember. David is old money."

I purse my lips, trying to understand the proverbial caste system that appears to be in place here in the Hamptons. "If he's old money and looks down upon people with found money, as you claim—"

"Which he does."

"Then why does he invite you to his parties?"

"They like to flaunt the fact that this has been their lives for as long as they can remember, that they're the equivalent of American royalty. Old money invite new money so there are warm bodies at their parties, at least more than the few dozen people who'd attend if they kept it strictly old money. Found money goes in the hopes to finally be accepted. It's a game that's been taking place for ages now. And I have a feeling it will continue even when I'm dead. The current found money will eventually become old money and a fresh batch of newly minted millionaires and billionaires will strive for acceptance."

"Well…" I settle into the black leather. "I suppose I'm in store for a rather eye-opening summer. Anything I should keep in mind? Should I act a certain way? Not swear? Stuff like that?"

He flashes me his debonair smile as he pulls his car up to an elaborate iron gate. "Just be your normal, charming self. Don't change who you are for these people. I chose you *because* of who you are. Don't blend into the crowd. Stand out."

"It's hard not to stand out with bright red hair," I joke.

"That's not what I mean. You'd stand out even if you had a black curtain tossed over you. I'd never ask you to change who you are to suit my needs."

I face forward, reminded of my breakup with Trevor.

"I like you as you, and that will never diminish. Anyone who takes for granted how incredible you are doesn't deserve you. Remember that."

"But aren't you trying to convince these people you're someone you're not?"

"I'm not trying to convince them I'm someone I'm not." He returns his eyes to the driveway, continuing up an even more extravagant and impressive paved path than the one leading up to his estate. I didn't think such a thing were possible. Again, I'm proven wrong.

"But you said it yourself. You're not cut out for the relationship thing."

He pulls to a stop in front of a sprawling home that rivals many of the mansions I'd seen in Newport during a trip I'd taken with Trevor. When a valet attendant approaches the car, opening my door, Julian leans toward me. "And I'm not. But that doesn't mean I sleep around, either. Because I don't. I don't lead women on. I am upfront and honest with everyone from the beginning, just like I was with you."

He steps out of the car and I do the same, allowing one of the attendants to help me to my feet. When Julian reaches me, I part my lips, wanting to press further, but the warning in his gaze reminds me we're on display for everyone. I glance past him to see other cars pulling up behind his, curious eyes observing us. Some indifferent, others tainted with animosity.

179

"Ready?"

I nod quickly, swallowing down my nerves. He rests his hand on my lower back, steering me up a grand staircase leading into a palatial home that screams money. Crystal chandeliers. Marble tiles. High ceilings. Pristine furniture. Rare art. It is the quintessential display of wealth.

After navigating our way through the house, we step out of a pair of French doors and onto the back patio, the pool party already in full force. There must be over two hundred people in attendance, not to mention a band set up on a stage in the corner, playing hits of the 80s and 90s.

You know those cliché scenes in coming-of-age movies when a girl moves to a new school and walks into the cafeteria that first day, knowing absolutely no one? That's how I feel now. Except I'm at a five-star cafeteria and naked. At least I *feel* naked. That could be the only thing to explain the dozens of eyes that instantly zero in on us, the whispers washing over my skin.

Able to sense my nerves, Julian turns toward me and grabs my chin, tilting my head back.

"Be yourself. These first few days will be the hardest. People will wonder who you are. And some women here today will most likely be catty. Don't let them get to you."

He brings a thumb to my lower lip, brushing against my flesh. One touch and I'm completely intoxicated by this man and the way my body responds to even the slightest graze of his skin against mine. I crane my head back, the distance between our mouths diminishing with each heartbeat. I'm no longer paying attention to the band rattling off Jenny's phone number or the people squeezing past us to get through. It's just Julian. Just this. Just us.

"Don't let anything they say or do make you think you're anything less than the amazingly beautiful and vibrant woman you are. In my opinion, you're the most beautiful woman here."

He runs a lithe finger down the curve of my neck, the warmth of him so close unhinging me. My eyes flutter into the back of my head, my skin flushing, my knees weakening.

"I think that's enough to get them talking. Let's go enjoy the party."

When I no longer feel the heat of his breath so close, I open my eyes, struggling to calm my racing heart and act as if Julian hadn't brought me to the edge of complete and utter bliss with his words alone. After taking several deep breaths to compose myself, I link my hand in his.

"If whatever project you're working on doesn't pan out, you'd make a damn good escort," I joke in a husky voice as he leads me past a crowd of curious onlookers.

"Is that right?" His tone is amused.

"That's right."

"And what makes you say that?" He leans toward me, whispering into my ear, "Do I turn you on?"

"You could probably make a lesbian want to have a go with you just to be sure she really is gay."

He's silent for a moment before he bursts out laughing, the sound carrying over the band. It's so natural and addictive. How can anyone not feel a pull toward this man?

"Thanks for your vote of confidence, but I doubt I could ever be an escort."

"You never know. You could give August Laurent a run for his money. He's got a great voice, too, but not like yours."

We approach a bar and he places our drink order — manhattan for me, scotch for him. Then he faces me. "You've spoken to him?"

"I have."

His eyes brighten in genuine enthusiasm. "How did you manage that?"

"I got lucky." I shrug. "Someone mentioned I was looking for him…a little birdie, as he put it. He tracked me down, called my office line, and *bam*. Now we're email pals."

"Email pals?" He brings his glass to his lips as he steers me away from the bar and toward a vacant table tucked out of the way. For someone who needs to conduct business, he seems to be paying a great deal of attention to me.

"Yes." The perfect gentleman, he helps me into a wood slat chair. "We've been exchanging emails the past few days."

"Getting good material for your story?"

I bring the chilled martini glass to my lips, savoring that first sip of my drink. "He's a bit…aloof. He doesn't like to share much. But I'm working on it. I just need to establish a rapport with him. Then he'll open up."

"Good."

"Good." I watch as he shifts his attention away from me, searching the partygoers.

An unnerving silence settles between us as he rests his hand on my thigh like he did in the car. And just like in the car, I know it's not real. There's no emotion behind his fingers as they delicately brush my skin. No yearning building deep inside as he steals a glance at me. No unyielding desire as he leans toward me and nuzzles the crook of my neck. It's all for show. That's become my mantra these past few minutes. I have a feeling that will become my mantra these next few months, too, a constant reminder there's absolutely no meaning behind anything he does or says, despite what my heart wants to believe.

"Julian!" a voice shouts, snapping me out of my thoughts.

I follow his line of sight to see a man approach. He has short, shaggy, copper hair, fair skin, and a slight five o'clock shadow, although it's not too noticeable due to the light hue. His nearly six-foot frame is dressed in a pair of swim trunks and an open, white button-down. That appears to be the unspoken uniform amongst the men, while the trend with women seems to be who can wear the smallest piece of fabric and still be able to call it a bathing suit. Despite all the females being dressed as if ready to go for a swim, not a single one of them is in the pool. In fact, *no one* is in the pool. I wonder if that's customary at these things. Have a pool party, wear a bathing suit, but don't think about getting into the water.

"Christopher! Good to see you." Julian stands from the table, appearing genuinely happy to see him. Then again, it could be an act, too. I never know what to think with him.

"So this is her? The girl you haven't been able to stop talking about?" He looks from Julian to me, then back again.

"Sure is. Christopher, this is Guinevere Fitzgerald. Guinevere, this is Christopher Albright."

"Nice to meet you." I stand up, holding out my hand.

He grasps it. "You, as well. I've heard a great deal about you, Guinevere. Please. Sit. Sit." He gestures to my chair as he occupies the free one across from me.

"You can call me Evie," I instruct as I return to my seat. "Everyone else does. Except this guy." I jab Julian playfully in the stomach once he lowers himself back to his chair.

"He's always been pretty formal, at least as long as I've known him, which is since freshman year of college."

"Is that right?"

"Sure is. I can tell you some incredibly embarrassing stories about the guy. Trust me. He used to be awkward. And scrawny."

"Please tell me you have pictures."

He smiles. "Of course."

"If you want to keep my company's 401k account," Julian interrupts, gritting a smile, "you'll keep those photos to yourself. And you were just as awkward."

At that moment, a stunning brunette wearing a yellow two-piece sidles up to the table, placing a kiss on Christopher's temple before turning her attention to me. Her eyes are the color of honey, her hair full with perfect beach waves falling to mid-back. Her smile is warm, which makes it difficult for me to hate the fact she has the physique most women would kill for — tall, slender, but still with a classic hourglass shape.

"Is this her?" she asks excitedly.

"Now I know why my ears have been ringing the past few days," I answer, holding my hand toward her. "Hi. I'm Evie."

"Sadie. And try weeks." She plops down on the last free chair, taking a sip of what appears to be a cosmo.

"Weeks?" I furrow my brow. "What do you mean weeks?"

"That's how long Julian's been talking about you. It's about time he found a good girl, instead of playing the

184

perennial matchmaker."

"Matchmaker?" I look back at Julian. I never would have pegged him for a guy who'd go around setting people up on dates, considering he seems rather averse to being in a relationship himself.

"He introduced me to Christopher several years ago. Now we're about to celebrate our fifth wedding anniversary."

"Sadie is one of the first friends I made out here in the Hamptons," Julian explains.

"Is that right?" I smile nervously, looking between them. I can picture them as a couple. Both gorgeous with incredible bodies. They look more like a couple than Julian and I do. And Sadie and Christopher.

"Not like that," she interjects quickly, her eyes wide. "No, no, no. We never... Ya know. Our relationship's always been strictly platonic."

"Even if it hadn't, it's okay." I place my hand on Julian's thigh. It's the first time I've initiated contact between us. But it's what feels natural, what I would do if Trevor were here with me and we were having this conversation with one of his friends. I meet his eyes. "He's here with me now. That's all that matters. Not the past. Not the future. Just right now."

I keep my gaze locked with his, the outside world seeming to melt away. It's not until I hear Sadie that I look back at her.

"Aww..." She covers her heart, her eyes bright and smile wide. "That is the sweetest thing. Isn't it, babe?" She glances at Christopher.

"It's about time," he jokes in response. "Maybe now I won't have to field this asshole's phone calls about reinvesting portions of his portfolio at all hours of night or on weekends." He brings his beer to his lips, looking at me from over the bottle. "Promise me you'll keep him occupied outside regular office hours, okay?"

I lean into Julian, giving him a demure look. "I'm sure I can keep him *very* busy."

Christopher whistles as Sadie claps, but I don't look their way. I can't, the raw need covering Julian's expression catching me off-guard. If I didn't know any better, I'd think he were about to throw me over his shoulder and haul me into the house so we could find somewhere private. My thighs squeeze involuntarily at the notion.

Remembering where I am, I clear my throat, looking back at Sadie and Christopher. "So, how did Julian play matchmaker?" With a trembling hand, I bring my drink to my mouth, needing the alcohol to cool the flames building inside.

"At one of his parties," she answers.

"Sadie is what you'd call old money," Christopher adds.

"Well, used to be," she corrects.

I pull my brows together. "Used to be? How's that?"

She shrugs. "Marriage."

"What—"

"I'm old money, but married no money."

"Thanks for emasculating me, sweetie," Christopher quips as he drapes an arm across her shoulders, but the smile never leaves his face.

"Anytime." She lowers her voice. "You'll eventually figure it out, but there's a bit of a hierarchy out here."

"Julian's already given me the Cliff Notes." I glance at him, about to rest my hand on his thigh once more, but stop myself, his heated stare still trained on me. We're definitely playing with fire. I think he's finally realized that. "About old money and found money," I finish, facing Sadie once more.

"Well, I grew up in old money. Granddaddy was big in steel in the early 1900s. Made his fortune and was smart, so he didn't lose much during the Great Depression. Anyway, some of the more conservative families prefer their offspring to marry within their 'station'," she explains, using air quotes. "Like my parents."

"But you didn't."

"They may view love and marriage as a business relationship, one for profit, but I don't. When I first met Christopher, I couldn't help but feel a connection. He was smart, charming, funny, a breath of fresh air from all the stuffy people I've always known. My parents thought it was just a phase." Her expression drops as she toys with the ring on her left hand. It's stunning and a decent-sized rock, but not nearly as extravagant as some of the jewelry I've seen on other women here. "I think they sometimes think it's still a phase."

She smiles at Christopher, but it doesn't reach her eyes this time. I sense she still struggles with the tension that must exist between her parents and the man she loves. I couldn't imagine having to choose one or the other. I was lucky to have a boyfriend my parents adored.

"But that doesn't matter. They can drop my social standing a few pegs all they want. It won't change anything."

"Then why do you still come to these things?" I wave my free hand around. "I could be wrong, but it sounds like you're pretty fed up with the way things are and want no part of it."

187

She leans toward me. "That's true. But I love showing off the fact that I'm genuinely happy. Most of these people wouldn't know happiness if it slapped them in the face. And it ruffles their feathers to know I've found it. That no matter what they do, they can't take that away from me."

"Wow." I shake my head, absorbing Sadie's story. "It all seems a bit antiquated."

She raises her drink. "Welcome to the Hamptons, where the caste system is alive and well." After she takes a sip, she returns her glass to the table. "So, did you two really meet in a bar?"

I'm about to confirm this when Julian's voice cuts through. "We sure did."

I turn my head, meeting his eyes. There's still an intensity within, but it's not as pronounced as it was. He pulls me close, his fingers tracing a delicate circle on my bicep. I attempt to melt into his embrace, wanting it to appear as natural as possible.

"Her ex had just broken up with her and she decided to share her story with the entire bar."

Sadie's eyes widen. "You didn't!"

I blanche as Julian continues. "It was far more entertaining than any stand-up routine I've seen." Pride drips from his statement, his hold on me tightening. "Guinevere has a gift with words. So I suppose I should thank her ex for being a complete idiot. If it weren't for him, I wouldn't be sitting next to this incredible, amazing, captivating woman who seems to have weaseled her way into my heart practically overnight."

He speaks with such passion, such fervor, such affection, it's hard to imagine this is simply an act. But as Shakespeare so succinctly put it in *As You Like It*, "All the world's a stage, and all the men and women merely players." Now is my time to play the part of Julian's girlfriend. Come September, the curtain will close and I'll go on to the next act of my life.

Chapter Nineteen

"AND THAT'S IMOGENE Joyce," Sadie says under her breath as we sit at the same table a while later. Julian and Christopher excused themselves earlier. I haven't seen them in over an hour. At least they left me in good hands. Sadie seems to know the dirt on everyone. And being the Hamptons, there's more dirt than usual. "She claims to be James Joyce's great-niece or some shit."

"Is she?"

Sadie shrugs. "Who knows? One can never be too sure of anything around here. People constantly say whatever they need in order to secure an invitation to the next big social event, or to make someone jealous, or to appear better than someone else. Hell, if you wanted, you could say you were a distant relative of F. Scott Fitzgerald and people would probably believe it. You'll soon learn that everything out here is a façade. Nothing is real. It's all for show. The smiles. The clothes. The houses. It's all a competition, a game we play every summer to see whose dick is the biggest."

"Then why do you come year after year?"

As she relaxes back in her chair, she crosses her legs. "It's too entertaining a show to miss. Not to mention it's good for Chris to network, considering he works in wealth management. Plus, Julian asked me to hang out this summer, as a favor to him."

"He did?" I furrow my brow.

"Yes." She smiles warmly. "He didn't want you to feel lonely. Thought you could use a little female camaraderie." She's silent for a moment. "He's a good guy. A *really* good guy. Loyal to a fault. Caring. If you have a problem, he'll do whatever he can to help you, regardless of what he has going on in his own life at the moment. He may look like he's this tough bad ass, and he's definitely perfected the mystery man persona he seems to exude, but to those of us who know the real Julian Gage…" She reaches across the table and clutches my hand in hers. "Well, you've hit the jackpot because there's no one better." She pulls back. "Well, except Christopher, but Julian comes in a very close second."

She winks as she sips on her drink. It warms my heart to hear someone talk about Julian with so much affection. It solidifies my original assessment of him. He truly is a good guy, not the playboy con artist some would have me believe.

"And I'm so glad he's finally met someone who makes him happy."

"That's all I want." I force a smile. "To make Julian happy."

It's not a complete lie. I *do* want to make Julian happy. If I didn't care about him, I wouldn't be giving up my weekends to be his proverbial arm candy, as ridiculous as the idea of me being anyone's arm candy sounds, especially when I'm surrounded by several women who actually *are* models and only here to be some rich guy's arm candy for the night.

"And this may be the alcohol talking," she continues, her voice slurring more and more with every word she speaks, "but I think you could be the one. Ever since I was a little girl, I had these…feelings about people. Like

191

I could see a couple and know instantly if they were made to last. And you and Julian…" She slowly nods, waggling her brows. "You two are made to last. I saw the way he looked at you. That man could not take his eyes off you." Her playful expression grows serious. "Every woman deserves to find a man who looks at them the way he does you."

I chew on the inside of my cheek as I lower my head, a blush blooming on my face, wishing I could tell her it's all fake, but I can't.

"And every man deserves to find a woman who looks at him the way you do Julian," she finishes. "It seems I've been waiting for him to find a girl for years, at least someone who's more than a passing fling." She reaches for my hand and squeezes it again. "I'm so glad he found you."

"Me, too," I whisper, wishing I'd met her somewhere else. I could see us being real friends. I could see her joining Nora, Chloe, and me at our Thursday evening get-togethers. I could see her dropping whatever she has going on when one of us has an emergency. But that won't be possible, an unfortunate side effect of this arrangement I hadn't anticipated.

Needing to cut through the growing tension, I lift my eyes back to the growing crowd of people swarming around the pool, dancing as if the world is watching. In a way, I suppose the world *is* watching.

"So…who else do you have dirt on?"

"Everyone."

After draining her drink, she sets the glass back onto the table and scoots her chair even closer to mine, continuing to give me the rundown on the who's who in the Hamptons. Every so often, a few women approach, fabricated smiles on their faces as they hug Sadie, claiming it's good to see her. Then their disdainful stares settle on me. It doesn't take a genius to conclude that they know who I am. They probably came to talk to Sadie as a pretense to getting a closer look at Julian Gage's girlfriend.

"You should write a book," I joke after a while of soaking in the stories she's relayed. I used to watch soap operas during high school and college, thinking the plot lines were far-fetched. Or so I thought. These people have proved that soap operas aren't as ridiculous as I presumed. Secret babies. Amnesia. Arranged marriages. Mistaken identity. Faked deaths. It's all here, and then some.

"The thought's crossed my mind. I doubt anyone would actually believe any of the stuff is plausible. It all sounds crazy, don't you think?"

"Before today, I would have thought the same thing. Now I get the feeling the stories you've shared are only the tip of the iceberg."

"Oh, honey. You have *no* idea."

We both laugh and I finish the rest of my manhattan, standing up. "I'm going to get another drink. Want one?"

"Sure. Would you like me to come with you?"

"Nah. You stay here so we don't lose our table. We've secured a prime piece of real estate to people-watch." With a wink, I spin from her, squeezing through the throngs of people to make my way to the bar, ignoring the stares as I do.

Now that the party's in full force, the bar is much busier than when we first arrived. While I wait to place my order, I scan the pool area, amazed that this kind of party is an everyday occurrence here. Most people would plan all year to throw a celebration of this magnitude. Here, it's just Wednesday.

As I continue soaking in the atmosphere, I stiffen when I see a familiar face a few yards away. My heart drops to my stomach as he wraps his arm around a petite woman's waist before raising a scotch to his lips. Lips I once kissed. Lips that once told me how much he loved me. Lips I used to make smile daily. I'm no longer the reason they smile. The woman at his side is.

He leans down and kisses her forehead, bringing her even closer, as if he can't stand to be any farther from her than necessary. An ache builds in my throat, in my limbs, in my soul as I'm forced to witness their exchange. Sensing my stare, Trevor flicks his eyes in my direction. When he sees me, he flinches, his muscles growing taut.

I remain frozen in place, dumbstruck, unsure what I'm supposed to do. I should have anticipated running into them, considering Julian *did* mention Theresa is a friend of his neighbor. I just didn't expect to come face-to-face with them at my first party. Based on the confusion covering Trevor's brow, he didn't anticipate this, either.

Just then, an arm snakes around my waist and I snap my head up, meeting Julian's concerned gaze.

"Guinevere?"

I blink, wishing something as simple as a kiss didn't have this effect on me. But we were together twelve years. How can I just forget that? I'm on a see-saw. One minute, I want to write off Trevor. The next, I want him to tell me he's made a mistake.

"Are you okay?"

With a quick nod, I avert my eyes, hiding the emotions coming to the surface. But Julian won't let me, grabbing my chin and tilting my head back.

"He's a fool," he whispers, leaning toward me.

"He looks happy, doesn't he?"

"So what if he does?"

I pull my lips between my teeth to stop my chin from quivering, trying to avoid making a scene in front of all these people…and Trevor.

"Because *I'm* supposed to be the one who makes him happy. That's always been my job. How can he—"

"Like I said, he's a fool. You make me happy," he offers in consolation.

I lower my voice to barely above a whisper. "But it's not real."

"My happiness when I'm with you? It's more real than anything I've felt in a long time, even if the rest of this is only for show. And I want you to be happy, too. So tell me what it'll take to make you happy, and I'll do it."

I laugh as I blurt out the first thing that comes to mind. "A dartboard with Theresa's face on it."

"Consider it done," he responds in a lively voice. "Would you like another with Trevor's face? Or perhaps a punching bag?"

"I certainly wouldn't send it back." I wipe the few tears from my eyes. It's surprising how quickly Julian can make me smile, even when facing heartbreak.

"Good."

I peer into his eyes, his compassion seeming to mend the rips caused by Trevor. "Thank you."

When he brings his hand to my face, rubbing his thumb under my eye to erase one last tear, a shiver trickles through me, my sadness and despair turning into something else.

"I don't care what it takes. I want to show you that you deserve more than he gave you. No woman deserves to be with someone who doesn't appreciate them. And Trevor didn't appreciate you, not if he broke up with you because you no longer fit into his idea of perfection. You deserve someone who *will* appreciate you. Never settle for anything less. Okay?"

"It's not as easy as you make it sound, not after twelve years."

"I know. But with time, it will be."

I nod, unsure if I like the idea of getting over Trevor. Since I was eighteen, he's been a part of me. It's hard to picture life without him. Divorced couples must go through this, still sleeping on the same side of the bed, even though the other person's no longer there. Still sitting in the same chair at the dining room table, even though you now have your choice. Still using the same bathroom sink to brush your teeth, even though they're both now yours.

Feeling another crack in my armor, I look back at Julian. "I need to use the ladies' room. I'll be right back." I go to turn from him, but he grabs my arm, stopping me, forcing me to face him once more.

"Are you okay?"

"Yes," I insist. Sensing curious eyes watching us, I place my hand on his chest, then raise myself onto my toes, inching toward his neck. "Never better," I murmur. When my lips touch his cheek, he inhales a sharp breath.

All afternoon, we've shared more than a few sensual touches — a brush of his hand on my leg, a finger smoothing an unruly wave behind my ear, his hand intertwining with mine. But there's been nothing more. Until now. In fact, I've never had the pleasure of

196

experiencing the warmth of his skin on my lips, the scruff from his unshaven jaw harsh and piercing, but invigorating at the same time. I didn't think I'd like it, considering Trevor always kept his jawline smooth. But something about Julian's two-day beard stirs me to life, replacing my despair with yearning, desire...hope.

When I pull back, Julian's eyes find mine, both of us powerless to look away. It was only a chaste kiss on the cheek, but in it I felt something I hadn't in a long time...a spark. Based on the bewilderment in his expression, I surmise he felt it, too.

"Bathroom," he says, finally finding his voice, snapping me out of my daydream.

"Right. Bathroom." I peer at him for a few more seconds, then spin from him, trying with everything to regain my composure.

As I'm about to duck into the house, I glance over my shoulder, a jolt of electricity coursing through me when I notice Julian's eyes glued to my body. In that moment, I don't even notice Trevor standing just a few feet away. Maybe this is why Julian walked into my life. Not to take Trevor's place, but to help mend my heart so I can move on. Maybe Chloe was onto something when she formulated her motto, "You live. You learn. You upgrade." Perhaps Julian is my chance to upgrade, even if for just a few months.

Feeling hopefully optimistic, I continue into the house, navigating the long corridors to the guest bathroom, which is just as spacious and luxurious as the rest of the house. To my surprise, there's no line. I step inside, allowing myself a minute to breathe for the first time all afternoon.

Once I'm refreshed and ready to face the party, I walk back through the stunning home. I didn't have a chance to truly admire its beauty when I first arrived, but now that I'm alone, I take a moment to soak up my surroundings. While Julian's house is impressive, this place makes it look like a shack. High, decorative ceilings. Crown molding. Furniture that looks like it's merely for show. Artwork. Sculptures. Fountains. I feel like I'm in a museum, not a person's home.

As I reach the ornate living room, my eyes focus on a painting hanging on the far wall. From the limited exposure I've had to art, it appears to be impressionist. Broad brushstrokes and muted colors. I step toward it to get a better look.

"Do you like art?" a voice inquires.

I whirl around to see a man I estimate to be in his forties approach. He has a touch of silver in his beard, making him look distinguished. He has a full head of dark hair and mesmerizing gray eyes I'd recognize anywhere.

"Holy crap," I say, covering my heart with my hand. "You're Ethan Ludlow."

"Guilty as charged." He winks, approaching me. "And you must be the lovely Guinevere I've been hearing about all afternoon."

"Trust me, I doubt anything you've heard is true."

"Not much you hear about in the Hamptons is." He leans against the wall, crossing his arms. "But it's not all bad. And it's not all lies. I can now confirm a few things with my own eyes."

"And what's that?" I smooth a strand of hair behind my ear, trying not to freak out over the idea that I'm standing here, having a casual conversation with Ethan Ludlow, child actor who rose to fame playing on one of the longest-running sitcoms in the 80s. He had a leading role in a few movies during his teens and twenties, then decided to try his hand directing and producing. The movies with his name attached are some of the most popular ones out there. And I'm standing next to him. I want to pinch myself to make sure this is real.

"You have some incredible...assets." He waggles his brows and a chill instantly envelopes me as he advances. The stench of alcohol wafts from his breath, and I back up as my heart drops to the pit of my stomach.

I grit out a smile, brushing him off as Sadie's warning about this kind of thing plays in my head. While there are some good guys here, a lot of them think their overflowing bank accounts allow them to have anything they want. They don't realize there are things in this world that *can't* be bought. And what they can't buy, they simply take.

"I suppose they could be saying much worse. If you'll excuse me, I should be getting back to the party."

"I heard you're a writer for a magazine," he says, preventing my retreat. "I'm always interested in meeting new writers to see what kind of ideas they have. Ever consider working in the film industry?" He leers at me.

I wish I had more than this flimsy coverup on. Every time Julian had stolen a glance, he gazed at me in a way that made me feel like the most beautiful woman around. This guy makes me feel like I'm a piece of meat. Is that how he looks at every woman?

"I'm happy at the magazine." I attempt to sidestep him, but he mirrors my movement, blocking me again.

"Come now. There's a vast difference between working for a women's magazine and working on a script for the next blockbuster. Who wouldn't want to be involved in something like that? People would kill to be in your shoes right now." He closes the distance, the heat of his breath like the blade of thousands of knives. "In more ways than one."

I swallow down the bile rising in my throat, unable to believe this is actually how Ethan Ludlow behaves. Growing up, he had the persona of being a wholesome kid from a great family. Hell, he's married to Sonia Moreno. They're *the* Hollywood power couple. Why would he be hitting on me when he has someone as stunning as Sonia at home?

"Like I said…" I attempt to mask the tremor in my voice, peering over his shoulder in the hopes of finding a familiar face. Unfortunately, no one here is familiar. "I'm happy at the magazine."

When he places his hand against the wall, I duck underneath it, walking as fast as my legs can carry me. I only make it a few feet before a pair of arms wrap tightly around me, pulling me against a hard body. Instinct kicks in and I struggle, thinking it's Ethan. But it's not, the arms holding me warm and familiar. When I look up, I stare into Julian's frantic and concerned eyes. He rakes his gaze over me, trying to figure out what has me so rattled. Then he glares over my shoulder, every muscle in his body tensing.

"Julian," Ethan says as he approaches. Julian's protective grip tightens around me. "Good to see you again. I was just getting to know your girlfriend here." He continues past us, smirking, holding his head high and acting as if he can do whatever he wants. "I'm looking forward to getting to know her even better over the next few months."

Julian doesn't utter a single word, staring him down until he disappears through the living room. Once he's out of view, Julian returns his attention to me, scanning my body for any hint of harm.

"Are you okay? He didn't hurt you, did he?" His voice sounds frenzied, desperate.

"I'm fine," I assure him. "He's just like every other asshole here who thinks they can treat women like property."

"Except for me."

I open my mouth to agree, but he *is* using me as a pawn in whatever game he's playing.

"Except for me," he repeats, this time firmer. "Right?"

"It doesn't matter." I push away from him, but he's in front of me before I can return to the party.

"It does, Guinevere. It matters to me. I don't..." He runs a hand through his hair, tugging at it.

"It's okay, Julian." I cup his cheek, offering him a comforting smile as I lower my voice so no one overhears. "I knew what I was getting into when I signed up for this. We're both using each other. We're both pawns in this game. Nothing more."

I drop my hold on him, exiting the house and immersing myself back into the party. The sun's begun to set, casting a glow on the pool deck. Without the hot rays beating down on me, the air is comfortable, especially with the gentle breeze coming off the ocean wrapping around my skin.

As I search for any sign of Sadie, a hand clutches my bicep, forcing me around to see Julian's determined stare.

"Don't ever think you're a pawn to me, Guinevere." His voice is harsh, powerful, yet sincere. As much as I want to think this is just another part of his game, something about it feels too convincing, too...real. "You're not." He takes a breath. When he speaks again, his words come out barely above a whisper.

"Yes, we may be putting on a show to get what we need, what we *both* deserve, but don't ever think for a second I view you as a piece of property. I respect you, more than you realize. Just because we have a bit of an unconventional relationship doesn't lessen that." He runs a soft finger along the contours of my face. I shiver, the reaction as surprising and unexpected as everything with Julian seems to be. "You are so much more than any of that. You are…"

"Yes?" I lick my lips as I tilt my head, losing myself in the depth of his eyes.

"You are…" He places a hand on the small of my back, pulling my body against his. My heart pounds against my ribcage. No longer out of fear or dread, but out of desire and anticipation. My chest rises and falls in a quicker pattern, every inch of me desperate for his next move. I shouldn't be this turned on by him. I shouldn't want his hands on me. Still, I can't help but wonder what *could* be.

"Yes?"

"You are…unexpected."

"Good unexpected or scary unexpected?"

He chuckles. "Good unexpected." His buoyant expression turns serious as he pulls his bottom lip between his teeth. I can see a war raging within. "*And* scary unexpected," he adds, releasing his hold on my lower back and bringing his hand to my face.

When he runs his thumb along my bottom lip, I plump it out. Electricity courses through my veins as the heat of his breath grows closer and closer. I brace myself for his kiss. I *welcome* his kiss. In twelve years, I've only known one man's kiss, one man's arms, one man's body. Perhaps it's time I experience something new, too. I may regret it tomorrow. Hell, I may regret it in a few minutes. But right now, I just want to be kissed again.

As I inch even closer, a body unexpectedly slams into me. Everything seems to play in slow motion as I struggle to regain my balance. Julian reaches out, scrambling to grab onto me, but gravity is not my friend, and with unceremonious grace, I fall into the pool.

When I resurface, I wipe at my eyes, seeing all the partygoers staring in my direction, and my cheeks flush in embarrassment. I normally don't care about making a complete fool of myself. But here, I'm self-conscious, especially when I notice everyone whispering amongst themselves as they gawk at the poor girl who got bumped into the pool.

Thankfully, Sadie soon emerges from the crowd, a cool confidence about her. "Well, it *is* a pool party, isn't it?"

She steps out of her sandals that I can only imagine cost a small fortune. Leaving her drink on a nearby table, she dives into the pool with the practiced expertise of a swimmer. When she pops her head above the water, she meets my eyes, winking.

I pass her a grateful smile, unsure how I'll ever repay her for doing this. I shrug out of my now soaked coverup and take my shoes off, tossing them onto the pool deck just as I notice Julian removing his shirt. I keep my eyes trained on him, unable to look away from his chiseled physique, everything about it near perfection, except for the scars on his abdomen. In my eyes, those scars are part of the fabric that makes up who he is, although I'd love to learn the story behind them.

With a smirk, he cannonballs into the pool, disappearing beneath the surface. Before I know it, dozens of people jump in, some of them wearing their street clothes, the alcohol encouraging them on.

As my eyes scan the sudden festive environment, I notice Theresa and Trevor standing off to the side. She pulls on his hand, attempting to get him to join in the revelry. He refuses, excusing himself and heading into the house. I shouldn't feel partly responsible for his sour mood, considering he broke up with me. But despite everything, I still care about him.

I'm about to find my way out of the pool to talk to him when an arm loops around my waist. Spinning around, I meet Julian's eyes, smiling. Like two puzzle pieces locking into place, I drape my arms over his shoulders, making anyone think we've done this dance dozens of times before. I do my best to ward off the electricity flooding through me as we remain chest to chest, our wet flesh pressed against each other.

"I thought you wanted people to take you seriously," I remark.

"I do."

"I'm not sure this accomplishes that."

"That's true, but I couldn't resist."

"Resist what?"

"Getting wet with you."

"Is that right?" I run my hand through his waterlogged hair, scratching at his scalp. He bites his bottom lip, groaning from the contact.

"I have a feeling I'm going to have trouble resisting a lot of things about you over the next few weeks."

I bring my mouth toward his, remaining just out of reach. "Only time will tell."

Chapter Twenty

"LET ME HELP you," Julian says once the valet attendant pulls up with his car. We approach the Ferrari and he reaches for my hand. The instant he touches my skin, he flings his eyes to mine. "Jesus! You're freezing!"

"That's what happens when the air cools down and you're wearing nothing but a wet two-piece."

"Why didn't you say anything?" His brows pull together in concern.

"It's not a big deal," I insist as I climb into the passenger seat. "I can take care of myself."

"I don't doubt that, but if you're uncomfortable, you need to tell me." He takes the key fob from the valet attendant and pops the trunk. After rummaging around in it for a minute, he closes it, then ducks into the driver's seat, handing me a sweatshirt.

I look at the big, bold letters printed on the front. "SUNY?"

He shrugs. "What did you expect?"

"I don't know. Harvard. Yale. Columbia." As I pull the enormous sweatshirt over my head, I inhale, instantly bathed in a scent that can only be described as Julian. It reminds me of waking up in his bed that first morning, panicked. I don't even recognize him as that person anymore. I don't recognize myself as that person, either.

He finds my hand and brings it onto the shifter, our fingers intertwined as he puts the car into first. "Nope. I enjoyed my higher education years out here in Stony Brook."

"Interesting," I muse, settling against the cool leather as he pulls around the elaborate driveway, navigating onto the quiet road, my hand glued beneath his as he shifts between the gears.

"Interesting? How so?"

"I had you pegged as more an Ivy League guy."

"I guess you had me pegged wrong." When he glances at me with a sparkle in his blue eyes, I can't reel in my smile.

"I guess I did."

"I'm surprised you didn't find out about this when you Googled me."

"I must have gotten distracted by other information that your college education didn't seem all that interesting in comparison."

"Like what?"

"Like Theodore Price."

When I say the name, he swallows hard, the mood shifting from playful to somber. He passed away over ten years ago now, but by Julian's unfocused stare, it's apparent he still grieves the loss of the man who, according to many reports, molded him into the person he is today.

"He sounds like a good man," I offer when he remains silent.

"He saved my life."

I want to ask more, my mind immediately going to the scars on his abdomen.

"Did he——"

"I want you to promise me something, Guinevere," he interrupts, his voice determined. His hardened expression is at complete odds with the way he clutches my hand, his thumb brushing against my skin haphazardly, as if it's second nature.

"What's that?"

"That you'll stay as far away from Ethan Ludlow as you can. That you'll come find me if he so much as breathes on you the wrong way. No matter what I'm doing, who I'm speaking with. I don't care if I'm in the middle of some negotiation."

I shiver as I recall my earlier exchange with Ethan. The excitement of standing next to this Hollywood legend. Then the sickness filling me when I realized what kind of person he truly was.

"I knew I'd need to warn you about him eventually, but thought I could put it off. Obviously not, because he's already interested. Word's gotten out you're a writer."

"I'm not really——"

"You are. Don't let anything Trevor said make you believe otherwise. You *are* a writer. That's probably why Ethan tracked you down. That, and you were there with me."

"Why? Is he one of the old money people who likes to constantly knock you down a few pegs?"

"You can say that. He's one of Theodore Price's children."

I can't hide the utter shock when I hear this. "What? I mean——"

"He uses his mother's maiden name in the industry. An homage to her legacy, I suppose. So yes, he has a tendency to make it difficult for me to get things done, considering he's a shareholder of the company, albeit a minority one. Outside of that, he's still a Hollywood slimeball. He'll offer you the moon and the stars, success, money, everything you've ever dreamt of. But trust me when I say it will come at a high price. Do you understand what I'm trying to tell you?"

I nod, swallowing down the bile rising in my throat at what could have happened if I hadn't taken the opportunity to get away from Ethan when I did. How did I not know he was one of Theodore Price's kids? I really need to read up on all my celebrity news.

"I don't want you to worry about me. You're trying to network at these events. You shouldn't have to stop what you're doing to make sure I'm okay."

"But I *will* worry about you." He laughs nervously, and I sense a chink in his armor, revealing a vulnerability I've yet to see. "It's a personality flaw. I worry. I always will. I just want you to be okay."

He briefly glances at me, his eyes pleading. His grip on my hand tightens, like he's scared something will happen if he lets go. I wonder if this protectiveness, this fear, is tied to those scars. I want nothing more than to ask about them, how they got there, if they're connected to Theodore Price and how he supposedly saved Julian. Instead, I simply murmur, "Okay."

"Okay," Julian breathes, as if my acquiescence allows a weight to lift from him. He brings my hand to his lips and places a soft kiss on the flesh, repeating, "Okay."

When he pulls his car into what he refers to as the carriage house a short while later, his property is devoid of all activity.

"Are these like your day-of-the-week underwear?" I ask as he helps me out of the Ferrari. They're the first

208

words either one of us have spoken since our tension-filled conversation about Ethan.

"Day-of-the-week underwear?" He cocks a brow.

"Yeah." I gesture to the line of luxury cars. It's all I can do not to salivate over them. I've been living in New York so long I almost forgot what it's like to drive. It's one of those things I took for granted before moving to the city. Like grass. Now I yearn for that feeling of independence. "Monday is the Land Rover. Tuesday the Porsche. Wednesday is obviously the Ferrari."

"Obviously." He smirks, linking his fingers with mine as he leads me up to the main house.

"So what's the deal with all the cars? Most people I know only have one. Well, now that I live in New York, most people I know have zero."

"I like cars."

"I gathered as much."

"We all have our guilty pleasures." He narrows his gaze on me as he grins slyly. It's sinful to hear the words guilty and pleasure roll from Julian's tongue. I fight to silence the voice in my head telling me how nice it would be to be one of his guilty pleasures, if just for a day. "What's yours?"

"Sex," I answer, not even thinking.

He inhales a sharp breath, his eyes widening. I pull my hand from his, slapping both of them over my mouth, my face reddening to a shade that would probably rival my hair color.

"I mean—"

"Why would you consider sex a guilty pleasure? The term in and of itself infers it's not essential. If you ask me, sex is essential for the continuation of the human race."

"I didn't mean that," I flounder. "It just popped out.

209

That happens sometimes. I don't have a brain-to-mouth filter."

He regards me in quiet contemplation as he opens the front door to the house, allowing me to enter before him. It's dark, apart from a few dim lights illuminating our path to the bedrooms.

"So you were thinking about sex?"

"What? No!" I exclaim. "I..." Trailing off, I exhale deeply, trying to calm my frazzled nerves. "I'd like to retract my original response. Books are my guilty pleasure, okay?"

"Books?"

"Yes." I face forward as we crest the top of the stairs. "Books. Final answer."

"Are you sure you don't want to phone a friend?"

Pinching my lips together, I smile coyly. "Did Julian Gage just make *another* joke?"

"What can I say? I think you're rubbing off on me."

As we come to a stop outside the door to my room, I'm about to reply with a flirtatious retort. Before I can do so, he faces me, zeroing in on my mouth. It reminds me of the tension sizzling between us when he dropped me off Friday night. But it's more pronounced, more intense this time. We've only spent a few hours together, but in those few hours, I have a better insight as to who Julian Gage truly is. Friday I was attracted to him. Now I *like* him. He's more than just a pretty face with an enormous bank account. And I want to know even more, despite the voice in my head warning me against it.

"So..." I chew on my lower lip as I fidget with the hem of the sweatshirt. Then I realize I'm still wearing *his* sweatshirt. "Crap. You probably want this back." I start to pull it off my body when he touches his hand to my arm, stopping me. I drop my hold on it, allowing it to fall back down.

"As fantastic as you looked in that bathing suit, I like you in my sweatshirt more." He advances toward me, the heat in his eyes forcing me to back up against the wall. He leans his forearm on it, curving toward me. "I had a wonderful time with you tonight, Guinevere."

"Me, too." I close my eyes as lust blinds me, the same craving that's teased me all day flickering through me, my skin, my core, my soul aching for this man's touch.

I hold my breath, bracing for his lips to meet mine. Instead, the warmth disappears and I flutter my eyes open. Julian steps back, readjusting his composure, clearing his throat.

"You have a spa appointment tomorrow at noon." It's like he's flipped the switch from fun, lighthearted, sensual Julian Gage to the practical and pragmatic businessman.

"A spa appointment? You didn't have to—"

"Yes, I did. It's part of the ritual, so to speak. If I want people to take our relationship seriously, you need to spend the afternoon at the spa with all the other wives and girlfriends. Sadie will be there. It's all part of the act we need to put on."

"Well then, who am I to complain?" I smile, but it's forced.

"Reed will be waiting for you out front at 11:30. Before then, make yourself at home."

"And where will you be?" I ask flirtatiously in an attempt to bring playful Julian back, but he's gone.

"I need to attend to business-related matters during the day. I'll be back in time to escort you to the gala." Without giving me a chance to ask any more questions, he turns, continuing down the hallway before disappearing into his bedroom.

"Good night," I murmur once I hear the click of his door.

I stare into space, trying to reconcile the two very different versions of Julian Gage. One minute, he tells me how much he worries about me. The next, he runs from me as if he can't stand the sight of me. What could cause these wide swings in demeanor in such a short time? I can't shake the feeling it's all related to the scars marring his perfect skin.

Chapter Twenty-One

"OH, MISS GUINEVERE...," Camille breathes after she finishes zipping up my gown, clasping her hands together as she admires my reflection in the mirror. "You are absolutely exquisite."

The person staring back at me may as well be a stranger. My red locks are pulled out of my face and curled into loose beach waves. The cosmetologist at the spa gave me a natural look, only emphasizing my eyes with smoky shadowing, which if I were to try and recreate would end up making me look like a raccoon on a bender.

As amazing as my hair and makeup is, the real attention grabber is the sapphire blue dress. It's something I never would have taken a second look at, with the plunging neckline and slit that goes up to my mid-thigh, but it's a gorgeous gown. The fitted bodice is encrusted with jewels before ending at the waist and transitioning into a flowing tulle skirt. It's unlike any dress I've ever worn, and I doubt I'll ever wear anything this elegant again.

"Mr. Gage will be quite pleased."

I force a smile, pretending to be enthusiastic about the notion. It's a little bittersweet to know I currently feel more beautiful than I ever have, yet it's being wasted on someone who will never appreciate it. This is what I signed up for, though. There are worse ways to spend my

Fourth of July than being pampered at a spa, then attending *the* social event of the summer on the arm of a dashingly handsome man. Who cares if he switches from hot to cold in the blink of an eye?

"Thank you, Camille."

"Of course, dear." She meets my eyes in the mirror as she smiles at me in adoration, like a mother would a child. Her excitement strikes me as odd. She knows the truth of what's going on. So why is she acting as if I'm about to leave for a ball to meet Prince Charming?

"Well…" She steps away, grabbing the shoes Dana selected to go with the gown, placing them in front of me. I slide them on, trying not to think about the fact that my entire ensemble probably costs more than my college education. "We shouldn't keep him waiting any longer. He's already on the brink of exploding in anticipation."

"He is?"

"Why wouldn't he be?" She hurries out of my room, striding down the hallway. I practically have to run to catch up. "You're a beautiful, charming, enigmatic woman he appears to be quite taken with."

"You and I both know appearances can be deceiving." I give her a knowing look, silently reminding her this isn't real. Reminding myself of that fact at the same time.

"They certainly can be. In more ways than you think. Sometimes we act a certain way because it's all we know, because we believe it's the only thing that can protect us." She glances at me, her eyebrows raised.

I slow my steps, my mind racing with questions. It's obvious she knows something.

"Camille!" I call out, running toward her. When I reach her, I ask, "How long have you known Ju— Mr. Gage?"

She stops walking, turning to face me. "Since he first met Mr. Price, God rest his soul."

"You worked for him?"

"I did. Started as a housekeeper before he made me his head of household."

I chew on my lower lip, then quickly release it, not wanting to smudge my lipstick, although I'm confident this stuff could survive the nuclear winter.

"And when did Julian enter the picture?"

She exhales and stares into the distance, searching her memory before looking back at me. "Oh, over twenty years ago now. Mr. Price became like a father to Mr. Gage. And he was the son Mr. Price's own sons refused to be. At first, I was skeptical about Mr. Gage's intentions. I guess a part of me thought he was just someone else who wanted to prey on a wealthy, lonely man. I'm normally not one to judge or assume, but when you see a boy of barely sixteen, who looks like he hasn't had a decent meal in ages, befriend an older man, you assume the worst. But Julian proved me wrong, proved us all wrong."

She smiles warmly before continuing down the hallway. My brain buzzes with even more questions. Julian Gage is a puzzle I'm eager to solve.

Bunching the fabric of my skirt in my hands, I walk quickly, following her down the stairs. Once we enter the living room, she faces me, doing one last check of my dress to make sure everything's in place.

As she brushes away a thread, I whisper, "Where did he get the scars on his abdomen?"

She stiffens, inhaling a sharp breath. When she meets my pleading eyes, she slowly shakes her head, conflicted. "Do you believe in soul mates, Guinevere?"

215

"You can just call me Evie. And yes." I nod. "I did at one point."

"I do, as well, but not like most people. I like to think soul mates can include more than just a romantic relationship. I truly believe Mr. Price and Mr. Gage were soul mates. They were both in need of a certain kind of companionship, and they found it in each other." She clutches my hands in hers. "Julian hasn't had the easiest life. There's a darkness that continues to hang over him. Just… Be patient with him. He'll come around." She passes me a reassuring look before turning to walk out of the room.

"But I don't want him to come around." I spin to face her, then lower my voice. "This isn't real."

She glances over her shoulder, smiling. "Whatever you need to tell yourself, dear."

I open my mouth, about to argue my point further, when Julian rounds the corner, coming to a stop the instant he sees me standing in front of the large windows overlooking the ocean. The two-day scruff he's been sporting is gone, his face clean-shaven. His hair's wayward in a sexy sort of way, curling slightly over the collar of his jacket. And his tux… It should be a crime for a man to look this exquisite without being naked. The lines accent his chiseled physique in a way that almost makes me never want to see him with his shirt off again.

Almost.

I'm not that much of a sadist.

I didn't count on missing him as much as I did throughout the day. I shouldn't have longed for his touch, craved his scent, considering the brush-off he gave me last night. I tried to blame it on the fact that I spent the afternoon at the spa with Sadie where we talked with a few other women about my whirlwind romance with Julian. Some of the women, whom I expected to greet me with cold shoulders and upturned noses, ended up gushing over what they viewed to be a real-life Cinderella story, one I could sense they secretly wished for themselves.

"Guinevere…," Julian exhales, his gaze holding steady with mine, his pupils dilating. No one's ever admired me the way Julian does, even when I'm dressed more casually. No one's ever made me feel so beautiful.

Emboldened, I twirl, the layers of the skirt flaring around me as I show off for him.

"I stand corrected."

I stop spinning. "Regarding?" I arch a brow.

With determination, he strides toward me. In an instant, his hand palms my lower back, pressing my body to his. I wonder if this is what Cinderella felt like. If she struggled against hope, knowing once the clock struck midnight she'd have to go back to her ordinary life. Just like I'll be forced to return to the pieces of my life once the summer's over. But that didn't stop her from dancing, from dreaming, from living. Why can't I do the same thing?

Because life isn't a fairy tale. If you wake up missing a shoe, you're not a princess. You simply drank too much. There won't be a prince showing up on my doorstep, a glass slipper in hand, promising to make all my dreams come true. This is the real world, and in the real world, I have to chase my dreams myself.

"Dana."

"Dana?"

"She doesn't just deserve a raise. She deserves everything she could ever want."

217

He links his hand with mine and spins me around, his motions graceful as he soaks me in. I'm so swept up in this moment, I don't even have to concentrate on maintaining my balance or not tripping over my own feet, as I'm sometimes prone to do. Under Julian's watchful gaze, I feel like I'm flying.

"You look…" He stops twirling me, then brings my body back to his. One hand remains clasped with mine as the other returns to my back. He begins swaying to no music at all, except the song in our heads. And I hear it. It's low and struggling to break through the other noise, but it's there. "You are stunning, Guinevere." The hunger in his gaze softens as he lowers his voice. It's gentle, benevolent, earnest. "I won't be able to leave you alone for a second tonight, not with you looking like this." He leans in, his breath warming my neck. "I won't *want* to leave you alone for a second."

I do everything to keep my composure. Inside, I want to scream at how perfect Julian can be when he wants. He seems to always know exactly what to say so I'll never want to leave his side. I'm still supposed to be heartbroken over Trevor. But in the span of only a few days, Julian's completely endeared me to him. What will he do by the end of the summer?

Placing my hand on his chest, I push against him, needing to put a little distance between us for my own sanity.

"We should go. We don't want to be late, do we?"

He stares at me for a moment. I notice the subtlest hint of his shoulders dropping at the loss of contact. Or perhaps I simply imagine it, my desperation for him to feel this growing connection between us forcing me to see things that aren't real. Then he fixes his expression, that flirtatious smirk I remember from the first time I saw him crossing his mouth.

"I suppose that would be a bad thing." He holds his elbow out for me to place my arm through. "Come on, Princess. Time to get you to the ball."

Chapter Twenty-Two

DURING MY FIRST month at the magazine, Viv insisted I attend the opening of an art installation at an eclectic little gallery in SoHo. It was the most upscale event I'd ever attended. Waitstaff in tails and gloves. Men in beautiful suits. Women in gorgeous gowns. And Champagne flowing like it grew on trees, which I suppose one could argue it does, since grapes are grown on vines and Champagne comes from grapes.

Nevertheless, that gallery opening was mere child's play compared to the posh and glamour of the annual Red, White, and Blue Gala. Anyone who's anyone is here. And if you don't get an invitation, you're not someone worth knowing.

Which is why my already antsy nerves are even more so, considering the importance of tonight, especially for Julian. As the newcomer to this elite group, all eyes will be on me. Because of that, I need to do everything in my power not to embarrass him. As long as there's not a pool nearby, I think I'll be okay.

The gentle sounds of a jazz band fill the air as Julian leads me through the foyer of a magnificent home situated on the beach. I expected this to take place at a function hall, but I've once again been proven wrong. Why rent a hall when you can show off the grandeur of your home in front of several hundred of your closest friends? That's all life in the Hamptons seems to be. One

220

giant competition. And this place is the crown jewel. It's like a mansion straight from the Gilded Age. Lush tapestries. Grand staircases. Painted ceilings. Now I really do feel like Cinderella.

We follow the flow of guests, smiling polite hellos every few feet before emerging into a large ball room. Waitstaff are in abundance, circling the room, carrying trays of Champagne and *hors d'oeuvres*. I tilt my head back, admiring the intricate detailing on the ceiling.

"It's like the Hall of Mirrors in Versailles."

"*La Gallérie des Glaces*," Julian says in the perfect French accent. "You've been?"

I look back to him, laughing slightly. "No. I've never been out of the country. But I've always dreamed of visiting Europe, particularly Paris."

"You've never traveled abroad?" He sounds genuinely surprised by this fact. I suppose in his circles, it's an odd occurrence.

"Can't say as I have."

"You were with Trevor for twelve years and he never took you?"

I open my mouth to defend him, but Julian interrupts me before I can utter a word.

"You can't tell me he didn't have the money, because I know what that firm pays their attorneys. He could have afforded it."

My eyes shift nervously around the room. Have I really been so blind as to overlook so many of Trevor's shortcomings? "We've both been so busy," I respond, but my words lack any conviction.

"You need to go to Paris. Everyone should experience the city once in their lives. There's nothing like it anywhere else in the world." The more he speaks, the more excited he becomes. There's a boyish gleam in his eyes as his obvious adoration for the City of Lights shines through. "When the summer is over, I'll take—"

I quickly hold up my hand. "Don't."

He scrunches his forehead, perplexed by my sudden change in demeanor. "But—"

"No." I lean toward him, my voice nothing more than a low whisper. "I can pretend to be your girlfriend all summer. I've agreed to that much. But I won't do the fantasy game with you. I won't have you making me promises you have no intention of fulfilling."

"Who said I have no intention of following through?"

"Me. That's who. You're so accustomed to being able to just hop on a chartered jet and fly off to Paris for lunch. That's not my reality. That will *never* be my reality. It's already difficult to remain grounded when I'm surrounded by all this." I wave my hand around. "I don't need you making this any harder than it has to be."

I pull my bottom lip between my teeth, fighting against the lump in my throat. I wish I hadn't revealed this vulnerability to him, but this is challenging enough. The more I remind myself that this is nothing more than a fantasy, the easier it will be when the dream ends.

"Guinevere, I…" He shakes his head, running a light finger down the curve of my face before cupping my cheeks in his hands. He rests his forehead against mine. It's such a tender moment, one I wish were real. "I'm sorry. I guess I got swept up in the moment. I didn't realize…"

"It's okay. But I feel like some lines have been crossed that I may not have originally anticipated. Don't get me wrong," I add quickly. "The past few days have been great. Better than great. And you've been…great." I laugh. "Better than great." My eyes turn back to his, serious again. "And that's why I don't want to blur the lines anymore. It will only set ourselves up for failure. At least me. Because, at the end of the summer, you'll walk away without a single look back, and I'll still be picking up the pieces of a life I don't even recognize right now. Years down the road, we'll both remember this summer and smile. You from your palace overlooking Central Park, and me from whatever apartment I can afford, which will probably be somewhere in New Rochelle. Hell, one day, maybe I'll be able to tell my kids about the summer I experienced a real-life fairy tale. But that's all this is. Just a fairy tale. Not real life."

He opens his mouth, his expression pensive as he gazes at me. I can almost sense him wanting to tell me I'm wrong, that the fairy tale *can* be real. That this *doesn't* have to end after the summer. Instead, he blows out a long breath, nodding.

"I can respect that. I know what it's like to be surrounded by constant disappointment. I won't lead you on. No more fantasies."

"No more fantasies," I repeat, a pang in my heart at the idea.

"No more fantasies," he says once more, then pulls back, smiling a small smile. We return our attention to the party, everyone oblivious to our emotional exchange. Resuming the roles we're here to play, he links his hand with mine. When a waiter carrying a tray of Champagne passes, Julian swipes two flutes, handing me one.

"For the record..." He lifts his glass and I do the same. "I know you'll soon meet someone who will give you the trip to Paris you deserve." He sips the effervescent liquid, his eyes unwavering as they remain glued to mine.

"I hope so," I murmur absent-mindedly.

223

"Evie!" an excited voice exclaims as I'm about to take a sip.

I search for its source, seeing Sadie and Christopher gliding toward us. That's exactly what it looks like. As if Sadie is walking on air, everything about her poised and put-together. She looks as stunning as I expected she would, wearing a pale white silk gown that hugs her slender frame. Her brown hair is pulled into a bun at her nape, a few strands framing her face. And around her neck is a dazzling diamond necklace that must have cost a small fortune.

"Oh, my goodness..." Grabbing my hand, she spins me around almost in the same fashion as Julian did earlier. "You look incredible. This dress..." She shifts her attention to Julian. "Dana?"

"Who else?" he answers with a laugh.

"Who else indeed. She truly is the best. You'd better keep your eyes on this one tonight, especially around Ethan." She laughs, indicating she's simply making a joke, but Julian knows it's not.

He shifts, wrapping an arm around my waist. For once, I'm certain it's not just for show but his innate need to protect me. The fear streaming from his eyes when he saw Ethan around me last night was far too real to simply be an act.

"He has a thing for the ladies. That's probably why Sonia left him."

This is news to me. I wonder if Chloe knows. "She did?"

A smirk forms on Sadie's lips as she leans closer, her eyes brimming with excitement. She would get along famously with Chloe, both of them bonding over a shared love of gossip. Maybe that's why I've formed such a strong bond with Sadie after only a few days. She reminds me so much of Chloe.

"It's quite the scandal," she whispers. "Last summer, after the Fourth of July, she was mysteriously absent from all festivities, forcing Ethan to attend alone. Then, earlier this year, she was rumored to have been staying with another man while on location for an upcoming movie that was shooting in Vancouver."

"That's not exactly a scandal, Sadie," Christopher interjects, rolling his eyes.

"That's not the scandalous part," she insists, her gaze floating to his before returning to mine. I'm with Christopher. Two celebrities ending their relationship isn't newsworthy these days. "It's rumored this man was a male escort."

My interest piques at this tidbit of information.

"Which sounds ridiculous. I mean, why would someone like Sonia Moreno need to hire an escort? Any man would love to be with her, so why should she pay someone to sleep with her?"

"Maybe it's not about sex," I argue, my own words surprising me. All eyes instantly zero in on me, so I explain, using information I'd gleaned from my brief conversations with August Laurent. "Men and women are programmed differently. As such, they typically hire escorts for different reasons. Yes, most men do so in order to have a quick romp in the sack. Women are different, and I would argue far superior to the male species." I wink as I bring my Champagne flute back to my lips, taking a sip.

"I won't argue with that," Christopher quips. "Not if I want to sleep in the same bed as Sadie tonight." He looks to Julian. "And I wouldn't argue if I were you, either, not if you want to share Evie's bed with her."

"Duly noted." Julian's eyes find mine, wistful and eager. A part of me wonders if he wishes he could share my bed, too.

"As the superior gender," I continue, tearing my gaze from Julian's, "our reasons for hiring an escort are much more complicated than simply wanting to get laid. We do so to feel a connection, to feel adored, to feel beautiful."

The instant I say the words, the air is sucked from my lungs. That is precisely what Julian's done for me. After only twenty-four hours with him, I'm no longer clinging to a life I may never have again. All because he made me feel beautiful. And if Julian, an amateur, can make me feel like this, I can only imagine what August Laurent could do for someone over the course of a month.

"If it's true, I understand why she did it. An escort is discreet."

"Especially this one," Sadie says. "Apparently, he's the most sought-after escort in the country."

My eyes practically bulge out of their sockets as I choke on my Champagne. "August Laurent?" I cough out.

She smiles deviously, waggling her brows. "You've heard of him."

"Evie's working on a story about him for her magazine," Julian explains, his tone boastful. "She hopes that giving the world the inside scoop on the elusive escort will land her a promotion to assistant editor."

"I'd pick up the magazine for that article alone."

I clear the last remnants of Champagne from my throat. "That's what I'm hoping for."

"How's the research going? From what I hear, the guy's an enigma."

"You seem to know a lot about him, Sadie," Christopher teases.

She playfully jabs him in the stomach. "I need to stay educated in case I ever need to use his services." She winks, then turns her gaze back to mine.

"Somehow, he caught wind that I'd been looking for him and reached out to me. I won't reveal too much of what he's told me because I want you to buy the magazine." Everyone laughs politely. "But based on the little information I've gathered so far, I can understand why someone like Sonia Moreno would hire him, especially if she were in the middle of a problematic separation. My boyfriend of twelve years just broke up with me. Ending a long relationship is difficult, even if you've fallen out of love. You think no one will ever love you again, that you're past the age where anyone will find you beautiful. That's what Julian's done for me."

I tilt my head, meeting his eyes. The past twenty-four hours have been a whirlwind, a constant battle of not wanting to get swept up in the fairy tale. Maybe I deserve the fairy tale, regardless of the fact that it's bound to end. That didn't stop Cinderella from going to the ball and dancing with her Prince Charming, even though she knew it was over at midnight. Maybe it's time I take a page out of her book. Stop planning for a future. Live in the moment. Not care about what awaits me a month, a week, a day from now. Right now, I've never felt so cherished, even if this man was a stranger mere days ago.

"He's made me feel beautiful," I continue. "Even if this is just a fleeting romance, I'll always have that."

Staring into his deep pools of blue, everything around us seems to disappear into the background as we share in this moment, this realization that, no matter what happens, I'll forever be grateful to Julian for the gift he's given me. His lips curve into a smile, our mouths inching toward each other.

"Ah, young love," Christopher sighs playfully.

Julian and I snap our heads forward, reminded that we're not alone. He wraps his arm around my waist, then kisses the top of my head. "That it is."

Chapter Twenty-Three

JULIAN AND I spend the next few hours dancing and mingling among the upper crust of the Hamptons. He's unmistakably surprised by the familiarity with which I speak to several of the women, ones who had their noses turned up at me yesterday because I was the new girl. But, just like in high school, people eventually come around.

"And here I was, worried about how you would get on without me," he jokes after dinner as we all file to the expansive exterior verandah to watch the fireworks display.

"I suppose knowing that I'll never see these people after this summer relaxed me a bit. Yes, some of them still don't like me, probably because they secretly wish they were sharing a bed with you instead of their overweight, balding husbands. But the others…" I shrug. "Once they heard our story, they couldn't get enough. I had them swooning and sighing in the salon. They're not much different than anyone else. They want the same things all women do."

"And what's that?" His blue eyes sparkle as he smiles down at me, everything about him relaxed.

"Love. Happiness. And the occasional mind-blowing orgasm."

Julian's throaty laugh fills the air, music to my ears. "Is

that all?"

"It's not too much to ask, is it?"

We come to a stop at the stone ledge and I lean on it. "Of course not. We all deserve love and happiness."

"Don't forget mind-blowing orgasms. I'm pretty sure those will inevitably lead to love and happiness. Let's face it. If I found someone who could give me a mind-blowing orgasm, I'd fall in love with him. Which is probably why I've fallen in love with Mr. Winky."

Julian passes me a bemused look. "Mr. Winky?"

I love how easy conversation is with him. Now that I've stopped worrying about a future and am simply living in the moment, I'm no longer on edge. Yes, there are still intense moments between us, but I don't care whether it's real. It doesn't matter. All that does is that I'm happier than I've been in a long time, all because of Julian.

"Please don't tell me you nicknamed Trevor's dick, because I'll never be able to look at him the same way again."

My core clenches when I hear him say dick in his gruff voice. I can only imagine what he's like in the bedroom. Based on the way he acts around me while we merely pretend we're madly in love, I presume he's just as impassioned, if not more so. And I bet he's one hell of a dirty talker.

"No." I fight against the heat washing over my face at the idea of Julian's bedroom voice. "I didn't nickname his dick. And he certainly never gave me mind-blowing orgasms." I add the last part as an afterthought.

"So who's Mr. Winky?" he inquires, and I'm grateful he doesn't push the Trevor issue. In fact, until Julian brought him up, I haven't thought of Trevor all night, regardless that he's also here with Theresa. I'm simply too consumed with Julian and everything he is. The way he dotes on me and takes care of me doesn't leave any room to worry about Trevor.

"Only the best battery-operated boyfriend I've ever had."

He laughs loudly and slings his arm over my shoulders. "I love that you're not embarrassed to talk about this stuff."

I shrug. "It's my job to talk about sex. Literally. Nothing fazes me anymore. I've seen it all. Some things I wish I could unsee."

"I'm not sure I want to know."

"You definitely don't. All I'm saying is there's a fetish for everyone and everything. And I do mean *ev-ry-thing*."

"Duly noted."

I turn my eyes back to the shore, able to make out the sound of the crashing waves and the fizzling of foam as the saltwater spreads across the sand. It's a cloudless night, the stars twinkling above us against the dark. There's a slight breeze, as there usually is along the coast, causing a chill to run through me, despite the moderately warm temperatures.

Noticing me shiver, Julian shrugs out of his tuxedo jacket, draping it over my shoulders. I glance behind me, offering him a smile of thanks. I expect him to return to my side. Instead, he wraps his arms around my body, pulling me against him, my back to his front. As if this were a dance we'd done dozens of times before, I melt into him, reveling in his embrace. Nothing about this feels stilted or awkward. It's so natural, so familiar, so effortless.

Bathing in his warmth, I smile at a few nearby guests

as they assemble to watch the fireworks. Out of the corner of my eye, I spy Trevor standing with Theresa. I must admit, he's rather handsome in his tuxedo, his hair freshly trimmed. Twelve years together and this is the first time I've seen him in a tux. The thought should anger me more, but it doesn't. Maybe if I'd never met Julian I'd be sitting on Chloe's couch, lamenting about how Trevor could leave me for someone boring like Theresa, but it no longer bothers me. Julian's right. So is Chloe. Why should I want to be with someone who doesn't appreciate me for me?

As I observe their awkwardness, struggling to see any connection between the two, Trevor glances in my direction and our eyes meet. He swallows hard when he sees me safe and secure in Julian's arms. Julian must notice Trevor staring. His embrace tightening, he caresses my stomach with his left hand, the one closest to Trevor. The gentle contact sends a rush of exhilaration through me, each brush of his thumb moving higher and higher. I hold my breath as he nears the curve of my breast.

"Is this okay?" he murmurs into my ear, his breath hot on my neck. "I'll stop if you say so. No hard feelings."

"Don't stop," I exhale. There's no way I could tell him no. Not now. Not when I'm wound this tightly. I'm fully aware it's just for show, to make people think we're a real couple, but if that's the only reason Julian's putting on this display, so be it. Who cares if it's not real? All I *do* care about is savoring in this moment. And in this moment, I just want Julian's hands on my body.

"Goddamn," he hisses as he grazes the bottom of my breasts. When he pulls my body even tighter against his, he groans, grinding against me.

"Down boy," I joke. Feeling how turned on he is gives

my confidence an added boost. Say what you will, but there's nothing as empowering for a woman as knowing she has the ability to turn on a man, to bring him to his knees, to make him desperate for just a taste, a feel, a touch.

"I can't help it. He has a mind of his own, especially when you're around."

Music fills the exterior speakers and, seconds later, a loud boom echoes. Everyone "oohs" and "aahs" as their attention shifts to the horizon, the brilliant colors of the fireworks bright against the dark canvas. But Julian's attention remains focused entirely on me.

When his hips circle a slow, sensual rhythm against my body, I moan, leaning my head against his chest. I try to concentrate on the fireworks in the sky, not the ones erupting in my core at the sensation of his seductive teasing. My nipples strain against my dress, my body's reaction at odds with the warning my brain sounds, telling me to retreat, that I'd drawn lines for a reason. I couldn't retreat now if I wanted to, a carnal need to experience more of Julian driving me forward, regardless of the possible consequences.

"Do you have any idea how many times I've thought of you these past few weeks?" His teeth skim against my neck, causing a jolt of electricity to rush through me, hot and needy. Surrounded by all these people, I fight to maintain my composure. With each word, each nip, each touch, it's becoming more and more impossible.

"How many?" I manage to squeak out as I keep my eyes glued to the gorgeous display in front of us commemorating our country's independence. I can't help but feel that this weekend marks the start of *my* independence, too. The start of a new chapter in my life.

"I lost count. At the office. In the shower... In my

bed."

I bite my lower lip, fantasies clouding my brain. Barging in on Julian when he's at work and seducing him at his desk. Surprising him in the shower and having him slam me against the cool tile, the way he fucks me hungry and insatiable. Then crawling in beside him in the middle of the night. Without a word, he'd show me the tender lover I sense is hidden somewhere beneath the mask. I barely know this man, yet the fantasies in my head are so real, as if someone's able to show me a piece of him I'll never be able to have.

"Have you thought of me?"

"Y-yes," I stammer, squeezing my legs together as pressure slowly builds inside me, on the brink of bubbling over. I fear if it's not released, I'll explode into a vibrant show more brilliant than the fireworks in the sky.

He runs his hands along my stomach, my muscles clenching. With each journey north, he retreats with a path traveling farther south. He presses me into the ledge, shielding curious onlookers from noticing when he dips his hand into the slit of my dress.

"Have you thought of me during one of your dates with your so-called Mr. Winky?"

Normally I'd giggle at the sound of anyone else calling my battery-operated boyfriend by his name. But I'm too turned on to find humor in anything right now. Instead, all I can do is answer truthfully.

"Yes."

"When was the last time?"

"Last night."

"Fuck." His grip on me tightens. The warmth of his hand brushing against the waist of my panties causes my breathing to increase, my chest to heave at the promise of what's to come. "Is this okay?"

"Yes." I adjust my stance, parting my legs slightly, signaling him with my body how much I want this. Chloe and Nora have done the no-strings thing. I can do that, too. I hope. "God, yes."

When he slips his hand beneath the line of my panties, I grip the ledge harder, my jaw clenching as I do everything in my power not to draw attention to us.

"Is this okay?" he asks once more as his fingers leisurely make their way farther south.

"Yes." I'm no longer standing on the verandah of a ridiculously opulent mansion in the Hamptons overlooking the ocean as we watch an excessive fireworks display. I'm flying, the ground nothing but a speck of dust.

He groans again as he brushes his fingers against my skin. "He really did make you get waxed, didn't he?"

"He did."

When he grazes my center, I whimper, in another place, another time, another universe. "Is this okay?"

"Yes."

"I was hoping you'd say that."

His touch becomes firm as he explores me, this entire experience completely out of character for me. Or maybe it's simply because my ex never would have so much as entertained the idea of doing something like this in public. I think that's what makes it even more exciting. The notion that, at any moment, someone could look our way and realize what's going on. But they don't, everyone too immersed in the fireworks, the musical accompaniment being piped in through the sound system loud enough to drown out my pants and pleas for more.

"Guinevere," he growls as he explores me with more intensity, pushing one finger inside before adding another. "Did Trevor ever turn you on like this?"

"No." It's the truth. Never. Not once. There was no spontaneity with him. I thought I liked that. I knew when we'd be having sex. I knew what position we'd be in. I'm starting to think that certain things can't be planned.

"I love that I do this to you. Because you have no idea how fucking hard I am right now. How hard I get every time I think of you. You do it for me. And this isn't me saying it as part of our game. This is me saying it because it's true. I'm starved for you."

"Oh god." My eyes roll into the back of my head as the thunder of fireworks becomes more and more fevered. I was right. Julian is a damn good dirty talker. I'm pretty sure I could come from his words alone. Add in how expertly he massages me and brushes his thumb on my clit and I soon climax in time with the grand finale of the fireworks display, screaming out in utter bliss as applause and cheers fill the air.

Every inch of me trembling, I struggle to make sense out of what just happened, how I should feel about it when I desperately wanted to keep the lines from being blurred. Not only did I just blur them, I pretty much eviscerated them, all because I got swept up in the moment.

"Don't," he rumbles into my ear as he removes his hand, adjusting my dress to hide our indiscretions. I stare forward, my mind racing, chest heaving. "Don't think this is anything more than what it is — two consenting adults enjoying each other's company."

I nod subtly, swallowing hard. How does he know my thoughts are currently clouded with guilt and embarrassment over what we'd just done, how easily I'd allowed him to touch me like that when only one man has in over a decade? I haven't even been single a full month, yet am already spreading my legs for someone else, a relative stranger. Granted, Trevor doesn't seem to be bothered by the idea of being with someone new so soon, but it feels…wrong.

"You deserve to feel beautiful, to feel desired, to feel adored. That's all I wanted. Okay?"

I turn around, locking eyes with him, his expression a mixture of hunger and remorse, a near mirror image of the war currently battling inside my own heart. How can I tell him I want him, but with every second we spend together, the harder it will be to walk away from him at the end of the summer? That if he keeps touching me like that he'll ruin me for all the men who come after him? And there will be men who come after him. He made sure of that. We both did.

"The ball's in your court, Guinevere. If you want to explore this connection further, I'm more than willing. If you're not comfortable with having a strictly physical relationship, I understand that, as well. Just know that I am insanely attracted to you. And I will be no matter what you choose."

My breathing is still labored from the after-effects of the orgasm rolling through me as I peer into his eyes, desperately wanting to crush my lips to his, wrap my arms around him, and allow him to consume me in a way I believe only he can. But can I really do this? I feel like I'm standing in the door of a plane, torn between jumping out and experiencing the exhilaration of flying, or returning to the ground from the safety of my seat.

I'm about to share my fears when Sadie's familiar voice cuts through. "There you two are!"

I jump away from Julian, as if we'd just been caught

237

doing something we shouldn't. I'm not Catholic, but I have a feeling this is what the Catholic guilt I've heard so much about must feel like. I search the area, my eyes settling on her approaching with Christopher and a man I estimate to be in his fifties.

"I've been looking everywhere for you. I wanted to introduce you to my uncle Clinton." She leans in, lowering her voice. "He's my cool uncle." She winks an exaggerated wink as he laughs politely.

"Trust me," Clinton says. "It's not a stiff competition. Most in the family are—"

"Uptight," Sadie offers.

"Pricks," Clinton interjects immediately. "I was going to say pricks." He beams down at Sadie, an affection between them I haven't seen much out here. It's obvious she has a great deal of respect for her uncle, and he has a great deal of admiration for his niece, regardless of any fallout from her marrying Christopher. "But I suppose uptight is more agreeable." He returns his attention back to us, extending his hand toward Julian. "Clinton Alderman."

I stare at it, horrified over the idea of Julian shaking his hand after what he just did, then realize he used his left one with me. If he was that talented with his left hand, I can only imagine what he could do with his predominate one. A blush heats my cheeks as they shake politely.

"Julian Gage."

"Nice to finally meet you, Julian."

"And you." He turns his attention toward me. "This is my girlfriend, Guinevere Fitzgerald."

Clinton looks toward me, his eyes finding mine. But unlike so many other men I've met here, he doesn't appraise me like a piece of meat. He looks at me like I'm

238

a human being. It's refreshing.

"Lovely to meet you, Guinevere."

"Evie," I correct. "You can just call me Evie."

"Evie."

After we all exchange pleasantries, Clinton turns back to Julian. "Sadie mentioned you're in the process of expanding your charitable branch overseas and are trying to get the ball rolling to open up shelters for women in high-risk areas."

I snap my head toward Julian, surprised by this. I'm not sure what I thought this big project of his was. I simply thought it was to build some ridiculously luxurious hotel in Dubai, something that could increase his income substantially. But to find out it's a charitable project? Another piece of the Julian Gage puzzle snaps into place.

"I'm sure I didn't get all the details correct," Sadie adds. "Just what I picked up from Christopher."

"It's something I've been wanting to do for a long time." He turns his attention to Clinton, his demeanor becoming serious, flipping the switch from seductive Julian to businessman Julian. "When I inherited Theodore Price's fortune, the first thing I did was begin a charity here in the States. Our mission is to provide a safe haven for women in abusive relationships. At least here, we get some assistance from criminal justice agencies. Which got me thinking about what it must be like for women in countries and cultures where this kind of abuse isn't frowned upon. In fact, it's *encouraged* as part of their customs. I want to do something to help these women, but expanding overseas isn't as easy as I thought it would be. There's quite a bit of red tape I have to cut through to even consider the possibility."

239

"Well, I may just be able to help you. I'm not sure what Sadie's told you about me, but I'm in the oil industry."

"I know."

"And in the oil industry, red tape is our specialty." He winks, then jovially slaps Julian on the back. "Come with me. A few of us are digging into Graham Salazar's cigar stash. You should join us."

"I'd love to." Smoothing the lines of his shirt, he steps away from me, exuding all the confidence and poise I've come to expect from him.

"Chris, you should join us, as well."

Christopher's dark eyes widen. He drops his hold on Sadie, joining Julian and Clinton.

"Great to meet you, Guinevere," Clinton offers with a smile.

"Likewise." My gaze shifts from him to Julian. We haven't finished our conversation about the unexpected fireworks display earlier. Maybe it's for the best. Maybe it's one of those things we shouldn't discuss, that we should just forget happened. "You boys enjoy those cigars."

Clinton tips his imaginary hat, then turns, leading Julian and Christopher away from the verandah.

When the men are out of sight, Sadie winks. "That never would have happened if you weren't here."

"What do you mean?"

"My uncle. He's great, don't get me wrong, but he's from a different generation. He recognizes things aren't how they once were, but he's still from old money. He hasn't fully embraced this new dynamic. It shouldn't matter if Julian *were* a bit of a playboy. But it does to these people. They don't want to be associated with someone like that. So seeing him with a woman..." She shrugs.

240

"Some of them are coming around and accepting him as someone who *will* be around for the foreseeable future, someone they could benefit from doing business with. They're starting to see what I see."

"And what do you see?" I ask, although I'm unsure I want to know the answer.

"I see a man falling hard for a fun, down-to-earth woman."

My face reddening, I avert my gaze, looking back out over the ocean. A breeze picks up and I pull Julian's jacket tighter around my shoulders, basking in the warmth and earthy aroma from it.

"And I see a woman living the fairy tale we all secretly hope for. Enjoy it."

I meet her eyes, smiling a small smile. "I am."

We remain on the verandah for a little longer, making the rounds as Sadie introduces me to even more people. After a while, I politely excuse myself, wanting to take a moment to freshen up. I feel as if my earlier indiscretions with Julian are plastered on my face, in my eyes, on my complexion.

Once my makeup is refreshed and I ensure it doesn't appear as if I'd just had one of the best orgasms of my life, I make my way out of the bathroom and back toward the ballroom. As I skirt past dancing couples, I spy the bar and decide to make a detour before rejoining Sadie.

Approaching the counter, I catch the bartender's eyes and order a manhattan, draping Julian's jacket along the surface of the bar. When he places the drink in front of me, I thank him, opening my clutch to leave a tip. All I have are a few hundreds that Julian left me this morning to use for gratuity at the spa. With a shrug, I place one down. The bartender doesn't even flinch. I surmise he must get that a lot at these kinds of parties.

"You really love those things, don't you?" a voice comments as I take my first sip. I look over the top of my glass to see Trevor standing before me.

"It's a step up from the Boone's Farm we drank freshman year."

He laughs at the memory, a boyish glint in his eyes. It reminds me of the Trevor I first met all those years ago. The one who used to paint his face red for football games. Who used to drag me out to have snowball fights during the winter. Who stood on one of the tables in the dining hall and shouted to the world, or at least a small portion of the student body of the University of Nebraska, how much he loved me.

Then his expression hardens, leaving the man he's turned into. A serious, workaholic who bears no resemblance to the Trevor I fell in love with. Does he feel the same when he looks at me? Is that why he ended things? Did we really commit the awful crime of being too blind to realize we'd fallen out of love with each other?

"You look good, G."

"You clean up pretty nice yourself." Spying a piece of lint on the lapel of his tuxedo jacket, I reach for it and brush it off, an old habit. Once, it felt normal to do something like this. Now it's different. It's not my job anymore. I don't *want* it to be my job anymore.

I raise my glass to my lips, looking around the ballroom. A few weeks ago I would have done anything to have a chance to talk to Trevor like this. Now all I can think is that I hope Julian won't be upset I'm speaking to him, as ridiculous as that sounds.

"I mean it. You look… Wow. I barely even recognize

you."

"I could say the same about you."

He furrows his brow. "What do you mean? I wore suits nearly every day the past few years. But you... You seem like a completely different person than I remember."

"That's the problem then, isn't it?" I place my drink on the bar, squaring my shoulders. "Because I'm the same exact girl I was when you broke up with me, Trevor. I haven't changed much in the past twelve years. Sure, I may have a few more pounds and bigger breasts, but everything about me is the same. The way I sleep. The way I talk..." I trail off, my voice wavering, more out of frustration than heartache. Frustration I didn't see the truth years ago. "The way I love. It just wasn't enough for you."

I'd kept my feelings locked up for years, even though I constantly advised my readers not to, that the hallmark of a solid relationship is being open and honest, that keeping your feelings hidden is simply a ticking time bomb. I did just that. I smiled and pretended to be someone I wasn't so Trevor would love me. Nothing about our relationship was ever real. This thing I have with Julian is more real than the love I thought I shared with Trevor.

I lean toward him, my eyes fierce, the veins in my neck strained as I finally tell him exactly how I feel.

"At least now I'm with someone who thinks I *am* enough, who thinks I *am* serious enough to be with. He appreciates me, quirky sense of humor and all." I grab Julian's coat off the bar and turn from Trevor. I only make it a few steps before I stop, whirling around to face him once more.

"You know what? Maybe I *have* changed. Maybe I was

tired of having to be someone I wasn't just to make you happy. I'm done with that. Now is the time to make *myself* happy. And Julian makes me happier than you ever did." My chest heaves as emotions overwhelm me. Then I lower my voice. "I'm just sorry it took me twelve years to realize this. Goodbye, Trevor."

Chapter Twenty-Four

"OKAY, TELL ME everything," Chloe orders as she flies into my cubicle a little before five on Monday.

She plops onto the free chair, interrupting me from sorting through more of my scribblings about August Laurent. We exchanged several emails over the weekend, in which he revealed more information about his background. Now I'm trying to organize everything into an outline to make it easier to determine which direction to go with his story.

"Nice to see you, too," I respond sarcastically. "Where have you been? And why are you just getting in when it's practically time to leave?"

She smooths her hair behind her ear, avoiding my eyes, which is the Chloe tell that she's purposefully being evasive. "This isn't about me. This is about you. How did it go?"

I study her, unable to shake the feeling she's keeping something from me, but I've been itching to see her since Julian dropped me off at her apartment yesterday afternoon. A nice surprise since I expected Reed to drive me again. When she wasn't home, I had no option but to obsess over every little thing that happened, which resulted in the conclusion that Julian is obviously bipolar. Or, better yet, suffering from multiple personality disorder. What other explanation is there?

"Come on, Evie! Dish!"

"I don't even know where to begin." It's true. It seems like a lifetime's passed since I stepped into that chauffeured town car and was whisked off to the Hamptons for a weekend of excess and privilege.

"Start with what happened when you got there."

I sit back in my chair as I stare into the distance, trying to collect my thoughts. "To be honest, I wasn't sure what to expect, how Julian would act around me, considering this is just supposed to be a business relationship. But when I saw him and he saw me…" A blush builds on my cheeks as I recall the adoration in his eyes when they fell on me wearing that two-piece.

"Yeah?"

"There was a spark."

"But…" She arches a brow, sensing there's more.

"But every single action, every word made me question his motivation. I constantly got swept up in the moment and believed it was all real, only to be reminded it wasn't the next minute. The entire weekend, I felt like we were on a see-saw or playing a constant game of tug-of-war. He'd have me so wrapped up in him I'd forget the reason I was there. Then he'd retreat, acting like I had some infectious disease. And at the gala…" I trail off.

"Yeah?"

"It's just…" I fidget with my hands, still struggling with how to process what happened on the verandah during the fireworks display. Once we left the party, we hadn't spoken of it. For the rest of the weekend, it was as if it had never happened. At first, I considered it to be a good thing. Now I'm not too sure.

"What is it, Evie?" She places her hand on my knee,

her voice filled with compassion. "You know you can tell me anything."

I blow out a breath, lifting my eyes to meet hers. "Things got a little...heated." Butterflies flit in my stomach at the memory. "Actually, things got *very* heated."

"Heated?" This catches Chloe's attention. "Heated how?"

I chew on my lower lip, trying to find the right words.

"Come on, Evie!" she all but shrieks. "You're a sex and dating columnist for crying out loud. This shit is what you do for a living."

"He touched me," I blurt out.

She waggles her brows as a slow smile builds on her mouth. "Where? Your arm?"

"You know where," I scoff, rolling my eyes before swooning from the memory. "God, Chloe..." I squeeze my legs together. Just discussing this leaves my body desperate for more. "It was so wild, so crazy, so out of character for me." I lower my voice, inching closer to her. "We were on the verandah. It was a little chilly, so he draped his tux jacket over my shoulders. Then he wrapped his arms around me, keeping me warm. One thing led to another and before I could stop the train from derailing, he slipped his hand under the slit of my dress and took me to pleasure town."

She stares at me, processing my story.

"I wore this dress with a long, flowing skirt. There was so much fabric, it masked what was really going on."

She waves me off. "I know what you were wearing."

I blink at her. "You do?"

"Of course. Photos were all over the gossip websites as everyone tried to figure out who the mystery woman on

Julian Gage's arm was. That's not what I'm questioning."

"It's not?" I ask, unsure what to think of my photo being plastered all over the Internet. I knew this would happen, but I'd been living in my fantasy world all weekend. This explains why my mother's been trying to get in touch with me. She probably saw my picture with someone other than Trevor. I make a mental note to call her and tell her we broke up, considering I no longer have any interest in getting back together with him.

"Pleasure town, Evie?" Chloe bursts into a giggling fit. "Really? That's what you're going with? Did you ride his rocket all the way there, too?"

"No! There was no rocket riding. There was no rocket fondling. Hell, I never even caught a glimpse of the launch pad, although I certainly felt it." I laugh along with Chloe. This is exactly what I needed, a few moments with one of my best friends to make sense out of the weekend.

"But he worked your...command center?"

"Did he ever. The fireworks in the sky were nothing compared to the explosions down below. He knows his way around...ground control."

"Okay, okay." Chloe waves her hands in front of her, tears forming in the corner of her eyes as she struggles to breathe. "You need to stop with all these spaceship references or I'll never be able to watch *Apollo 13* again, and you know how much I love Kevin Bacon."

It takes a few minutes, but our laughter gradually wanes. When it does, she comments, "So you broke the no kissing rule."

"What? No."

"But you let him——"

"Explore ground control," I interrupt with a smile.

"Find your pleasure center," she corrects, "yet you still refuse to kiss him?"

"It worked for Julia Roberts' character in *Pretty Woman*."

"Actually, it didn't. She still ended up falling for Edward."

"Because she kissed him. I haven't kissed Julian; ergo, I won't fall for him."

She assesses me with her analytical stare, then states, "Are you sure you haven't already?"

"I'm not sure of anything, Chloe," I admit after a pause. "All I do know is being with Julian made me realize I haven't been true to myself. I put on an act for Trevor so he'd love me. You were right. I shouldn't waste my time on someone who doesn't appreciate me for me. And Julian does. He makes me happy, makes me feel beautiful. Even if it's only for a few months, it'll be worth it."

Her eyes brimming with enthusiasm, she wraps her arms around me, planting a kiss on my temple. "I'm happy for you. Don't think about the future. Have fun. Live in the moment. Let Julian explore your command center until he has all its functions worked out properly. Hell, maybe you can even play on his launch pad."

I laugh, this entire conversation bordering on ridiculous, but in a way that makes me feel incredibly grounded in reality.

Pulling away, she holds me at arm's length, her eyes trained on mine. "You've always been a planner, and I love that about you. Your obsession with planning out every second of every day with stickers and notes is quirky and adorable and what makes Evie...Evie." She drops her hold on me, then continues. "I'll admit, I was skeptical of this arrangement at first, since I know how you are, but now… I don't know. You're…different. I *like* this side of Evie. You're confident and self-assured."

I give her a sanctimonious look. "I've always been confident and self-assured. Need I remind you I got up in front of an entire bar a few weeks ago and told them all about my embarrassing breakup?"

"That doesn't make you confident and self-assured. All that evidences is the fact you've been screaming for someone to notice you because Trevor never did. Now someone finally has. So who cares if nothing comes out of this? Stop making plans for the future. Enjoy the ride." She pulls me closer again.

"On his rocket ship," I add, then we both burst out laughing.

"Come on," Chloe says when she sees it's after five. "Izzy's off today. Let's all go surprise Nora at the yoga studio and hijack one of her classes."

I get up from my chair, grateful for one night of normalcy in a life I have trouble recognizing these days. "That sounds perfect."

I gather my things, and within a few minutes, we're in the elevator on our way to the lobby. As it descends, I steal a glance at Chloe and smile. She scrunches her brows, knowing I'm about to do something crazy. When I start singing Elton John's "Rocket Man", she stifles a laugh, covering her mouth with her hand. Everyone else in the elevator glances sideways at us. Then Chloe joins in, which causes me to sing louder. Much to my amusement, a few of our fellow passengers join in. By the time the elevator reaches the lobby, we're all singing the chorus. But we don't stop once we exit. We continue belting out the lyrics as we all make our way toward the doors.

I'm so wrapped up in the strange, impromptu moment that could only happen in a place like New York City, and in a building that houses a slew of magazine offices, I almost don't recognize the man leaning against a column in the lobby until Chloe grabs my arm, forcing me to stop.

My breath hitches when my eyes fall on Julian. He looks rather dashing in the charcoal gray suit he makes casual by foregoing the tie and leaving the top few buttons of his shirt undone. Sunglasses obscure those deep blue orbs that are permanently ingrained in my head, but I can still feel their heat. Everything about him is so effortless, so confident, so compelling. It's no wonder everyone passing him pauses to look. A few women even giggle, probably wishing they were lucky enough to spend time with him. But I'm the lucky one. I think...

He pushes off the column and walks toward me, lowering his sunglasses. "Guinevere..."

The way my name rolls off his tongue is incredibly erotic. Even more so now that I've been treated to a taste of his bedroom voice.

"Julian." I straighten my posture, doing everything to make it appear as if his presence doesn't have my stomach in knots.

"Do I want to know what caused that impromptu rendition of 'Rocket Man'?"

"Definitely not." I can only imagine his reaction if he were to find out Chloe and I reduced what happened on the verandah to aeronautical terminology.

"I didn't think so."

I attempt to slow my racing heart as we stare at each other. I hadn't expected to see him again until Friday

251

morning when I'm to head back to the Hamptons to attend a charity art auction aboard some heavy hitter's ridiculously large yacht. At least I didn't think I was supposed to see him. Perhaps I overlooked something.

"Good to see you, Chloe," Julian says, finally acknowledging I'm not alone.

"You, as well, Julian. To what do we owe the...pleasure?" She discreetly pinches my side. I bat her away, struggling to maintain my composure.

"I came to collect Guinevere." He shifts his gaze back to mine, a mysterious aloofness about him.

"Did I forget about something?" Frantic, I reach into my commuter bag to retrieve my planner, where every event I'm set to attend has been written down and color-coded. "I could have sworn—"

A hand reaches out, forcing me to let go of my planner, my life. Glancing up, I'm met with Julian's smirk.

"Put the calendar away. You didn't forget anything."

I blink, swallowing hard at the intensity in his stare. "I didn't?"

His lips turn into a playful smile as he shakes his head, slow and flirtatious. "No."

"Then—"

"I stopped by to see if you wanted to do something."

"Chloe and I were planning on dropping by Nora's yoga studio—"

"But I was just telling Evie how exhausted I am from a crazy weekend," Chloe interrupts, faking a yawn before winking conspiratorially. Squeezing my arm, she passes me a sly grin, then leans toward me, her voice a low whisper. "Don't think. Enjoy the ride...on his rocket."

I snort out a laugh, then instantly cover my mouth.

"Bye, you crazy kids!" Chloe calls out, waving as she heads off.

Once we're alone, Julian returns his attention to me. "So it's settled. We'll do something."

"What about the itinerary?"

"The itinerary?"

"Yes. The itinerary." Passing him a coy smile, I bat my lashes. "That was part of our deal. You promised we'd only have to see each other during pre-approved times."

In an instant, his playfulness disappears, his expression turning impassioned and carnal as he closes the distance between us. When his hand palms my back, forcing me against him, I gasp. My legs weaken as every synapse in my body fires at the same time.

It's official. Julian Gage is the most potent drug known to man. He should be regulated and come with a warning to all females...and perhaps a few men.

Side effects include wet panties, labored breathing, and irregular heartbeat. May cause multiple orgasms upon even the slightest touch. Consult a doctor prior to repeated use.

He leans toward me, his voice a heady growl. "Fuck the itinerary."

Chapter Twenty-Five

FUCK THE ITINERARY indeed.

Over the next several weeks, that's precisely what Julian and I did. I still accompanied him to the myriad of events that seemed be the hallmark of summer in the Hamptons, where he continued to try to convince many of the power players that his project was worth them investing their time and connections, but we also spent time together away from the Hamptons.

On more than one occasion, he made the trek back to the city to take me to dinner, or for a walk through Central Park, or to see *Hamilton*…after I'd mentioned I'd yet to see it and doubted I'd ever be able to score a ticket. He claimed he needed to come into the city for work anyway, but the fact that he seemed to spend many work hours with me made me believe otherwise.

When I wasn't with Julian, I worked tirelessly on getting more of a feel for who August Laurent truly is. Now I know why Viv was so eager to green light this story. He's incredibly tight-lipped. Yes, over the course of our phone conversations and email exchanges, he's given me some insight into what he does and why, all revolving around the theme of empowering women and making them feel beautiful during a difficult time. But the article is missing something. No matter how many times I've written and rewritten it, it's not the gripping exposé I'd originally envisioned. Not without more than he's given me.

I tried to press for details about his clients, even asking if I could talk to a few with a guarantee of complete anonymity, but he denied my request instantly. Without any other option, I asked if the rumors about him and Sonia Moreno were true. I thought perhaps that would encourage him to open up more. I may have overplayed my hand because an entire week has gone by without so much as a response to any of my emails.

Before Viv approached me regarding this promotion, I'd always enjoyed my work. Writing for the sex and dating columns has been one of the least stressful jobs I've ever had. Yes, there are deadlines and Viv can be particular with how the articles are worded and presented, but after a while, I learned what she liked and adjusted my style to match her preference. Now I can't help but feel like a complete failure, like I'm not cut out for this. Maybe my parents are right. Maybe I'm better suited to teach.

When Julian picks me up on the second Friday in August for my obligatory weekend in the Hamptons, I try not to let this roadblock affect my mood, but it's obvious something's bothering me. The instant I'm in the front seat of his Porsche Spyder...or as I've affectionately renamed her, Monday...Julian notices.

"You okay?" He steals a glance at me as he merges into traffic.

I float my eyes from the trendy buildings that make up the East Village, forcing a smile. "Of course."

"Are you sure? You seem...off." He shifts into third as he continues up First toward the interstate.

"I'm fine. Everything's fine."

"Fine?"

"Yes. Fine."

"Hmm."

"What?" I tilt my head.

"During his lifetime, Mr. Price offered a great deal of advice, most of it regarding operating and building a successful business. But he also gave me real-world advice." Licking his lips, he glances at me, our eyes locking before he returns his attention to the road. "One of the things he told me was if a woman ever says she's fine, I should run for cover."

I laugh softly as I gaze at him, a nostalgic twinkle in his eyes.

"You're not fine, Guinevere. Remember what I said at the beginning. No lies. It's the only way this will work. Tell me what's bothering you." His voice is soft and comforting as he grasps my hand in his.

"I thought we weren't going to do the whole sharing of our sob stories?"

"Is it a sob story?" he asks hesitantly.

"No. Just some trouble at work." I grit out a smile. I've tried to keep my troubles to myself, considering Julian has his own problems with getting his project up and running. "Nothing to concern yourself with. Don't worry. I'll be my usual charming self this weekend. I need to figure out my next step. That's all."

He abruptly pulls the car to the side of the road, putting on his hazards. In typical New York fashion, horns blare and drivers shout expletives as they pass, flipping him off. It doesn't deter him.

"What are you doing?"

Once he shifts into neutral and engages the parking brake, he faces me, his eyes hardened. "I never intended this arrangement to cause you problems at work. You don't have to come with me this weekend."

"It's not," I insist. "This is a me issue. It has nothing to do with our arrangement. I guess I didn't realize how difficult…" I trail off.

"How difficult what?"

"Don't worry about it."

He brings his hand to my cheek and I melt into him. He tenderly grazes his thumb over my bottom lip. It's a subtle, gentle touch, one most may not react to. But that's all it takes to ignite the spark, the unquenchable thirst building inside me. Now that I know exactly how it feels to have Julian's hands on the most intimate parts of my body, that thirst has only increased. There have been so many instances I've been on the brink of initiating something more.

Like when he took me to a pottery class. I thought it would be fun to recreate the scene from *Ghost*, complete with appropriate background music, which I sang myself. The way he stared at me, his eyes dancing with amusement as he tried not to laugh at the spectacle I made, only increased the connection I felt to him. Trevor would have tried to hide out of embarrassment. Not Julian.

Like when he surprised me with a trip to one of the most beautiful bookstores I'd ever seen. He barely took his eyes off me as I roamed the aisles in wonder of all the stories filling the gorgeous space. I'd asked Trevor to take me there dozens of times. I never even had to ask Julian. He did it because he knew I'd enjoy it.

Like when he realized I started waking up early to watch the sunrise over the ocean. He began getting up, too. Now, whenever I open the French doors and step onto the balcony of his exquisite home, he's waiting for me, holding a cup of coffee prepared the way I like it. Trevor never made coffee for me.

Regardless of how close we've become, the ball's remained firmly in my court. There have been countless opportunities for me to toss it back to him. But I haven't, scared it will ruin what we've built.

"I told you. I'll always worry about you. If you'd rather stay in the city to focus on work, I understand."

"Thank you." I sigh, finding comfort in his words. There are so many sides to Julian, I can't decide which I like best. One minute, he can be mysterious and aloof. The next, sweet and compassionate. And still the next, tortured and defeated. All parts that make up this man who's unwittingly found his way under my skin where he's burrowed so deeply I'm unsure whether I'll be able to let go. But, in less than a month, I have to do just that.

Swallowing hard, I pull back, forcing him to drop his hold on me. "Maybe a weekend away to clear my head is what I need. Sometimes the best medicine is a little sun and sand." I turn my lips into a small smile.

"Are you sure? I really don't mind—"

"It's fine," I interrupt, crossing my arms in front of my chest as I tap my foot, feigning annoyance. "And if you don't take me, I'll hop on a train and show up at your house, so you may as well enjoy my company for another two hours." I pass him a playful look, winking. "Plus, as if the hair weren't a dead giveaway, I'm Irish, and I have the stubbornness to prove it. You're not going to win this battle with me, Mr. Gage."

Pinching his lips together, he studies me for a moment, then pushes out a breath. "Fine. We'll compromise."

"Compromise?"

"Precisely." Disengaging the parking brake, he presses

258

his foot on the clutch before shifting into first and pulling back into traffic without signaling. Horns honk all around us, but Julian ignores them.

New York drivers.

"And what would that be?" I lean against the seat, tilting my head to admire him. God, I love the confidence he exudes when he drives, the way he handles the car stirring too many fantasies to the surface of my subconscious.

"You can spend the weekend with me in the Hamptons, but just me." He lifts his brows.

"Just…you?" I swallow hard, my pulse increasing.

"Exactly. No parties. No dinners. No distractions. Just us and whatever we want to do. We'll be on our own schedule. No one else's."

"Just us?"

Approaching a traffic light, Julian presses on the brake, coming to a stop. As he licks his lips and curves toward me, I almost combust right there, the proximity of his mouth to mine making me want to erase the last bit of space between us and finally have a taste of what I've fantasized about since my first weekend in the Hamptons. Since he picked me up for our first dinner together. Since I first saw him from across the bar on what I thought was the worst night of my life.

"Just us," he confirms.

On a hard swallow, I slowly nod. "Okay. Just us."

"Perfect." He grins, pulling away from me. "Oh, and by the way…"

"Yes?"

"You have no idea what hearing you call me Mr. Gage does to me, Guinevere," he growls, the husky rumble hitting me deep in my core. I open my mouth, stunned, unsure how to respond to his brazen flirting. Thankfully, the light turns green and he puts the car back into gear, following the flow of traffic.

I blow out a long breath, smoothing a ringlet behind my ear as I squeeze my legs together, praying he doesn't pick up on how on edge I am. If he does, he doesn't say anything.

When we walk into Julian's house after an uneventful drive, it's unusually quiet. Normally the foyer is bathed with light, heavenly aromas of whatever Camille has prepared for me to eat upon my arrival meeting me. Now it appears like a ghost town.

"Where is everyone?"

"I gave them the weekend off," he explains as he heads toward the stairs.

"You did?"

"Yes."

"When did you do that?"

"When you dozed off on the drive."

"I'm sorry. I'm a horrible fake girlfriend. I've just been really tired lately, and—"

"Has anyone told you how adorable you are when you snore?" He continues up the stairs and down the corridor leading to the wing where our bedrooms are located.

"I do *not* snore."

"You do. Don't worry," he adds quickly. "It's not this big, gravelly snore that makes me worry you're about to keel over and die. It's this little snore, almost like a whistle."

"A whistle?"

"Yes. A whistle. Music to my ears, baby doll."

When we reach the door to what's become my room,

he doesn't stop, continuing toward his, leaving me confused. Every other weekend, there's been an itinerary full of events for us to attend. Without that, I'm uncertain what to do, how to act, who to be.

"Julian?" I call out. He spins around, arching a brow. "What are we doing?"

"You wanted a bit of sun and sand. Go put on a swimsuit. I'm taking you out on my boat."

I chew on my lower lip. "I'm not sure I have one for this weekend. This wasn't on the itinerary, so I doubt Dana set one aside. There are a few outfits in case of emergency, but I didn't see an extra bathing suit."

"Just put on one you've already worn. If I can make a suggestion…" He grins a devious smile. "That two-piece you wore your first day here was…" His eyes harden as his pupils dilate, the vein in his neck throbbing.

"Yes?" I bat my lashes.

"Hot, Guinevere. It was fucking hot."

Chapter Twenty-Six

"HOLY CRAP," I moan as I revel in the flavors dancing on my tongue. Garlic. Butter. The spiciness from the bold cabernet Julian opened to complement our meal.

"Why do you sound so surprised?" he replies in a smooth voice, smirking as he raises his wine glass and takes a sip, swirling the liquid around his mouth. His eyes never leave me as I indulge in his exquisitely prepared dinner. I sense he likes watching me enjoy the fruits of his labor.

"I never pegged you for the type who could cook." I tear my gaze from his, looking at the darkened ocean from the small bistro table on the patio overlooking the pool where we currently dine. The breeze wraps around my skin that's sun-kissed after spending several hours relaxing and reading on the deck of Julian's boat. But any chill that would normally find me is chased away by the fire pit.

Everything about today has been perfect. For the first time since we began this charade, it felt authentic, like we were a real couple enjoying each other's company instead of putting on a show for everyone. He took me out on his boat, then let me drive one of his cars into the downtown area, where we indulged in ice cream. Seeing a farmer's market, we stopped and picked up the steaks we're currently savoring.

"Especially this well," I add as I slice into the filet mignon once more, the preparation rivaling that of any steak I've had in recent memory.

"I guess there's a lot about me you don't know."

"There certainly is, Mr. Gage. So why don't you tell me something else most people don't know about you."

After a moment of contemplation, he shakes his head. "You first."

I lift my brows. "Me first?"

"Precisely. You just learned I enjoy cooking. I want to know something interesting about you, Miss Fitzgerald."

"Okay." I adjust my posture, squaring my shoulders. "What would you like to know?"

He pinches his chin, studying me. "What would you like to tell me? What are your likes, dislikes, hobbies, stuff like that?"

"I enjoy saying 'You're welcome' loudly when someone doesn't say thank you."

Julian bursts out laughing. "I'd love to be around to see that. But how about something serious?"

"That is serious."

Not saying a word, he narrows his eyes.

"Fine." I push out a breath. "I speak four languages."

"Is that right? And here I was trying to impress you with my knowledge of French. Which do you speak?"

"English."

"Obviously."

"But I'm also fluent in profanity, sarcasm, and pirate."

He chuckles, but it quickly fades, his expression contemplative. "Why do you do that?"

"Do what?"

263

"Use humor as a mask."

I blink repeatedly, his words surprising me. "I don't use humor as a mask," I insist as I avert my gaze.

"You do. Over the summer, I've picked up on that. Anytime we broach a subject you're uncomfortable with, you make a joke. Granted, I think your sense of humor is incredibly sexy, but I often wonder what you're hiding, what skeletons lurk in your closet to cause this uncertainty or apprehension."

"There are no skeletons in my closet."

"Everyone has skeletons."

"Do you?"

Julian's jaw hardens, his stare becoming distant. I'm reminded of the scars on his abdomen, of Camille's warning that there's a darkness hanging over him. I've seen it firsthand. One minute, things will be great. Better than great. Then something happens to force him to withdraw into himself.

"I do," he finally says, surprising me. I expected him to avoid the question. "Like I said. Everyone has skeletons."

"Well, I don't." I stab one of my brussels sprouts with my fork, bringing it to my mouth. "I had the perfect life. My parents are still married and live in the same town. Dad was my high school principal and Mom's an Honors English teacher in the next town."

"Siblings?"

"An older brother."

"And what is it he does?"

"He's an English professor at the University of Nebraska."

"And you studied English, as well, didn't you?"

264

"Yes."

"But you're not a teacher. Excuse me for saying, but it appears as though that's the normal track, at least in your family."

"That's true, but——"

"But you didn't want to teach, did you?"

I shake my head as a small smile forms on my lips. "That was *their* dream for me, not mine."

"Then tell me…" He leans back in the chair, his eyes bemused. "What is Guinevere Fitzgerald's dream?"

"This conversation feels awfully one-sided."

"How so?"

"You're giving me the third degree, yet you don't have to answer my questions?"

"You can find anything you'd like to know about me on the Internet. The same doesn't go for you."

"Not everything…," I draw out, but he ignores my comment.

"So tell me your dreams, baby doll."

When he uses such an endearing term, I'm cast under his spell, opening like a flower, urged to spill my secrets, hopes, frustrations, things I never even shared with Trevor, mainly because I didn't want him to worry about my problems when he had his own worries with college, law school, and his career.

I've often told my readers that relationships aren't fifty-fifty. Sometimes you have to do a little more heavy lifting to help your partner through a difficult time, just like they'll have to do the same for you. It's more like a see-saw. There are ups and downs, but it eventually evens out.

It was never really even with Trevor. I was always the

one using all my weight to lift him up, sacrificing my dreams so he could achieve his own. I deserve better than that. Now, thanks to Julian, I realize that. This makes me want to share things I've kept inside.

"Ever since I was a little girl, I've dreamt of being a writer," I say finally. "That's all I wanted. I remember sneaking into my parents' room and stealing one of my mother's romance novels when I was only twelve or thirteen. I'd hide away in my room and devour it in hours. That's when I fell in love with…love. And unrealistic expectations." Laughing at how naïve I was back then, I look at the ocean waves with an unfocused gaze. When I sense the heat of his stare on me, I return my attention to my dinner, taking a bite of my steak before I continue.

"Sure, I read the classics, like any person who loves the written word. But like my mother, sometimes you want the fantasy, too. Although I don't think I realized it was just a fantasy. So, being the planner I am, I made a list of who my dream man would be. I pictured it all in my head. I'd meet the love of my life in college when I was old enough to have some experience, but young enough that we'd both come into adulthood together. We wouldn't rush into getting married right after graduation, as I researched the statistics and the success rate of marriages increase as you near thirty. He'd be a professional of some sort. A doctor…"

Julian lifts a brow. "Or lawyer…"

"Yes. Or a lawyer. We'd spend our twenties finding out who we are individually and as a couple, as we'd both navigate our chosen career paths."

"And what would your chosen career path be? In this plan you made for your life, I mean."

"I always wanted to write for a magazine. Being a

writer is often considered a lonely profession, and it is. I love the idea of being part of a team, so that's why I wanted to go the magazine route."

"Then why didn't you study journalism?"

"I did my research. Many of the columnists at the top magazines had non-journalism degrees — English, political science, art design. So I studied English, despite my parents insisting I study education with an emphasis in English, if only to have it as an option in case things didn't work out. For a while after graduation, I thought maybe I should have taken their advice. I moved out to New York. Yes, it was to be near Trevor, but also to be in New York, where so many magazine offices are located. I had so much hope and drive those first few months...until I realized how difficult it was to crack into the industry. They were all looking for someone with experience. I had none, apart from working on the university newspaper and magazine. It was by pure luck I even landed the job at *Blush*. When I saw the posting, Trevor told me I was crazy for applying since I lacked any of the qualifications. But that didn't stop me. I figured it was better to get rejected by the magazine than myself."

"If you weren't qualified, how did you get the job?"

I shrug. "By doing what it appears I do in all uncomfortable situations." I pinch my lips together, giving him a knowing look. "I made Viv laugh. I used humor in my cover letter. It caught her attention, so much so that she brought me in for a chat. She was trying to shake things up at the magazine, bring in fresh talent. So she told me to come back in a week with a piece she could run in the sex and dating column. That was when I concocted a tongue-in-cheek article about what all women should do for the first thirty days of any relationship in order to keep the guy interested. It starts out pretty innocent, but as you continue reading, you realize it's satire."

"I'm not sure I want to know what's in it."

I smirk. "You probably don't. But Viv loved it. Better yet, readers loved it. It was the most read article on the website the week it published. So Viv hired me, much to my parents' chagrin. Like Trevor, all they think I do is write about sex without any substance. So having a chance at this promotion and writing an article about something other than the best sex position for maximum pleasure is exactly what I've been searching for ever since I told my parents I didn't want to pursue teaching. But now…"

"Yes?" He places his elbows on the table, leaning toward me.

"The story's falling apart and there's nothing I can do to stop it."

"I'm sure it's not that bad."

"It's not to the level I need it to be if I want this promotion."

"This is the August Laurent piece?"

I nod. "All I have is his perspective, his side of things. It's too one-dimensional. There's no drama, no compelling reason people would want to know more about this guy. But I know there's a story there, that there's more to him than he's told me. But to figure that out, I need to talk to some of the women who've hired him. Unfortunately, he flat out refused to reveal any of their identities, even when I guaranteed their names would never be disclosed. I thought I'd try to encourage him and mentioned I'd heard the rumors of him and Sonia Moreno, asking if it were true. He never responded. It's been over a week.

"So not only is the piece complete crap, he's no longer cooperating. There's no way I can submit this story to Viv like it is and hope to be promoted. Hell, as it stands now, she won't even publish this piece as a column, let alone a feature story."

"You sure about that? There must be another way, a different angle you can take to make it compelling."

"I've tried." I push my now empty plate away. "Boy, have I tried. I've written and rewritten that article a couple dozen times. No matter what I've done, it still falls flat." I stare into space, trying to figure out a solution, but it remains out of reach. I shake off the thought, smiling at Julian, my voice brightening. "But I don't want to think about that right now. The idea that my parents were right about teaching being the best career path for me will only depress me. For the rest of the weekend, I want to pretend I'm not a complete failure."

"You're not a failure, Guinevere. You're an extremely talented writer. You just need—"

I shoot up my hand, silencing him. "Not now."

"Going to pull another Scarlett O'Hara?" He smiles slyly as the memory of the night we met fills me with warmth. We certainly have an unusual story, one most people would never believe, one you read in romance novels and fantasize about. Like I've said from the beginning…it's a real-life Cinderella story. Except this version won't end with Julian tracking me down after he finds my glass slipper. It will end when the clock strikes midnight, no matter what.

"Why, Mr. Gage…," I coo in my best Southern accent, burying the thought. Maybe he's right. Maybe I *do* use humor to mask my emotions. "That is absolutely what I plan to do. Because—"

"I know, I know. 'Tomorrow is another day.'"

When I hear Julian speak with a Southern drawl, I practically come in my chair. It's almost as beautiful as listening to him speak French. Truth is, the mere sound of his voice sets my heart aflame.

"Yes, it is."

He pushes back from the table and takes a few steps toward me, extending his hand. I eye him as my fingers link with his, standing up.

"So what would you like to do *tonight*?"

"We can always make a fashionably late appearance at whatever party's scheduled. That way, you're not sacrificing your entire weekend."

"Out of the question. This weekend is all about you. If you weren't here, what would you be doing? How did you spend most of your Friday nights before we met?"

"Usually watching a movie and being a complete couch potato."

"Then let's be couch potatoes."

I step back, brow furrowed. "Really?"

"Yes. What's so surprising about that?"

"You don't strike me as the couch potato type."

"Didn't that steak teach you?"

"Teach me what?"

Leaning toward me, his breath tickles my neck. "I'm just full of surprises."

With that, he pulls me away from the patio and into the house, despite my protests that we need to clean up. He assures me he'll take care of it later, then leads me to a part of the house I've yet to spend any meaningful time in...the theater room. It's impressive, an enormous projection screen across the far wall. About a dozen leather recliners fill the tiered setup, along with a lush sectional in the front, which is where he heads.

"What do you want to watch?" He settles into the corner of the couch, draping his arm over the back. "Name the movie and it's yours."

"Any movie at all?"

"Any movie at all," he confirms.

"Even a chick flick?" I walk toward him, sitting next to him on the couch, but leaving a few inches between us. "You'd seriously be happy watching some sappy romance?"

"Like I said, this is *your* night. If you want some sappy romance, sappy romance you shall have."

"And if I wanted to watch porn?"

His eyes grow intense as he narrows them on me. "*Do* you want to watch porn?"

"If I did?"

"Whatever Evie wants, Evie gets." The sensuality in his tone has me squirming in my seat. "What does Evie want?" He toys with a few tendrils of hair in my ponytail, the light touch sending a shiver down my spine. "What movie makes you happy?"

A slave to his touch, I say the first thing that pops into my mind. "*Breakfast at Tiffany's.*"

His mouth gradually curves into a brilliant smile. "You got it." He grabs a remote and presses a few buttons. The screen sparks to life. After sorting through a few menus, he hits play and the familiar strains to the opening measures of "Moon River" fill the room.

"We don't have to watch this if you don't want to," I say quickly, crossing my arms. "I'm sure you'd much rather watch something with big explosions and lots of

271

boobs."

Shaking his head, he wraps his arm around my shoulders, enclosing me in his embrace. "Absolutely not." He props his long legs onto the cushioned ottoman in front of us. "Actually, this is one of my favorite movies."

I tilt my head, meeting his eyes. "It is?"

"It is."

I peer into his deep blue pools. "Why is that?"

"I like the story. How even someone who didn't think she was worthy of being loved eventually found someone who did love her."

"Everyone deserves to be loved," I whisper as my gaze remains locked on his. He reaches out, brushing an errant curl behind my ear, his finger tracing the lines of my face. My heart rate increases as desire heightens deep in my core. I focus on his lips, what they must taste like. I've thought of little else the past few weeks, how much I want to kiss him, but I fear I won't be able to stop at just a kiss. I'd want more. I'd want everything he's adamantly insisted he could never offer me.

"Come on." He clears his throat, the moment breaking before it had a chance to begin. He gestures to the screen. "Watch the movie."

I peer at him for a moment longer, then shift my eyes to the movie, watching as Holly Golightly, wearing an oversized nightshirt, accessorized with an eye mask and earplugs, meets Paul Varjak. I laugh at the absurdity, reminded of my own initial meeting with Julian, how I was thrust into his life just as Holly and Paul were thrust into each other's.

I nuzzle into Julian's chest, inhaling a deep breath of his familiar scent. The first time I smelled this soothing aroma, I nearly had a heart attack, thinking I'd just had a one-night stand. Heat radiates through me as I reflect on how far we've come since the night I expelled the contents of my stomach all over my dress and his shoes.

He rests his hand on my hip, lightly tracing different patterns on the small slice of exposed skin between my tank top and maxi skirt. It relaxes me even more than Julian's mere presence does.

"I like this," I murmur, no longer worried about how he'll respond to my admission.

Leaning down, he places a soft kiss on the top of my head. "I like this, too."

That's the last thing I remember before dozing off, the gentle beating of his heart the perfect metronome to lull me to sleep.

Chapter Twenty-Seven

A SOFT SNORE rips through my slumber and I flutter my eyelids open, my surroundings unfamiliar at first. Then the day trickles back... Spending the afternoon with Julian. Having dinner with Julian. Falling asleep cocooned in Julian's warm embrace as we watched *Breakfast at Tiffany's*, where I remain. The movie still plays on the screen, but it's the final scene where Holly Golightly frantically searches for Cat in the alley, rain pouring down on her.

When she locks eyes with Paul, I lift my own to Julian, observing the gentle rise and fall of his chest as he sleeps peacefully. The sight brings a smile to my face. Despite practically living together these past several weeks, I've yet to see him sleep. I should feel like a creeper, watching him like I am, but there's something so tranquil about his expression, I can't look away. It's the most relaxed I've seen him. The darkness can't find him there, allowing his brain a moment's rest.

As the music in the movie swells, I float my eyes back to the screen as Audrey Hepburn slowly walks up to George Peppard, Cat stuffed safely in her trench coat. When they kiss, my heart expands with the emotion between them. I've seen this movie more times than I care to admit, can probably recite most of the lines from memory. But the kiss in the rain between Holly Golightly and Paul Varjak, once she finally realizes love isn't such a bad thing, is one of my favorite kisses of all time. So much passion. So much heartbreak. So much hope.

Looking back at Julian, I stare at his face, his eyes still closed, deep in slumber. His lips part with every exhale before his chest expands on a short inhale. My gaze remains transfixed on his lips, unable to look away. I've exhibited extreme restraint all summer by not kissing him, by keeping the ball firmly in my court. How much longer can I hold out?

Chloe's been pushing me to step out of my comfort zone and do something I didn't plan. Thanks to Julian, I've done just that. I haven't opened my planner once in the past two weeks, a tremendous feat for someone who usually spends several minutes of every day updating and meticulously planning out my life months in advance. Lately, I haven't given much thought to what awaits me down the road, mainly because I know what awaits me… Life without Julian. Do I really want to walk away without knowing how his lips taste? I know the answer to that. It's been evident from the beginning.

Shifting in his arms, I carefully adjust my position, my eyes unwavering as I admire him. I inch toward him and my pulse increases, my racing heart thundering in my ears. All I can do is pray my clumsiness doesn't decide to make its presence known and turn what I want to be a moment full of passion into one I'll never live down. There's no going back after this. I'm about to cross the line I insisted remain firmly drawn. But as I gaze upon Julian's breathtaking face, I realize the reason I'd kept the line firmly drawn is no longer applicable.

I've fallen for him. I've allowed him to burrow deep under my skin and into my heart. Kissing him won't change any of that, won't make it any less painful when the clock strikes midnight and I turn back into a commoner.

Resolved that this is the path we were always meant to take, I graze my lips against his. They're warm, soft, electrifying. It's the slightest hint of a touch, but it still sends a shiver through me, the dull ache that settled in me during our first meeting growing more intense and prominent. I've fantasized about this moment on more than one occasion, but nothing could have prepared me for the real thing, the fireworks in my core, the music filling my heart. If this is how I react to the mere whisper of his lips against mine, I can only imagine what would happen if we took this further.

Lost in the sensation, I almost don't realize when Julian's body tenses beneath mine, his breath hitching. I should pull back now that he's caught me stealing a kiss, but I'm physically unable to retreat. And he doesn't push me away, either. We remain in place, our lips barely touching, neither one of us moving. The meaning behind this isn't lost on either of us.

We're at a crossroads.

I can pull back, apologize, and pretend this never happened. Or I can take a risk on something new, something exhilarating that will inevitably end in heartbreak. I've spent all my adult life planning every second of every day. I allowed myself to be locked in a cage, feigning happiness in a life that made me miserable. It wasn't until Julian, until I took a leap and did something out of character, that I finally felt alive. I want more of that.

Threading my fingers through Julian's wayward locks, I press my mouth more firmly against his. With a groan, he wraps his arms around my waist, pulling me into his lap, forcing my legs on either side of him. His embrace is powerful, dominating, consuming, yet he allows me to remain in control, to decide how far to take this. There's no question that the ball's still in my court. I get the feeling that's exactly where it will stay.

I brush my tongue along his bottom lip, begging for entrance, which he's more than eager to grant me. A hand goes to the back of my head as he digs his fingers into my scalp, urging me on. Moaning, I deepen the exchange, my nerve endings stirring. He tastes of mint, wine, and something unique to Julian. A flavor I'll crave long after we say our final farewell. The way he kisses me, his tongue sweeping against mine, exploring me as if trying to imprint every tiny sensation to memory, only increases my need for more.

My fingers digging deeper into his hair, I press my body against his. But no matter how I try, I can't get as close to him as I want, as I need. Even a whisper of air between us is too much.

I circle my hips, desperate to satisfy the ache building inside, but I doubt anything can ever extinguish the fire within. Julian's kiss has sparked an inferno, one I fear will continue to burn for years to come.

I rip my lips from his, panting, pressing my hand against his chest as I struggle to catch my breath. Chests heaving in near unison, we stare at each other as if seeing one another for the first time. I try to tell myself it was just a kiss. People kiss all the time. But deep down, I know this isn't just a kiss. Not with him. Not with us.

"Does this mean I can finally kiss you now?" he asks when I don't say anything immediately.

I peer into his blue eyes, a brow raised in question. He doesn't close the distance between us, indicating this is my decision and mine alone. But it's not even a decision. Not anymore. Not after a taste.

"Yes," I breathe.

He brings a hand to my face, cupping my cheek. I fuse into the contact, closing my eyes. "Even though that's all this will ever be?"

His voice is soft and timid, almost as if he doesn't want that any more than I do. I wish I understood why he seems to deprive himself of love, of happiness. But now's not the time for that conversation.

"I don't care about that," I insist. "All I care about is this, right now." I bring my lips back to his, skimming them. I feel him harden against me. "You taught me that, Julian. You taught me it's okay to live in the moment, to stop planning for every minute of every day. And right now, in this moment, I just want to kiss you." I swallow hard, grateful he can't see the truth in my eyes. "Nothing more."

"Nothing more?"

"Nothing more," I confirm.

"Nothing more."

There's something in his voice as he repeats our promise to each other. Sadness. Remorse. A reminder. I can't quite pinpoint what it is. Before I can dissect it further, he loops his arm around my waist and flips me onto my back, hovering over me.

I'm breathless from the sudden shift, my heart rate spiking. As our eyes meet, I smile a small smile, a glow washing over me. He rests his elbow by my head, leaning toward me. Then he kisses me, fully, madly, completely, reminding me why I chose this path, why I want to live in the moment.

Because this moment is everything.

Chapter Twenty-Eight

MONDAY MORNING, I walk into the office with a smile on my face, still in the clouds from my weekend of making out with Julian. After these past few days, I doubt anything can burst my bubble. It was one of the most enjoyable weekends I can remember in recent history. It allowed me a peek into yet another side of Julian Gage...the *real* Julian Gage.

We got up to watch the sunrise over the ocean. He made me breakfast. We walked along the beach, fingers intertwined. He even took me to some local bars most of the people in his circle would never be caught dead in. We ate fish sandwiches as he shared stories of going there with Christopher during his college days. Throughout the weekend, it felt like we were a real couple, especially when he'd steal a kiss as we cooked dinner together, or lounged by the pool, or sunbathed on his boat.

By the time he dropped me off at Chloe's apartment, leaving me with a sweet goodbye kiss, I didn't think anything could dampen the high I'd been on...until I sit down at my desk and open my latest draft of the August Laurent feature and am reminded of how lackluster this story is. Julian's kisses are magical and make me feel things I never thought possible. But they can't fix this. Only I can.

So that's what I attempt to do, spending hours toiling over my notes, looking for anything that could spice up a story that should sell itself, but it still falls flat. It's nothing more than a piece about how a man went from helping a friend at a wedding to being a highly sought-after escort, empowering women who are going through a difficult breakup or divorce, making them feel beautiful again. Why? Why would a woman believe she has no other option but to hire him? And why does he do this? Why does he sacrifice having a personal life of his own to help women, help strangers?

I'm about to throw in the towel and refocus my attention on writing articles for my column when I hear a ping from my computer, indicating an incoming message. I glance at the alert on my screen, my breath hitching when I see it's from August Laurent.

Navigating toward my email program, I find the message and click on it, bracing myself for him to back out of the article altogether.

To: Evie Fitzgerald
From: August Laurent
Subject: On Second Thought...

Dear Miss Fitzgerald,

I hope this message finds you well. I'd like to apologize for my somewhat rash behavior as of late. I was quick to shoot down your request to interview some of my past clients without giving it the careful consideration it deserves. I've spent the weekend doing just that, and after reading a rough draft of the article you sent with your latest email, I'm in agreement with you. It's missing something.

Attached is a list of times and locations for four interviews I've set up between you and a few of my former clients. I hope speaking with these four women in particular will give you a greater insight into why I do what I do, more so than I've been able to provide you.

I look forward to reading a revised draft of your story upon completion of the interviews.

All the best,

A

A renewed hope builds inside me as I click on the attached document. When it pops up, I scan the contents. It's a simple one-page file, but in that one page is everything I've been searching for. I get to work, alerting Viv to this new development so she can have the proper legal documentation drawn up. Before I know it, it's past two and I'm rushing out of the office to get to my first interview.

When the cab slows to a stop in front of a five-story brownstone in the Upper West Side a few minutes before three, I crane my head, my mind reeling. I have no idea who I'm about to meet, considering the document August sent only contained places and times, no names. Based on this house, whoever I'm here to see has money…and a lot of it.

After I pay the driver, I step out of the cab, double checking the address on the bronze plate beside the door with the one August provided. It matches.

Taking a deep breath, I ascend the steps, doing my best to settle my nerves at the idea of walking into a situation I doubt anyone can properly prepare for. I press the buzzer, then smooth the lines of my dress as I listen for footsteps. After a few seconds, the door opens, revealing an older woman I estimate to be in her sixties. Her hair is short and graying, her face devoid of any heavy makeup.

"Hi, I'm Evie—"

"Yes. Yes. I'm Margaret, the housekeeper. Come in. Come in." She ushers me inside, quickly closing the door behind me and leading me through the foyer. I barely have a chance to take in the ostentatious surroundings of the late nineteenth-century home as I'm led into a small cage elevator. I can just imagine the parties the walls of this house have probably seen during its time.

"I've never seen one of these," I comment, running my finger along the intricate latticework of the screen door. "It's beautiful."

"It's the original elevator. The motor and cables have been replaced over the years, but the owner insisted the house retain its original charm. Too many people buy these homes, gut them, then design them in a style in complete contradiction to the history within. If you want sleek lines and modern furnishings, buy an apartment in Central Park West. Don't buy one of these historic homes and destroy it."

I love the passion with which she speaks. I surmise this isn't the first house she's been in charge of. Hell, just a few months ago, I wouldn't have known how to act in the presence of a housekeeper or head of household staff. Now I do. I've had the pleasure of being waited on hand and foot all summer, thanks to Julian. Although those days are numbered.

"And who exactly is the owner of this home?"

"You'll see."

"So much secrecy."

"It's for good reason." Margaret narrows her gaze on me. It's a look of warning, telling me whatever I'm about to learn will make me rethink everything, open my eyes to what's truly going on.

The elevator slows to a gradual stop on the top floor and we exit into the hallway, which is bathed in natural light. I follow Margaret toward a sunroom, then step onto a rooftop terrace.

If it weren't for the woman sitting at an outdoor patio set, I would have taken a moment to soak in the stunning views of New York City, the Hudson to the west and Central Park to the east. But as I slowly walk toward the poised woman sipping her tea, I'm speechless.

I rewind to the information Sadie shared with me at the Red, White, and Blue Gala, thinking her story about Sonia Moreno was just sensationalized gossip. Now I know it's not.

Not when I'm staring at Sonia herself.

Chapter Twenty-Nine

"SO YOU'RE GUINEVERE Fitzgerald." It's a statement, her tone showing her knowledge of me isn't tied to the article I'm writing about August Laurent, but because of my connection to the world in which she normally resides during the summer months.

"Sonia...," I breathe, momentarily dumbstruck. Her dark hair falls to her mid-back, barely a strand out of place. She wears a fitted, thigh-length black shift dress, her skin olive-toned and tanned. From what I know of her, she's around my age, but has a sophistication that makes her seem older, even if she doesn't look it. "I mean, Ms. Moreno." I reach my hand toward her and she takes it, her hold delicate. "It's wonderful to meet you."

"You, as well." A hint of her Spanish accent comes through. "Please..." She gestures to the chair across from her, indicating for me to sit down.

"Is there anything else you need, Ms. Moreno?" Margaret asks.

"We're okay for now."

"Very well. Call if anything comes up."

"Certainly." Sonia offers the woman a smile as she turns from us, then focuses her attention back on me. "Tea?" She raises the teapot.

"That would be lovely."

Lovely? I don't even sound like myself. I've never called something lovely, apart from a brief period during high school when I became obsessed with all things related to British literature. I refused to speak in anything but a British accent, which I'm sure sounded horrendous when coupled with my subtle Midwestern tone.

Sonia pours a bit of tea into a small cup, then places it on a china saucer with a floral design, handing it to me.

"I have to say," she begins as she leans back in her chair, bringing her tea to her lips, "I was quite surprised to learn August had agreed to an interview, considering how private he is."

"I've assured him I'll protect his anonymity, along with everyone else I speak with. This isn't a sensational story meant to reveal who the mysterious August Laurent is. It's simply a piece about the man, what makes him tick, why he does what he does…" I hesitate before adding, "Why women feel compelled to use his services."

"Well, now that I see you and realize who you are, it makes sense."

Her statement catches me off-guard. "Who *I* am?"

"Of course."

I shake my head, placing my cup back onto the table in front of me. "I'm not sure I follow."

"You *are* dating Julian Gage, aren't you?"

"Yes." Normally, I probably would have thought it odd that a complete stranger…a celebrity, no less…would be familiar with my personal life. But there's been nothing private about that this summer, not with all the photos of Julian and me that have graced the pages of the gossip websites.

She squints, studying me, as if attempting to put a puzzle together. Then her expression brightens. "Well, that must be why August agreed. He probably saw you with him and figured if anyone would understand, it would be someone who's been thrust into the lifestyle."

"And why is that important?" I lower my voice. "Are many of his clients from this…lifestyle?"

"You mean famous?"

"Yes."

"Some are. Some are ordinary housewives."

"And they can afford his fee?"

"What fee?"

"His fee…" My words lack the conviction I wish they had. I want to kick myself for never asking him about this. I assumed he charged. It never even crossed my mind he didn't. My curiosity only grows. Why would he do this if he wasn't getting paid?

"He doesn't ask for a single dime in return for his services."

My jaw becomes slack as I swallow hard. "He doesn't?"

"Not anymore. Yes, August Laurent was, at one time, a bona fide escort, but several years ago, it turned into something more. It's no longer about the money. It's about something bigger."

That's all it takes for me to become enthralled with this story, my mind spinning from this small piece of information, something I could have learned if I'd known to ask.

"Do you mind if I record this?" I swiftly remove my phone from my purse. "Your identity will never be revealed and the recordings never published. I just don't want to miss anything or get something wrong."

"August mentioned I'd get approval before

publication?"

"Absolutely." I retrieve a document the legal team gave me and push it across the table toward her. "Everything's stated in there. Essentially, I'll never disclose anything to anyone without your approval. Anything published in the article will be done in a way to ensure no one can connect you to this story. And you'll get approval rights. If we publish anything you disagree with, you can sue the magazine for everything it's worth."

She scans the papers, her eyes glossing over the legalese before she returns her attention to me. "Okay. You can record this."

"Thank you." I open the voice recorder app on my phone and place it on the table. I pull out my notepad to take notes of our conversation, as well. I scratch the date on the top of a fresh piece of paper, then look up at Sonia. "How did you meet August Laurent?"

She smiles, contemplating. "I think a better question might be how I met my husband."

"Your husband?"

"Yes. Had I never met Ethan Price...or, as the world knows him, Ethan Ludlow...I never would have needed August Laurent."

"Okay." A chill trickles down my spine. "How did you meet your husband?"

"It's your typical Hollywood romance. I was an actress trying to catch my big break. And Ethan was a big shot producer who could make those dreams happen. We met at a cliché party in the Hollywood Hills. The guest list included a mixture of nobodies dying to be somebodies, and somebodies who wanted to take advantage of those nobodies. I just didn't realize that then."

"Is that what happened? Did Ethan take advantage of you?"

"Not at first, no." She looks into the distance, as if recalling happier times. "He was sweet, exactly as I thought he'd be from the characters he played on the sitcom when he was a young boy. Back then, he had a reputation in Hollywood as being down-to-earth and compassionate, someone who would bend over backwards to help those he cared about. And he cared about me, a girl who left a small town in Texas to chase her dreams in Hollywood. He made those dreams come true.

"Those first few years, I was so wrapped up in everything that I missed the little signs. I made excuses, saying he was just under stress, or I shouldn't have been so friendly to one of his associates, or I should've worn a less revealing dress. I was only twenty-one when we met. He was forty-five. I figured the tension could have just been due to the age difference. Regardless, with his name attached to mine, I started getting calls for auditions. And not just crap, two-bit parts like before. These were real roles, ones that eventually made me a household name."

Instead of smiling, as one would think when telling the story of how she finally achieved everything she could have imagined, her expression falls, her lips forming a tight line as her chin trembles.

"What happened?"

"About five years ago, I was in romantic comedy where I played opposite Matthew McConaughey. It was one of the biggest hits of the year. Made millions. Before then, I was known as Ethan Ludlow's girlfriend. After that, I was simply Sonia Moreno. Worse…" Her voice becomes strained through the obvious lump in her throat. "He became known as Sonia Moreno's boyfriend."

"I take it he didn't like the blow to his ego."

She laughs slightly, crossing her legs in a practiced way that makes it appear smooth and swanlike. "He certainly did not. How would you feel if you were a child star desperately trying to stay relevant as a producer and director and your newbie girlfriend was now more popular than you ever were?" She brings her tea back to her mouth, taking a sip. I do the same, allowing her a moment to collect her thoughts.

"He increasingly grew more and more controlling, possessive, angry. I couldn't even give an interview without him having a meltdown over something I said, regardless of how meaningless it was. He found something wrong in everything, something to make him think I was being unfaithful, that I was going to leave him. I insisted I'd never leave him, that I owed him everything, that I loved him. Because I honestly thought *I* was to blame for his insecurity, I did what I thought I had to in order to fix it and assure him he was the only man I wanted.

"So the next week, we boarded a plane to Bora Bora and got married in front of our other celebrity friends. It was so different from the wedding I imagined when I was a little girl."

"Why was that?"

Her eyes light up at my question. All women love talking of their childhood fantasies. It brings us back to that time in our lives when we believed the world was our oyster.

"I'd always envisioned marrying the man of my dreams in the church in Mexico where my parents said their vows, then have a reception at this gorgeous restored farm near my grandparents' house there. Instead, our guests were Hollywood types there just to say they were. I remember having second thoughts, thinking I could just fly away and start over again, but it seemed impossible. I was too recognizable. I couldn't disappear. It was the first time I felt trapped. And that only increased over the years.

"Don't get me wrong. Ethan and I had some wonderful times, times when I did love him. There were moments he was so full of life and excitement. But as I learned, for every up, there would eventually be an even bigger down. And when that happened, it was near impossible to reason with him. He'd find something lacking with me, something that made him lose his mind. In those moments of mania, I believed that to be the case, believed I was at fault."

I lick my lips as I prepare to ask my next question. "Did he hurt you?"

She lowers her eyes, nodding slightly.

"How often?"

Blowing out a long breath, she looks up. "I lost track over the years. After a while, I could predict when it would happen. It was a cycle. Things would be great. Then he'd grow increasingly irritable. It was only a matter of time before something set him off and he'd lose all control. The next day, he'd apologize, beg for my forgiveness, promise to get help, to never drink, to make it right, and he'd be the man I remember him to be when we first met.

"This went on for years. Each cycle got increasingly shorter and more volatile. In retrospect, I should have jumped ship ages ago, but when Ethan was in a good mood, he was sweet, charming, endearing." She laughs to herself, a shimmer in her eyes. "I used to joke he could

290

charm the skin off a snake. He had this energy you wanted to be around. And when he looked at you in a way that made you think he saw no one else, well... There's nothing like that."

"I've heard a few rumors that he..."

"Cheated on me?" she finishes. "I blamed myself for that, too. *He* blamed me for it, told me if I was the type of wife he needed, he wouldn't have to seek comfort in another. I should have expected this, considering he was still married to his previous wife when we met. So I did what I could to be the perfect wife just to save some poor girl who was trying to make a name for herself in this industry from suffering the same fate I did."

My mouth grows dry at her words, a chill enveloping me. "What made you seek out August? There must have been some triggering event, something that made you say enough."

"The premier of my latest movie." With shaky hands, she places her cup back on the table. "Until then, I'd done mostly upbeat romantic comedies. But my latest film was more of a romantic drama. A very sexy romantic drama."

I nod. "I've seen it."

"Honestly, I was surprised when Ethan suggested I throw my name into the hat for the lead, but he claimed he was okay with the nudity and intimate scenes. It wouldn't be my first sex scene, but all my previous ones were lighter and more fun. When I got the part, he was thrilled for me. But after we got home from the premier, he was different...aloof, sinister. He accused me of enjoying those intimate moments too much, more than when *we* were intimate. I told him he was crazy, that I was merely acting. Things spiraled out of control, and before I could make sense of what was happening, he

291

forced himself on me, demanding I tell him he's the best lover I'd ever had."

I cover my mouth with my hand, shaking my head. I can't even begin to comprehend what she's been through. I never would have imagined it was something like this. She's been dubbed America's Sweetheart, a gorgeous woman who came from nothing and made a name for herself in an industry that's notoriously exclusive. I may have complained about Trevor's lack of attention, especially later on in our relationship, but he always treated me well, always respected me. I couldn't imagine feeling so trapped, so degraded, so worthless.

"You'd think that would have been enough for me to leave."

"It wasn't?"

She shakes her head. "No. I stayed, mainly because I believed his threats that I'd never work again, that he'd use his sphere of influence to make sure no producer or director ever hired me again. Not only did he have a long history in the movie industry, his father was Theodore Price, owner of half the world, it seemed. It didn't matter that his father had been gone several years. Ethan was still connected to many of his powerful friends. It wasn't until the Red, White, and Blue Gala in the Hamptons last summer that something changed."

"The gala?"

"Often, the household staffs from the surrounding homes work the event, as well. During the fireworks display, I politely excused myself, the weight of the lies I'd been forced to tell all night suffocating me. Every time someone else congratulated me on my latest role, all I heard were Ethan's threats, all I felt was the burn of his body covering mine as he forced himself on me, destroying my soul."

"Why didn't you go to the police?"

"I didn't think they'd believe me. Ethan had me so brainwashed that I honestly thought they'd dismiss me. I was his wife. I'm supposed to want to have sex with my husband."

"But that wasn't sex. Regardless of any marriage vows, consent is still required."

"I know that now," she says. "I knew it at the time, too. I was worried what he'd do if I said anything. Acting was all I had. I couldn't lose that."

"What happened at the gala?"

She straightens her spine. "I went to the ladies' room. It was vacant, apart from one attendant."

"Who?" I press, my gut telling me this woman might be integral to the story, someone I could potentially speak to this coming weekend.

Pulling her bottom lip between her teeth, she considers what to tell me. "I'd rather not say. I don't want to put anyone else in Ethan's line of fire, so to speak. I'd never be able to live with myself."

My shoulders fall as I blow out a breath. "I can understand that."

"After I finished washing my hands and reapplying my makeup, she stopped me. Without saying a word, she carefully lifted the flutter sleeves of my gown, revealing the bruises on my biceps from where Ethan had restrained me the previous evening during one of his rage-filled moments. I could have said we were into the rough stuff, but there was no masking the fear in my eyes. Then she withdrew a business card from her back pocket. No name. No address. Nothing. All that was on it was a phone number. She said when I was done living in fear to call it. After that evening, I left the Hamptons and

293

locked myself away, trying to figure out my next move. I didn't call until February twenty-seventh."

"Why did you wait so long?"

"I wish I had an answer," she exhales, shaking her head. "There are times I wish I could go back and shake myself, force myself to wake up, but it's not that easy. Ethan manipulated me to the point that I truly believed I'd be nothing without him, despite the fact I now had a career of my own. I never saw myself as this successful celebrity. I still saw myself as the struggling actress who would do anything just to get an audition."

"What caused you to finally call?"

A blank look crosses her face as she stares straight ahead. "A photo of me from a movie I'd shot a few months earlier appeared on the front page of some tabloid with a headline about me leaving my husband for someone younger. Ethan saw it and flipped out. He wouldn't listen to reason, didn't care that the actor was gay or that it was a scene from the movie. He pulled out a knife, brought it up to my throat, and told me the only way he'd ever allow me to leave him was in a casket.

"The following day, after he'd apologized profusely and promised yet again to seek treatment for his anger issues, I kissed him goodbye, then called the number. In a matter of hours, I was on a plane to Vancouver where I spent the next two months with August Laurent.

"What did you tell Ethan? He had to notice you were gone? Did you tell him you'd had enough?"

She pinches her lips together, slowly shaking her head. "I told him I'd just gotten a project thrown into my lap and would be on location shooting for a few months. I offered to fly him out, knowing he'd never take me up on it. Once my star got bigger than his, he balked at the idea of joining me on set."

I sit back, trying to wrap my head around the story she just shared with me. Whenever I saw Sonia and Ethan together on TV, I assumed they were the perfect couple, the one everyone aspired to be, that their love was what we all hoped to find. As with everything, appearances can be deceiving. I got my first taste of that earlier this summer when he came onto me. I figured he was just drunk. I suppose Sonia made the same excuse I did when, in reality, there's no excuse for that behavior.

"And what was your time with August like?"

"Exhilarating." The tension seems to roll off her shoulders in waves as she reflects. "He was exactly what I needed. He took care of me and made me feel beautiful, something I hadn't experienced in years. I would talk about my time with Ethan, and he wouldn't judge me for staying with him. He had a level of understanding I never expected. He showed me what a real relationship should be like, what real love should look like."

"Do you love him?"

She scrunches her brows, chewing on her lower lip. "It's an interesting question, one I've never really thought about, but I suppose you can say I do. I love how his encouragement empowered me, how he helped me realize I *do* have worth, how he gave me the strength to walk away from it all.

"You see, hiring August Laurent isn't about a fleeting physical attraction. It's more than that. It's about sharing a connection, something I hadn't had in years. He gave me that. He gave me the greatest gift anyone could. If it weren't for him, I shudder to think where I'd be right now. I wouldn't be on the brink of finally saying goodbye to my past. And it's all thanks to August Laurent's influence on me. Because now I know I have worth. Even if Ethan's threats are realized and he makes sure I never work in this industry again, he can't take away the most important thing, not anymore."

"And what's that?"

A brilliant smile forms. "My freedom."

Chapter Thirty

A HEAVINESS SETTLES in my chest as I stare at my overnight bag, packing up the few essentials I'll need for my final weekend with Julian. I'd been dreading this for weeks, especially once we kissed. Thankfully, I haven't had time to think about it too much lately. Most of my free time has been filled with interviewing other women who'd been referred to August Laurent. Every single one of them helped me view him as who he truly is — a man who used his notoriety for good. He could have continued as a traditional escort, someone women called if they needed a date for a wedding to make their ex jealous or didn't want to sit through another Christmas with family members asking why they're not married or in a serious relationship just yet. At first, that's what he did, smiling, playing the role he'd been hired to play. But then something changed. I can't help but wonder what that was.

As I grab a few of my toiletries out of my vanity, I pause when my eyes fall on a strip of photos. On our way out to Southampton last weekend, Julian made a surprise stop at Coney Island. He couldn't believe I've lived in New York for nearly ten years and had yet to go. It was exactly as I'd imagined — cheesy, dirty, obnoxious…and magical. We played carnival games and ate food I'm sure will take the rest of my life to work off.

Neither one of us wanted to leave. So much so that we

ended up being three hours late to the dinner we were scheduled to attend. That didn't seem to faze us. Nothing mattered much lately, except for being with each other. Now I'm on the brink of never seeing him again.

Despite the shift in our relationship, Julian's carried on as if it's business as usual, that he's still planning on walking away after this weekend. Two months ago, I looked forward to having my freedom back, as well as a beautiful new wardrobe. Now I'd trade all of that for just one more night, one more hour, one more minute with Julian.

Tears well in my eyes and I fall onto the bed, my throat closing up as I look to the ceiling, frustrated with myself. I'm not supposed to cry over him, not when one of the reasons he asked me to help was because I'd remain detached, because I wouldn't get emotionally invested. But I have. Regardless of what he wants me to believe, I know he has, too. How can he walk away now? How can anyone walk away after forming this kind of connection, this amazing bond? Isn't it human nature to want to pursue something like this and see where it leads?

As I consider the predicament I now find myself in, I'm reminded of August Laurent and how every single woman I've spoken to has admitted they love him. Surely after spending a month or two with these women, he must have formed feelings for them, yet he still walks away every single time. How does he keep his heart guarded? How can he leave them, knowing there's something there?

Grabbing my phone, I open my email. I may regret this, but I need words of encouragement. As much as I love Chloe and Nora, I can't talk to them about this, not when I've refused to admit I'm falling for the guy. Despite the change in me they've both picked up on, I insist there's nothing between us, that I'm still looking forward to the end of the summer. I need advice from someone who's been in my shoes. There's only one person who will understand.

> *To: August Laurent*
> *From: Evie Fitzgerald*
> *Subject: ???*
>
> *How do you do it?*

Short and to the point. I hit send, then continue packing up my things. Only a few seconds pass before my phone rings. I snap my eyes toward it, the familiar Blocked appearing on the caller ID.

"Evie Fitzgerald," I answer, although I know who it is. By now, it's become a routine with us.

"I thought we were past this, Miss Fitzgerald. Haven't you figured out by now I'm not taking advantage of vulnerable women?"

"It's not that," I respond quickly. "That's not what I'm talking about. I understand now."

"Then what is it?"

I draw in a shaky breath. "How do you do what you do and not feel like you lose a piece of yourself every few months?"

"A piece of myself?"

My chin trembles and I struggle to speak through the lump in my throat. "How do you find the strength to walk away from someone you've grown to care for?" I choke out in a strained voice, one that evidences my frustration and sadness.

There's a brief pause on the line before he speaks again. Everything about his words exude the compassion

I surmise is why women are desperate for his companionship.

"Is this line of questioning coming from somewhere…personal?"

I exhale deeply as I swipe at my eyes, erasing my tears only for new ones to fall. "Let's just say I find myself in a somewhat similar situation. Apart from the whole escort thing." I laugh slightly and look down, surprised to see the strip of photos from Coney Island clutched in my hand. I can't even remember grabbing them. My chest tightens and I swallow hard. "I agreed to help out a friend for the summer…"

"And now that summer's ending, you're having trouble walking away."

My words caught in my throat, I nod. It doesn't matter he can't see me. He knows what I'm going through. This is why I reached out to him. I *need* his reassurance that I'll get through this.

"Listen, Evie…" His tone softens, taking on a friendly, more familiar quality. Until this point, we've been fairly professional in our correspondence and discussions. This is the first time he's called me Evie, despite my insistence he do so. It's always been Miss Fitzgerald. "I never said I didn't struggle with walking away."

"Then how do you do it? How do you form this amazing connection with another person, one that makes you truly believe you're soul mates, and still leave?"

"Because I remind myself I'm there to serve a purpose."

Now his own voice trembles. It's not as prominent, but it's obvious his words are laced with emotion, proving he's not this detached machine who has no trouble

300

jumping between women. He truly does care about each one. The world needs more people like August Laurent.

"I'm there to give women the companionship they desperately need to put them on the track to what's next. Perhaps that's what you need to focus on. That whatever arrangement you had was just to get you to the next step in your life. It won't be easy. You'll find pieces of him in places you never expect, and it will knock the breath out of you. Like when a commercial you laughed over comes on the TV, especially all those pharmaceutical commercials where the side effects seem worse than the condition it's meant to treat."

I close my eyes, remembering doing the same thing with Julian just a few weeks ago. Now the tears that fall are no longer tears of sorrow but of joy, of comfort, my heart expanding.

"Or you hear a song on your playlist and remember dancing to it. Or you see a car that looks like his, only for your heart to deflate when it's not. But I assure you, the memories will eventually stop being painful, and you'll look back on this time with fondness instead of heartache. It won't happen right away. But it *will* happen."

"But—"

"My advice to you, since I'm assuming these are your last few days together?"

"Yes."

"Don't dwell on the future. Enjoy the present. Savor every last second you have together. Create more memories instead of lamenting on old ones. I promise these memories will carry you through the difficult road ahead, where you'll question everything. Everyone comes into our lives for a reason, Evie. This…friend.

Maybe he didn't come into your life to be your soul mate. Or maybe he is your soul mate, but not in the way you think. Maybe he's like Virgil guiding Dante through Hell and Purgatory, showing you who you are so you can start living."

As I hang up and continue packing my things for the last time, I do everything to follow August's advice. I try not to dwell on the idea of the sun setting on this magical summer, focusing instead on enjoying the little time I have left with Julian. Maybe he came into my life to help me realize I deserved so much more than what Trevor gave me. That I deserve to be with someone who supports my dreams, regardless of how ambitious and out of reach they may seem. Julian gave that to me. For that, I'll forever be grateful. The notion keeps the tears at bay.

Until the buzzer sounds and I step out of the building to see Julian standing on the front stoop, the car I've nicknamed Thursday, the Jaguar, idling by the curb. He looks as beautiful and captivating as when I first saw him from across a bar during what I thought to be the worst night of my life. But now that I know his inner beauty matches that on the outside, he appears even more beautiful, more captivating. It forces the ache to return, tears sliding down my cheeks.

Julian's quick to pull me into his chest, holding me tightly as my tears soak his white linen shirt. His arms comfort me at the same time they remind me this will be the last time they'll be here to do so.

"It'll be okay," he murmurs, his own voice showing signs of strain. "This was always how it was going to end. Nothing will change that. You deserve more than I can give you, Guinevere."

I lift my head and peer into his eyes. "How do you

know?"

He brings his thumbs up to my eyes, wiping at them. "It's the truth. I am not a good man. I won't bring you down with me. You deserve the sun and moon and stars." He brings his forehead to mine. "I can't give that to you."

I cup his face, relishing in the scruff of his unshaven jaw. "What if you already have?"

He swallows hard as his eyes lock with mine. I can see the internal struggle through those vibrant blue orbs, ones I've seen look at me in a way I never thought another man would. So much admiration. So much devotion. So much...love?

Before I can react, he swallows me in his embrace, crushing his lips to mine, his kiss ravenous, desperate, needy, as tears slide down my cheeks. I arch into him, returning his kiss with the same intensity, wanting to remember every groan, every circle of his hips, every swipe of his tongue before the candle is extinguished.

Chapter Thirty-One

THEY SAY TIME seems to drag when you're excited about something. The opposite is true, as well, because my final weekend with Julian flies by, time rushing when I'd love nothing more than for it to slow down.

The myriad of events I attend on Julian's arm are marked with a celebratory atmosphere reminiscent of the last days of school. I hate lying to all these people as I make plans to get together with several of them in the city. But that won't happen, not once word of our breakup gets out. I'll be back to my normal life, and my summer with Julian will be nothing but a distant memory. In my heart, I know that will never be the case. Not for me. And not for Julian. He's struggling with this, too. I can see it in his eyes as he looks upon me with a hint of longing, feel it in his arms as he holds me a little tighter, taste it in his lips as he presses them against me with a bit more desperation.

As I stare at my reflection in the full-length mirror as Camille helps zip up the stunning charcoal-colored ballgown I'm to wear to the final gala, it's bittersweet. I've kept my emotions at bay all weekend in front of everyone, only allowing Julian to see them in the hopes he'd change his mind. Now that it's almost over, a tear escapes at the knowledge that this is it, my last night by his side. It's not about the glitz and glamor. What's killing me is never experiencing the same adoration, devotion, or affection I have this summer. Even if it's not real. In my heart, it is. It has been since the beginning.

"It'll be okay." Camille fetches a tissue and holds it out when she notices the tear sliding down my cheek. I offer her a smile as I bring it to my eyes, grateful I'd worn waterproof mascara. "He's struggling, too."

"Right," I scoff. All weekend, Julian's been his usual charming self. Yes, there's a hint of sadness surrounding him, but not enough to make a change.

"Trust me, sweetie. I've known Mr. Gage a long time. I've never seen him this...unsure."

"Then why doesn't he say something? Why does he insist he can't give me what I deserve? Who is he to make that determination?"

Camille clasps my hands in hers as she leads me toward the sitting area, both of us lowering ourselves onto the couch. "Did you know that Mr. Gage spent his younger years in the foster care system?"

Swallowing hard, I shake my head. After those first few days, I tried to steer clear of all articles about him, mainly because I was mentioned in a lot of them. The last thing I wanted was to read gossip about myself, something Julian had warned me against earlier in the summer.

"How did he end up there?" I lower my voice. "Does it have something to do with the scars?"

She pinches her lips in contemplation. "That's not my story to tell, but being in the foster system can change you. The system failed him, didn't get him the help he needed after what he went through... Didn't give him the *love* he needed. That boy spent his most impressionable years desperate for love, only to never have it bestowed on him. It's my belief he gave up and decided he's undeserving of love."

I stare straight ahead, absorbing her words. Julian never spoke of his childhood much. Whenever I asked, he closed up, saying it was unimportant. Now I understand why. The scars have never fully healed. Physically *and* emotionally.

"Maybe if you show him he's deserving of love, if you tell him how much you love him—"

Whipping my eyes toward hers, I inhale a sharp breath. "I never said I loved him."

She pats my hand affectionately. "You didn't have to. It's written all over you, dear. You love that man, probably more than you've loved any other person in your life."

"I—"

"And he loves you, but refuses to admit it…to himself or anyone else. Yes, he's a grown man, but at times, he's still that lost little boy desperate for even the slightest show of love, the one who cries himself to sleep because he doesn't think he deserves to be loved. Prove him wrong. Show him he is." She holds my gaze a moment longer, her eyes pleading with me to love Julian like he deserves. *Do* I love him? I don't want to admit the answer. It will only make tonight more difficult than it already is.

"Come on, Cinderella. Let's get you to the ball," she says, ripping me out of my thoughts.

"Except Prince Charming won't be hunting me down afterward to see if the glass slipper fits."

"Cinderella didn't think that would happen, either, but that didn't stop her from enjoying herself. Don't let the knowledge of what tomorrow brings stop you."

With a nod, I silently follow her out of my room,

walking this path for the final time. Earlier in the summer, I'd given myself the same pep talk Camille just did. It was easier then, back when we still had time.

As I round the corner into the formal living room, my Christian Louboutin heels clicking on the wood flooring, a figure in a black tuxedo turns from peering out the windows, Julian's gaze settling on me. On a hard swallow, I blink back a new wave of tears. My throat constricts over the idea that this is the last time he'll ever look at me in amazement as he soaks in the dress Dana selected for the evening's festivities. Even when we were just scheduled to attend a casual barbecue or beach bonfire, he still had a way of admiring me as if I were bathed in priceless diamonds.

"Hey," I say with a smile, cutting through the silence.

"Guinevere…" His voice catches as he says my name. He clears his throat, taking slow steps toward me. Just like all those weeks ago, he grabs my hand in his, spinning me around to get a better view from every angle before tugging my body against his. He places his free hand on the small of my back, and I drape my arm over his shoulder, toying with a few tendrils of hair that hang over his jacket collar. We remain still for what feels like an eternity, but in reality is only a second. Our eyes lock, midnight blue to my emerald green. Neither one of us utters a single word. There's no need. In this silence, in this moment, in this space, we say everything we want to.

A low hum cuts through the quiet. It's a familiar song that will always remind me of the moment I finally succumbed to my desire and kissed him. He squeezes my hand, then leads me around the room. Unlike our first weekend together, when dancing with him felt stilted and awkward, we move with practiced grace.

Julian begins to sing the lyrics to "Moon River", husky

and deep, and it takes every bit of willpower I possess not to burst into tears. I've never truly paid attention to the words before. It was just a song that reminded me of one of my favorite movies about two drifters who were wrong for each other, but so right at the same time. Just like Julian and me. But we weren't meant to see the world together. Our rainbows' end isn't the same, and I'm not sure anything can change that.

We slow our steps as the song comes to an untimely end and we stand in place, our hands still clasped together, our bodies a breath away. If this is our last private moment together, I want to savor it. The way he holds me, admires me, cares for me.

Too soon, he releases me from his hold. "Guinevere, I…"

"Yes?" I respond, hope building in my voice.

"I…"

"Yes?" I rest my hand on his cheek, his clean-shaven skin soft against mine. I wish I knew he planned to shave. I would have loved one last kiss with his scruff scraping against my lips, jarring and bruising, yet making me feel more alive than anything else in my life. Never again. The thought rips at my heartstrings.

"I, uh…" He licks his lips, blinking rapidly. "I got you something."

"You didn't have to get me anything." I drop my hold on him. "You already bought me a wardrobe that could probably pay for the first year's rent at the apartment of my choosing in the city," I joke.

"You're not going to sell it, are you?" he asks frantically. "Because if that's what it takes for you to afford your own place, I'll buy you an apartment. I—"

"It's a lovely gesture," I interrupt. "But not necessary.

308

Now that I've had the opportunity to revamp my piece on August Laurent, at least I have a decent shot at that promotion. It'll be nice to have my own bathroom again."

"And a door."

"Yes. And a door," I laugh, grateful for the short reprieve of tension. "It's amazing how we take those little things for granted until we no longer have them. I'll never take doors for granted again."

He smiles, but it doesn't reach his eyes.

"So..."

"Right." He spins, heading toward the wet bar. After retrieving a square white box, he walks back to me with a smile on his lips. "This is for you."

"What is it?" Taking it from his outstretched hand, I feel the weight, knowing it must contain more than just a t-shirt, as the size of the box would normally indicate.

"Open it."

Eyeing him suspiciously, my heart thumps in my chest. With trembling fingers, I pull at the red ribbon. When I lift the cover, I gasp at what I see inside. It's another box, but that's not what surprises me. It's the Tiffany's blue shade that steals my breath.

"I was planning on getting you something from Cartier, but I figured Tiffany's would have more meaning."

"It could be an empty box and it would be infinitely better than even the most expensive piece you could get from Cartier," I gush.

"Phew," he exhales, swiping at his brow. "That's a relief, because it really is just an empty box."

Laughing, I shake my head and pull out the square blue box, placing the other one on a nearby table. "No, it's not."

"You're right." His expression turns serious, his eyes trained on me. "It's not," he admits in a soft voice. "Open it."

I hold his gaze for a moment, then shift it to the box. Butterflies flap their relentless wings in my stomach as I slowly raise the lid. When I set my eyes on what's contained within, all the wind is knocked from my lungs. An exact replica of the necklace Audrey Hepburn's character admires during the scene when she takes Paul to Tiffany's for the first time. The light reflects against the stunning yellow-colored diamond in the center, the intricate latticework of diamonds along the neckline like a vine surrounding a lone flower.

"Julian…" I cover my mouth with my hand, speechless.

This isn't the first piece of jewelry he's purchased for me. I have an entire jewelry box in the dressing room filled with pieces to accent the various outfits I've worn over the course of the summer. This one is different. It's something he's given to me because he wanted to, not as a complement to my wardrobe.

"Now I know why Camille insisted I not wear the necklace Dana had paired with this dress."

He grins a devious smile. "It's good to have her on my side." He winks, then extends his hand toward the box. "May I?"

I remain motionless as he takes it. He removes the stunning necklace, then stands behind me. I catch a glimpse of my reflection in a mirror hanging over the fireplace, watching as he brings it to my neck, securing it. When he's finished, his hands stay on my shoulders. I touch my fingers to the stones. I've never worn such a weighty piece of jewelry in my life.

"Wow," I murmur. "I'm not sure I want to know how much this cost, or how many carats I'm currently wearing around my neck."

"The large stone is a forty-carat yellow diamond. A rarity. Ten carats in white diamonds accent the neckline."

"So fifty carats worth of stones." My breathing becomes labored as I try to grasp onto the concept. "*Please* don't tell me what this cost you."

"It's not about the money. Not to me—"

"Because you have money."

"All the more reason for me to do this for you, to give you something to show how appreciative I am for everything you've done for me this summer. This is the least I could do."

I practically choke on my saliva. "I could understand giving me a Starbuck's gift card or something, but this?" I spin around to face him. "I don't feel right accepting."

"You will accept it." He grabs my hands in his, bringing them to his lips. He places a gentle kiss on each. "Please. Let me do this for you. Let me give you something to remember our time together."

"I'll never forget." I lock eyes with him, silently pleading for him to acknowledge that our time together doesn't have to end, that *we* don't have to end. Why should it have to? Why should we walk away from each other because the summer's over? Yes, that was the original plan — an end date so I could have my life back, so I could *plan* the rest of my life. Now I want nothing more than to deviate from the plan, to throw the planner out the window and see where this could take us.

"It doesn't have to end," I say, one last attempt as I

touch my mouth to his. He kisses me softly, gently, but in his tenderness is more emotion than any of Trevor's kisses could even hope to contain.

"It does, Guinevere. You deserve to be happy." He pulls back, his fingers digging into the skin of my cheeks as he cups my face. "I can't give that to you. I can't give you more than this."

I've heard the same thing all weekend whenever my emotions got the better of me in his presence. I want to push it more, but not at the risk of marring our last few hours together. Instead, I simply nod, my lips finding his once more.

The sound of the ocean waves fills the room from the open windows and we melt into each other, our kiss passionate, yet restrained, two words that describe Julian Gage perfectly. Despite how much I can tell he wants me, he'll never admit it. To me, or himself.

When he pulls away, a hint of moisture dots his own eyes. "We'll always have Tiffany's."

I pull my lips between my teeth as I struggle to swallow through the pain in my throat. "We'll always have Tiffany's."

~~~~~~~~~~

The Farewell Gala is exactly as I expect it to be — filled with glamour, pretension, and bravado, yet another display of extreme wealth amongst the country's upper crust. But tonight, as opposed to the previous few weeks, Julian doesn't leave my side to talk business with someone interested in investing in his project. Whenever anyone approaches, he requests they reach out to his assistant to set up a time for a meeting or a phone conference when he returns to the city on Tuesday.

The entire evening, he's the perfect date, doting on me, making sure I have everything I need. More than once, part of me considers the possibility he's acting like this because Ethan Ludlow seems to circle like a hawk, although to anyone else, he's no more harmful than a parrot. Not to me, not after the story Sonia shared. And not to Julian, either. Despite that, I truly believe he stays with me because he doesn't want to waste a second of the little time we have left.

Before I know it, Julian and I are dancing to the final song of the night, then saying our goodbyes to the friends I've made over the summer, some of them women who turned their noses up at me during that first pool party. It's amazing how much can change in just a few months.

After a silent limo ride back to Julian's house, we head through the dimly-lit living room and toward the staircase for the last time. His hand finds mine, our fingers interlocking as we walk those final steps toward my room. When we reach the door, he drops his hold, turning to face me. Our eyes meet, neither one of us saying a single word.

I've been dreading this for weeks. It's not just good night. This is goodbye. I'd insisted it be a term of our arrangement. As did Julian. A clean break.

There's nothing clean about this.

I open my mouth, about to make one final plea for him to reconsider his position, that he *can* give me what he believes I deserve, but before I have a chance, his lips are on mine, stealing my words. His touch is so light, it's akin to kissing a ghost. And tomorrow, that's precisely what Julian Gage will be.

Desperation takes over and I wrap my arms around him, curving my body into his as I deepen the kiss. He's more than eager to match my intensity, pressing me

313

against the wall. He kisses me as if he needs it to breathe, as if his lips were made just for mine, as if it's the last time he'll ever taste me. Because it is.

He releases his hold on my face, his hands traveling down my frame, exploring, needing, wanting. When he brushes against my breast, I moan as he hardens, grinding against me. There's so much longing, so much yearning, so much despair in this kiss, electrifying and satisfying me in a way I fear no one else will ever be able to do. Pulling him closer, I claw at his back, drawing everything out of him I possibly can. And I give him everything I have. My devotion. My respect. My love. I don't need to tell him exactly how I feel. I show it in the way I worship him, hold him, cherish him.

He moves his lips from mine, kissing a hot trail along my jawline, his hands teasing and torturing as he tries to imprint everything about me to his memory. I throw back my head, savoring in the warmth of his mouth on my skin as he nibbles on my neck. Our heavy breathing fills the hallway, my heart racing. Regardless of what tomorrow may bring, I know one thing... I need this man. His kisses. His touch. His soul.

My fingers thread into his thick hair, tugging as his mouth journeys along my collarbone, his hand squeezing my breast. With my body pressed against the wall, I hook a leg around his waist, gently thrusting against him, urging him to continue, telling him I'm ready for whatever he's willing to give.

Eventually, his lips find mine again. At first, the kiss is impassioned and animalistic, but transitions into something...different. It's full of pain and heartache as his tongue sweeps against mine, slow and measured.

When he pulls back, he stares at me with a haunted look, as if on the verge of telling me something but can't seem to form the words. It reminds me of the same tortured expression in his eyes my first night in this house.

And just like that night, instead of saying a single word, he drops his hold on me and retreats with quick steps, disappearing into his room before I have a chance to whisper "goodbye".

Chapter Thirty-Two

I STARE AT the bright moon over the ocean as I lay awake in bed, sleep evading me. Since my first night here, I've slept well, the room designed to emphasize maximum comfort and relaxation. Tonight, nothing can get my brain to shut off, not when I wonder if I blew it with Julian. What if I'd made one final plea for him to reconsider? Would it have changed anything?

I'll never know.

Feeling like the walls of this luxurious bedroom are suffocating me, I throw the covers off and my feet find the cool floor. I grab my silk kimono robe off the bed post and toss it over my tank top and sleep shorts, securing it around my waist. When I open the French doors and step onto the balcony, I inhale a long breath. The ocean breeze kisses my skin as I walk toward the ledge, leaning my arms on it. It's so tranquil and serene, the sound of the waves soothing the fire and indecision within.

As I smooth a few tendrils of hair behind my ear, I spy a figure standing at the end of the deck, staring at me. My breath hitches and my body shoots upright. His eyes, bloodshot and tired, find mine. It's clear Julian hasn't been able to sleep, either.

He pushes himself away from the ledge, walking toward me with slow steps, a heat in his gaze. Hungry. Ravenous. Desperate. I straighten my spine, facing him, the tension between us mounting with every inch he erases. When he's a breath away, he stops, his expression wrought with turmoil. It's reminiscent of the indecision covering his face earlier tonight when he left me in the hallway. I worry the same thing will happen, that he'll retreat instead of push forward. I can't let that happen.

Without saying a word, I reach for the sash of my robe, pulling at it, allowing the material to fall to my feet. A chill washes over me as the breeze wraps around my exposed skin, but the raw need covering Julian's expression chases it away, empowering me. Finding the hem of my tank, I pull it over my head, leaving me in just my shorts.

He sucks in a breath, his eyes breaking from mine as they rake over my chest. This is a bold and rash move, especially for me. I've never had to put it all on the line and risk rejection. But this is the eleventh hour. There's no tomorrow, not if I don't take a leap.

When he returns his gaze to mine, there's something unfamiliar in it. It's more than lust or desire. He's not ready for me to walk out of his life any more than I am. But is that enough for him to ask me to stay? Or will the demons that still haunt him return, forcing him to withdraw back into himself?

I don't have a chance to think about it as he tugs my body to his, his mouth covering mine. His kiss is fevered, intense, wild. He seems to feed on me, needing me for sustenance. He breathes into me, causing a flutter in my chest. His hands shift to my ass and he squeezes, his raspy groan satisfying and electrifying. When he lifts and places me on the ledge, my legs wrap around his waist, his fingers digging into my skin. Desperate to feel every inch of him, I kiss him with more force, pulsing my hips against him. It feels like we've done this dance thousands of times before, our bodies in tune with each other so perfectly, so succinctly. A growl rips from his throat and

317

his grip on me tightens. Before I can make sense of what's happening, we're moving, his lips never straying from mine as he carries me into my room.

Once he deposits me onto the bed, he leans back, peering at me, a question in his unwavering gaze. Not a single word has been spoken between us since we left the gala. We don't need them. After spending this amount of time together, we can read each other. We started out as strangers and became so much more than simply friends. I struggle to see a world without Julian in it.

I don't *want* to know a world without Julian in it.

As I nod in silent confirmation that this is what I want, I grab the back of his head, capturing his lips once more. When our tongues meet, he moans, and I hook my legs around him. Moisture pools between my thighs as I squeeze them, desperate for Julian to extinguish the flames he sparked months ago.

His mouth moves from mine, traveling along my jawline, nibbling on my earlobe before beginning the journey down the rest of my body. He takes his time to worship every inch of me, every curve, every dip, every valley, feasting on me as if I'm the finest delicacy known to man.

When his tongue swirls around my nipple, I fist the sheet in my hands, lightheaded. But that's nothing compared to the immense pleasure shooting through me when his teeth scrape against the sensitive flesh. My breathing increases, my pulse skyrocketing. Unmatched need fills me and I close my eyes, thrusting against him with increased urgency.

"Patience," he finally says. "I want this to last."

Taking several deep breaths, I try to slow my racing heart. But he's already struck the match. He did so the night I first saw him at the bar in Manhattan. All summer, he's fueled the flames to the point where I'm now ready to combust.

He returns his mouth to my nipple, sucking before continuing his exploration of my body. Every nip, every scrape, every lick pushes me higher and higher. When he reaches my hips, he hooks his fingers into the waistband of my shorts. A single brow arched, he peers up at me. I nod quickly, lifting my ass off the bed, desperate for him to hurry. With a sly grin, he leisurely lowers my shorts and underwear down my legs, tossing them to the floor, then settles between my thighs. Not a single self-conscious thought fills my mind as he seems to admire me from this vantage point, like a man who's been starved for too long.

He gradually breaks his gaze from mine and licks his lips. Every muscle in my body tightens as I hold my breath, waiting for the warmth of his mouth on my most sensitive spot. I've spent the summer in a perpetual state of heightened arousal. I fear all it will take is the slightest swipe of his tongue for me to shatter.

I close my eyes, gripping the sheets even tighter, my core clenching in anticipation. Finally, he presses his tongue against me, and I moan, relaxing my body as I lose myself in this sensation of bliss I've only fantasized about. I do everything to prolong it, but it's impossible. The past two months have been one big buildup to this moment. Now I regret what I've deprived myself of to keep my heart guarded, when Julian was able to burst through those walls without even a brush of his finger against my skin. In my heart, I know this was the path we were meant to take. We were meant to wait until this moment to experience this mind-blowing passion neither one of us believed possible...until now.

My breath quickens as that familiar sensation of warmth and ecstasy fills me, the peak in sight. As if able to read me like a book, Julian increases his motion, filling me with a finger, then another, pushing me to the brink until I succumb to his touch, convulsing around him. But that doesn't make him stop. He continues worshiping me until the last of my tremors cease.

As he crawls up my body, a smirk on his lips, I grab his face, crushing my mouth against his. The taste of me on his tongue reignites the flame and I'm instantly desperate for more of him, for all of him.

"I need you," I plead in a throaty voice, frantic and delirious.

He simply nods, pushing his shorts down his legs. As he's about to toss them to the floor, he reaches into one of the pockets, retrieving a foil packet.

"I was standing out there for over an hour before you walked onto the balcony," he answers the question written on my face.

"So this was your plan all along?" I ask coyly.

He releases a short laugh. "I don't think anything about this was ever planned, Guinevere." I smile at how true his words ring. Nothing about this summer went according to my original plan. Maybe that's the beauty of it. Because it was completely unexpected in the most satisfying of ways.

He touches his lips back to mine, treating me to a soft kiss. "I never planned this." His voice is contemplative.

"Me, either."

"Now I can't think of anything I want more."

"Me, either," I repeat, running my fingers through his hair and down his back, relishing in the feel of his skin. He briefly closes his eyes, melting into my touch, arching his back before returning to a kneeling position. He secures the condom, then positions himself between my thighs. I swallow hard, this moment bigger than I ever thought it would be.

Julian arches a brow, silently asking if this is what I truly want. I nod once more. He pushes into me, slowly, deeply, completely. My body fuses to the mattress as a sensation of absolute fulfillment washes over me. He leans down, cupping my face in his hands. His eyes sear mine as he moves so reverently inside me, taking me by surprise. I expected sex with Julian to be...different. Less emotional, less passionate, less...intimate. But this isn't sex. Not with him. Not with us. It would never be just sex.

I move with the steady rhythm he sets, relishing in every gentle thrust as he fills me to the brim, stretching me in a way no man ever has, then pulls back before continuing the same pattern. Neither one of us speaks a single word. There's no need, no requirement to fill the vacant space with declarations of lust or desire. The silence is more striking, the unspoken words more poignant than insignificant ramblings just to make it seem as if we're in the moment. Because we both know we're there, that we've finally made it to this place we fought against for too long. No more.

Julian rolls his hips into me, his motions measured and penetrating, delivering the utmost pleasure. As he nuzzles the crook of my neck, he finds my arms, pinning them on either side of my head.

"I don't know how much longer I can hold back." His voice is strained.

"It's okay." I wrap my legs tighter around his waist, circling him. "Let go," I whisper, taking his earlobe between my teeth, nibbling on it. That's all it takes for his muscles to tighten, his harsh grip on my wrists painful, yet satisfying. As his movements become increasingly more intense, I close my eyes, my core clenching as another wave of desire washes over me, much to my surprise.

"Don't fight it," he murmurs into my ear, his own breathing labored. "Just let go."

He drives into me with even more ferocity and I scream out, shattering around him as explosions of light obscure my vision. His mouth clamps onto my neck as he finds his own release, his body trembling and jerking. He thrusts one final time, then loosens his grip on my wrists, collapsing on top of me, spent and sated.

My fingers drift up and down his back, savoring the grooves of his tattoo, toying with his hair as I try to calm my breathing. I stare at the ceiling, everything seeming different now.

"Wow," Julian exhales, struggling to catch his breath just like me.

I laugh. "You can say that again."

He rolls off me and stands, removing the condom and tossing it into the trash bin next to the nightstand before crawling back into bed, draping the duvet over our bodies. His arms wrap around me and I blow out a contented sigh.

But I still don't know what this means for us, if this changes anything. I open my mouth, about to ask, when Julian places a soft kiss on my shoulder blade, tightening his hold on me.

"Shh," he soothes. "I'll be right here when you wake up. I'm not going anywhere."

All the tension immediately leaves my body as I melt into his embrace, his promise filling me with hope.

Chapter Thirty-Three

THE MELODY OF the lapping ocean waves and Julian's gentle breathing meet my ears as I slowly rouse from a restful sleep. The sun shines in the room as seagulls squawk, the sheer curtains blowing near the open French doors we never shut last night in the frenzy of finally experiencing each other. And experience each other we did. At least four times.

Sensing I'm awake, Julian traces a delicate circle around my hipbone. I moan, relaxing into his touch as he stirs my desire once more. I flip over to face him and place gentle kisses on his chest. He's so warm. So virile. So...perfect.

He grabs my chin, tilting my head back and leaning down to kiss me. I tear away, covering my mouth with my hand.

He cocks a brow. "What is it?"

"Morning breath," I say from behind my hand. "No one likes morning breath."

He chuckles, the rumble hitting me deep in my core. He wraps his arms around me, bringing me closer into his body, the heat coming off him electrifying.

"I like morning breath."

"Then you're weirder than I thought."

"Nah. I'm just weird for you." He grabs my chin once more. When he leans in for a kiss this time, I don't hide, his mouth touching mine. "Mmm," he moans, tongue tracing along my lower lip, coaxing me open. A slave to whatever he wants, I part my lips, our tongues meeting in a gentle dance.

I hook my leg over his waist, inching as close as I can. As our kiss becomes more heated, his hold on me tightens and he brings my body on top of his. Straddling him, my hips circle a slow rhythm against him. He groans as he hardens even more, craving me as much as I hunger for him.

"Do you feel what you do to me?" He grips the back of my neck, fierce, jarring, intoxicating.

"Yes." I close my eyes, continuing to tease him.

"Do you want me?" His hands find my waist, controlling my motions as he thrusts against me.

"God, yes."

That's all he needs to hear. He reaches for the nightstand, grabbing the last condom. He's about to open the packet when I rip it from his hands. Passing him a flirtatious grin, I tear it open, my eyes remaining locked on his as I carefully roll the condom on him. My touch on his length causes his nostrils to flare, his jaw to clench.

Once the condom is in place, I hover over him, my mouth a whisper from his. Our breath intermingling, I lower myself onto him, taking him as deep as I can before pulling back. He brings his lips toward mine, but I escape them. I'm no longer concerned about morning breath. I like this game, the playful desperation as Julian tries to capture my mouth with a kiss, to no avail.

My motions remain slow and sensual as I savor in him. Just like he did to me the night before, I grab his wrists, pinning them on either side of his head as I shade his face with my hair. He flexes his fists, and I can tell it's killing him not to be able to touch me. I know all too well. I was in his place last night.

Our eyes linger on each other as we remain in this moment. I give Julian everything he deserves as I take everything he's willing to give me until neither one of us can take anything else and I collapse on him, both of our bodies quivering and trembling.

In the aftermath, I remain locked in his embrace, my head nuzzled into his chest as I relish in the sound of his steady heart. He delicately traces circles on my shoulder blade, my arm slung over his waist. As we lay there in solitude, my attention is drawn to the scars on his abdomen.

"What's the story behind these?" I ask as I shift my hand to the three circular marks, brushing my fingers against them.

The instant I do, he grabs my wrist in a harrowing grip. I snap my eyes to his, wincing in pain. But he doesn't relent. Something inside him snaps and he's not himself, an old defense mechanism kicking in, forcing him to become someone else.

"Don't." It's not a plea. It's a demand. A warning. The atmosphere changes as he glares at me. Gone is my charming, endearing Julian. In front of me is a broken man. A haunted man. A shattered man. His entire body seems to tremble, his stare darkening as he squeezes my wrist so hard I yelp, tears forming in the corner of my eyes.

When he hears my piercing cry, he releases his hold, his eyes widening as he stares at me in confusion, as if snapping out of whatever trance he'd been in. Then he quickly pushes away from me and jumps out of the bed. I rub my wrist, flexing it, able to discern the place where each individual finger was wrapped around it. He focuses

325

on my skin where a bruise is already forming, then looks back at me, turmoil covering his expression.

"Why don't you want to talk about your scars? What happened?" My brain tells me to retreat, to drop it, but I can't. I reach for him again, but he steps away, grabbing his shorts off the floor and yanking them on.

"I don't talk about them."

"But I want to know. I want to know this part of you. I want you to open up."

"Why?" His tone is harsh, one I've never heard him use with me, with anyone. "Why do you need to know about this? It doesn't matter."

"It *does* matter! It's a part of you. Based on your reaction, it's a big part of you. This is what people do when they care about each other. They share themselves. The good. The bad. And the gritty darkness."

He stares at me, his jaw tight, then lowers his head. "I can't do that." He avoids my eyes as he walks toward the door.

I scramble off the bed, rushing to pull on his oversized SUNY sweatshirt. When his hand touches the doorknob, I blurt out the first thing that comes to mind, the only truth I know that will make him see that whatever idea he's concocted in his head is ridiculous.

"I love you!"

He stills, his body stiffening as my declaration hangs in the air. The silence is so penetrating, you can probably hear a pin drop from a mile away. My heart thumps in my chest as he remains motionless, staring at the door.

"What did you say?" he asks in a soft voice, peering over his shoulder at me.

I advance toward him, my eyes unwavering. "I said I love you."

326

"No, you don't." He digs his fingers into his hair, yanking at it, pained at the mere notion. "You can't."

"I didn't want to believe it at first, either, but I can't avoid it anymore. I've fallen in love with you, Julian."

"No. You're just in love with the *idea* of me. None of this is real. That hasn't changed just because we slept together." He opens the door, storming away from me, but I follow him into the hallway.

"Aren't you tired of it all?" My words carry through the empty space. I can make out the typical morning sounds of the household staff cleaning and preparing breakfast, but I make no attempt to lower my voice. "Aren't you fucking exhausted of constantly running away from anything that *is* real? I know *I'm* exhausted *watching* you do everything you can to remain closed off to everyone who actually matters. Everyone who cares about you. Everyone who loves you."

He pauses, his lips curling, his fists clenched. A few weeks ago...hell, a few days ago, I would have dropped it, thinking it wasn't worth the argument. But I'm tired of this. Of him pushing me away the second I open up. I won't do it anymore.

I approach on timid steps, grateful when he doesn't try to escape. "Take it from me... It is *exhausting* pretending to be someone you're not just so you're accepted. I did it for twelve years of my life...until *you* showed me I was good enough as myself."

"This is who I am." He remains in place, but his voice lacks any conviction.

"No, it's not. I know it's not. I don't believe the Julian Gage who asked me to pretend to be his girlfriend for the summer is the real Julian Gage. I don't believe the only reason you needed me to pretend to be your girlfriend was to get your project up and running. I see how you are. You're resourceful. You already have hotels in several countries, so you know how to navigate all the bureaucratic bullshit."

He shakes his head. The more I speak, the more tension seems to mount inside of him.

"So that got me thinking. Why would you possibly want me on your arm? Then it struck me. You only did it because you thought it would help you be accepted into these people's inner circle. That's all. Not for some project, as noble a cause as it is. You just wanted them to accept you. Why? Why do you care? Why is this so important to you? Why, Julian?!"

"You wouldn't understand!" he shouts back. "You don't know what it's like being an outcast, of never being accepted!"

"So... What? You decide it's worth sacrificing happiness and who you are just so some asshole one-percenter will talk to you? That's not who you are. I know it. You're not that self-centered. I saw pieces of the real you through the cracks in your armor."

"No. No. No." He continues shaking his head, his body trembling with the force of his anger.

"That's the real Julian Gage!" I state over the lump in my throat, my voice becoming louder as relentless tears fall down my cheeks. I let them fall. At least I'm not hiding my feelings. At least I'm finally being true to myself. "Not this person standing in front of me lying through his teeth because he's too scared to admit he has feelings for someone. That, God forbid, he might just *love* someone!"

My words must have hit a sore spot because he punches his fist against the wall. The noise startles me and I jump, my heart ricocheting into my throat.

"You can't fix me, Evie!" he thunders, his eyes red as the vein in his neck strains against his skin. "No one can. So stop—"

"I don't *want* to fix you!" I scream, my chest heaving through my heavy sobs. The house has grown eerily quiet as my words seem to echo against the lifeless walls. Drawing in a deep breath, I lower my voice. "I just want to love you. Why is that so hard for you to accept?"

"Because love doesn't last," he chokes out. "The second you get a glimpse at who I really am, at all the shit I've done, you will run for the hills. So let's save each other the hassle now and cut our losses. You wanted a firm end date to our agreement. We've reached that point. It's come to an end."

"Is that truly what you want? To end it? To walk away and keep pretending to be someone else?" I look at Julian through my tears, desperate for him to admit he's never felt anything as real as he has with me.

He swallows hard, his Adam's apple bobbing up and down as the harshness in his expression softens. "This is all I know."

I hang my head low, emotionally and physically exhausted. I want to shake him out of this, to slap him and make him wake up. Will it work? Is it worth it? I don't know if I'm strong enough to pull him from the depths to which he's already fallen.

When I don't say anything else, he takes a step back. "Goodbye, Guinevere."

I float my eyes to his, not saying anything. I just stand there, studying the apprehension on Julian's face. He starts to turn from me, but hesitates, a flicker of indecision in his eyes. If this is what he wants, I'm not going to beg him to reconsider. Not anymore. I'm too drained to stay on his path of self-destruction, fighting against hurricane-force winds that will only pull me under and drown me. I won't do that to myself. I don't deserve it. Julian taught me that.

With a heavy sigh, he eventually turns from me and continues down the hallway. Just as he's about to disappear into his room where he can hide away from the world, I call out one last time.

"You were right."

He pauses, lifting his head, his eyes filled with sorrow.

"I do deserve better than you."

He nods, his shoulders falling.

"You deserve better than you, too."

I allow my words to linger for a moment, then step into my room, slamming the door behind me. Throwing myself onto my bed that still smells of Julian, I hold out hope that he'll change his mind and knock on my door.

He never does.

Chapter Thirty-Four

"**Y**OU SERIOUSLY DON'T want any of this stuff?" Izzy asks in disbelief as she sorts through hangers filled with the clothes I was treated to over the summer. "Why would you want to get rid of it?"

As much as I've wanted to share what happened between Julian and me, I couldn't bring myself to do so. Yes, my friends are aware we fooled around that first weekend, but I insisted that was the only time. I never even told them we'd kissed. And often.

When we all got together the Tuesday after Labor Day and they asked about my final weekend with Julian, I lied and said it was just like every other weekend, that I was thrilled to put the summer behind me and focus on my possible promotion. I must be a good actress because none of them questioned me, not even when my phone would ping with an incoming text and I'd jump to my feet in the hopes it was Julian apologizing for his behavior.

It never was.

Now, nearly two weeks later, I'm beginning to think I'll never hear from him again. Which is why I need to get all these clothes out of here. Not only do I have nowhere to store them in Chloe's tiny apartment, but I can't bear to look at them. Every time I do, the memories of my time with Julian come rushing back.

Like the way he looked at me the first time he saw me in that navy blue-and-white polka-dot two-piece. The way his mouth felt against mine the first time we kissed when I was wearing a beige maxi skirt and loose white tank. And the way we danced to him singing "Moon River" when I wore the stunning gray ballgown on our last night together.

"It's not my style," I say. "Take all the clothes you want. Or shoes." I gesture to another trunk filled with dozens of shoes I only wore once. "Jimmy Choo. Manolo Blahnik. Christian Louboutin."

Nora's eyes widen as she darts toward the trunk, throwing it open. "You have Christian Louboutins?" A peacefulness crosses her expression as she pulls out a pair and examines the signature red sole.

"Take them. We're the same size."

She grins dreamily. "I love you, Evie. If I swung that way, I'd totally whore myself out for you."

"I love you, too, Nora." I return her smile, although it's not as full as normal. How can it be when I'm surrounded by memories of Julian? And this is precisely why I need all this stuff out of here. I never wanted it to begin with. I purposely left them at Julian's place, but the day after I returned to Manhattan, a delivery man appeared on my doorstep. I'd hoped Julian had sent flowers to apologize for his behavior. Instead, he had the contents of my room packed up and delivered here. No note. No apology. Nothing.

"Are you sure you don't want anything?" I ask Chloe.

Standing, she gestures down her petite body. "If you haven't noticed, you're at least six inches taller than me. And have boobs. Whereas I, well... I'm lucky to fit in a B cup most days."

I nod toward a smaller trunk. "There's jewelry. And sunglasses. That stuff will fit. Check out some of that."

Chloe's hesitant at first, but her curiosity eventually gets the better of her. I lay back on my bed as I watch my friends pillage the spoils of my own war.

"You really don't want any of this stuff?" Chloe inquires yet again, a hint of skepticism in her tone.

"I really don't want any of that stuff," I confirm for what feels like the hundredth time.

"Even this?"

I glance up as she pops open the lid on the signature blue Tiffany's box, revealing the exorbitant necklace Julian gave me.

Everyone's eyes zero in on the brilliant stones encrusted in the intricate neckline, leading to an obscenely large yellow diamond.

"Holy fuck!" Nora gasps.

"Is that *real*?" Izzy asks.

Chloe lifts the necklace out of the box. Instantly, her gaze settles on a sheet of paper beneath it I hadn't noticed before.

"What is it?"

"Certificate of authenticity," she replies, reading it. "Fifty carats worth of diamonds. The stone is a forty-carat fancy vivid yellow diamond, with an additional ten carats of flawless diamonds in the neckline." She looks up, meeting my eyes. "Appraised value…one million."

I try to hide my utter shock at her words. I knew it was an expensive piece of jewelry, but I estimated maybe a hundred grand or something like that. Shows you how educated I am about the value of jewelry. But a million dollars? I can't even wrap my mind around that amount of money. Does it matter? Chloe routinely reminded me of Julian Gage's net worth during my time with him. A million dollars barely puts a dent in it. It's akin to most people buying flowers for their loved one. All Julian cared about was making an impression. He used me to do so.

"Take it. I don't want it."

My friends share a look before turning their inquisitive stares on me. They simultaneously advance toward me, sitting on the edge of my bed in concert.

"Okay. What the hell is going on?" Nora starts.

"You haven't been yourself since Labor Day," Izzy adds.

"And now you want to give me a necklace from Tiffany's worth a million dollars?" Chloe continues. "Are you out of your fucking mind, Evie? How do you even *have* a necklace worth a million dollars? I mean, the rest of this stuff is nice, maybe worth a grand here and there, but a million dollars? What aren't you telling us?"

"That she has a magic pussy," Nora jokes.

"You guys know everything," I argue, my face heating as I try to convince them the lies I've told are true. "Our entire relationship was for show. Julian needed a companion to conduct business and make deals over the summer months. And like you mentioned, Chloe, this was a great way to clear my mind and help me forget about Trevor. We'd agreed it would only last through Labor Day. It's after Labor Day, so the agreement has ended. Plain and simple. Nothing more to tell."

Chloe squints, analyzing my demeanor. I've seen that look before. The look of disbelief mixed with annoyance, the one that means she's about to unleash an interrogation worse than I'd be subjected to if arrested for murder. Thankfully, the buzzer rips through the space and she exhales, pointing a finger in my face.

"This isn't over. You're not off the hook just yet."

She jumps up from the bed and leaves to answer the door. I watch her disappear into the living room, then blow out a long breath. When I shift my eyes to Nora and Izzy, forcing a smile, they harden their glares.

"That's right, Evie." Nora pinches her lips, trying to frown.

I stifle my laugh at the idea of her being some badass bitch. She doesn't even like it when I kill spiders, preferring to set them free instead. This woman doesn't have a bitchy bone in her body. She's all about peace and tranquility, the balance of mind, body, and spirit. She is the typical yoga instructor. So to see her trying to appear angry and annoyed only causes me to giggle.

"You're not off the hook yet."

"Oh, Nora. I almost forgot!" Scrambling to my feet, I head to one of the racks and flip through the hangers, grabbing an adorable shoulder dress in a subdued tropical print. "I'd set this aside for you earlier. I thought it would be great pre-wedding wear."

She protests at first, but stops when I say wedding, allowing me to pull her off my bed. Since her engagement, I've learned discussing her upcoming nuptials to Jeremy is a surefire way to distract her. Normally, I hate discussing her wedding. Now it's my saving grace.

"Don't you think?"

Holding the dress up to her body, I spin her so she's facing the full-length mirror propped against the far wall that's surprisingly not obstructed with the array of trunks and boxes filling the space. The fire department would have a field day if they ever saw what a fire hazard it is.

"You're right!" Her voice oozes excitement as she flips the switch from suspicious friend to glowing bride-to-be. "This would be great for the rehearsal dinner! Did I tell you?"

She whirls around to face me in full wedding planning mode. I widen my eyes, feigning enthusiasm. Izzy simply laughs, fully aware this was just a diversionary tactic.

"We're doing it at a luau. Figured everyone's making the trip just for us, we should make sure they all get a taste of the islands." She leans toward me. "And there are dancing Samoans blowing fire. Maybe you can nab yourself a hot local while you're there." She winks, then turns back to the mirror.

"The only hot local I'm interested in is Jason Momoa, but I think he's already spoken for." I smile, expecting Nora to swoon with me over his tattoos, which I know she's a complete sucker for. Instead, her body becomes taut, her breath catching as her eyes widen.

I look into the mirror, wondering what could account for her sudden change in demeanor. The instant I do, my heart drops at the reflection of Julian standing in the doorway.

Chapter Thirty-Five

"GUINEVERE," JULIAN BEGINS in a shaky tone as I remain frozen in place, barely able to breathe. My mouth agape, a heaviness settles in my stomach. Ever since I walked away, I hoped for this moment. I didn't think it would actually happen. Things like this only happen in fairy tales.

When Nora squeezes my arm, I snap out of my shock, floating my gaze to her and Izzy, who both smile in encouragement. I suppose that's the thing about best friends. I don't have to tell them a single word. They'll still see the truth, despite my lies. Just like I see the truth in Julian's eyes right now...despite *his* lies.

Slowly, I turn around. The confident, self-assured man I spent my summer with is nowhere to be found. He looks like a different person, a shell, broken, defeated.

"You know what, Nora?" Chloe's voice cuts through the tension in the room. "I just realized I haven't seen any of the invitation samples you received."

"Me, either," Izzy offers.

"I thought you both didn't care which one I chose. That—"

"What kind of maid of honor would I be if I didn't give you my honest opinion on which type and style of paper will eventually end up in a landfill?"

"But I don't have them with me. I left them at my

337

apartment. You said you wanted one day where I didn't mention the 'w' word."

"Nora…," Izzy says through clenched teeth, glancing between Julian and me, urging her to put two and two together.

It takes a few seconds, but realization finally washes over her. "Oh! I get it." She winks conspiratorially, following Izzy out of the room. As she walks past Julian, she pauses, lifts herself onto her tiptoes, and leans toward him. "Good luck."

"Thanks." He laughs slightly, then refocuses his unwavering stare on me. "I have a feeling I'll need it to fix the mess I've caused."

The girls glance back at me, giving me a hopeful look before making their way out of the apartment, leaving me alone with Julian. Neither one of us moves for several long moments. I want to ask why he's here, but I keep my mouth closed, simply staring at him with a blank expression. I've already said everything I wanted to. The ball's in his court.

Anxious from the awkward tension, he shoves his hands into his pockets, tearing his eyes from mine as he takes in the disaster that is my room. With a furrowed brow, he walks past me and toward all the trunks. My lungs expand as I inhale the aroma that is quintessentially Julian, memories flooding back.

"What are you doing with all your things?"

He stops in front of a box labeled GARBAGE and reaches in, retrieving the familiar polka-dot two-piece. I've always been self-conscious about my body…until I met Julian. I'd never felt as beautiful as I did when he first saw me in that bathing suit…except it wasn't real.

"They're not mine," I say dismissively. "I have no need

for them, so I told Nora, Izzy, and Chloe to take anything they'd like before I donate what I can to a women's shelter. I figured you'd appreciate that."

He faces me, narrowing his gaze. Out of the corner of his eye, he spies the open Tiffany's box and flinches. "All of it?"

"All of it." I hold my head high, squaring my shoulders.

On a long sigh, he lowers himself onto my bed, his head hanging. I'm about to berate him for being so bold as to make himself at home when he interrupts me.

"I was in Paris this morning." He peers up at me through his long lashes, the confidence he typically wears like a shield absent. He still looks amazing in his dark suit, and smells even more sinful, but he's pale, dark circles under his eyes from an obvious lack of sleep.

"Did you come here to rub that in my face?" I press my lips in a tight line, my tone sharp. "If that's the case, mission accomplished. I've never had the luxury. I hope you enjoyed some macarons while you were there."

He shakes his head, briefly lowering his gaze. "I didn't mean it like that. You see what you do to me? You make me so…flustered."

He runs his hand through his sandy locks, tugging at them. My fingers twitch at the memory of what his hair feels like.

"I was there for work. This morning, as I went through my routine of reading the newspaper while having coffee, the TV was on as background noise, some classic movie channel. Do you know what was playing?"

I swallow hard, not saying a single word. My heart echoes in my ears as my eyes fixate on the despair and remorse hanging over him.

"*Breakfast at Tiffany's*," he says in a measured tone. "It was the final scene. You know the one when Paul finally calls out Holly Golightly for who she really is, for being scared of falling in love because she doesn't want anyone to put her in a cage?"

Tears form in my eyes as I recite one of the most poignant lines from the film. "'No matter where you run, you just end up running into yourself.'"

"Exactly." In an instant, he's on his feet, striding the short distance toward me. When he cups my cheeks in his hands, a current runs through me, my body waking after a nearly two-week slumber.

Drawing in a deep breath, he rests his forehead on mine. "I don't want to run into myself anymore. I am absolutely petrified of this, of you, of us. But I'm even more scared of not feeling this anymore."

I close my eyes, allowing his words to fill me with the hope and promise I'd been yearning for since it all came crumbling down. But is it enough? Does it change anything? How do I know it's real?

Shaking my head, I release myself from his hold. I need more than that, more than him being scared of losing me. I need…him. All the broken, damaged pieces that make up who he is.

"Thank you for finally admitting that. I can only imagine how difficult it is. But just because you're scared of losing me isn't enough reason for me to stay, not after…" I trail off.

"Guinevere…" He grabs my hands in his, pleading with me. "You have to believe me when I say I'm willing to try. For you. That's all I can give you right now. Please understand."

"I do understand." I pull away, glancing at all the

clothes he spoiled me with, all of it as artificial as he is. All glamour, no substance. "But I need more than that. Just two weeks ago, you wanted me to believe you'd never change who you are for anyone."

"I lied." He rubs his temples, his jaw clenching. "Okay? You *know* I lied, too!" He returns his impassioned gaze to mine. "You saw the truth."

"You're right. I did." I sling my purse over my shoulder, retreating from him into the living room and toward the front door. When I reach the foyer, I pause, glancing back at him standing a few feet away, looking confused. "The truth is, I don't know what to believe. You can say you made a mistake today, but how do I know it's because you truly believe it, not because you have some ulterior motive?"

"Please, Guinevere." He closes the distance between us, his chest heaving in desperation. "I want this. I want *you*. I can't function without you in my life. Nothing is right in the world. And I'm sorry I was a fool and pushed you away. I promise. I won't push you away again. Just please... Give me a chance to prove it to you."

Pulling my lips between my teeth, I consider his plea. Then I place my hand on a hip. "Okay."

"Okay?" His eyes light up as he goes to close the last bit of space between us, but I step back, holding up my hand to stop him.

"Prove it. Now. Prove you won't push me away again."

He parts his lips, his brows pulling together. "How?"

"You say you want this, that you want something real with me."

"I do." He reaches for my hands, clutching them in his. "More than I've ever wanted anything."

341

"Real relationships aren't all romantic dinners and snuggling on the couch. They require a connection, sharing yourself. *All* parts of yourself, even the ugly ones. That's what makes it real. Looking past the ugly at all the beauty hidden beneath the surface."

Julian swallows hard, his fingers growing cold as understanding of what I'm asking rolls over him. He drops his hold on me and turns from me, staring blankly into space.

"I want your ugly, Julian. It's the only way this will work. The only way I'll know you're in it for real. So I'm going to ask you one question. Whether you respond will determine whether I walk into your arms or out that door." My voice trembles as I struggle to hide the emotion at the thought of walking away from him yet again. But I can't be with someone who only allows me part of the way in. I made that mistake with Trevor. I won't do it again. "How did you get your scars?"

Julian slowly glances over his shoulder, lifting his eyes to mine. Moisture pools in the corners as he pleads with me to ask him another question...*any* other question. But I can't. This was the question that started it all. And it may be the question that ends it all, too.

I'm unable to move, my heart caught in my throat as I wait for him to finally answer me. He doesn't. Instead, he faces forward, shaking his head.

My shoulders fall as my heart deflates. "I understand," I manage to squeak out. I turn from him, heading toward the front door. I only make it a few steps when his voice stops me.

"My step-father shot me." His words are low, devoid of emotion. He speaks so softly, I'm unsure I heard him correctly.

I whirl around. "What did you say?"

"The scars." Facing me, he pulls his shirt out of his pants, lifting it and revealing the marks on his abdomen. "From my step-father."

"Why?" I return to him as he tucks his shirt back in.

He rubs the back of his neck, drawing in a pained, shaky breath. "I was trying to protect my mother." He slumps onto the couch, the truth weighing him down.

"Your mother?" I sit beside him, unable to take my gaze off his remorse-filled expression.

"It wasn't enough. He killed her. She was trying to get us away from him so he couldn't hurt us again."

I lean into the cushion, briefly closing my eyes as I put the pieces together. No wonder he used a large portion of the inheritance he received from Mr. Price to open a women's shelter. He lost his mother to domestic violence.

"The instant she slumped to the floor, all I saw was red. I charged at him. He pointed the gun at me, warning me not to do anything stupid. But I didn't care. And he was drunk. So I grabbed a knife out of the butcher block and stabbed him, but not before he got off three shots. Thankfully, a neighbor, who was a paramedic, heard and burst into the house. If he hadn't, I probably wouldn't have made it."

"And that's what landed you in foster care." I tilt my head at him, studying him.

He shoots his eyes to mine, surprised at my statement. Then he pinches the bridge of his nose, exhaling. "Camille."

"You didn't have any other family you could live with?" I press. I come from a rather large extended family. The idea that there was no one else Julian could count on boggles my mind.

"Mom was young when she got pregnant. The result of an affair with a college professor. Her parents were well-respected, affluent members of their community. They saw her pregnancy as a blemish on their reputation. When she refused to get rid of the baby, they cut her off. She raised me on her own. We were all each other had. When she died, there was no one to claim custody of me, so I was put into foster care. Since the system's so overworked, none of the foster parents wanted to deal with an adolescent boy suffering from emotional trauma. Sure, I was in therapy, but I got moved around between therapists, too."

"Julian…" I shake my head, unsure what to even say. I'd learned about pieces of his past in the research I'd done on him. I could never have anticipated this was the real story.

"I push people away, Guinevere." His eyes intensify, the blue hue becoming darker. "It's what I've always done. Actually, I've never let anyone get remotely as close as you. No one's cracked the shell. Until you came into my life." His expression softens as he leans toward me, grabbing my hand in his. "You saw through me when no one else ever could. You were right about all of it. How I acted the way I did because I was scared. I knew it was true, and I hated you for calling me out on it. Worse, I hated myself because I thought it made me appear weak."

I bring my free hand up to his cheek, reveling in the scruff. "It doesn't make you weak. It makes you human."

He covers my hand with his, my heart swelling with the longing I feel in his touch. "I understand that now. I've spent my entire life running from anything real…including love. I'm just not sure I know *how* to love."

344

"Oh…" My heart deflates as I pull my hand from his cheek. I begin to slink away, my eyes watering, but he grabs my chin, forcing my gaze to his.

"But I want you to show me how."

I part my lips, my brows furrowed. "Show you how?"

"Yes, Guinevere. I need you more than I've needed anyone." He releases his grip on me, then stands and starts to pace. "But I'm messed up. *Really* fucking messed up. I wasn't lying when I said I'd hurt you. I probably will. Just please…" He stops, dropping to his knees in front of me, his hands clasped together. "Be patient with me. I have a lot of scars, ones that will take me a while to finally share with someone after keeping them all to myself for years. But I *want* you to know all these things about me. I *want* you to know my ugly."

"That's all I want. Just you." I bring my hand to his face, brushing my thumb along his cheek. "The real Julian Gage. No more lies. No more pretending. No matter how bad you think it is, lying is worse. So just be honest with me. And if I ask something you're not ready to talk about, don't push me away. Just say you're not ready. That's all I ask. Just be honest."

A flash of hesitation crosses his expression as he chews on his lower lip. I want to question it, but before I have a chance, he's on his feet, pulling me up with him. His arms swallow me as his lips find mine. Any doubt is instantly erased as his kiss consumes me, heart, body, and soul. For the first time, I feel like I'm actually kissing Julian, not the man he pretended to be all summer long.

"I like this better," I murmur against his lips, a tingle trickling down my back from the subtle contact.

"Like what?"

"Kissing you. Not the other person you were."

"And I like kissing you like this, too." He circles his hips, then yanks my body, hard and fast, against his. His erection pushes into my stomach, making me gasp. "And I'd like to do more than just kiss you. You have no idea how hard these past few weeks have been, especially now that I've gotten a taste."

I pass him a coy look. "Oh, I have a pretty good idea just how *hard* it's been." I palm his erection, which only causes the fire in his gaze to burn brighter.

Before I can protest, he lifts me up, forcing my legs around his waist. His mouth slams against mine, his kiss voracious, hungry, desperate as he carries me toward my makeshift bedroom.

When he reaches the doorway, he pauses, looking around. "Where the hell's the door?"

"I told you. This is just a den."

He glances at me, then out to the open living room before back at me again. "Oh, fuck it," he growls, practically tossing me onto my clothes-covered bed.

"Julian!" I squeal, laughing at the playful deviousness in his expression.

He hurriedly shrugs off his suit jacket while I rip my t-shirt over my head, both of us frantic to scramble out of our clothes. Finally, once his boxer briefs land on the top of our discarded things, he retrieves a condom from his wallet and climbs onto the bed, crawling up my body.

Impassioned lips find mine and I melt into him. He tastes as I remember…citrus, spice, and Julian.

"Guinevere…," he pants.

"Yes," I exhale.

"I'm buying you a fucking apartment with a door. And a better bed than this pullout sofa."

I laugh, the sound echoing through the room. "And

why would you want to waste your money on that when I can just crash at your place?" I bat my lashes, passing him a demure look.

"So I can show up at your place anytime I want." Leaning back, he rips the packet open with his teeth, then rolls on the condom.

When he teases me with his length, I grab the back of his neck, every inch of me alive with anticipation. "And why would you want to do that?"

"So I can have you anytime I want." He exhales as he pushes into me, slow and restrained, filling me in a way only he can.

Our eyes meet as our bodies connect, but unlike before, it's not just the joining of our bodies. It's the joining of our hearts, our minds, our souls. I thought Trevor made love to me all those years we were together. He never did. But Julian... This moment, this feeling. This is exactly the love I've been searching for my entire life.

Maybe four isn't such a bad number, after all.

Chapter Thirty-Six

My fingers draw light circles around the grooves of Julian's scars as we lay in his bed, the motion now as innate as breathing. It's a far cry from the morning I woke up in this same bed and had a panic attack about where I was, *who* he was. Now, this is the only place I want to be. It has been for the past two months.

As summer made way for fall, our relationship truly blossomed. We've opened up to each other in a way I never did with Trevor. I want Julian to know everything about me. And I want to know everything about Julian. Thankfully, he wants me to know everything, regardless of how sad and horrible. He shares these things because he knows I won't judge him. I'll love him in spite of it.

I'll love him *because* of it.

It doesn't matter that he still hasn't uttered those three magic words to me. He will when he's ready. In the meantime, I shower him with my own love.

"How did you meet Mr. Price?" I ask in a lazy voice, spent and sated after our latest round of lovemaking. As much as I enjoy going out with him and being seen on his arm, my favorite place is still in his bed. He's an exciting and enthusiastic lover, one I can admit I'm incredibly addicted to.

"Mr. Price?" He peers down at me from where I rest in his embrace, relaxed from the steady rhythm of his beating heart.

"Yeah." I continue tracing circles around his scars. At first, it made him self-conscious. Now, I like to think it offers him the comfort he needs, that he deserves. "I know what Camille and you have shared, but I get the feeling there's more to it."

"What? You don't think I'm some criminal mastermind who took advantage of an old guy, like his children do?"

His words bring a smile to my face. Now that I know the real Julian Gage, thinking of him as a criminal mastermind is absurd.

"Absolutely not." I shake my head. "Plus, I did the math. When you met him, he was in his sixties, not this elderly, feeble man his kids made him out to be."

"That's for sure. He had more energy than I did some days. Thankfully, the judge realized his kids were greedy and pissed off their father didn't give them the bulk of his wealth."

"But I also think there's more to the story than you befriending a lonely man over a game of chess."

"I can't get anything past you, can I?" he comments on a long sigh.

"No, you can't."

His lips curve into a small smile, eyes sparkling as he stares into space. He pulls me closer into him as he sighs, relaxing. If I asked this same question a few months ago, he would have closed up. Now he talks about his past with no hesitation. It hasn't been easy. There have been moments he's struggled to share certain things, especially when I asked about the aftermath of his mother's death and he told me about the six months he spent in a juvenile detention facility before the judge ruled he acted in self-defense. Regardless, he's slowly learning how to open himself to me.

"No one really knew how to handle me in any of my foster homes. I never got the help I should have when I was first placed in the system. I went to therapy, but it didn't work…at least not for me. I kept blaming myself for what happened. When I got to be too much for my first family, they sent me on to the next home. The cycle repeated for years, so much so that I thought this was my penance for taking another man's life."

"Julian…" I tighten my arm around him, kissing his chest. "You don't honestly believe that, do you?"

"I did at the time. And I'll admit there are times I still do. I had no direction in life. When I first arrived at a new home, my foster parents would care for a little while, hoping to save some poor kid from becoming another statistic so they could brag to their friends about all the good they were doing. Until they realized how difficult it was. They'd quickly lose interest and wait for Child Services to come and take me to a new placement so they could try all over again with a new kid. By the time I was sixteen, I was so used to the cycle, I stopped caring, stopped trying. I'd been through so many foster homes, I'd lost count."

"It couldn't have been all bad. I'm sure you had friends at school."

"I was never in the same one long enough to make friends. Child Services did everything to keep me in the same district, but it wasn't always possible. I always had to start over again in new schools. After a while, I stopped trying to form friendships with anyone there, since I knew it would only be a matter of time before I was uprooted again. Plus, I hated being teased by everyone about the fact that I didn't have real parents. I acted out, allowed my anger to get the better of me. I was suspended from school a lot. And that's actually what brought Theodore Price into my life."

"How so?"

"I was living in a foster home with five other kids in Fort Lee, just across the Hudson from New York. My foster parents had their hands full, so they never realized when I wasn't there. Hell, when I brought home my notice of suspension, they signed it without even reading it. They were just going through the motions, knowing the clock on me was ticking. I was a few years from being eighteen and aging out of the system, with no hope for a future.

"When my mother died and Child Services came to take me away, they let me bring a few items with me. I'm not sure how, but my mother's old address book ended up in my things. I think I just wanted something with her handwriting on it and that was the first thing I could find. Well, as I grew older, I became more and more angry about the shitty hand I'd been dealt. I figured everything would be different if I had a real family, people who actually cared about me. So I looked in my mother's address book and paid her parents a visit at their multi-million dollar home in the Upper West Side."

"Did they know who you were?"

He exhales loudly. "Yes, but they turned me away. Said my mother's death was due to all the bad decisions she'd made. That she was dead to them years before her actual death. That I never existed in their eyes."

"My god." I cover my mouth, struggling to understand how anyone could say that, especially to their own blood. No wonder he has trouble accepting love.

"I had a lot of problems, Guinevere. A lot. I battled

351

depression, anxiety, along with a slew of other things. After they said that to me, I started to think maybe it *would* be better if I didn't exist."

Tears well in my eyes at the pain I hear. I squeeze him tighter, reveling in his warmth, reminding myself he *is* alive. I can't imagine a world without Julian in it.

"I never went back to my foster home that night. I just walked and walked. Hours passed as I tried to think who would care if I weren't alive. I couldn't think of a single person…" He trails off, his voice wavering before he clears his throat and continues.

"As I crossed the George Washington, I came to a stop. I remember standing there, looking at the Hudson swirling below, wondering if I could actually do it, if I could really jump. I kept wondering if it would hurt, if dying would be painful. Regardless, I knew it would be nothing compared to the pain I lived with every day.

"I was about to hoist myself over the railing when I heard someone say, 'The bravest thing I've ever done is continue to live when I wanted to die.' It stopped me cold. I looked to my right. Mr. Price stood a few feet from me. And that's exactly where he remained for the next hour, talking to me about everything and nothing. By the time the sun rose, I was no longer interested in jumping. But that wasn't enough for him. He made a phone call and got me in to see his therapist, the man who helped him with his own depression after his youngest son had jumped from that same bridge years before."

"Oh, my god."

"That's why he was out there. It was the anniversary of his death, so when he saw me in the same place, he felt compelled to save me. And that's exactly what he did. He was the first person to take a genuine interest in me. Everyone else only did because they were getting paid to do so. But not Mr. Price. He had nothing to gain, yet he still cared. Not only did he get me the help I needed, he encouraged me to focus on school. He told me if I graduated, he'd pay for college. Before then, I never put any effort into my education. By the time college rolled around, I'd no longer be considered a ward of the state and would be on my own. Why bother studying when I couldn't afford college? But Mr. Price did something no one else had. He made me see I had potential outside my life circumstances."

"You went to SUNY, right?"

"Not the typical Ivy League school you hear most successful men attend, but that was an accomplishment for me in and of itself. Once Mr. Price offered to fund my college education, I buckled down and raised my grades. Having a great therapist helped.

"After I turned eighteen, Mr. Price helped me find an affordable apartment near campus. He even offered me an entry-level job at his company to earn money. He wanted me to learn how to take care of myself, how to budget and pay bills. With him, everything was a lesson. Yes, he had more money than I could even wrap my head around, so he wouldn't miss a measly $800 a month that was the rent on my studio apartment. It wasn't about the money. It was about teaching me to live on what I made."

"My parents did the same. When I got my license, they made me get a job so I could pay for car insurance. I had to give them $20 every week. They wanted me to understand that everything has a cost, that we have to work for things we want."

"And that's what Mr. Price taught me. The life lessons he shared with me were more valuable than anything I learned in school."

"So you remained close, even in college?"

"We did. Every Sunday, he invited me to his place in Manhattan…" He looks around. "Here, actually," he adds with a smile. His brows scrunch in contemplation. "It's funny, isn't it?"

"What is?"

"When he first passed and I inherited everything from him, I still called this his place. I thought I always would."

"I'm sure he'd want you to think of it as your place, don't you?"

He pulls his lips between his teeth. "I suppose."

"So… Sundays?"

"Right. Every Sunday, I came over here and Camille would cook us dinner. I often found myself hating to leave. He shared his story with me, how his success was due to simply being in the right place at the right time. He told me about his wife and children. His wife died from breast cancer ten years earlier, just a few months after he lost his son to depression. She was the glue that held the family together. Once she passed, his kids drifted away, leaving him mostly alone, except when they needed money."

"That's so sad."

"I guess you could say we both needed each other."

"He sounds like a really good man."

"I owe him everything." He shifts to his side, his hands cupping my cheeks as he stares intently at me. "Just like I now owe *you* everything."

I swallow hard. "Me?"

He slowly nods as he brings his lips to mine. "Yes, Guinevere. Mr. Price showed me I was deserving of love, but he never did what you did. He couldn't."

"And what's that?"

I feel his lips turn into a smile. "You taught me *how* to love. If you never did what you did, if you never had the balls to call me out on my shit, I doubt I'd be here, that *we'd* be here." He covers my mouth with his as he pushes me onto my back. "And I *really* like being here with you."

His deep kiss leaves me breathless, a panting bundle of hormones. When he moves to the crook of my neck, I moan, closing my eyes, relishing in the roughness of his day-old scruff against my skin. I bring my hands up to his back, digging my fingers into the flesh, my nerve endings firing as he travels down my body.

"Are you only using me for sex?" I breathe.

"Never," he croons. "Although I *really* like having sex. But it's not just sex with you." His lips circle around my nipple, his tongue torturous as he tastes me. "It never was. It never will be."

I throw my head back, my hand moving to his scalp. My fingers dig into his hair, guiding him as he worships me in a way only he can. "Never."

"Never." He flicks his eyes to mine. I grin deviously as I place my hands on his broad shoulders and push him down my body. "Can I help you with something, Miss Fitzgerald?" His voice is playful and coy. As much as I love learning about his past, I love this side of him more. The flirtatious man I found him to be during our time together.

"You know there is." Spreading my legs, I prop my feet on the bed.

"And what would that be?" He blows out a long breath as he settles between my thighs, the warmth driving me wild.

"Your mouth on me."

"Anything for you, baby doll."

I brace for his tongue to work the magic it always does when a loud ringing cuts through the room.

Julian stiffens, his eyes widening as he remains motionless for several seconds. This isn't the first time a phone's rung when we were about to go at it, but this ring… It's not coming from either of our phones. It's coming from down the hall.

"Ignore it," I whisper, running my hands through his hair. That's normally all the encouragement it would take. Not this time. He pulls his bottom lip between his teeth, visibly torn about what to do. Then he sighs.

"I have to get that." Rolling off me, he grabs his discarded boxer briefs from the floor and yanks them on as he darts out of the room.

My mouth agape, I sit up, staring at the door in disbelief. What could be so important that he left me when he's rarely answered a phone call in my presence, and certainly never during sex? He's been adamant in his insistence that when we're together, he wants to devote all his attention to me. What changed? And what phone was that? His cell is sitting on the nightstand.

My curiosity getting the better of me, I throw my legs over the side of the bed and grab my robe, pulling it over my body. I carefully tiptoe down the hallway, stopping shy of the open door to his study.

"Slow down. Slow down. Tell me what happened." His tone is calm and compassionate as he pauses. I can faintly make out the voice on the other end — a female voice. "Where are you right now? … Shh. Shh. It's okay. It'll all be okay. You're stronger than this. Don't let him get into your head."

My heart's caught in my throat as I listen to his

conversation. A sickness forms in my stomach at the idea that he hasn't been faithful, but my rational side screams for me to slow down and look at the situation realistically. We've spent practically every night together the past few months. If Julian were sleeping with someone else, I would have known about it. I would have at least smelled the perfume on him. Since he confided in me about his past, the only perfume I've smelled on him is my own. But the secret cell phone doesn't ease my worries any.

Lost in my own thoughts, I almost don't hear him end the call. When the sound of footsteps meets my ears, I hurry back toward the bedroom on light feet, tossing my robe to the floor and jumping back into bed.

When he appears in the doorway, I smile, but it doesn't reach my eyes. "Everything okay?"

He parts his lips as he steps toward me, hesitant. Then his shoulders drop. "Actually…" He worries his bottom lip and my heart deflates. "I have to go."

"Go?" I prop myself onto my elbows, doing my best not to act dejected, but it's impossible, especially with the knowledge that he was speaking to a woman.

"Work thing. It's an emergency." He heads to the closet and retrieves a pair of jeans and a sweater, pulling them over his body. "You know I'd never put work ahead of you. You're more important than that, but this is a matter of life or death…" His voice trails off as he swallows hard. "So to speak. I don't know how late I'll be, but stay. You don't need to leave just because I'm not here."

Returning to the bed, he leans down, kissing my forehead, then steps back. In the silence, we hold each other's gaze. Something in my expression must tell him I'm not convinced this is a work thing. Regret creases his brow.

"I'm sorry, Guinevere," he says in a soft voice. He looks as if he's about to say something else. Then he shakes his head, turning from me and hurrying out of the room.

Chapter Thirty-Seven

I CAN'T SHAKE my melancholy mood as I shuffle from the elevator toward my cubicle. The atmosphere at the magazine office usually fills me with energy, especially this time of year when Christmas lights and decorations seem to hang from every available surface. But nothing lifts my spirits.

As I lay in Julian's bed last night, I tossed and turned, unable to shut off my mind. The smell of him on the sheets was anything but comforting as I came up with a thousand scenarios about where he was and what he was doing. They all seemed so outrageous, so out of character for him…except for the truth that he abandoned me to go see another woman.

I try not to dwell on that as I stare at my laptop screen, needing to focus on my work, but it's impossible. I'm so consumed with what's really going on, I almost don't register Viv's voice saying my name.

I glance up from my computer, doing my best to force a smile as she leans against the wall to my cubicle. "Good morning, Viv."

"I was hoping it would be; unfortunately, I just read the rough draft of the escort piece you sent over."

I swallow hard, my stomach rolling. To Viv, it was a rough draft. For me, it was the result of hours of writing, rewriting, revising, and editing. I wanted Viv to be so impressed by the initial draft that her suggestions were merely stylistic. Based on the displeasure on her face, that's not the case.

"And?" My voice is shaky, hesitant. I brace for her to rip it apart, as she's been known to do.

"It's good. But good doesn't sell magazines, Evie. The picture of this August Laurent character you've drawn is compelling, and the idea of a male escort empowering women is one that will intrigue readers. Many women will empathize with what his clients have experienced. He's helped all kinds of women, from the single woman left in a circle of friends to women whose spouses never appreciated them. You've painted him in a light that will make readers think twice about judging him as merely a male escort taking advantage of women. Hell, *I've* thought twice about judging him as a male escort who takes advantage of women."

"Thank you?" My voice lifts, waiting for the punchline.

"But it's one-dimensional. I want more August Laurent."

"The whole article's about August Laurent."

She smiles a thin-lipped smile. "No. It's about the women who've hired him."

"And through each of them, you learn something about him."

"I learn about the man he is when he's with each woman. That's not who he really is. I want the *real* August Laurent. I want to know what makes him do what he does, what makes him want to sacrifice friends, family, *love*."

"The article talks about that," I protest, although she's right. There's no big insight into who August Laurent truly is, which is why I pressed to talk to some of his clients. There's still a piece missing. The *why* is missing.

"Something must drive him to choose this path, to help the women he does. There's a story there. I want to know what that is. And so do your readers."

She holds my gaze for a moment longer, then turns, walking away. I open my mouth to argue, but it won't do any good. After all, this is her magazine. If I want this promotion, I need to give her the story she wants...and then some.

Mentally exhausted, I return my attention to my laptop, opening the file I'd amassed on August Laurent and the handful of women who agreed to let me interview them. My notepad in hand, I scour through everything once more, searching for something I may have overlooked or deemed unimportant. The more I review my email exchanges and phone conversations with August, the more it hits me. He seemed to evade all my questions about his younger years, often shifting the focus back on me. It almost reminds me of how Julian used to do the same thing until I convinced him to open up.

As I consider what I can do to persuade August to share what caused him to get into this line of work, Chloe flies into my cubicle, her eyes wide, expression grave. "Did you hear?"

"Hear what?" I peer at her, brows furrowed. This level of excitement could mean Diego in accounting finally asked out Rachel in design. Or it could be actual news.

"Sonia Moreno was murdered. She was a friend of Julian's, wasn't she? I thought I saw a photograph of them together at some fundraiser earlier in the year."

Blinking repeatedly, my heart drops to the pit of my

stomach as a chill rushes over me.

"Yes," I answer in a small voice. But her connection to Julian isn't what has me out of sorts. It's the fact that she's a client of August Laurent's. And not just any client. A woman who claimed he saved her from an abusive marriage. During a few follow-up interviews, she mentioned she was getting her affairs in order before going public with her abuse and officially filing for divorce. I wonder if she finally did it.

"How was she killed?" My voice trembles, tears forming in my eyes. She seemed so confident, so happy, like a weight had been lifted off her shoulders at the thought of starting over, even if she never worked another day in Hollywood again.

"Details are still sketchy, but a few of my sources say she had stab wounds covering her chest and abdomen. Police are operating under the theory it was a burglary gone wrong. She'd just returned from being on location for the past month, so authorities think her place had been scouted for a break-in. She must have surprised them by being home."

I shake my head, my heart squeezing under the weight of everything I know. It could have been a robbery, but my gut tells me it's not. Not after everything Sonia shared with me.

Jumping to my feet, I grab my coat and my bag, needing to do something, *anything*. I can't remain silent about this.

"Where are you going?" Chloe calls after me.

I whirl around, meeting her questioning stare. She probably came into my cubicle to share the juicy gossip before it hit the airwaves. Never could she have predicted my response, or the fact I may hold the missing link to what happened. I refuse to believe Sonia went through everything she did, *survived* everything she had, just for some thugs to kill her. It's too much of a coincidence.

"I have to go." It's all I can tell her, at least for now.

I spin on my heels, about to race to the elevator when Viv approaches, her own expression frantic. She doesn't even have to utter a word. I know she's here because of the news about Sonia. Viv is the only other person who's aware of the identity of the women I interviewed, including everything they've been through.

"It's okay." Her voice is a low whisper. She squeezes my biceps, giving me a reassuring smile. "Go. Be her voice."

I nod, then hurry from the office, doing everything to keep my emotions under control. I barely knew the woman, but in the brief time we spent together, I felt a connection to her. I can only imagine how August feels, if he even knows.

I stop in my tracks, imagining him watching this story break on the news. I can't stomach that. No one deserves to learn about the death of a loved one that way. So I reach out to him the only way I can.

To: August Laurent
From: Evie Fitzgerald
Subject: Sonia Moreno

Dear August,

Please call me as soon as you receive this message. It's about Sonia. News just came over the wire. I'd rather tell you over the phone instead of through email.

E

I stare at my phone the entire ride toward Police Plaza, waiting for him to call.

He never does.

By the time the cab drops me off a block from police headquarters, news of Sonia's death must have already spread. Reporters are camped out front, setting up cameras and preparing to go live to break the news, all for better ratings. As I hurry up the stairs and into the lobby, the place is a madhouse. Everyone passing appears as if they know exactly where they're going. I'm lost and out of my element, unsure if I'm even in the right place or if they'll take me seriously.

"Can I help you?" a woman asks in a thick New York accent as I look around.

I turn, my stare falling on a young brunette sitting behind a pane of what I imagine is bulletproof glass. My heart breaks a little at how far our society's fallen that you can't even feel safe in a police station anymore.

Straightening my spine, I step toward her. "My name's Guinevere Fitzgerald. I work for *Blush* magazine."

Rolling her eyes in annoyance, she points to the front doors. "Reporters have to stay outside and wait for the press conference."

"No," I interject. "I'm not here to *get* information. I'm here to *give* information. I just recently interviewed Sonia Moreno. I may have evidence to help in finding her killer."

"The detectives already have someone in custody who was seen in the vicinity of her house."

"Have you questioned her husband?" I press.

"Her husband?" She arches a brow. "The director?"

"Yes." I retrieve my cell phone from my purse, unlocking the screen and scrolling through the audio files until I find the one I need. "She spoke of him. How she was getting ready to file for divorce, but was worried about what he might do." I hit play. Sonia's voice fills the room. Her subtle Spanish accent leaves no question that it's her.

"Turn that off," the desk sergeant orders, glancing at people lingering close by. She gets up from her seat and walks away. A few seconds later, the secure door opens and she holds it for me. "Are you coming or not?" she presses when I don't move.

"Right. Of course." I walk toward her and follow the sergeant down several long corridors. I stay as close to her as possible, worried I'll get lost or trampled by people rushing around if I stray. I barely breathe until we step into the elevator and the doors shut, allowing me a reprieve from the chaos. I love the busy atmosphere at the magazine, but it's never like this.

When the elevator stops, we exit onto the twelfth floor, the words "Homicide Unit" in bold letters hanging on the wall in front of us.

"This way."

We continue down several hallways, the sound of two-way radios and loud voices filling the maze-like space. Approaching a door labeled "Conference", she points to a line of chairs against the wall.

"Wait there. Detective Mulroney will be with you shortly."

"Thanks," I say, but she's already disappeared.

Taking a seat, I smile as a man in a dark suit with a buzz cut, a detective shield hanging from his neck, rushes past, carrying a bunch of papers. I pull my planner out of my bag, scratching down notes in one of the free pages. There's no doubt in my mind Ethan is involved, not with the threats he'd made. What I have to say may not be useful, but I must try. I'll never be able to live with myself if I don't and he continues to walk free. Julian would want me to do the same. He stood up to an injustice and protected his mother. I need to protect Sonia's legacy.

When the door to the conference room opens, I snap my head up, looking in its direction, my hands growing clammy. I'm innocent of committing a crime, but I'm just as nervous as I would be if that weren't the case.

"Thank you for coming in and sharing this with us, Mr... What do I even call you? Now that I know who August Laurent is…"

My pulse skyrockets when I hear that name.

"Call me whatever you'd like," a familiar voice interjects. But it's lacking the normal vitality I'm used to hearing during our conversations. It's somber, solemn, not to mention the subtle French accent seems to have disappeared, as well.

The door widens and two men step out. I freeze, unsure how to act, whether August would want me to acknowledge him. He knows what I look like. But I have no idea what he looks like. Every single woman I've interviewed has remained incredibly tight-lipped about his appearance, about his true identity.

But as the detective moves to the side and I meet the eyes of the man I've spent months obsessing over, my heart plummets. The room spins, my grip on my planner loosening. It falls to the floor, pages spreading in every direction as the world seems to give out from beneath me.

Chapter Thirty-Eight

"JULIAN?" I SAY through the thickness in my throat, fighting to capture a breath as I stand. Chills rush through me, my limbs trembling as flashes of the past several months play before me. What I thought was a coincidence when I ran into him at the Steam Room. August calling me because a "little birdie" told him I was looking for him. His sudden change of heart after he'd adamantly refused my request to interview a few of his clients. His agreeable attitude wasn't because of any skillset I possessed. It was all because he wanted to sleep with me.

"Julian?" I squeak again when he only stares at me, his jaw slack. My expression pleads with him to finally say something. But he doesn't. He simply bows his head, shaking it, silently confirming the awful truth. My eyes burn with the betrayal filling me and I spin from him, running down the hall, searching desperately for the elevator.

"Guinevere! Wait!" he calls out, but I continue, wheezing as my sobs remain trapped in my throat.

With each step I take, the more it makes sense. I often mentally remarked about the parallels between the two men. But I never considered Julian *was* August Laurent. He would have told me. Wouldn't he? A voice in the back of my head reminds me he wouldn't if he were trying to hide the truth. And there's only one reason he would do that… Because on the nights he wasn't with me, he was keeping another woman company. The thought turns my stomach.

I somehow find the bank of elevators and send a prayer of thanks to the big man upstairs when there's already one waiting. Once inside, I repeatedly hit the button for the lobby. Julian's voice grows closer, calling my name, begging me to stop. I bang the button faster, willing the doors to close. They finally do just as he reaches the elevator, the echo of his fists slamming against the doors filling the car. I release a relieved breath and slink against the wall, needing the support to keep me upright.

When the elevator arrives on the main floor, I dash from it, keeping my head lowered, refusing to look over my shoulder in case Julian…or August…or whoever he is manages to catch up. I barrel past the front desk, ignoring the desk sergeant's questions about how it all went, and continue through the large glass doors.

The instant I step outside, a coldness hits me like a wall, and not just from the frigid temperatures on this December morning. There's a strange feeling in the air. The sky is a foreboding shade of gray, one I've grown accustomed to over the years.

I inhale a breath, tasting the impending snow in my mouth. Based on the weather report I caught earlier, that's exactly what's supposed to happen over the next few hours. The first snowfall of the season. Normally, I'd play hooky from work and enjoy the beauty of snow falling around New York City. But my mood's been drastically altered.

Tugging my jacket closer, I do my best not to slip on the slick brick as I hurry past the growing number of reporters, evading their shouts asking if I know anything about Sonia Moreno. I ignore everything, until *he* bellows my name, his voice carrying across the plaza, echoing against the tall skyscrapers.

"Guinevere!"

I glance behind me, watching as Julian frantically runs toward me, panic and desperation covering him. His stare is distressed, neck stiff, jaw tense.

"Leave me alone!" With quick steps, I continue toward the corner, raising my hand to hail a cab. When one pulls up to the curb, I open the door to get in, but come to an abrupt stop when an arm blocks me.

"Guinevere, please. Just hear me out."

I keep my eyes forward for a moment, my vision obscured with tears. This truth is worse than Trevor walking away after twelve years. He may have had his faults, but he never lied to me, never misled me, never used me.

"Hear you out?" I squeak, biting down at my bottom lip, hoping to transfer the pain from my heart to another part of my body. "Why? So you can make up an excuse about why you lied to me? I've heard them all before. I don't need to listen to you go on about how you wanted to tell me the truth but didn't know how. That's a bunch of bullshit. You just wanted a guaranteed piece of ass every goddamn night." A shiver rolls through me, acid burning my stomach. "Nothing more."

I go to duck under his arm and into the cab, pausing when I hear his voice again.

"I haven't taken on a client since the beginning of June."

I have no reason to believe him, but something in his tone makes me second-guess myself. I still, one foot in the cab, one foot on the ground. So what if he hasn't taken on a client since June? Does that change anything?

369

"Lady, are you in or out?" the cabbie asks in a thick Middle Eastern accent, glancing at me. I look at him, then back at Julian, torn.

"Don't run from me, Guinevere. Not without knowing the truth. Please."

I close my eyes, squeezing them tightly. Once again, I'm entangled in a battle between my brain and heart. My heart screams at me to stay, but my brain tells me to walk away and never look back.

"Please," he says once more, this time softer. "'No matter where you run, you just end up running into yourself.'"

The instant Julian utters that quote from *Breakfast at Tiffany's*, I exhale a protracted breath, shaking my head. I hate that he's using that movie against me. It's unfair, but it still makes me stop and think rationally for a moment. And a moment is all it takes for me to realize I'll never move on unless I have answers.

Blowing out an exasperated sigh, I step away from the cab and close the door, but don't turn around. If I peer into Julian's eyes, I fear I'll crack. "You wanted to explain. Here's your chance. Explain."

"Please, look at me."

"Explain," I repeat, this time harder.

At first, it's silent, then he exhales deeply. I picture him running his hands through his hair in resignation. "I never intended things to get this messed up."

"No? What was your intent then, Julian? Or is it August?" Spinning around, I throw my hands up in frustration, paying no attention to the snow beginning to fall around us. "I don't even know your real name."

"Julian Gage is my real name. I was born August 10, 1980, in Jersey City. I never lied to you about that."

"But you failed to mention you also go by August Laurent, the man I was doing a story on." With each word, my voice gets more and more agitated. "You called me repeatedly, pretending to be this other person, when all along it was *you*. Hell, you even used a fake French accent so I would be none the wiser. You had so many opportunities to come clean, yet you deliberately kept the truth from me. Why? Why would you do something like this?"

"I never meant to hurt you, Guinevere."

"*Bullshit*! Bullshit, Julian. You *did* mean to hurt me! The second you made a conscious decision to lie to me, to deceive me, you intended to hurt me. You know what they say about secrets, don't you?"

He remains silent.

"Two can only keep a secret if one of them is dead. At some point, the truth was bound to come out. Or were you going to wait until we were married to tell me you had to leave on occasion to go screw some other woman?"

He grabs my biceps, his eyes imploring. "I know I fucked up. I knew it the second I walked into the guest room of my beach house and saw you wearing that stunning two-piece. That entire weekend, there were so many times I considered telling you the truth. Because I had started falling for you. Even in those early days. For the first time in my life, I wanted somebody to know every part of me. The good. The bad. The ugly. You know my ugly. The reason I *am* August Laurent is because of that ugly."

"Tell me this, Julian…" My voice wavers as my next question remains on the tip of my tongue, my throat closing up at what his response will most likely be. "When you approached me with your proposition, did

371

you only do so because you knew I was on the hunt for August Laurent?"

He briefly closes his eyes, hanging his head as he drops his hold on me. "I wasn't planning on calling you as August Laurent that Monday after our first dinner. I was just going to let it go. But I found myself forming feelings for you. And I liked the idea that I could help you get promoted. So I picked up the phone and did the one thing I swore I'd never do. I called a journalist who was hoping to do a story about me."

"Did you not even stop to think about what this would do to *my* career?" I shriek, pacing in front of him. "All along, I honestly thought I did something right to get the elusive August Laurent to agree to an interview when he's refused everyone else for years. I thought that maybe, just maybe, I could prove everyone wrong and show them I *am* good at what I do. But all along, the *only* reason August Laurent agreed was because Julian Gage wanted to get into my pants!"

"That's not true. That's not the only reason." He advances toward me, but I step away.

"Oh really? If I weren't the one sitting at that coffee shop trying to get a lead on August Laurent, if it were someone else, would you have reached out to them?" I lean into him, my nostrils flaring and fists clenched as I wait for his answer. "If I hadn't shared my frustrations over the direction of the story, would you have granted me access to some of your clients?"

He averts his eyes. His silence is the only confirmation I need.

I push past him once more and hail a cab, keeping my back turned. I can't stomach the sight of him, of the visible reminder I'm not enough, that I never would have gotten this far with this story, with this promotion, if he hadn't made it so.

When a cab pulls up, I go to pull the passenger door open.

"I love you, Guinevere!"

I stop in my tracks, choking out a sob at his admission. I've waited months for him to finally say those three beautiful words. I pictured him sweeping me into his arms, showering me with kisses as he declared his love for the first time. Instead, it tastes of desperation, one final act to make me stay.

"That's the truth. That hasn't changed. You taught me that. *You.* That has to count for something."

"Maybe. But you know what you taught me?" I look over my shoulder at him, but he doesn't answer. "That being spontaneous comes at a cost, one I'm no longer willing to pay." I hold his gaze for a moment, watching as the snow falls around him.

"I'm ready to give it all up for you. All of it." His voice is strained and wrought with emotion.

I bite my bottom lip to stop my chin from quivering. "I wish I could believe you. I just don't know what's real and what's not. Goodbye...whoever you are."

Chapter Thirty-Nine

"Are you certain this is the direction you want to take?" Viv looks at me from over her horn-rimmed glasses.

I rub my clammy hands along my pants, glancing out the window of her office. The city is dark, despite it only being three in the afternoon. A downpour soaks Manhattan, the weather matching my mood.

"Like I said, I've given this serious consideration over the past few weeks. I didn't get the story because of my talent or tenacity. I got it because…" I trail off as I attempt to compose myself. The last thing I need is for Viv to see how the truth of who Julian is has affected me. "Because I had a personal relationship with my…subject, although it was unbeknownst to me at the time. That still doesn't change anything." I straighten my spine, rebuilding the wall around my heart. "I would have never gotten remotely close to landing that story had he not had a personal interest in me. You should choose your new assistant editor based on their talent, not luck…or the fact that the subject hoped to get something out of our agreement."

Telling Viv I no longer want to be considered for assistant editor has been one of the most difficult things I've ever done, but it's necessary. I could never accept a promotion I didn't earn.

When she doesn't respond, I stand, heading toward

374

the door.

"Do you honestly believe that?"

I turn around. "What do you mean?"

She removes her glasses, chewing on the end of the frames. "That you didn't get the interview with Mr. Laurent based on talent."

"Of course I do, Viv. I dated him without realizing it. He admitted he—"

"I understand that. But do you really think people agree to be the subject of a story based on the goodness of their heart?"

I step away from the door, sucking in my lower lip. "What are you saying?"

She stands from behind her desk and walks toward me, her mouth formed in a tight line. "I've been in this industry for more years than I care to admit. It's one of the toughest jobs out there, especially for a woman. No matter what you do, how much you try to present yourself as serious, there are times when you'll only get the interview if you turn on the charm, if you make them think there's a chance of something...more."

"I didn't just make him think there was a chance of something more. I gave him something more. And then some."

"No. You gave that to Julian, not August."

"I still didn't get the story based on my talent alone, regardless of whether the man I slept with was Julian or August. I didn't plan for it to happen this way."

"Evie..." She runs her hands down my arms. "Life sometimes doesn't go as planned. It's how we handle the unexpected that determines our strength. Do you go on to fight another day? Or do you give up because it's too hard?"

"I'm not giving up," I mumble.

"No?" She spreads her arms. "Then what do you call this? So you were lied to. It doesn't lessen your ability to do your job and do it well."

"But I'd know the truth." I point to myself, my jaw tensing. "If I continued on and, by some miracle, you gave me the promotion, every time I walked into that office and saw my name on the nameplate, assistant editor below it, I'd question whether I earned it. I *need* to know I earned it. I'd never…" I stop short. I can't tell her the other reason. That every time I walked into that office, I'd be reminded of Julian. Ever since I learned the truth over two weeks ago, I vowed to erase him from every aspect of my life. That includes my work life, too.

"I've always known you were stubborn," she says when I don't finish my thought. "I just didn't realize you were stupid, too." She spins and grabs a large envelope off her desk, shoving it at me.

"What's this?"

"An early proof of the February issue. It's not final yet, but it has the feature story and the layout you designed. Figured you'd want to see the fruits of all your hard work."

"Oh."

She crosses her arms. "Yeah. Oh."

After several long moments pass and she doesn't say anything further, I take it as my cue to leave.

"You're damn good at what you do, Evie," she offers as I reach the doorway. "You should be proud of everything you've accomplished, regardless of *how* you did so."

I glance over my shoulder and smile, wishing I could be as proud of myself as it appears Viv is. I walk out of her office, returning to my cubicle and the only thing that makes me feel grounded in a world that seems to have fallen to pieces around me. I pull my new planner out of my desk drawer and make new plans...better plans. *Happier* plans.

But it still doesn't heal the gaping hole in my heart. I wonder if anything will.

~~~~~~~~~~~

"Coming to Nora's to help her decide on centerpieces?"

When I hear Chloe's voice, I pull my attention away from my planner, which is now covered with decorative stickers and color-coded based on my itinerary for the day. I've even started making daily, weekly, and monthly goals for the next three months. It makes me feel like I'm slowly regaining control of my life, like I will move on from this little hiccup.

"The hotel..." She focuses on my desk, then snatches the planner off the surface. "What in the holy hell is this?"

"You know what it is." I tear it away from her, hugging it to my chest like a baby would a security blanket. "It's my planner. A new planner. For new plans."

"Oh, I know that. But what is it doing out here?"

"Nothing." I hold my head high. "I just like being organized. I dropped the ball the past few months and am now suffering the consequences. Life is better when it's planned. No surprises. So that's what I'm doing. Making a new plan for the new year."

"Does this new plan include finally growing a pair and talking to Julian? I'm not sure how many more bouquets of roses we can fit into the apartment before the city zoning committee tries to evict us for running a floral shop out of a residence. Or are you *planning* on ignoring him forever?"

"I'm not ignoring him," I answer calmly. "I just have absolutely nothing to say to him. Eventually, he'll move on. He'll go back to being August Laurent, screwing whatever rich socialite calls him that month, and forget I even exist."

She considers my words for a moment, then sits on the spare chair. "But will you?"

"Will I what?"

"Move on? Forget about him?"

"Yes. I have a plan."

She rolls her eyes. "Of course you do. And what does that entail?"

Flipping my new and improved planner open to the correct page, I push it toward her, keeping a protective stare on her the entire time to ensure she doesn't do something crazy.

"What is this?"

"New requirements for a potential partner."

"You're joking, right?"

"No. Goals are important. Of course, I set the bar a little lower than I did when I first did this in high school. I'm thirty. Most women are twenty-seven when they marry, and the men are twenty-nine. So I can't be as selective as I was twelve years ago. Ideally attractive, a decent job—"

"I can read," she shoots back. "It's all here on your list."

"And not a secret escort."

"Well…" She closes my planner and pushes it toward me. "I don't think you have to worry about that."

"I wouldn't be so sure. I didn't take that into consideration last time and look where it got me."

Chloe glares, her lips pinched together as she leans toward me. "Did you ever stop to put yourself in his shoes? Try to figure out *why* he did what he did?"

I open my mouth, shaking my head. "What are you—"

"Julian!" She slams her hands on the desk, her eyes fierce. "Have you considered what *he's* gone through during this pity party you've thrown for yourself these past few weeks?"

"I know why he did it. So he could have his cake and eat it, too." I look away from her heated stare, crossing my arms over my chest.

"You know that's not the case. You said yourself he claimed to have stopped taking clients the beginning of June. When you met. The *first* time. Before you ever agreed to be his fake girlfriend."

"Who knows how true that is?" I mutter under my breath.

She brushes off my comment. "If he told you who he was back then, would you have given him a shot?"

"No." I chew on my fingernails when I notice a word spelled wrong on my itinerary for January second. My hands itch to reach out and grab my planner to fix it, but I have a feeling Chloe would toss it into the incinerator if I did that.

"Then maybe that's why he did what he did. Because he knew lying to you was the only chance he had to get to know you. Trust me, as much as I was initially skeptical of the whole arrangement, that man has always had eyes for only you. I saw it that first weekend when the photos of Julian Gage's mystery woman started appearing online. The way he looked at you… Well, it's

379

a way all women yearn to be admired, revered, worshiped. There's no question in my mind he worships the ground you walk on. That he would do anything for you." A smile lights up her face. "I've never seen you as happy as I have when you were with Julian. Trevor certainly never made you that happy."

"At least Trevor never lied to me. He didn't have a secret escort business he never told me about. Remember this…"

I open one of my desk drawers, shifting through the contents until I find the list I'd scratched out after Julian called to take me to dinner all those months ago. On one side are Trevor's pros and cons. On the other are Julian's. I haven't updated this list since that day. I could probably add many more cons to Trevor's side and dozens of pros in Julian's. But there's one con that outweighs everything else. The con he played on me.

I shove the list at Chloe. "Trevor's a much better choice than some man I'm not sure I ever knew."

"On paper, maybe, but I recently read this dating advice column where the author said that love is fickle and makes no sense. That just because someone has all the traits you deem important, it doesn't mean you love them. That only the heart decides that. Sound familiar?"

I lower my eyes, pulling my lips between my teeth. "Maybe."

"So tell me…" Chloe places her hand on my arm. I lift my head. "What does your heart say about Julian?"

"That none of it was real," I answer in a quiet voice, my throat pained.

"I think it was as real for him as it was for you."

I shake my head, refusing to believe it. "This entire thing taught me that life is better when you stick to your plan. Trevor was my plan. I should never have let a pair of beautiful blue eyes and a smooth-talking mouth stray me from that. Not only do I have to live with the knowledge I messed up, but I also destroyed any chance I had at making Trevor realize he made a mistake."

Chloe glares at me before sighing and standing. "He came to see me."

"Who? Trevor?"

"No. Julian." She pulls on her jacket, securing it with a belt. "When you refused to talk to him, he reached out to me. You know what he told me?"

I remain silent.

"That even if you never speak to him again, he doesn't regret what he did, not when you gave him the greatest gift imaginable."

"Guaranteed sex?" I quip back sarcastically, but it's missing my usual bite.

"No. He said you taught him how to love." She pauses, allowing her words to linger. "But I think he gave you an even greater gift."

"And what's that?" I ask hesitantly.

"He taught you how to *live*. If he had to lie to get you to stray from this picture-perfect life you imagined for yourself, from constantly making lists of pros and cons of every decision, from micromanaging everything, I'm grateful he did so. And I think if you looked hard enough, you'll realize you feel the same way."

Chapter Forty

I LOUNGE ON the couch in Chloe's living room, glaring at the envelope Viv gave me earlier while *It's a Wonderful Life* plays on the television in the background. In retrospect, it probably wasn't the best movie choice, considering I'm currently going through my own internal crisis. I wish I had a guardian angel who could come down and show me what *my* life would look like had I never met Julian Gage. Would it help matters any?

Always a glutton for punishment, I grab the envelope off the coffee table and lift the flap. I'm most likely going to regret looking at this. Then again, I *did* just wish for a guardian angel. Maybe that's Viv. Unexpected and impractical, but so was Buster Poindexter as the Ghost of Christmas Past in *Scrooged*.

My stomach tenses as I pull out the magazine and flip it over. When I stare into a pair of familiar blue eyes, my throat tightens. I haven't seen Julian since Sonia's funeral, and even then, I kept my distance, disappearing before the end of the service so he couldn't approach me. At one point, whenever I peered into these eyes, I saw a man willing to take a risk and love me. Now all I see are his lies.

As Jimmy Stewart begs Clarence to take him back to the life he'd wanted to end, I thumb to the page Viv marked with a sticky note, landing on the featured article — *August Laurent: Unrobed*. The initial two-page spread is a combination of photos of him along with the text of the article I'd poured everything into the past several months.

I peel the note off and read it.

E,

I made a few adjustments to the final draft you submitted. Mr. Laurent requested additional information be included to give the reader greater insight into why he does what he does. This piece will still run, regardless of what decision you make, but I hope I won't have to change the byline. The ball's in your court.

- Viv

I shift my eyes to the caption beneath the title, running my fingers over the glossy page.

By: Guinevere Fitzgerald, Assistant Editor
Contributor: Chloe Davenport, Columnist

It's strange to see my full name in print. I've always gone by Evie Fitzgerald. In a way, it's satisfying, like I'm turning over a new leaf, starting a new life. No longer writing about the best condoms for maximum pleasure, but about subjects of value.

Encouraged by George Bailey shouting about wanting to live again, I turn my attention to the opening paragraph of the story I pitched on a whim, thinking nothing would come of it. I can't help but smile at how wrong I was. In more ways than I care to admit.

When I first pitched the idea of getting the

inside scoop on the man who, over the past decade, has become one of the country's most sought-after escorts, I selfishly did so because a story about a male escort would appeal to a large percentage of female readers. I envisioned the cover in my mind... A man dressed in a suit, tie draped around his neck, white shirt unbuttoned revealing chiseled abs, head cut off to keep the mystery alive.

I suppose that's how I assumed this man's story would be. All eye candy. No substance.

Well, dear reader, you're in for quite the ride, just as I was.

August Laurent's tale is one you can't truly appreciate until you have the full picture. I confess, I didn't have that until now. I assumed he was a womanizer, a heartbreaker, a philanderer... Someone who had no qualms about taking advantage of women for monetary gain.

I couldn't have been more wrong.

My heart squeezes as I zero in on that one line. When I first wrote it, I believed it with every fiber of my being. Has any of that changed because I know *who* August Laurent is? Maybe I'm wrong about him again.

Bringing my eyes back to the article, I lose myself in the world I spent my summer living. But it's better now, the pieces Chloe contributed adding another dimension. Now, instead of being a story that seemed to focus on the women August helped, I'm left with a tale of a boy forced to become a man when most kids his age only cared about the latest video game. A boy who had to say goodbye to the only family he had when the rest of us were at an age we wished our parents would disappear. A boy who refused to get close to anyone because he didn't think he deserved to be loved.

But that didn't stop him from giving love when it was needed, despite his insistence that he didn't know how to love. He did. In giving that love, he helped so many women realize their true worth. Some of them just wanted to feel secure in their decision to focus on their career instead of getting married and having kids. Others needed to feel as if they were worthy of love after being with someone who took them for granted. And others needed him to save them, just as he was saved. Regardless of the fact that it was strictly a business arrangement, he still made them feel beautiful, made them feel worthy, made them feel loved.

He did the same thing for me, too, but as Julian.

Can I learn to look past his faults because of the way I felt when I was with him? The way I *still* feel when I hear his name, look into his eyes, recall the heat of his hands on my skin? I want to. God, I wish I could run into his arms and start over again, like he's begged me to do over the weeks that have passed. But this is a man who's made a living out of giving the women who've hired him the fantasy they need, learning how to read them and tell them what they need to hear. How do I know anything he's told me is real?

I'm so consumed with indecision, I barely register the sound of the buzzer, thinking it's the apartment next door. When I hear it again, I shoot my gaze toward the door, holding my breath as I stare. I've ignored that buzzer for weeks now, regardless of Julian's pleas from the front stoop to talk to him. A few hours ago, I was happy to continue to ignore him. Now, I wonder if I can give him the second chance my heart urges he deserves.

Placing the magazine on the coffee table, I stand, taking measured steps toward the entryway, my pulse increasing the closer I get. I place my hand on the knob, able to feel the electricity. When I open the door, I expect to stare into pleading blue eyes. Instead, the eyes looking back are hazel.

"Trevor…" I wrap my arms around my stomach, warming myself as I walk out onto the front step, remaining out of the rain. "What are you doing here?" I hug myself, Julian's SUNY sweatshirt providing me with warmth.

He shoves his hands into his pockets, nervously rocking on his heels. "I, uh… I was in the Village for a meeting with a client and thought I'd stop by to see how you're doing."

"How *I'm* doing?"

I haven't seen Trevor since my final weekend in the Hamptons at the Farewell Gala, which he attended on Theresa's arm. And I haven't spoken to him in even longer, both of us happy to ignore each other all summer. Truthfully, it wasn't a conscious effort on my part. Julian's presence consumed me to the point that I ignored everything else…including the ex-boyfriend often standing only a few feet away.

"No plans with Theresa tonight?"

"We broke up around Thanksgiving." He laughs slightly. "Mom and Dad came to visit, like they do every year."

"And how did that go?"

"Let's just say it made me realize how different Theresa and I are."

"Sorry to hear that."

He lifts his eyes to mine as he shakes his head. "No, you're not."

I part my lips, about to argue with him, but snap my jaw shut. "You're right. I'm not."

"I deserve that, especially after the way I handled things."

Neither one of us says anything for several long seconds, an awkward tension building. I used to feel comfortable around him. This is a man with whom I had no qualms, even sharing all the dirty details of my period...much to his chagrin. Now I don't know how to act.

"How's Julian?"

I hold my head high, doing my best to maintain my composure at his question. "We're not together anymore."

"I figured as much."

"You did?" I arch a brow.

"You were both at Sonia's funeral but didn't acknowledge each other. I wasn't aware you were friendly with her."

"I could say the same about you," I shoot back, not wanting to discuss the fact that my connection to Sonia is actually through Julian's alter ego, August Laurent.

"The firm represents her." He pauses, then corrects, "*Represented* her."

All I can do is nod, silence falling between us once more.

"Can I come in?" Trevor finally asks, his eyes imploring me as he hunches his shoulders, trying to shield himself from the rain. "Just for a minute. I just...

I just really want to talk to you. If you don't like what I have to say, I'll leave and never bother you again. Okay?"

I study him in quiet contemplation. After the way he ended things, I don't owe him anything. But my curiosity gets the better of me.

"Fine."

Turning from him, I enter the apartment, the warmth thawing my cold fingers. After shaking the water off his coat, Trevor leaves it in the entryway, then follows me into the living room. I grab the proof copy of the magazine off the coffee table and shove it back into the envelope, keeping the identity of Julian's alter ego a secret for now.

"Do you know what today is?" Trevor asks.

I scrunch my brows together, wracking my brain, but nothing comes to mind. A few months ago, I would have been able to remember every anniversary we shared. Now those memories have faded.

"December fifteenth?"

"Exactly." He steps toward me, a heat I haven't seen in years crossing his expression. "Do you remember what happened on December fifteenth twelve years ago?"

I shrug. "I don't know."

"We were at a football game. But not just any football game. It was a momentous game, and not because of any Bowl placement for the Huskers. Something else happened at that game. Do you remember what that was?"

Closing my eyes, I chew on my bottom lip, the memory of the game he's referring to returning with striking clarity. I can almost hear the roar of the crowd in the stands. Smell the hot dogs and beer. Feel the frigid wind whip against my face.

"You told me you loved me, and not just as a friend."

When I open my eyes, there's a smile on Trevor's mouth. It reminds me of the carefree, spirited person I met my freshman year, not the Trevor he turned into. He's *my* Trevor again.

"And do you remember what happened after that?"

"The game went into double overtime. By the time we won, I was so cold. I joked I had hypothermia and the only way to make sure I didn't perish was by stripping so we were skin to skin."

"You sure did." As he continues closing the distance between us, our chests rise and fall in sync. Suddenly, everything about him becomes familiar, simple, easy, like riding a bike. Despite the passing of time, you don't forget how to hop back on, even after a nasty fall. It may take some time to build up the courage to ride full on again, but you eventually do.

"I didn't really have hypothermia," I say in a breathy voice.

"I know. But I would have been an idiot to turn away your offer for some skin-to-skin time." He adjusts his stance, his hand going to the small of my back and bringing my body flush with his. He lowers his mouth toward mine, the warmth of his breath dancing on my lips. "I was such an idiot to push you away, Evie. I knew it was a mistake, but refused to admit it. I hated seeing you with another man. It drove me crazy to think someone else was enjoying *my* laughs, *my* smiles...*my* lips."

Hypnotized by his heartfelt plea, I succumb to the pull Trevor has on me, all reason leaving me as his lips brush against mine for the first time in over six months.

"I don't care what I have to do to win back your heart, I'll do it. You'll never have to doubt me again, just please... Give me a chance."

He doesn't even allow me to respond as he presses his mouth even firmer against mine, kissing me like he did for so many years. When he first broke up with me in June, this was exactly what I wanted. But now, it feels lacking, foreign...wrong. It's missing something...something only Julian's kisses ever provided me. A feeling of love. I'm no longer thinking of kissing Trevor, but of Julian, recalling the magnitude of his blue eyes in the photos Viv selected for the article. I'd expected to see all shots with his head cut off, recalling the numerous times the man I thought to be August Laurent insisted his anonymity was all he had. Instead, every single photo was of him, August...

Trevor kisses me deeper, but his hand roaming my frame lacks the confidence Julian's touch had. I'm transported to the Steam Room the day I received that first phone call from August Laurent, his voice still strong in my memory.

"If I ever find someone worth giving this all up for, I'll gladly grant your magazine an exclusive photo shoot and you can plaster my face from here to kingdom come."

The realization hits me like a freight train. Breathless, I stumble away from Trevor, as if he holds some contagious disease. I stare into his eyes, but all I see are Julian's. The same deep pools of sorrow and pain staring back at me from the pages of the magazine. It's not August in those images. Not to me. It's Julian.

Bringing my hand to my lips where the ghost of Trevor's lackluster kiss lingers, I step back. The truth has been glaring at me all along, but I was too stubborn to open my eyes. Yes, I was angry at Julian for lying, but what really irritated me was the idea of him sharing himself with all those women. He never did that. They only got to know August Laurent...mysterious, enigmatic, aloof.

I got to know Julian Gage.

My broken, damaged, tortured Julian.

My lascivious, passionate, amorous Julian.

My beautiful, caring, kindhearted Julian.

"Evie?" Trevor's concerned voice cuts through. "Are you okay? I thought—"

"He's showing his face."

He tilts his head to the side and pinches his lips together. "What are you talking about?"

"He's showing his face," I repeat, this time louder. My heart pounding, I snap out of my stupor and grab my boots, tugging them over my leggings. "He said it himself." My voice grows increasingly excited and frantic with each word I speak, my heart ready to burst. "He would only reveal who he was when he found someone who made it worth giving up. He's willing to walk away just to have a chance with me. If that's not love, I don't know what is."

I whirl around, heading toward the front door. As I'm about to open it, I pause, facing Trevor once more. His brow furrows in confusion at my sudden change of demeanor. I don't know how to explain it, either.

Flinging my arms around him, I plant one last kiss on his cheek. It's fitting, in a way. Trevor is the reason I met Julian in the first place. Now he's the reason I finally opened my eyes to what's been staring at me all along.

"Thank you, Trevor!"

I spin from him, dashing out of the apartment. As I run into the rain, I feel a little like Jimmy Stewart in *It's a*

Wonderful Life when he rushed through the streets of Bedford Falls, desperately trying to get home to the people he loved. And that's what I'm doing, too...trying to get home.

Julian is my home.

Chapter Forty-One

ADRENALINE COURSES THROUGH me as I jump out of the cab in front of Julian's building. The entire drive from Chloe's, I tried to figure out what to say. I'm not sure any words will be adequate, but I suppose apologizing for my behavior, admitting I was wrong, is probably a good start. He claimed he'd give it all up for me, but I refused to listen, insisting I'd never be able to believe another word out of his mouth. So he did one better. He *showed* me. Now it's time I show him how much he means to me, how sorry I am for all this wasted time.

I'm a nervous wreck as I ride up the elevator to his penthouse apartment. I don't know what to expect when he opens the door. I *hope* he opens the door. I never even stopped to consider he might not be here or, worse, is here but refuses to speak to me. After all, I deserve it. I refused to speak to him.

When the elevator slows to a gradual stop and the doors open, an emptiness settles in my stomach, my mouth growing dry. This is it. My grand gesture. I like to think Julian wouldn't want those photos to be published in an article revealing August Laurent's identity if he'd given up on me. Then again, I could be wrong. It could all be a ploy by Viv to get me to agree to the assistant editor position. I have no way of knowing anything for sure, not until I see Julian again. And for the first time in weeks, I *do* want to see him.

Heading toward his door, I square my shoulders, summoning every ounce of courage I possess to swallow my pride and admit I made a colossal mistake. I was the one who had the balls to admit my feelings to Julian in the first place. Now I have to be the bigger person and admit I was wrong about him, about both August and Julian.

I bring my hand up to the door, but before I have a chance to knock, it swings open. I still, momentarily taken by surprise before a familiar smile greets me warmly.

"Guinevere," Camille sighs, holding out her arms and taking me in them, hugging me. "It is so good to see you." She pulls back, not a hint of disapproval in her gaze as I'd expected to see. I'm more than aware of how close she is to Julian. I have no doubt he told her what happened. "Although I suspect you're not here to see me."

I laugh. "While I have missed you and your cooking, no. I've come to talk to Julian."

"He'll be so happy to learn you're here. He's been an absolute bore these past few weeks." She smiles, then her expression falls flat. "But he's not home."

"He isn't?"

"No. He left about an hour ago. He's at a charity auction for the foundation Sonia's sister started in her name."

"Of course." I chew on my lower lip, contemplating my next move. Now that I've had my big epiphany, I hate having to wait another second.

"It's just over at the Four Seasons."

I glance down at my clothes before lifting my eyes back

to hers. "I don't think I'm dressed for that kind of event."

"So? That didn't stop Cinderella from going to the ball."

"She had a Fairy Godmother. And a bunch of talking mice as friends. I don't exactly have any of that."

Camille's eyes dance, her expression turning conniving. "I don't think I can help you with talking mice, but I have something better than a Fairy Godmother."

"Oh yeah? What's that?"

"Come see for yourself." With a wink, she turns from me and walks back into Julian's home. I hesitate at first, then step inside.

The instant I do, his warmth and energy fill me. For the past few months, this place was like a home. I felt more comfortable here than I ever did in the apartment I shared with Trevor. Julian never reminded me he was the main bread earner in our arrangement, as Trevor so often did. The difference is just another reminder of the person Julian is. He never flaunted his money, except to spoil me. Our relationship was never a competition. It was a true partnership.

Camille stops outside one of the guest rooms, then pauses before pushing open the door. Curious as to what's going on, I walk inside, my gaze instantly falling on a stunning sapphire blue ballgown hanging outside the closet. The fitted bodice has a sweetheart neckline and off-the-shoulder sleeves. Jewels overlay the satin material down to the waist, then the dress juts out into a flowing skirt Julian seems to like, considering most of the formal gowns I'd worn all summer were of a similar style.

"Like I said," she sings as she approaches me from behind. "I may not have a magic wand or mice that can sew, but I do have a dress."

My mouth agape, I spin around, my mind reeling with various thoughts, the most pressing being why there's a dress waiting for me when I haven't spoken to Julian in several weeks.

"He had Dana set something aside," she explains, answering the question written on my face. "He'd hoped you'd have a change of heart by tonight."

I can't fight against the smile pulling on my lips. I want to be angry at him for being so arrogant and assuming, but I can't. It's further proof that I never left his mind, that he wasn't lying when he insisted I was the only woman he thought of since he met me.

"He's a bit cocky, isn't he?" I mutter in a playful tone.

"He certainly is. I've known Julian Gage over twenty years now. The one thing I've learned is when he sets his eyes on something, he doesn't stop until he has it."

"And he wants me." I look back at the dress.

"Yes, sweetheart. He does. He has since the night you met." She places her hands on my shoulders, forcing me to face her. "He may have lied to you, things may not have gone as planned, but I don't think your story could have been written any other way. Do you?" She cocks a brow.

There's only one answer that seems fitting. "No, I don't."

"Good." She beams. "Now, let's get you ready for the ball, Cinderella. This time, there's no turning into a pumpkin at midnight."

Chapter Forty-Two

I LOOK DOWN at my dress, a hint of the same inadequacy I experienced my first weekend in the Hamptons with Julian washing over me. Curious eyes float in my direction the instant I enter the elaborate ballroom at the Four Seasons. I summon every ounce of courage I possess, aware most of the people present have learned of our breakup and are probably wondering why I'm here. Men don crisp tuxedos. Women wear stunning gowns, glittering jewels covering their necks and ears. Impressive crystal chandeliers hang overhead, the ambient lighting not too bright as couples dance to a jazz band playing an old Ella Fitzgerald tune.

As I continue farther inside, my eyes zero in on the bar. My nerves are at an all-time high and I need something to help settle the butterflies in my stomach. With each step I take, I feel the whispers of the other guests against my skin. All summer, I never felt as out of place as I do now. I had Julian at my side back then. This is just another reminder of everything he did for me, how he made me feel empowered amongst those who view it their duty to judge others.

Once I have a manhattan in my hand and take a sip, I return my attention to the enormous ballroom, searching for Julian. But it's hard to find him in a sea of what I estimate to be over five hundred people.

After Sonia's passing, I'd received word of this event to raise funds for the foundation her sister had started in her name with the purpose of providing help and resources to other women in similar situations as Sonia found herself in.

Thankfully, the police brought Ethan in for questioning based on the information I, as well as Julian, provided. When the robbery gone wrong angle didn't pan out, they took a closer look at Ethan and ended up arresting him after his alibi fell through. Once I learned that, I felt a bit of vindication for Sonia, knowing Ethan wouldn't get away with what he'd done. But there are times I turn on the TV and listen to newscasters discuss recent developments in her case that I can't help but feel I could have done something to prevent this from happening in the first place. I can only imagine what Julian must be going through, the guilt that must consume him over the fact he tried to help, but it wasn't enough. Just like with his mother. I should have stood by his side and comforted him during this difficult time that must have reopened old wounds. I hope it's not too late to do that.

As I search for Julian, or at least a friendly face who could point me in the right direction, a voice comes over the speakers and everyone turns their attention to the stage in the center of the room. Cameras flash, reporters lifting audio recorders to get a few snippets. That's how it usually is at these functions. The media is invited to ensure the event makes headlines, padding egos. But here, it's not about that. It's about sharing Sonia's story and encouraging more people to help those in similar situations.

"Hello, friends," the woman says in a slight Spanish accent. Her olive-toned skin and dark hair make it apparent she's Sonia's sister, their appearance nearly identical. "My name is Isabella Moreno. I wanted to take a minute to thank all of you for coming out tonight to support this foundation." She smiles, but it doesn't reach her eyes. "Sonia would have wanted to know her death wasn't in vain, that something good could come out of it, that perhaps she could have a hand in preventing the same tragedy from happening to someone else. It's because of your generosity that can become a reality."

There's polite applause from the crowd before she continues. "I had no idea what was going on in her personal life. When the cameras were on, she was all smiles, telling everyone how happy she was in her marriage. We all believed it was the perfect love story. It wasn't until this past year that I learned the truth. It all started when she told me she'd hired an escort named August Laurent. Or, as many of you know him, Julian Gage."

She steps away, revealing a man in a perfectly tailored tuxedo, like many of the other men here. But he's not like any of the others, not to me.

Low murmurs and a few gasps ring out as he steps up to the podium, many of the attendees just as surprised about this revelation as I was when I first learned the truth.

"Good evening." Placing his hands on the podium, he pauses in contemplation, briefly closing his eyes before looking at the assembled guests. "Since Sonia's death, I've debated what to do, what to tell all of you. I've kept this secret for years. My work depended on me being able to maintain my anonymity, and it worked. But losing Sonia made me reconsider things. It made me realize the importance of telling those you care about how you feel. You may not get another chance."

He momentarily averts his gaze, drawing in a deep breath. "Sonia was surrounded by people she thought were her friends and was in a marriage that, on its face, was the picture of perfection. But she'd never felt so alone. That's why she sought me out. And over the weeks we spent together, she confided in me. I think she just wanted someone to talk to, someone who would listen and not judge her for staying in an abusive relationship. Because of our time together, she finally found the strength to file for divorce."

He grips the podium tighter, his expression fraught with emotion. When he looks at the audience again, tears are visible in his eyes and his voice wavers.

"Unfortunately, despite the courage she demonstrated, her husband carried out his threat. She called me that night, panicked. I tried to get to her. But I was too late."

My heart drops to the pit of my stomach as I recall the night he left me for what I thought to be another woman. He claimed it was a matter of life and death. I can't believe how true that was.

He clears his throat, his voice becoming strong once more. "And that's why this work is so important. Sonia had her freedom ripped from her, but our hope is that other women won't have to suffer the same tragedy.

"Sonia isn't the first victim of domestic violence, and she certainly won't be the last. But we can try to combat this epidemic, this idea of patriarchy and male dominance that seems to permeate society. Yes, men can be victims of domestic violence, too. It's the idea of exerting power and authority over another person that needs to stop. It happens far too often and to people we never expect because of how happy they appear on the outside. Hell, Sonia always smiled, no matter what. I should have known something was off, considering my mother did the same thing...until she was murdered by her husband, my step-father, when I was twelve."

An eerie silence falls over the room as people absorb his confession, his truth. This is a man who's spent the past decade in these social circles, pretending to be someone he wasn't so they'd accept him. It warms my heart to witness him finally discuss his past so freely. I hope it will encourage more to do the same.

"I haven't spoken about my mother in years, not until a few months ago when I had the pleasure of meeting a woman who made me rethink everything." He laughs slightly, a sparkle in his eyes, as if recalling happy memories. "She had this strange habit of being herself all the time, which completely captivated me, considering we all have a tendency of pretending to be someone we aren't. Not this woman. And by being herself, she helped me see that it's okay to talk about my past, about the skeletons in my own closet. All the past trauma, torment, hurt... She called it my 'ugly'. And she embraced the ugly. It's what makes us who we are. We can't erase it. Do we wish we could? You bet your ass. Instead of doing everything to bury it, we should embrace all the pieces that make us uniquely us.

"So tonight, in honor of Sonia, I'd like to announce the groundbreaking of a project I've been working on. For those who may not be aware, when I inherited Theodore Price's fortune, I used a great deal of that money to open women's shelters here in the Tri-state Area. A few years ago, I wanted to do something bigger, so I expanded my charitable foundation reach into every state in the country. But it still wasn't enough. I wanted to do more. Now, thanks to all your generosity, I'm able to do that. Working with Isabella, we'll be going overseas, helping women born in cultures where abuse is so pervasive, it's considered normal. It's not. And it's my mission to help even more women realize this. Thank you."

Thunderous applause erupts as he steps away from the podium, pausing for a few photos before making his way from the stage. Reporters descend on him, all of them shouting questions about his identity as August Laurent. Instead of humoring them, he responds that they'll have to wait until the February issue of *Blush* magazine hits the newsstands to get the answers they're looking for. My heart expands, thinking how those magazines will now fly off shelves even more so than they would have.

I'm so lost in the gift he's given me I almost don't realize he's leaving. Snapping out of my stupor, I rush toward him, but after his revelation, it seems everyone wants to know more, people swarming him as he makes his escape. He must have predicted this would happen because two bodyguards flank him, ushering him out of the room as other security personnel escort the media from the event now that the speech portion is over.

I call Julian's name, but he can't hear me over everyone else. All I can do is watch as he's whisked away, without a single glance in my direction. As the excitement comes to an end, the sound of saxophones and piano playing a jazz standard fills the space. Out of nowhere, I hear my name.

I whip my head up to see Sadie rushing toward me. I don't have a second to brace myself before she barrels into me, hugging me enthusiastically. Thankfully, I'm quick enough to save the remnants of my drink from spilling.

"I've missed you!"

I still at first, surprised by her sudden attack. Then I melt into her embrace. "I've missed you, too, Sadie."

She pulls back, her eyes frenzied. "Did you know?"

"Know what?"

"About Julian being August Laurent? My god!" She loops her arm through mine, not taking a breath. "You were together while you were doing a story on August Laurent!" She gasps as she puts two and two together, facing me once more. "That's why you broke up, isn't it?"

"It is."

Her brows furrow as she surveys me. "But if you broke up, why are you here?"

I take a long sip of my manhattan, draining it. "I realized I made a mistake and came here to tell him." I shrug in defeat. "But I missed my chance."

She gives me an encouraging smile, squeezing my bicep. "It's okay. It'll all work out. Trust me." She winks.

"Thanks, Sadie." I sigh as I place my glass on a nearby hightop table. "But now that Prince Charming has left the ball, there's no reason for Cinderella to hang around. It was great seeing you again." I start to turn from her.

"Wait!" she yells, forcing me to stop. I look over my shoulder at her, an eyebrow raised. Her frantic expression softens. "Since you're already here, how about a drink? I'm buying," she jokes, considering it's an open bar.

"Honestly, I'm not sure I'll be the best company right now. I should just—"

"Come on, Evie. One drink while I update you on all the gossip, and there is some *juicy* gossip. For old time's sake."

On a long exhale, I reluctantly nod. "Okay. One drink. Then I'm going home and curling up on the couch with a plate of Christmas cookies."

"One drink. That's all I need."

403

I follow Sadie to the bar. She orders two manhattans, then we find a hightop table in the corner. The out-of-the-way location reminds me of the day we first met when we sat at a table hidden away, which allowed her to give me the dirt on the who's who of the Hamptons. She does the same now, updating me on affairs, unplanned pregnancies, and even a few paternity tests. It's like being brought up to speed on my favorite soap opera.

As she's telling me about one of the guest's affairs with the nanny, the music changes and the opening notes to an all-too-familiar song in three-quarter time fills the room. I stiffen, my breath hitching as memories of dancing to this song with Julian return.

The lighting in the room lowers, apart from a spotlight on the dance floor. When I look in its direction, my heart catches in my throat at the man I see standing there, a small smile forming on his mouth. His eyes locked on mine, he extends his hand toward me.

Sadie swipes the drink out of my hand and pushes me away from her. After passing her a look of appreciation, I slowly walk across the ballroom, the sea of people parting for me. With each step, my heart beats a little faster, my lungs struggle to capture a breath, my skin tingles with the memory of Julian's touch.

Approaching him, I float my gaze to his outstretched hand, briefly hesitating. His expression falls, panic overcoming him at the idea of me walking away.

"Got ya," I tease as I link my fingers with his.

Relief rolls off him in waves and, like so many times during our summer, he twirls me around to get a better look at the dress before yanking my body against his. He places his hand on my lower back and I drape my free arm over his shoulder. Then he leads me around the dance floor to the band leader singing "Moon River", neither one of us saying a word. There's no need. We share a connection, one that allows us to say everything we need with a simple look.

Months ago, it would have bothered me to share such a personal moment in the company of others. Now it doesn't. All I see is Julian. He's all that matters. This moment is all that matters. Not his past. Not my past. Just us. Just now. He taught me to embrace the moment, to stop living life according to a predetermined itinerary. Life doesn't always go according to plan. Julian's living proof of that. *I'm* living proof of that.

"You came back," I finally say once our song ends and we stop moving.

"I'll always come back for you, Guinevere. Always."

I run my hands through his sandy hair, relishing in the sensation I'd deprived myself of these past few weeks. "And I'll always come back for you, Julian." I bring my lips to his. "Always."

He cups my cheeks, his grip firm and demanding. Then he covers my mouth with his, his kiss soft, sweet, and delicious in all the ways I remember it to be. But he doesn't stop at a simple exchange, despite our audience. He sweeps his tongue against my bottom lip, begging for entrance, which I can't deny him. His hold on me tightens as he pulls me closer, exploring my mouth in a way that makes it feel like it's the first time. And that's what this is. I'm finally kissing every side of Julian Gage. And I'm willing to accept every piece of him.

Pulling back, he rests his forehead on mine. "A symphony," he murmurs.

"What's that?" I ask in a breathy voice.

"That's what I hear when I kiss you. Have since the

very first time. And I have a feeling I will until our very last kiss, which I hope is when we're both old and gray."

"Is that right?" I flirt.

He nods slowly, his eyes locked on mine, the fire sending a chill down my spine. "That's a promise. No more lies. No more games. Only the truth. Only you. You're all I want. All I need. And I hope I can be that for you, too."

It takes every ounce of resolve I have not to melt into a puddle on the floor. The only reason I don't is because he's supporting me, just like he always has, both as August and Julian. Truth be told, I love both men. They've molded the man in front of me into the person he is. For that, I'll always be grateful.

"You're more than that." I beam, then chew on my bottom lip, my expression falling. "There's just one thing."

"Anything. Whatever you want, it's yours," he promises in desperation.

"Can we still play a few games?" I waggle my brows, giving him a coy smile. "Because I'd really like to try some roleplay with you."

His jaw clenches as his eyes widen. Then he brings his lips back to mine, his kiss ravenous and insatiable. "What am I going to do with you?"

"I have a few ideas."

Before I have a chance to register what's happening, he hoists me over his shoulder in a fireman's hold. The entire place erupts in cheers and applause. When I hear a familiar whistle, I crane my neck up, meeting Sadie's infectious smile. I beam at her, grateful she encouraged me to stay. The moment fills me with so much joy, I don't even care about the scene we're making as he carries me out of the gala, through the hotel lobby, and down the busy Manhattan sidewalk, tourists staring. It's not until we're a few blocks away that he finally puts me down.

Always the gentleman, he shrugs out of his tuxedo jacket and places it over my shoulders. When I glance at the storefront to see where we are, I fall in love with him a little more.

Tiffany's.

For someone who said he wasn't cut out to be in a relationship, he sure knows how to make a woman happy.

Brushing my hair behind my ears, he brings his hands up to my face, admiring me as the tension between us shifts from one of playfulness to one of devotion. "I love you, Guinevere Fitzgerald."

"And I love you, Julian Gage. And August Laurent. And any other personalities hiding in there. I love them all."

He chuckles, the sound exactly what's been missing. There's nothing like hearing him laugh. I used to be desperate to make everyone around me laugh to mask the fact I wasn't happy with the life I'd planned. Now I only care about making Julian laugh.

"That's good to know, but from this moment forward, there's no one else. Now that I finally have you, I don't need to be anyone other than myself."

He brushes his lips against mine and kisses me in front of the display window of Tiffany's. I couldn't think of a more perfect spot to begin our story of forever. It just goes to show you. The greatest things in life can't be planned.

Love can't be planned.

Chapter Forty-Three

I STARE AT THE pink hue of the sky as the sun setting in the west casts a beautiful glow over the ocean outside the windows of Julian's home in the Hamptons. A smile curves my mouth as I consider how far we've come since the first time I stepped foot in this house. Back then, I never would have imagined I'd be kicking off another summer with someone who was only supposed to be a fun distraction, or my key to revenge. Now I can't imagine my life without him.

The sound of my phone ringing tears my attention away from the stunning view. I pull it out of my clutch, grinning when I see Chloe pop up.

"You made it!" I say as I answer her FaceTime call. "How are the islands treating you?"

She lifts the oversized sunglasses off her eyes as she brings a tropical concoction to her lips. She flew to Hawaii early this morning, but if I didn't know any better, I'd think she'd been there for days.

"I may never leave."

I smile. "I don't blame you. I'm counting down the hours until we hop on a plane tomorrow."

"Yeah," she scoffs, rolling her eyes. "Because you have it so rough, having to hold off on coming to Hawaii so you can go to some high-class party in the Hamptons. Let me get out my violin, Evie."

Shaking my head, I can't stop the grin from crawling across my lips. She's right. I do have it pretty good. Not only do I have an incredibly supportive man in my life, but I also have a job I only dreamed about. Thankfully, Viv knew I wasn't thinking clearly and refused to offer the assistant editor position to anyone until the beginning of the year. By then, I'd come to my senses.

My new position isn't without its challenges. I wouldn't trade it for anything, though, especially whenever I pass a newsstand and see the new edition of a magazine bearing my name as the assistant editor. You can Google me now, and the search will return information unrelated to my relationship with Julian Gage. I wouldn't have been able to say the same if I gave up and went home to become an English teacher, as I considered when everything fell apart.

"Have you seen Nora yet?" I ask.

"Yes." She rolls her eyes. "She's in full bridezilla mode, but in the best way possible. I think you've rubbed off on her."

"How so?"

She grimaces. "She has lists."

"Lists?"

"Lists," she repeats with a nod. "And itineraries. She has one for you when you get here. I've already warned Izzy."

"Do I want to know what's on these lists or itineraries?"

"I can't say for certain what's on yours, but based on mine, I'm convinced she's lost her damn mind. You need to come and run an intervention. Stat."

I grin. "Why's that?"

"I thought I'd enjoy a week of relaxation before the

wedding. That girl has shit scheduled every day. Sightseeing shit."

I stifle my laugh at the look of absolute displeasure crossing her face. I've often wondered how Chloe and Nora were such good friends. While Nora's idea of a fun vacation is packing as much sightseeing and adventure into as short a time as possible, Chloe would much prefer to sit on a beach and have attractive men bring her fruity drinks as she works on her tan.

"At least you're in Hawaii. It could be a lot worse."

"The fact that I'm in Hawaii is what makes it unbearable. I should be shacking up with some hot islander who will breathe fire in my pussy. Instead, do you want to know what I'm tasked with doing during what should be a sex-filled vacation?"

"What's that?"

"Making sure Jeremy's best man keeps his dick in his pants. Apparently, he flirts with anything with a pulse. And since Nora knows I have a low tolerance for bullshit and charm, I've been given this exciting task."

I laugh once more as Chloe brings her drink back to her lips. "I'm going to need this shit in an IV."

"Remember. It's all for Nora."

"Yeah, well, Nora owes me after this. Anyway, I don't want to take up much more of your time. I know you have a big thing tonight. I just wanted to call and wish you a happy birthday." She lifts her glass once more, toasting me. "Here's to thirty-one. May this birthday be more memorable than the last."

"Actually...," I begin after a moment of contemplation, "my last birthday was pretty amazing. It just took me a while to realize it."

"At least you finally did." She holds my gaze for a

moment longer, then seems to look past me. I glance over my shoulder to see Julian descending the staircase. I return my eyes to my phone. "Looks like Prince Charming's here to take you to the ball. Have a good night, Evie. And happy birthday."

"Thanks, Chloe. Love you."

"Love you, too."

I end the FaceTime call, then drop my phone into my clutch, whirling around as Julian approaches, his impassioned gaze raking over my body. It doesn't matter we've known each other a year and are past the so-called honeymoon phase. He looks at me with the same desperation and desire every time. I get the feeling he always will.

His hand finds mine and he twirls me around, wanting the full effect of the cocktail dress Dana suggested I wear to tonight's gathering. It's more of a low-key event to celebrate the opening of Julian's first overseas women's shelter in the Middle East, something that wouldn't have been possible without all the networking he did last summer.

He tugs my body into his as his free hand wraps around mine. Just like so many other times, I drape my arm over his shoulder, toying with the curls that fall over his jacket collar. Our bodies sway as he hums "Moon River", which has become our song. There are times I hear it even when he's fast asleep beside me. It's the song of our love, one I hope will continue until we're long gone.

He leans his forehead on mine, barely a breath between our bodies as we share this moment. We've done this same dance so many times over the course of our relationship. It's never gotten old. I still feel the same spark, the same fluttering in my heart, the same craving

411

to be in his universe. In fact, I feel it even deeper now that I finally know all sides of Julian Gage. And every day, I continue to fall more in love with every part of him.

When he stops humming, he lifts his head from mine and looks at me with a focused gaze. "You look beautiful, Guinevere."

I bring my hands to the lapels of his suit jacket, smoothing them. "You clean up pretty good yourself." I wink.

"I got something for you."

"I told you…" I narrow my eyes on him. "No presents. You spoil me enough as it is. All I wanted for my birthday was to spend it with you."

"What if I told you it's not a birthday present?"

"I still don't want it."

"How about we test it out? I bought it to go with your outfit. Dana said it would really accentuate the jewels on the straps of your shoes. If you don't like it, I'll return it, okay?"

I playfully roll my eyes, feigning irritation. As much as I hate the thought of him spending money on me, I love that he spoils me. I love that he thinks of me so much.

"Okay."

"Okay." He smiles, but it's not as confident as usual. Reaching into the pocket of his pants, he pulls out a small box in that familiar blue hue unique to Tiffany's. "I was planning on getting you something from Cartier instead, but figured Tiffany's would have more meaning."

My breath hitches as he repeats the same words he uttered on what was supposed to be our last night together. There's only one possible way for me to respond to that. Tears fill my eyes as I stare at the leather box, knowing all too well what's inside.

412

"It could be an empty box and it would be infinitely better than even the most expensive piece you could get from Cartier."

"Phew." He laughs nervously. "That's a relief, because it really is just an empty box."

"No, it's not," I whisper through the lump in my throat.

"You're right. It's not."

He drops to one knee and pops open the ring box, then grabs my left hand in his. I exhale at the stunning diamond that greets me. It's a princess-cut stone that's easily three carats, the band thin and inlaid with even more diamonds.

"Guinevere Shea Fitzgerald, I couldn't have planned for you to walk into my life even if I tried. I'll never forget sitting in the corner of a bar after meeting with a client, wondering if it's all worth it, hearing you tell the entire place how you were dumped. All I could remember thinking is that I needed to know you. I'd spent most of my life running from love. And then there was you.

"Our relationship may not have been conventional by any stretch of the imagination, but that's what I love about us. We broke the rules. We weren't supposed to find each other, but we did." He brings the ring up to my finger, unshed tears forming behind his eyelids. "We weren't supposed to fall in love with each other, but we did. And I fall in love with you all over again every day. I want to continue to fall in love with you every day for the rest of my life. Do me the honor of being my wife, of taking a risk on me, of loving all the pieces of me."

His words are everything I could have dreamed for a proposal, and more. I never expected Julian to drop to one knee after only a year. I thought he'd need more time to get used to being in a real relationship. But that's what makes this so exciting, so exhilarating. I never saw it coming. It was never planned.

"I'm not quite sure getting engaged was on the itinerary," I joke, remembering our early days when I insisted on a firm schedule of events. "At least, I didn't see it there." I grin, playfully batting my eyelashes.

He's on his feet in an instant, yanking my body hard and fast against his, stealing my breath. He doesn't even wait for me to say yes as he slides the ring onto my finger, where I plan to leave it for the rest of my days.

"Fuck the itinerary," he growls as he kisses me for the first time as my fiancé.

Fuck the itinerary indeed.

The End

Playlist

Memories Are Made of This - Dean Martin
Live Learn - The California Honeydrops
Little Black Dress - Sara Bareilles
S.O.B. - Nathaniel Rateliff & The Night Sweats
Showboat - Josh Ritter
Anybody Else - Jon McLaughlin
A Little Fire - Parker Millsap
Falling Slowly - Glen Hansard
Classic - MKTO
Fool In the Rain - Led Zeppelin
Fight Song - Rachel Platten
Run - Matt Nathanson
Without You - Parachute
Reaching - Jason Reeves
Moon River - Henry Mancini
Summer is Over - Jon McLaughlin
Always Midnight - Pat Monahan
Put Me Back Together - Grace Grundy
What About Us - P!nk
3 Hours - Canyon City
Scarecrow - Alex & Sierra
The Shape of Us - Ian Britt
This Will Be Our Home - John Lucas
Never Got Away - Colbie Caillat
Capital Letters - Halloran & Kate
Dammit - Jana Kramer
Dear John - Julian Sheer

Extraordinary Magic - Ben Rector
Guiding Light - Mumford & Sons
I Hear a Symphony - Cody Fry
Have It All - Jason Mraz
First Try - Johnnyswim
Say You Do - Graham Colton
You - A Great Big World

Acknowledgments

Phew. I did it. Finally. This has actually been the most challenging book for me to write, not because of the subject matter, but because I rewrote the dang thing THREE TIMES!

This was always going to be a story about a woman who was dumped by her long-term boyfriend. The premise remained, but the details changed. First, Julian was just a tech guru and it was set in San Fran. Then I decided a male escort would be a lot more fun, so he became just that and it moved to Manhattan. Then I decided to switch from Manhattan in the winter to the Hamptons in the summer. And boy did it open up a world of possibility for me. This is what I love about writing and allowing my characters to take control. They really do have their own ideas. If I tried to steer them in the direction I'd originally planned, this story wouldn't be as fun and endearing as it is.

As always, I have my husband to thank for putting up with my constantly bouncing new ideas off him, sometimes when he's trying to sleep. I couldn't do this without him, so a big thanks.

Another big thanks to my two nannies who help with Harper Leigh so I can get lots of writing time in — Brooke and Karissa. Thanks so much for loving Harper as much as I do.

There's only one woman I trust with my baby, ie., my manuscript, and that's Kim Young. She's edited every single one of my books so far, and I hope she'll edit all the books I have planned in the future, as well.

I'm fortunate enough to have an amazing team of beta readers who graciously take time out of their busy schedules to read for me and offer their input and advice. Oftentimes, it's difficult to see the forest amongst the trees, and they help me do just that. Stacy, Lin, Melissa, Vicky, Joelle, and Sylvia — thank you ladies. #BurnhamBitches4Life

As always, a huge thanks to my fantastic publicist - Emily from Social Butterfly. You make releases infinitely less stressful. Told this would just be one book this time around (although it is the length of two books. LOL)

Another big thanks to my fantastic Angels, who help promote my work everywhere. I truly appreciate it. And to my spectacular reader group — thanks for giving me somewhere to hang out when my brain feels like it's going to explode and I need a good laugh.

And of course, last but not least, thank you to YOU! Whether this is your first T.K. Leigh book or your eighteenth, I so appreciate you for taking a risk on my work. I can't wait for you to see what I have planned next.

Love & peace,
~ T.K.

Books by T.K. Leigh

ROMANTIC SUSPENSE
The Beautiful Mess Series
A Beautiful Mess
A Tragic Wreck
Gorgeous Chaos
Chasing the Dragon (Deception Duet #1)
Slaying the Dragon (Deception Duet #2)
Vanished: A Beautiful Mess Series Novel

The Vault
Inferno

Heart of Light

CONTEMPORARY ROMANCE
The Redemption Series
Promise: A Redemption Series Prologue
Commitment
Redemption

The Dating Games Series
Dating Games
Wicked Games
Mind Games
Dangerous Games
Royal Games

ROMANTIC COMEDY
The Book Boyfriend Chronicles
The Other Side of Someday
Writing Mr. Right

MATURE YOUNG ADULT
Heart of Marley

For more information on any of these titles and upcoming releases, please visit T.K.'s website:
www.tkleighauthor.com

About the Author

T.K. Leigh, otherwise known as Tracy Leigh Kellam, is the *USA Today* Bestselling author of the Beautiful Mess series, in addition to several other works ranging from sexy and sinful to fun and flirty. Originally from New England, she now resides in sunny Southern California with her husband, beautiful daughter, and three cats. When she's not planted in front of her computer, writing away, she can be found training for her next marathon (of which she has run over twenty fulls and far too many halfs to recall) or chasing her daughter around the house.

T.K. Leigh is represented by Jane Dystel of Dystel, Goderich & Bourret Literary Management. All publishing inquiries, including audio, foreign, and film rights, should be directed to her.

Made in the USA
Middletown, DE
17 August 2020

15673234R00255